RIGHT
BACK WHERE
WE STARTED
FROM

PRAISE FOR
RIGHT BACK WHERE WE STARTED FROM

"Joy Lanzendorfer has crafted a terrific first novel, one brimming with energy, wit, and emotional resonance...The novel captures, vividly, some of the crazier times in California's crazy history. Highly recommended!"

—PETER ORNER, author of *Maggie Brown & Others*

"This multi-generational novel speaks of regaining what's lost and which you believe is rightfully yours to begin with...There's a sadness inherent in these stories, perhaps a lesson in humility. Weaving back and forth between the generations, the moral may be to be careful what you wish for."

—*HISTORICAL NOVELS REVIEW*

RIGHT BACK WHERE WE STARTED FROM

JOY LANZENDORFER

BLACK STONE
PUBLISHING

Copyright © 2021 by Joy Rankin
Published in 2022 by Blackstone Publishing
Cover and book design by Alenka Vdovič Linaschke

The characters and events in this book are fictitious.
Any similarity to real persons, living or dead, is coincidental
and not intended by the author.

Printed in the United States of America
Originally published in hardcover by Blackstone Publishing in 2021

First paperback edition: 2022
ISBN 979-8-200-83425-9
Fiction / Historical / General

Version 1

CIP data for this book is available
from the Library of Congress

Blackstone Publishing
31 Mistletoe Rd.
Ashland, OR 97520

www.BlackstonePublishing.com

For Kyle

PART I

CHAPTER 1

"Everybody wants to come to California," Mabel said, stubbing her cigarette out on a china plate. Emma—for she was called Emma then and not Sandra—looked up.

"When I first moved here," Mabel went on, "there was nothing from these porch steps all the way to that mountain. Now look at it."

Obediently, Emma, who was about to turn seven, gazed through the screened-in porch where they were sitting. Across the lane, the neighbor's vineyard stretched in grasshopper-green rows to the foot of Fitch Mountain.

"We looked into buying that land once," Mabel said. "Back when we owned the prune empire, we considered that property for a possible expansion. Now the neighbors own that land and we live in a hovel."

Emma glared at the vineyard. It seemed unfair that the neighbors prospered while she and Mabel lived in a house with crooked floors and bug problems. Her family was destined for better. Mabel's parents, Vira and Elmer Sanborn, came to California during the Gold Rush. They knew a good thing when they saw it.

"Your real father, Arthur Beard, would never have let us get this close to destitution," Mabel said. "If he'd lived, things would be different."

"What happened to him?" Emma said, wondering if this time Mabel would answer the question.

But Mabel didn't seem to hear her. She lit another cigarette and held it between her fingers so that a trail of smoke followed her every move. It drew attention to her fingertips as they skipped along the pin curls on her head. *Like butterflies lighting*, Emma thought, remembering the way they flitted from leaf to leaf, never quite coming to a full stop. It was almost as if Mabel herself was a butterfly and one wrong move would frighten her away.

"You can't believe what people say, Emma," Mabel said. "Most people are liars. They destroy others out of jealousy or just plain meanness." And Emma wanted to ask who had tried to destroy them, but as she struggled for a way to phrase the question, Mabel reached with the hand holding the cigarette and cupped the child's chin.

"But don't you worry," she said. "Your Mama will always tell you the truth."

CHAPTER 2

The orange juice factory was empty. The only things in sight were immense containers of juice that hung from the ceiling like giant bladders. A crowd of women stood in a knot in the middle of the factory floor. Each wore a short dress with matching tights the color of a tangerine. Over the costume was a sandwich board that read:

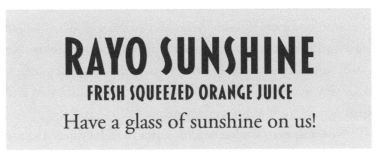

RAYO SUNSHINE
FRESH SQUEEZED ORANGE JUICE
Have a glass of sunshine on us!

A man wearing a straw hat with a blue-and-white ribbon around it stood before the girls, studying a list. Every time he called a name, his face disappeared underneath the hat brim. "Sandra Sanborn," he said.

"Here," Sandra answered from the crowd of girls. She

liked how her new name sounded in the man's mouth. Sandra
Sanborn was better than Sandra Guess, which was Billy's last
name, and far better than Emma Jones, the name her mother
had given her. Emma Jones sounded like a migrant picker's stepdaughter. Sandra Sanborn sounded like a movie star.

"Your position is the corner of Romaine and Vine streets,"
the man said.

Sandra suppressed a smile. Paramount Pictures was only a
few blocks from there. "Yes, sir," she said.

When the man finished calling out names, he yanked up
the factory door to reveal a pickup truck parked by a dumpster.
The girls climbed into the back of the truck, clutching the signs
and avoiding each other's eyes as the man handed out stacks of
coupons that said, "Good for one free glass of orange juice at
Rayo Sunshine's Hollywood kiosk."

"As you hand out the coupons, say our slogan, 'Have a glass
of sunshine on us,'" the man said. "During your shift, we ask
that you stay put. Don't leave your stations. We'll drop you off
and pick you up from your post."

Sandra shot him a look. The whole point of this job was to
get close to a movie studio. Wherever the orange juice people
stationed her to hand out coupons, she planned to adjust her
position so that she was in front of a studio or casting office.
That way she was upping her chances of being discovered and
getting paid for it at the same time.

Now this man—what was his name? Sandra wanted to say
it began with an "H"—was saying she couldn't do that. But he
wouldn't know what she did as long as she was at her post when
he dropped her off and picked her up. And what did he care
anyway, as long as the coupons got handed out?

Resolved, Sandra settled back as the truck zoomed
through Los Angeles. The broad streets were lined with purple

jacarandas and seemed to extend to the ocean. On either side of the road, movie theaters rose like art deco castles between construction projects. It was heartening to see signs of prosperity after the soup lines of San Francisco. She'd been smart to move here. Los Angeles really did seem to be the one place in the country that was, as the studios kept saying, "Depression proof."

At Vine Street, Sandra climbed onto the sidewalk. As the truck pulled away, a guy with a mustache came toward her, his eyes trained on her body. She remembered the skimpiness of the dress, which was shorter than some of her slips, and pulled the sign over her head before thrusting a coupon at the man. "Have a glass of sunshine on us," she said.

He tipped his hat and moved on. Sandra adjusted the sign and took in her surroundings. Although the four-lane road was jammed with traffic, the buildings around her were empty. The only thing to look at was a pharmacy across the street, which had an ad for gum in the window. A woman with gypsy-like hair was hugging a basket of oranges and pineapples. Behind her, miniature fruit trees stretched into a cinematic sunset.

"The taste of California in a gum," it said.

Sandra made a face and turned her back to the ad. As if that was any kind of advertisement for a California product. The state needed to move beyond such provincial images. She certainly intended to put such things behind her for good.

Now that Sandra was in Hollywood, she would shed her old selves—Emma Jones the migrant picker's stepdaughter, Sandra Guess the wife of a local bandleader—and become the person she was truly meant to be: a movie star. There was no doubt in Sandra's mind that she had "It," that illusive star quality the magazines were always talking about. Success was in her blood. She came from a long line of prosperous people, including her father, Arthur Beard, who headed an agricultural empire selling prunes across the nation.

On top of that, she had a plan to achieve her goals:

1. Get discovered by a director, producer, or other powerful studio man.

2. Get a contract with a studio.

3. Become a movie star through hard work and determination.

That last part was important. It wouldn't be easy to become a star, but if she worked hard, success would follow. Sandra knew it. And right now, it was time to go to the studio. Plastering a smile on her face, she moved backward down the street, handing out coupons to everyone she saw and chirping, "Have a glass of sunshine on us."

She knew from a map she'd memorized that Paramount Pictures was four blocks away, but she'd underestimated how long the blocks were. Each one took at least ten minutes to walk. Once Sandra was off the main road, she gave up handing out coupons and hurried as fast as she could toward the studio with the sign clapping against her legs. To pass the time, she thought about what she would say if Rayo Sunshine discovered she'd left her post. She could always say, "I thought I was allowed to leave for breaks." Or even better, "I had to use the restroom for female troubles." It was unlikely they would refuse to pay her because of female troubles.

By the time Paramount Pictures came in sight, Sandra's forehead was shiny with sweat. She stood near the base of a tree, fanning herself and studying the view.

The studio was a fortress of yellow stucco and red-shingled roofs set back from the road and surrounded by spindly palm trees that looked like upside-down mops. The way in was through a lacy wrought iron gate. A guard at a window opened and closed a panel for people to pass through. Above it all, water towers teetered on metal tripods, like sentinels watching over the scene.

You can do this, Sandra thought. *It's just handing out a piece of paper.*

As she crossed the street, she saw three women standing by the gate. They were roughly the same size and wore chintz dresses and matching white shoes. Only their hair color differed— one blond, one chestnut, and one dark brown. As Sandra approached, they burst out in a chord, their voices vibrating like buzzing bees. Then they launched into a three-part rendition of "I Got Rhythm."

I got rhythm, I got music, I got my man
Who could ask for anything more?

Sandra smiled at them as she passed. Without breaking a note, the singers' heads snapped around, their eyes as narrow as slots in a penny arcade, shocking Sandra so much she almost jumped. She dropped her gaze and walked down the sidewalk until the singing was muffled by traffic. When she looked up again, a crowd was forming around the group. Despite this, the blond was still watching Sandra with the same hard expression.

Clearly they didn't want another woman around the studio attracting attention. They saw her as competition. Well, they were right. She was. Besides, Sandra had more of a right to be here than they did—she had a job to do. Adjusting the sign, she got a coupon at the ready.

"Hello," she said to the first man who came by. "Have a glass of sunshine on me."

The man blinked at Sandra and took the coupon. "Thanks."

As he walked away, he glanced back at Sandra's legs in the orange tights, which she took as a promising sign. Maybe it was good that the dress was so short. Already, another man was emerging from the gate. She eyed him in what she hoped was a sensual way.

"Would you like a glass of sunshine?" she said. "On me?"

He took the coupon, looked at it, and then at her. "Thank you, miss," he said, tipping his hat.

This was working! Sandra straightened her shoulders and smiled in a way that would have flashed her dimples, if she had them. She considered herself the Greta Garbo type—sophisticated and elegant, yet relatable to the average woman—but that wasn't appropriate right then, what with the sandwich board and all, so she would be the gay comedienne instead. She'd be the singing telegram girl who wisecracks with Groucho Marx. She'd be the bright-eyed, all-American dancer waving a flag at the end of the Ziegfeld number.

More people came by, and Sandra handed out coupons, paying extra attention to the men. In between, she waved at the cars, looking for movie stars. Once a Rolls-Royce went through the studio gate, but she couldn't see who was in the backseat. The chauffeur did all the talking to the guard.

As the singers finished a song, there was a smattering of applause from the tourists. They launched into "Dream A Little Dream," their voices drifting underneath the traffic. "But in your dreams, whatever they be, dream a little dream of me."

Whenever Sandra glanced at the group, one of the girls glared at her in that same fierce way. It was making Sandra angry. Since coming to Hollywood, women were always giving her unfriendly looks. Of course they were all in competition for the men's attention, but that didn't mean the other girls had to be such pills all the time. It was exhausting.

A Ford pulled up to the curb and a woman dressed in a delivery outfit climbed from the passenger side. She was wearing a bellhop uniform with a square hat on her head. From the trunk of the car, she pulled out a gigantic flower arrangement and tottered over to the gate.

"Hey," someone said to Sandra.

She turned to see a boy of about eleven years old holding one of the coupons.

"Where is this place that I can get my free glass of orange juice?" he said.

Sandra glanced back at the delivery girl. "Doesn't it say on the coupon?"

"It says Sunset Boulevard. Where on it, though?"

"I don't know. Can't you look it up? The phone book?"

"I don't got a phone book."

Now the delivery girl was arguing with the guard at the gate, her tone sharp as she threw words over the top of the flower arrangement. Sandra strained, trying to grasp what the conflict was about.

"Hey, miss?" the kid said. He stared up with accusing eyes.

She sighed. "It's a building shaped like a giant orange. You can't miss it."

"But Sunset Boulevard is long. Am I supposed to walk the whole thing looking for a big orange?"

The delivery girl was staring at the guard in some kind of standoff. Suddenly she hurled the flowers down and stomped back to the Ford. Throwing open the passenger door, she said, "Let's go." The flower basket rolled on its side, the florist sponge sliding to the sidewalk.

As the Ford jerked around the corner, a man came out of the studio gate, stepped over the flowers, and stopped with his hands in his pockets. His eyes landed on Sandra, and the way he met her gaze made her heart thump in her ears. This wasn't a man going to lunch or taking a stroll. He was looking for Sandra. He didn't even glance at the girl group when they started singing "Happy Days Are Here Again" in his direction.

"Well?" the kid said.

"Go away," she hissed. "Where's your mother?"

"Please, miss? I want to know the address, that's all. I want my orange juice."

"Okay. The address is 10042 Sunset Boulevard."

The kid looked relieved. "Why didn't you say so in the first place?"

"Shoo, shoo," Sandra said, pushing him away before he realized she made the address up.

The man gestured for Sandra to come over to him. She put her hand on her chest, and mouthed, "Me?" He nodded and she headed toward him, clutching the stack of coupons. Now? He was going to discover her *now*? But she wasn't ready to be discovered. Was she? Did she even want to be an actress? Of course. Of course she did. That was a silly thing to think.

As she approached, she pulled out a coupon. "Hello," she said in her most sultry voice. "Have a glass a sunshine on me."

The man was big, with a beard cupping his chin. He took the coupon. "Thanks. What's your name?"

"Sandra Sanborn."

The singers were watching with their arms crossed. It filled Sandra with cool delight that they should witness this moment.

"Miss Sanborn, I'm sick of Rayo Sunshine sending you girls over here. We've had several talks with them about it, and they keep promising they won't send anymore. And yet, here you are."

Sandra's mouth fell open. So that was why Rayo Sunshine insisted their employees stay at their posts—other girls had done this too. So many had done it, in fact, that Paramount had asked Rayo Sunshine to stop it from happening.

"Oh," she said. "I wouldn't dream of bothering the studio, but—"

"But you are, Miss Sanborn. You're the fourth girl from Rayo Sunshine this month. And I'll tell you what I told each of them: There's no soliciting in front of the studio."

The sound of traffic filled Sandra's ears. Out of the corner of her eye, she saw the brunette whispering in the blond's ear.

"What about them?" she said, pointing at the singers. "Aren't they soliciting?"

He glanced over his shoulder. "They have permission to be here, but you don't. Look, I'm going to call this employer of yours. He can explain to me why you're here."

"What?" Sandra said, and then smiled. "You don't have to do that. I can just leave. It'll be like you never saw me."

He turned the coupon over, ignoring her. Desperately she tried to think how to turn this situation to her favor. She imagined saying something that would make the man soften to her, and soon they'd be laughing together. He'd say, "I'm sorry I was so rough about your being here. You seem like a nice kid." And she would nod understandingly and say that he was just doing his job and that she would leave now. No need to call anyone.

The man put a stubby finger on the phone number at the bottom of the coupon. "Wait here. I'm calling your boss."

Before she could reply, he headed toward the studio and disappeared behind a door in the guard station. Stunned, she stared through the gate at a yellow building with the words STAGE 4 painted on it. Then she whirled around and hurried down the street, the sign beating against her legs. She had to get away from here before he came back.

At the intersection, she ducked behind a family of overweight tourists until the light changed, then rushed across the street. That was when she heard laughing underneath the traffic.

By the gate, the singers were cackling and pointing at her. Sandra held herself erect, like Mabel had always taught her, and walked with as much dignity as she could muster until she turned the corner.

When she was out of sight, she heaved the sign off and stood in full view in the scanty dress, rubbing her shoulders. It felt wonderful, like removing a girdle after a night of dancing. She couldn't go back to the factory and get the dress and hat she'd worn to the job. By now, Rayo Sunshine would know what she'd done. She didn't have the money to throw away perfectly good clothes, but she felt too humiliated to face them. All she wanted to do was go home and hide.

With a sigh, Sandra headed toward the bus stop. Let Rayo Sunshine keep her dress, she decided. The cuffs on the sleeves were fraying anyway.

CHAPTER 3

The next day, Sandra and her neighbor Casey dragged lawn chairs around the front of Mrs. Pickler's boarding house, where they lived, and sat sunning themselves on the walkway. Casey had lived in the boarding house six months longer than Sandra. It was a shabby Victorian moored on an island of concrete and surrounded by factories. Sandra thought there must have been a meadow here once, full of sheep and chaparral with this house in the center of the scene, but now it just looked destined for a wrecking ball. Still, the rent was cheap and she didn't have to have a roommate.

As Sandra explained what had happened at Paramount Pictures, Casey lay with her freckled eyelids shut to the sun, her thin hair splayed around her head. She was bony and slender, and her girlishness was emphasized by her tendency to wear childish things, like ribbons in her hair or puffed sleeves. For the most part, Sandra was honest about what happened at Paramount, except she implied that Rayo Sunshine put her in front of the studio instead of going there by herself. That way she could complain about the situation without sounding like she'd done anything wrong.

The problem was that Casey kept bringing the conversation back to that very point, insisting that it was Rayo Sunshine's fault for sending Sandra to the studio in the first place. "I mean, to put you in that position," Casey said. "Especially since the studio asked them not to send any more girls."

"Yeah," Sandra said. "And when I asked the security guard why the singers could stay there when I had to leave, he said they weren't soliciting. So I said—"

"And you wouldn't have been soliciting either if Rayo Sunshine hadn't put you there. What did your supervisor say when you went back to the factory?"

"Nothing. I never went back. I just came home."

"Oh, you didn't, Sandra."

"Well, I was embarrassed."

"You poor thing. But you shouldn't let them get away with treating you like that."

"You're probably right. I mean, when I think about the way those singers were glaring at me, like I was taking away their business, if you know what I mean. So I said to the security guard—"

"You should complain, that's what you should do," Casey said, sitting up in her chair. "You should go down to this Rayo Sunshine Corporation and file a grievance for public embarrassment. I'll go with you if you like."

Sandra was starting to regret bringing the topic up. Casey looked as if she were about to drag her to the car this very minute. Of course, that was out of the question.

"That's okay," she said. "Maybe I'll stop by tomorrow when I go downtown."

"You'd better," Casey said, leaning back. "Honestly. The nerve of some people."

Sandra inhaled the cigarette she and Casey were sharing,

thinking that so far things weren't working out in Hollywood the way she'd expected. She'd been here for three months and hadn't even auditioned for anything yet.

"I expected it to be hard to get into pictures, but I didn't think it would be this hard," she said. "With all the competition, how can you get noticed?"

Casey shrugged. "Beats me. Date a producer?"

Although Casey was joking, Sandra considered this point seriously. While a producer might be difficult to access at this point, surely Sandra could date *someone* connected to the studios.

Of course, it would be easier to meet eligible men if she didn't live in a flophouse in an obscure part of town. When Sandra had more money, she would move to the Hollywood Studio Club where the starlets lived. According to the magazines, producers and directors were always visiting the club to play tennis or swim with the ingénues. Those were the kind of people Sandra should be meeting. She'd wasted so much time already, thanks to Billy. At twenty-six, she was almost too old to be starting out in Hollywood. Luckily, she looked much younger than she was. She could pass for twenty-two—maybe even twenty-one.

"I guess I'll try to go to Central Casting tomorrow," she said. "If it worked for you, it can work for me too."

"That reminds me," Casey said. "I got you something. Wait here." Jumping up, she ran into the house, her knobby arms bent at right angles. The studios used Central Casting to hire non-contract players for bit parts. When Casey first moved to Hollywood, Central got her a job in a mob scene for a film called *The Guardsman*. Along with twenty other extras, she'd stormed a castle wall. Since then, Casey called Central every morning, said her name to an operator, and listened while they checked if there was a part for her. There never was. To make ends meet,

Casey washed dishes at a diner, which made Sandra want to gag. She couldn't imagine anything worse than wiping down greasy dishes with people's spit all over them. It was much better to get a job as a secretary or a babysitter—if you had to get a job, which Sandra didn't, yet.

On the street, a Buick was rattling up to the boarding house and Sandra recognized her landlady, Mrs. Pickler, inside the car. She ground out her cigarette on the sidewalk and flicked it under the chair. The boarding house had strict policies against smoking, one of many rules Sandra ignored.

Mrs. Pickler, wearing an outdated squirrel coat, slammed the car door and shuffled toward the house. Sandra fixed the old woman with a smile as she approached. A white lozenge of a face gazed back at her. "What are you doing out here, Sanborn?"

"Getting some sun."

The old woman wrinkled her nose. "Do I smell cigarette smoke?"

"I don't think so," Sandra said in a mystified voice. "Maybe someone was walking by with one."

Mrs. Pickler put her hands on her hips. "Because if one of my tenants were to be caught with a cigarette, she'd be fined five dollars. We wouldn't want that, now would we, Miss Sanborn?"

"No we wouldn't, Mrs. Pickler."

"Good. Rent is due next week, you know."

"I'll have it."

Mrs. Pickler seemed satisfied and resumed her struggle up the walk. As she fumbled with her keys, the door flew inward and Casey barreled out, nearly knocking her over.

"Goodness!" Casey said. "Are you all right?"

There was a pause, during which Mrs. Pickler seemed to be trying to remember how to breathe. Her shoulders were raised like a startled cat's, and Sandra stifled an urge to laugh.

Slowly, Mrs. Pickler turned to Sandra as if Casey hadn't spoken. "Sanborn, please put those chairs back when you're done."

"I will."

Gripping her purse, Mrs. Pickler passed Casey and shut the door behind her with a firm click.

"That old bat," Casey said. "Rushing in for her afternoon gin, I suppose. Here, I picked this up for you at Central."

She handed Sandra a pamphlet titled, *Pay Rates for Women Players*. It had per diem rates for different categories of women registered with Central Casting. There were three groups based on looks, class, and wardrobe. A "Dress Extra" was paid fifteen dollars for parts including "society women and royalty." A "Character Woman" was paid ten dollars for "college girls, secretaries, and governesses." A "Woman" was paid seven dollars for "maids, nurses, and peasants."

She fingered the page, thinking that she would be a good Dress Extra. "Which category are you?" she asked Casey.

"Woman, mostly on account of my wardrobe. They want higher-paid extras to have furs and gowns so the studio doesn't have to provide costumes."

Sandra frowned. She didn't own any furs and her gowns were getting a little weathered. "Seven dollars isn't much pay for a whole day's work," she said.

"Yeah, but there's other ways to make money. A speaking part pays twenty-five dollars. And there are death scenes, which can go up to fifty dollars if the way you die is dangerous. Just lying there like you're dead is only three dollars though."

"For a day's work?"

"Yes. But think about it: three dollars for lying down all day. Where else can you get a job like that? And then there's being a screamer, which pays ten dollars."

"What does that mean, a screamer?"

"Screaming in fear, you know. Like this." Casey froze, focusing on something behind them. Sandra turned, but nothing was there except Mrs. Pickler's car. Slowly, Casey's hands rose to her face, her fingers curling like a baby's as she watched something approach her chair. She whimpered and tossed her head from side to side, eyes shut as if she didn't have the strength to keep them open. Just when the invisible thing reached her, she let out a theatrical scream and fell back in a faint. Sandra burst out laughing.

The door flew open and Mrs. Pickler stuck out her head. "What are you two doing?"

Casey sat up, choking with laughter. "I'm sorry, Mrs. Pickler. We're practicing for auditions."

"Well, stop it. Sanborn, you have mail. You two had better come in now."

Sandra and Casey exchanged glances. Neither of them liked that Mrs. Pickler was talking to them as though they were children. Still, Sandra was curious about the package Mrs. Pickler was holding, which looked like a shoebox wrapped in brown paper. When she took it, along with the rest of her mail, she saw that it was from Billy Guess.

"I have to attend to this," she said to Casey, and hurried past Mrs. Pickler into the house.

In her room, Sandra was confronted with a mess. Clothes lay on the floor and orange peels piled by the bed gave the room a pungent stink. On the bureau was a bag of groceries that she hadn't put away yet.

The clutter looked out of place next to Mrs. Pickler's feminine touches: organdy curtains, dusty silk flowers, a ruffled bedspread. The back of the door had a sign that said:

HOUSE RULES
$5 PENALTY

1. No men allowed.

2. No musical instruments.

3. No smoking or drinking alcohol.

4. The owner reserves the right to inspect room at any time.

Sandra sat on the bed with the package on her lap, feeling shaky. She hadn't heard from her husband Billy since she drove away in their car three months ago. Now he was finally sending her something. Maybe candy or a gift, with a letter begging her to come back.

Or money. God knew she needed it.

She unwrapped the box. On top was a jar of cold cream that she'd left behind and wished for many times. Underneath was a card of bobby pins, a mostly empty box of talcum powder, a coin purse, her Chinese-red lipstick—another thing she'd missed—and an old sketchbook. Below that were several letters.

That was it. No note begging her to come back. No divorce papers. Nothing more than forgotten things shoved in a box.

Billy wasn't coming after her.

Sandra let out her breath. Well. What did she expect?

The sketchbook was full of drawings from high school. She flipped past pictures of her feet, a cow chewing grass, a bunch of grapes in a bowl. It brought her back to those empty summers before she went to the junior college, when she decided to be an artist like Amy from *Little Women*. Like Amy, Sandra was always at a want for drawing pencils, and she liked how the novel made that sound romantic, as if being poor were honorable and not boring and awful.

All summer, whenever Sandra's stepfather wasn't making her pick prunes, she lounged around in her nightgown or wandered the back roads of Healdsburg, stealing figs and persimmons from people's yards. Always, there was a sketchbook by her side, and it struck her odd now that this was the only one she still owned.

She turned to the envelopes that were in the shoebox. They were addressed to "Emma Jones c/o Billy Guess." One was thicker than the other. The return address was from someone named John Hollingsworth. The name wasn't familiar.

Dear Mr. Guess,

My name is John Hollingsworth. I'm trying to track down my daughter, Emma Jones, who I heard was living with you in Santa Rosa.

I'm coming up on 60 years old and would like to meet her while I can. I'm living in Petaluma at the Parson's House on Kentucky Street. I'm a painter, and I have a studio that I'd like to show Emma. If you'd be so kind as to tell her about me and ask if she'd like to meet me, I'd apresiate it.

You can write me back at this address.

Respectfully,

John Hollingsworth

Sandra frowned at the letter. She'd never heard of this man. And what did he mean by his daughter? She was Arthur Beard's daughter. And her father certainly would know how to spell the word *appreciate*.

The second envelope was also from John Hollingsworth, dated a month later.

Dear Mr. Guess,

Thank you for writing me back. I'm proud to hear that Emma is such a success, first going to college and now making a go of it in Hollywood. It's exciting to think there might be an actress in the family.

You're mistaken to believe that Arthur Beard was Emma's father. I met Mabel in the '90s and knew her until the 1906 earthquake, when her husband Arthur Beard died. A romance blossomed, from which Emma came. I left when she was a baby.

I'm sorry to hear that your marriage to Emma is over. If you hear from her, I hope you'll be so kind as to tell her about me and ask her to please write.

Sincerely,
John Hollingsworth

Sandra reread the line, "*your marriage to Emma is over.*" So that was Billy's response to this creep spreading lies about her: My marriage is over. Sandra isn't my problem anymore. I'll just pop these letters in a box and move on with my life.

With a huff, Sandra tossed the letters in the trash. She'd only been in Hollywood a few months and already nuts were coming out of the woodwork. Mabel had warned her that people would lie to her, and here it was—a man claiming to be her father. Ridiculous. It had always been a fact: Sandra's father was Arthur Beard. He'd died in the San Francisco earthquake when Mabel was pregnant and she'd been forced to marry Daddy Jones, a migrant farmer who promised to take care of them, but didn't.

Sandra put the cold cream, lipstick, talcum powder, and bobby pins beside her makeup on the bureau, then unpacked the groceries: cigarettes in the drawer in case Mrs. Pickler came by, peanut butter on the windowsill to keep it cool, bread and apples wrapped tightly on the dresser. Then she hung her clothes in the closet, threw out the orange peels, and made the bed.

The room clean, she decided to do her exercises. Turning to the mirror, Sandra tilted her head to the right and tipped it so that her cheekbones were highlighted. Biting the inside of her cheeks, she held the pose, memorizing how it felt so she could reproduce it for photographers. She tried to do this once a day as practice, like a singer running scales. Around the mirror she'd pinned pictures of actresses from magazines for inspiration: Joan Crawford lazing on a sofa; Greta Garbo thrusting her jawbone at the camera; Jean Harlow gazing over her shoulder, her chin and nose rounded like a rubber doll's.

In the reflection, Sandra could see John Hollingsworth's letters on top of the trash and jerked her gaze away. She resented the suggestion that she was a person of illegitimate origins. She was the heiress of an empire—or would have been if her real father had lived.

Beside her on the bureau was the rest of her mail, which

she'd forgotten about. The new issue of *Photoplay* had the headline, IS MARLENE DIETRICH THROUGH? Sandra picked up the magazine, curious whether Dietrich was quitting Hollywood like they were saying. Underneath was another letter, this one from her mother.

When Sandra left for LA, she'd sent Mabel a breezy note saying that she was divorcing Billy and going to Hollywood to become a star. Since then she'd sent several equally breezy notes that said things like, "All's well! I've moved to a lovely apartment. LA is beautiful." She hadn't gotten a reply until now.

Hesitantly she opened the envelope and pulled out a sheet of thick stationery.

Dear Emma,

This was typical. Mabel refused to call her Sandra, even though she'd been going by the name since college.

I thought I'd write since I haven't heard from you in weeks. It's getting hard to explain to people. All I know, I tell them, is that she left her husband and moved to Hollywood. She doesn't keep me informed.

That wasn't true. Sandra had sent her mother postcards. Yes, they could have been longer, but it wasn't as though Sandra was ignoring Mabel. She was putting off correspondence until she had something to say about breaking into movies.

I'm shocked by your decision to leave Billy to chase a dream of becoming "a star." I didn't raise you to have a string of failed marriages.

Oh, that was rich. One failed marriage was hardly a "string."

Since your Daddy Jones passed away last year, money has been tighter than usual.

Ugh! Ezekiel Jones was not her daddy. He was her stepfather. Sandra hated when her mother said this.

I'll get by, however. I always do. Don't worry about your mother. Although it would be nice if you would write, if for no other reason than to spare me the humiliation of having to explain to people that I don't know where my daughter is, or what she's doing.

Your loving mother,
Mabel

Sandra tossed the letter on the floor. Her mother had no right to criticize the divorce. Mabel's marriage to Daddy Jones had been one long fight about money. Sandra had been teased all through school for secondhand dresses and lunches of bread and prunes that Daddy Jones got for free from his picking jobs.

The image of her mother in her raggedy tea gowns and Gibson hairdo floated in Sandra's mind like a sunspot. There was so much Sandra didn't know. Why had her mother left San Francisco in the first place? Her grandparents had died, but Sandra didn't know the details. And how had Arthur Beard died? Yes, there was an earthquake, but she didn't know the cause of death.

And why had Sandra never inherited any money? Where did it all go?

She retrieved the letters from John Hollingsworth from the trash, intending to reread them, and noticed heaviness in one of the envelopes that she'd missed before. Inside was a gray cardboard frame. She pulled up the cover to reveal a picture of Mabel.

Sandra's mouth fell open. In the photo, Mabel was younger than Sandra had ever seen her. She was turned toward the camera, her face at three-quarters profile. Her thick brown hair was swept under a hat and she wore a fur shoulder piece that emphasized a tiny, corseted waist. Even in her confusion, Sandra felt a tickling of pride to see her mother in all her beauty and wealth.

On the back was a date stamp: 1904. Two years before Sandra was born.

She hated how this was making her feel. She didn't want to think about any of it. Tomorrow she was going to Central Casting, and she should be focusing on that. This was all a distraction from her plan.

Standing, she went to the closet and pulled an orange hatbox from the shelf. It was empty because the hat that was supposed to go in it was still on the costume rack at Rayo Sunshine, along with the dress she'd worn that day. Sandra dropped the letters into the box and shut the lid, thinking that she would ask Mabel about John Hollingsworth later. She didn't have time right now—she had to get ready for Central Casting—but soon she would find out more.

The next time Sandra wrote her mother, she promised herself, she would bring the letters up.

CHAPTER 4

Excerpt from Chapter VI, page 7 from Medical Oddities and Other Horrors by Oliver Goldhammer, MD, PhD (Walter J. Black, Inc., Copyright 1947):

. . . Incan murals dating as far back as the fifteenth century give accounts of men who glowed "*azul*" before the "finger of god" knocked them down, suggesting ancient cases of this phenomenon. More recently in 1927, witnesses claimed that a New Jersey man named Alvin Elah turned periwinkle before his tie started zigging back and forth like a metronome. In 1941, an unnamed Indiana man not only turned "cobalt blue," according to *The Indiana Tribune*, but his socks flew out of the laundry basket and into the garden, where they proceeded to cling to him.

Yet these incidents might be dismissed if it weren't for Vira Webb. Her case is unusual in that unlike with Elah or the Indiana man, the event occurred at a society ball in Portland, Maine in 1851. There was an extraordinary amount of coverage at the time, including an article on the front page of *The Portland Heralder* with the headline: YOUNG LADY ESCAPES IN ELECTRICAL STORM SPECTACLE. Webb, unique among her fellow afflicted, is the only person to have survived the phenomenon to tell about it. Indeed, she went on to marry and her daughter, Mabel Sanborn, survives her.

It's a recorded fact that the Sanborn ball was held during thunderstorm season. While the weather might have been enough to cancel an ordinary party, this ball was much anticipated by Maine society because the respected judge, Luke Sanborn, was expected to announce the engagement of his son, James Sanborn, to Melissa Fletcher. On top of that, the judge had converted the attic of his three-story home into a ballroom.

When the guests arrived, they were directed up two flights of stairs to the third story, where the new ballroom spanned the length of the house. The maple floor gleamed, chrysanthemum bouquets hung on the walls, and refreshments were laid out beside a barrel of Mr. Sanborn's famous apple jack. At one end of the room, a small orchestra was setting up. At the other, a balcony overlooked a field. Someone in reckless spirits had thrown open the balcony doors and an energized breeze blew through the room. Every so often, lightning struck the field, and each time the guests exclaimed, "Oooh!"

Only Elmer Sanborn, James's cousin, remained unmoved. He had more important things to think about than lightning. In less than a month, he was planning to leave for the California Gold Rush.

His family was against the plan. They'd pleaded with Elmer to give up what they saw as a dangerous and foolhardy journey, and when that didn't work, they insisted he come to the ball, hoping that a young lady would distract him from his goals. But they could never understand how dull the twirling dancers seemed to Elmer. Compared to the sparkling promise of California gold, Maine society women were as colorless as wrens. As everyone danced, he stood by the wall with his hands behind his back, measuring the cost of the journey against the riches he expected to make in California.

The newspaper said that a man could net over $1,500 a day in the Gold Rush. That was more than Elmer could expect as a yearly salary after a lifetime of working at his father's bank. And that was just one figure. It was possible to make ten times that if you were lucky. Men were said to be able to stroll down the American River and scoop gold out of the water. A Frenchman had moved a stump on his land and found $15,000 in gold lying underneath it. Given this, Elmer couldn't understand why every man at this ball wasn't leaving for California this instant.

Take his cousin James, whose engagement to Melissa Fletcher this ball was celebrating. Everyone said James was going to be a great lawyer like his father, but Elmer could only pity him. James would spend every day rearranging papers in an office while Elmer would be living an autonomous life of wealth and adventure. Elmer had asked his cousin to come with him to California, laying out how easy it would be to get rich, but James had proposed to Melissa instead. To do something like that when there was a gold rush going on! Elmer couldn't fathom it.

Near the balcony, James was standing beside Melissa, who was patting the bottom of her ringlets so that they bounced upward. Elmer had seen her do this several times, once while talking to another lady at a concert and a second time while in line at a picnic. Each time, the gesture struck Elmer as vain. Now Melissa was talking to someone else, a woman. Who was that? Elmer could only see the side of her head. He strained forward, squinting through the dancers that separated him from the balcony until he recognized the girl. It was the piano player from church. Her name was Vira Webb.

Here Elmer tried to go back to thinking about the Gold Rush, but he kept trailing off to watch Vira. There was something arresting about her. It wasn't that she was prettier than the other girls here. Elmer wouldn't even have noticed her if she didn't get up in front of the congregation to play hymns every Sunday. No, something else was drawing Elmer's attention to Vira as she stood on the balcony with the evening sky streaked purple and gray behind her. He blinked to clear his vision.

Yes, it was still there.

Vira Webb was glowing blue.

It wasn't so much that Vira herself was blue as the blue was hovering over her skin, encircling her face and neck, and fading into her clothes. It was a soft blue, the color of forget-me-nots, but noticeable enough that Elmer could see it from across the room.

The feet of the dancers pounded to the rhythm of the Virginia reel as another gust of wind blasted the women's skirts. As if hypnotized, Elmer pushed through the dance floor to get closer to Vira. The blue outlined her body in a fuzzy radiance, like halos Elmer had seen in pictures of saints. She even looked a bit like a saint just then, smiling at Melissa with her hands clasped in front of her.

Then, as Elmer watched, one of Vira's blond curls rose off her forehead and stood straight in the air, as if someone was holding it there. She was laughing and the curl moved with her as she leaned forward and touched Melissa's arm with her icy blue hand.

If nothing else, Elmer was a man of action. Without

knowing why, he dove across the room and tackled Vira, pulling her into the ballroom. The dancers stopped in collective shock, but there was no time for outrage. As Vira's shoes cleared the balcony, there was a violent crack, like monstrous billiard balls slamming together. Lightning struck where Vira had been standing, hitting Luke Sanborn's balcony in a fierce stab as red and hot as a fireplace poker. Flames began to lick the balcony.

Before anyone could stop him, James Sanborn grabbed the barrel of apple jack and emptied it onto the fire. It was the wrong thing to do. Smoke billowed everywhere as the flames reacted to Mr. Sanborn's carefully attended liquor and traveled closer to the dancers. Women began to scream all over the room.

"Everyone, to the stables! The stables!" Luke Sanborn shouted.

The guests rushed toward the stairs. Though the newly hewn doorframe was wide enough for a man and woman to enter the ballroom in grand style, it wasn't wide enough for the minister's wife and two portly widows to shove through at once. For a moment the women were stuck like caterpillars caught in the beak of a bird. Then they burst into the hallway, their petticoats flying up in all directions.

While this was going on, Vira lay in Elmer's grasp, apparently having fainted. Undaunted, and rather enjoying himself, Elmer picked Vira up and carried her through the stampeding guests to the stables, where she regained consciousness in time to be laid in a carriage. For a moment she met Elmer Sanborn's hazel eyes with her own. He grinned and galloped off to help with the fire.

"That's a very brave young man," said a friend, watching Vira closely.

"Yes," she said.

She might have said something else then, but as the word left her mouth, rain began to pour down in a torrent. The balcony was doused and smoke rose to the sky. People hurried to their carriages, ball gowns slick like wet rose petals. The air was filled with the smell of burnt apples.

As the women gathered around Vira, her blue eyes followed the men rushing to keep the weakening fire from spreading. Onlookers noted how she watched one man in particular as he darted through the rain. Some later said she caused the fire by standing where lightning could hit her.

CHAPTER 5

The next day, Sandra stepped out of the car near Central Casting. The sky was a long way up and blocked by buildings. She was wearing her best daytime ensemble: a black silk skirt, white blouse, and jacket with cape sleeves. She knew she looked smart. Her one regret was the lack of fur trimming on the jacket. It was important to appear rich and elegant if she wanted to be a Dress Extra. At least she had the car from Billy. Most extras had to take the bus.

The building in front of her used to be a department store. Giant windows, which once displayed goods for sale, were now empty holes waiting to be filled. Some two dozen men were scattered on the sidewalk in front of the windows. Every one of them had a bushy beard and was wearing a checkered or plaid shirt. It looked like a busload of lumberjacks had been let out in front of the building.

Ignoring their curious glances, Sandra tried the Central Casting door. It was locked. A man with a brown beard smiled at her. "Too bad for you," he said in a German accent. "It's a men's day today."

Sandra didn't know what that meant. According to Casey, Central would take her information, register her in a database, and match her to the roles. No one had said anything about men's or women's days. Before she could ask if she should come back later, a clock chimed eleven o'clock and the men moved toward the building. Someone had appeared inside the display window, but even though Sandra was tall for a woman, she couldn't see over the men, most of whom were big with broad shoulders.

"Who's that?" she said to the man who'd spoken to her.

"You are green, aren't you? That's the casting director, Vachel Montgomery. He is about to pick someone for the call. Excuse me." He sprinted away and pushed toward the window.

Sandra walked around the crowd until she had a better view of Vachel Montgomery. He was bald and wearing a white coat like a dentist, and was standing in the center of the window, watching the men. This must be the person in charge of who got parts in movies. Sandra would have to get to know him. Not in the "casting couch" way, of course. She'd heard about women who did that sort of thing, but she was a lady. She drew the line at flirting. Or maybe dinner.

Vachel turned over a piece of cardboard that said:

Part: cowhand
Movie: riders of destiny
man, age 25–30. long beard. 6 feet tall

There was grumbling among the men. "Damn it," someone said. "Only one part?"

"There's no work these days," said another.

Vachel Montgomery paced back and forth in the window, his eyes never leaving the men on the other side of the glass. Finally he pointed to one with a strawberry-blond beard and twirled his finger in the air so that the man turned like a watch in a Neiman Marcus display case. Vachel studied him carefully, as though taking in every detail of his appearance. Nodding, he shifted his eyes back to the group, scanning the faces that tilted toward him like daisies to the sun. He pointed to a guy with a triangular goatee that looked like a devil's beard. He, too, stepped forward and rotated.

Now Vachel tapped the sign, indicating he was making his choice. There was an expectant silence, during which Sandra found herself rooting for the strawberry-blond, who was the handsomer of the two. A half minute passed as Vachel stared at the two men while gripping his chin, his pupils darting back and forth between them. Then he pointed to devil's beard, who triumphantly shot his arms into the air. There was good-natured razzing and patting on shoulders as he made his way through the crowd. The door to Central Casting opened and a woman in a polka-dotted dress stepped aside for him to enter. They disappeared inside.

Sandra turned back to the window, intending to catch Vachel's eye, but he was already gone. The rest of the men were dispersing down the block and she was alone as the heavy door swung toward the latch. Just before it shut, she caught the handle and slipped inside Central Casting.

The room she stepped into was loud. Telephones were ringing and operators were repeating, "Central?" "Central?" "Central?" into receivers. Sandra stood behind devil's beard as he talked to the woman in the polka-dotted dress, who was sitting at a small desk. Behind her, operators lined two long tables and shouted into telephones. Central Casting looked more like a polling outfit than anything to do with Hollywood.

As the man with the devil's beard finished up and hurried onto the street, she found herself face-to-face with the secretary, who leaned back in her chair, regarding Sandra.

"It's a men's day," she said coldly.

"I know," Sandra said, although she still didn't know what that meant. "I'm here to register. Should I come back on a women's day?"

"No, sorry. We aren't registering anyone through the end of the year."

Sandra wasn't sure how to respond to this. It hadn't occurred to her that Central might reject her outright. After all, they'd registered Casey.

For a moment it seemed there was nothing to do except leave. But on the drive over, Sandra had recited every motto she remembered about persistence. "The squeaky wheel gets the grease." "You have not because you ask not." "There is nothing impossible to him who will try."

She leveled a commanding gaze at the girl. "I'd like to discuss this with your supervisor."

"You're a riot," the girl said, pushing off the desk and heading toward the back of the room. "I'll get Mrs. Mel."

It struck Sandra that she'd seen nothing but girls since coming to Hollywood. This was a woman walking toward her now, with a round face and pearl earrings and a bosom like a shelf underneath a pink suit. Mrs. Mel stopped in front of Sandra and folded her hands. "What may I do for you?"

Sandra smiled brightly. "Hello. My name is Sandra Sanborn and I'm here to register for work."

At this, several operators looked up from their phones. Their faces were unreadable.

"I believe you were informed we're not registering anyone at this time," Mrs. Mel said.

"Yes, but can't you make an exception? I have a great deal of experience. I can sing, dance, do accents, drive—"

The woman shut her eyes. "I cannot and I will not. No. We

have five hundred calls a month and seventeen thousand registered actors. Even if I registered you, there would be no work for a year, and then it would be a crowd scene that pays three dollars for a day's work." She recited this speech as if she'd said it many times.

"What am I supposed to do then?" Sandra said. "Everyone knows Central Casting is how people break into pictures."

Mrs. Mel sniffed. "My advice is to think over your life, decide what you do best, and go home and do it. Hollywood doesn't need or want you."

Sandra's mouth popped open. All her arguments about why she should be registered felt weak against this woman's thorough dismissal of her. The girl in the polka-dotted dress dropped her eyes to her manicure and smirked. Meekly, Sandra turned to leave.

No one was around outside. The shadows from the building made Sandra shiver, so she leaned against her car, soaking in the warmth from the engine. She hadn't been here long enough for it to cool down.

Hollywood doesn't need you or want you. The words rattled in her head.

Maybe that woman was right. Maybe Sandra was just an ordinary person, not special or beautiful or talented. Just ordinary.

And if that were the case, what should she do? She was almost out of money. There weren't many jobs she could do as a woman that appealed to her. She didn't want to be a teacher or a nurse. She certainly didn't want to be someone's maid, or a waitress, or a shop girl. She wouldn't go back to Mabel in Healdsburg—she'd promised herself that she would never do that. While she liked to draw and paint, that wasn't a practical way to make money. The only other option was to become a secretary. She'd taken shorthand and typing in college. Secretaries in San Francisco made fifty dollars a week.

But Sandra had left Billy to become a movie star. It didn't count if she became a secretary instead.

"What kind of car is that?" said a voice. It was the guy with the German accent who'd spoken to her before. He bent to inspect her tires, although Sandra didn't know what there was to see down there.

"Oh," she said, distractedly. "It's a Ford."

He looked sympathetic. "What's wrong?"

"Central won't register me," she said, before she thought better of telling a stranger her problems. "This awful woman told me that they aren't registering anyone and that I should go home and that Hollywood doesn't need me."

She clapped her mouth shut. If she kept talking, she'd be sobbing all over this man's neck in a minute.

He leaned beside her with his elbow resting on her car. "Was this an older woman who said that to you?"

"Yes. Mrs. Mel."

"Ah. Marion Mel. She says that to everyone. Central wants extras to think of themselves as hobbyists so the studios can pay them low wages. I'm afraid you're the latest victim."

Sandra considered this. The woman's speech did sound rehearsed. Maybe Mrs. Mel was paid to discourage hopeful actors and destroy their dreams. If so, Sandra would be foolish to listen to her.

"But most of the studios use Central," she said. "You have to be registered if you want to break in as an extra, don't you?"

"You can get around that. Get an assistant director to call Central and ask them to add you to the registration. You're a pretty girl. Someone will do it for you."

Sandra nodded. This man was right. She wouldn't give up. This was just the part of the story where she struggled before achieving success. Many stars started out as extras—Norma

Shearer, Mary Pickford, Clark Gable. There was no reason why Sandra couldn't do it too. She'd been silly to listen to that woman's speech that she used to destroy people, probably out of jealousy.

"Thank you," she said.

He extended his hand. "My name is Frederick Bauer."

"Sandra Sanborn."

"Well, Miss Sanborn, I was going to get on a bus to go to the DeMille Studio. I understand they're casting for cowboy pictures and I don't want to let this beard go to waste. You could give me a ride and talk to them yourself. They don't use Central Casting for bit parts."

So, that was why he was so interested in her car. This guy was looking for a ride. People in Hollywood never did anything to be nice, she supposed.

But if it was true that DeMille didn't use Central Casting, she might be able to skip getting registered altogether. And if that didn't work, maybe she could meet an assistant director and have him call Central for her, like Frederick suggested. There was no harm in trying.

"Get in," she said, opening the car door.

The Cecil B. DeMille Studio was a Southern-style mansion with green shutters on the windows. A plaque said it had been built in 1926. Two Black men in purple livery costumes held open the doors for Sandra and Frederick as they entered a room with tile floors and large vases of horsetail ferns. A sign informed them that casting was located out back, so they turned on their heels and went through the doors again.

If the studio had been a real plantation, the casting

department would have been in the tool shed. Inside the cramped room, more men in beards were clamoring toward a glassed-in counter. Sandra thought she recognized some of them from outside Central Casting—they must have had the same idea as Frederick. A young man wearing a visor was yelling at them through the glass. "I'll pay you extras off, but the rest of you get out of here. There's nothing doing today. There won't be anything doing today. Get out!"

Frederick stroked his beard. "Nothing doing, the man informs us."

Sandra scanned the room and noticed a young woman in their midst, the only other girl in the room. She wasn't leaving, and Sandra felt that she shouldn't either, so she waved Frederick away. "I'll meet you outside." Following the girl's lead, Sandra got in line behind her. The girl was young, about sixteen years old. As the men pressed around them, her hair gave off the scent of violets. It was alluring. Sandra made a mental note to invest in violet perfume.

When the harried young man noticed the girl, his expression relaxed. "Oh, hello," he said in a different tone.

The girl had meek eyes. She smiled up at the man. "Hello, yourself. Do you think he'll see me?"

"Come on through." He opened the glass box and the girl disappeared inside the casting director's office. Sandra stepped boldly forward to speak to the man—would the casting director see *her*?—but he looked through her as if she weren't there. "The rest of you, get out," he said.

Defeated, she followed the men outside and stood underneath a fir tree that was dripping with Spanish moss.

Immediately, Frederick was beside her. "He wasn't very nice," he said.

"No, he wasn't," she said, thinking that she had two cigarettes left and if she smoked one in front of this vagabond, he'd expect her to share.

"And so," Frederick said. "Shall we go to Capitol Films?"

"Capitol Films? I never said I'd take you there."

"No, but they're also making Westerns, and they also don't use Central Casting. Therefore, I believe our partnership should continue."

Sandra sighed. Her feet were starting to hurt. These shoes weren't meant for all this walking around. "Where's Capitol Films?"

"Burbank."

"Burbank! That's at least a half hour away."

"More like twenty minutes by car. Come on, *schatzi*. You could use my help. Admit it. This is no life for a girl on her own."

That did it. Sandra turned and walked away. "No, thank you. I've had enough help for one day."

To facilitate her escape, she chose the shortest route to the car, which was to cross the lawn instead of going around it. Halfway there, her heels started to sink into the dirt. The lawn had been watered recently and was still wet in the center. Her shoes were covered in mud, but at this point, it was farther to walk back to the pathway and around to her car than it was to continue across the grass. She shifted her weight to her toes and took another wobbly step.

Frederick fell in stride beside her, his hands sunk in his pockets as if taking a stroll. He didn't seem to notice the mud, or her difficulty managing it.

"You know, a friend of mine is an assistant director at MGM," he said. "I could introduce you if you like."

Sandra took another step. "If you know an assistant director, why doesn't he get you a part in an MGM picture?"

He shrugged. "MGM isn't making Westerns."

"But they're making other pictures."

"No, no, *schatzi*. I only care about Westerns."

"What kind of actor only cares about one kind of movie?"

"Who said I'm an actor?"

Sandra stopped in her tracks so that they were both standing in the middle of the lawn. She could feel the grass blades poking into her silk shoes. "If you're not an actor, what are you then?"

Frederick shrugged. "I'm a photographer."

She shut her eyes. Why couldn't she ever meet a serious person? "If you're a photographer, why are you auditioning for movies?" she said in a deliberate tone.

"They're making a lot of Westerns right now, but they only cast you if you have a beard, so I grew one. It has always been my dream to be a cowboy."

"Now I've seen everything: an aspiring German cowboy."

He put his hand to his chest. "How did you know I was German?"

"Just your thick accent is all."

"I tell you what," Frederick said. "If you take me to Capitol Films, I'll carry you out of this muck."

It was a nervy thing to say. Sandra lifted her foot, and the mud made an alarming sucking noise. "No, thank you," she said.

"All right. Then perhaps I can offer my arm. I don't want you to fall down in that pretty suit."

He held out the arm, clad as it was in a flannel shirt. She had to admit he was right. She would never get mud out of this skirt if she fell. Her shoes were probably done for.

When Sandra reached to hold onto Frederick's arm, he swung it away with a smile. "Ah, ah, ah," he said, wagging his finger. "Only if you will take us to another studio."

Sandra took another step, and the ball of her foot slid

alarmingly. She sighed. "All right. One more studio and that's it. After that, I'm done."

It was late in the day when they arrived at Capitol Films. In addition to several bearded men in the casting office, there was a woman in a velvet evening gown, a man dressed like a clown, and a youth wearing a raccoon coat like a college boy from a decade ago. Again, Sandra asked to speak to the casting director and again, she was told he was unavailable. As she turned to leave, she noticed a bulletin board labeled CASTING OPPORTUNITIES and stopped to read the index cards pinned to it. One drew her interest:

OPEN CASTING CALL

for a feature film starring
Mr. Boris Karloff and Miss Barbara Pepper titled

MYSTERIOUS MANSIONS.

Seeking:
one female extra between 20 and 25 to shoot
in Los Angeles this May. Must be a screamer.

Physical description:
5'5"–5'7", thin, red or auburn hair, upper class, New
England demeanor. White dress, black shoes.

September 10, 10 a.m.–1 p.m.
413 Sunshine Street.

Sandra snatched the card off the board and hurried to her car, clutching her chance—her chance!—in her fingers. This part was perfect for her. She was a tall, thin redhead and had a classy demeanor in spades. She would go to this audition and be cast in her first movie. She could feel it.

As she reached the car, she remembered Frederick, who was still inside the casting office, and stamped her foot. He would want a ride back to Hollywood and she didn't know where he was or how long he would be. For a moment, she considered waiting, then decided she didn't owe him anything. He could take the bus back to Hollywood.

Just as she was about to make a break for it, Frederick appeared, whistling as he walked toward her. "No luck," he said. "You?"

"I got a lead on an audition. It's a casting call for *Mysterious Mansions*, a horror picture."

Frederick grinned from underneath his beard. "Look at you, *schatzi*. One day and you have an audition and a double date planned. Aren't you glad you listened to me?"

"Double date?"

"Yeah. You, me, my MGM assistant director friend, and one of your friends."

No one had asked Sandra out since she'd left Billy. She looked at Frederick carefully. He had nice eyes, but she couldn't tell what the rest of his face was like underneath the beard. Besides, he was pushy and unfocused. His career path made no sense. And she had a strong aversion to cowboy movies.

She put her hand on her hip. "I never said I'd go out with you."

Frederick leaned against her car. "But you *will*, won't you?"

CHAPTER 6

Elmer and Vira were married soon after the Sanborn ball. Prior to that incident, all Vira had expected from life was to marry a respectable gentleman and raise a family in good society. When Elmer saved her from the lightning, she became convinced he was that man—tall, strong, wealthy, the son of a banker, the nephew of a judge. The lightning strike was a romantic catalyst that had thrust them together, and a long, fruitful partnership would naturally follow. He would become a respected banker, she would have their children, and they would go on like that, their future as clear and broad as a river flowing to the sea.

So Vira was confused when one evening, Elmer informed her that they would be starting for the California Gold Rush the following month. "I've been working extra hours at the bank to afford a bigger wagon for the two of us," he said. "I think I've just about accomplished it. There's nothing stopping us from departing with the spring wagon trains."

Vira looked at her husband, who sat beside her on the settee with his legs a little farther apart than she thought was quite proper. A moment before, it had seemed that they were simply sitting together, with Elmer looking at maps of the United States and Vira embroidering and listening to the frogs croaking outside. Now she looked at the map spread before her on the table as her new husband traced the route to California with his finger. The longer he did this, the more Vira understood that he really expected her to go with him to chase gold.

"But," she said, "you aren't serious, are you Elmer?"

He took his finger off the map. "Why, yes. I told you I was going to the Gold Rush. Don't you remember?"

And Vira did remember. He'd mentioned the Gold Rush several times, but it had seemed hypothetical, like saying, "I want to find the Fountain of Youth" or, "I'd like to see the North Pole." It wasn't anything anyone *did*.

"I didn't think you meant it," she said.

He put his arm around her in a way that made her feel suffocated. "Well, I do, my dear. We're going to be Argonauts and seek life on our own terms." Abruptly, he released her and stood up to hang the map on the parlor wall. Taking up a charcoal pencil, he drew a line across the country, explaining that the trip to California would take three months.

Vira stared at the line and thought, *Three months.* "What about the bank?" she said. "Your father expects you to take his place when he retires."

Elmer snorted. "I can't abide banking. Counting other men's money is not for me."

This was so shocking that Vira could only stare. A jolt of fear went through her body, like a pit opening in her stomach. "What are we going to do for money?" she said.

Her husband laughed as if it were the cutest thing he'd ever heard. "We're going to strike it rich. There's gold lying on the riverbanks in California. We'll have so much money that we can live in a grand mansion far nicer than a lifetime of banking could earn us. Haven't you always wanted to be rich?"

In truth, Vira had never thought about it before. She'd never wanted anything more than a nice house, a family, and a long life. What she didn't want, she felt strongly, was to leave everything she knew to go across the country in a wagon.

"Can't we get a house here?" she said. "I was hoping to get one in town, like James and Melissa did after they got married. We could be their neighbors."

It was the wrong thing to say. Elmer stood up, flipping back his sack coat, and put his hands in his pockets. He swallowed several times while looking at the map, as if trying to control his anger. "My cousin James is a coward, if you'll excuse me, Vira," he said. "I asked him to come with me to the Gold Rush, and he did precisely what you describe—married Melissa and bought a house. Well, I want more from life than that. You didn't marry an ordinary man, you know."

Before, Vira had liked it when Elmer said he was extraordinary because it had hearkened back to the dramatic way they met. Now, with that same sinking feeling of terror, she understood that he expected her to be extraordinary too.

"I can't do that," she said, looking helplessly at him. "I can't go to the Gold Rush. Please, Elmer."

His mouth tightened and she felt that he was angry again. He looked at his shoes when next he spoke. "I don't think you understand. I'm going to California next month, and that's my final word on the subject. If you don't want to come along, you can stay with my mother."

Vira bit the inside of her lip, imagining herself locked in that big house with his mother, a weepy woman perpetually in mourning for a child she'd lost before Elmer was even born. As the daughter-in-law, Vira would have to wait on his mother in her dark sitting room, pouring tea and looking into her small face, clad in a lace cap, jowls drooping like tears. It would be months before she saw Elmer again—*if* she saw him again.

He sank beside her on the settee and pulled at her hands until he was holding them. "Let me tell you about the trip," he said. "I want you to come. I've earned extra money to bring you. I'm getting the nicest wagon there is, top of the line for my bride."

Vira dropped her eyes, telling herself to be a good wife and give his plans consideration. He was her husband, after all.

"All right," she said.

He handed her a book titled *The Emigrants Guide to the West*, which contained pertinent information about the trip, from what they should purchase to weather fluctuations to sights they might encounter along the way. Vira flipped through the pages while Elmer explained the journey. The way he talked made the Gold Rush seem like a romantic adventure. There would be dangers—Indians, wild animals, and such—but Elmer would protect her like he'd protected her from the lightning. And in the end, they would be wealthy.

"But how do we know there will still be gold when we arrive?" she said.

"Why, my dear," Elmer said. "Of course there will be gold. Don't you remember how we met? The lightning should have killed you, but it drew us together. We're special. Lucky. How can we help but triumph in anything we do?"

His faith in their love touched her. The guidebook had a picture of a rock formation that looked like a steeple reaching up to heaven. Chimney Rock, it was called. It would be something to see such wonders, especially if, afterward, Vira could return to normal life.

Elmer pushed two chairs aside, clearing a space in the room.

"This is where we'll put the 'Yes' pile, for things we're taking with us." He took a giant step to the left. "And this will be the 'No' pile, for things we're leaving behind. Don't worry," he added, seeing her expression. "We'll replace everything once we've made our fortune."

Vira watched him divide their things between the "Yes" and "No" sides of the room. Each time he put something in the "No" pile, she replaced it with a better version in her mind. The brass candlesticks would be silver. Her mirror had wavy glass—in California, she would get one with good glass. Her dress form was hard to adjust and always slipping out of alignment. She'd have one made in her size. Or better yet, she'd have her dresses tailored and give up sewing altogether.

She imagined other things too—a rosewood bed, hand-painted wallpaper, marble-top tables, an embroidered loveseat like Melissa had purchased for her new home. The house in California was nearly furnished in Vira's mind when she heard a scraping noise. She looked over to see Elmer pushing her piano to the "No" pile.

It was her mother's piano, a small upright with a panel of lavender glass on the front. As a child, Vira often awoke to her mother playing hymns on that piano, the music drifting upstairs to her room as she snuggled deeper into the feather bolster. Nothing could replace that, not even a grand piano made for a concert hall.

"Couldn't we take the piano?" she said in a small voice.

He laughed. "I should think not. Imagine that, a piano in a prairie schooner."

The full weight of what they were doing pressed on Vira again. This was no romantic adventure. They were leaving friends and family for the uneven gamble of striking it rich. What if it didn't work out? What if California was a terrible place? Or,

Vira thought, slipping the tips of her fingers to her neck, what if Elmer died and left her alone in the wilderness?

She looked down at the guidebook and saw the chapter heading "Crossing the Great Desert." With a gasp, Vira dropped the book and fled to the kitchen. Standing by the window, she put her face in her hands and breathed in the rose water on her wrists, trying to calm herself. She must trust her husband. He was wise and experienced, a full seven years older than she was. And he'd saved her from the lightning. Yes, there was that. He'd saved her life.

Elmer's face appeared in the reflection in the window. "What is it, dearest? You can tell me."

I don't want to go on this trip, she wanted to say. *So many bad things could happen. You hear about these bad things happening all the time.*

"It's just so much," she said. "It's too much to think about."

He kissed her cheek. "Then don't think. Leave it to me. I'll take care of everything."

But Vira couldn't stop thinking about it. No matter how she tried, her fears about the journey wouldn't go away. She kept telling herself to have faith in her husband. He was leaving for the Gold Rush and it was her duty to accompany him. Either that or she would have to wait, unwanted, in her in-laws' house for him to send for her, and then she would still have to make the trip to California, but alone. To soothe herself, Vira wrote lists of things to attend to before they left, and her days narrowed to the point of a pencil crossing out tasks. Still, she jerked awake from nightmares of wandering alone in ancient forests, chained to a trunk of frozen lace, Elmer nowhere to be found.

The Monday before they were to leave, Vira woke in the night worrying that all her needles would break on the trail and she wouldn't be able to sew. Where would she get a needle in the wilderness? In the morning, she went straight into town and cleared out the supply at the general store—twenty-five needles in all.

When she returned home, there, in front of the house, was the wagon. Vira had no idea it was coming today. She stood in the yard, clutching her shawl, thinking that she never knew what Elmer was going to do next.

The wagon was tall, about thirteen feet high, and looked like a crate balanced on four spinning wheels. White canvas stretched over the top, as pert and untried as the sail on a boat. It looked like a smaller version of the Conestoga wagons that pulled goods into the city. Soon it would pull them into the unknown.

Elmer was standing inside the wagon with both hands on his hips. Seeing her, he swung out his leg and pushed a wooden rectangle sitting on the wagon's bumper. It clapped to the ground, revealing a folding stair. "Come and look," he said.

Vira eyed the wooden step. It seemed treacherous, as if once she stepped on it she could never come down again. Yet when she looked at Elmer's face, she put a foot on the stair.

Her head brushed the top of the canvas as he slipped beside her and leapt to the ground. She cupped her hands over her mouth. Before her, taking up half the wagon, was her piano.

"I thought about it, and I think we can bring the piano along," Elmer said. "It'll be difficult, but we'll manage."

Vira knew what that meant: Another ox to pull the weight and all the complexities of a heavier wagon on the trail. And he was doing it for her.

Elmer took Vira's hand and tugged so that she was forced

onto her knees. It felt strange to be kneeling on the edge of the wagon, looking into her husband's ruddy face, which was soft and earnest, like a dog begging for scraps. "Vira," he said. "If you come with me to California, I promise I'll build you a grand house, far better than any home we could have here. You can have flowers and fine furniture and you can play your piano every day." He kissed her hand. "So what do you say? Will you accompany me to the Gold Rush?"

Vira looked over her shoulder at the piano. She'd always wanted to be like her mother—peaceful, obedient, full of quiet grace. No matter how she tried, Vira knew she wasn't like that, not in the deepest part of herself, where her faults lay. Maybe this trip would help her change.

Her wedding band shone on her finger, which was still imprisoned in his hand. She knew Elmer was waiting for her to say that it would be all right, and that she would go to California with a light and confident heart. And yes, Vira resolved, she would try harder to trust him. She would be the wife he wanted.

"Yes, Elmer," she said. "I will."

CHAPTER 7

Casey was leaning over Sandra as she sat on the bed, pinning her hair in place. As she did so, Sandra was confronted with a view of the inside of Casey's blouse. Her breasts in her bra looked like two eggs.

"What are these guys' names again?" Casey asked.

"Frederick is the guy I met. His friend, Harry, is the assistant director at MGM."

"That's studio code for errand boy, you know."

"Still. I'm going to make him get Central Casting to register me." Sweet-talking some guy into calling Central Casting sounded a lot easier than traipsing around to studios. Sandra had been so exhausted afterward that she stayed in her room all day yesterday to recover. Her silk shoes were ruined.

Casey stepped back, tilted her head to the side, and squinted. "Your hair looks good. Take a look."

Sandra held up a compact mirror and moved it around the back of her head. Her hair looked like wrinkles in a piece of velvet. Curls wound sensuously around her ear. "You should be a hairstylist," she said, touching a curl.

"Don't fiddle with it too much," Casey said, picking up a tube of lipstick and putting it on. "It's strange to meet these fellows at a restaurant. I don't know why they can't pick us up."

Sandra snorted as she reached for her cherry-red sweater. "We're lucky Frederick didn't ask me to pick him up. Actually, I'm surprised he didn't. Let's go."

At the bottom of the stairs, Sandra, who was behind in her rent, held her hand up to stop Casey while she determined Mrs. Pickler's location. Most days their landlady spent the afternoon in her sitting room, drinking gin and listening to the radio. To get out the door without being seen meant sneaking past her.

Luckily at this moment, her armchair was empty. The radio was droning to a vacant room.

"Let's go," Sandra whispered.

In the hallway was a desk with a slatted top that pulled down like a window shade. Casey reached underneath, produced a key, and unlocked the desk. The lid made a *tick, tick, tick* noise as each strip of wood folded into the next. Sandra winced, glancing toward the empty room.

"This is where she keeps the rent money," Casey whispered.

The desk's cubbyholes were stuffed with cash. Sandra couldn't believe the old woman thought this was a good place to store her accounts. On a stack of envelopes sat two quarters, which Casey slipped in her coat pocket. Then she pulled down the lid, locked it, and hurried into the late-afternoon sunlight.

Sandra ran after her. "You should put those back, don't you think?"

"Think of it as gas money. Our transportation is on Mrs. Pickler tonight."

Sandra shook her keys like she was shaking off water as she got in the car. While she disliked Mrs. Pickler's rules, Casey seemed to harbor a personal resentment against the old woman.

She'd muttered something about "knowing people like her," and it made Sandra wonder what kind of home Casey came from. She had a vague idea of people crammed into an Iowa farmhouse, but she didn't want to pry. She might discover something about Casey that she didn't like.

Frederick and Harry met them at a diner, as promised. It wasn't even a nice diner, but a touristy one on Hollywood Boulevard, with everything edged in chrome or red vinyl. It was like eating in a car lot, Sandra thought. The roast beef on her sandwich was dry and the pickle flopped weakly when she picked it up.

Harry, the assistant director, barely spoke during the meal. He was excessively tall with dark brown, somewhat greasy hair, and thick glasses. Still, Sandra wished she was paired with him instead of Frederick. She wanted to get Harry alone so she could sweet talk him into calling Central for her. Besides, Frederick was embarrassing. Not only did he have that silly beard, he was carrying what appeared to be a lady's purse. It lay at his feet throughout the meal. Sandra eyed it as she gnawed on her sandwich.

"So, Harry," she said. "Frederick tells me you're an assistant director at MGM. What does that entail exactly?"

He sipped his orange juice. "Whatever the director tells me to do. I got to pick out the rope they used in the *Don Quixote* picture. You can see it when he's riding along on his burro."

Across the table, Casey mouthed "errand boy." Sandra pinched her lips, swallowing back a laugh.

"Have you met any movie stars at your job, Harry?" Casey said.

He pushed his glasses up his nose. "Certainly. I've met lots of stars."

"Like who?"

"Oh, this person and that."

"But who?" Sandra said.

"Norma Shearer. I met her."

Sandra and Casey exchanged glances. This was something. Norma Shearer was the queen of MGM.

"We both met her," Frederick said. "At an industry party. She was a nice woman, that Norma."

Sandra didn't know whether to believe this or not. "Do you go to many industry parties?" she said to Frederick.

"Yes, yes, all the time. I'll take you to one if you want."

Demurely, Sandra sipped at her strawberry phosphate. She didn't want to go anywhere with Frederick Bauer, even though an industry party sounded like the sort of thing she should be attending. But he would bring his purse.

"You know, Harry," she said. "It so happens that I need an assistant director. I want to register at Central Casting, and they're not taking anyone. But if you'd asked them to put me on the list, I'm sure they'd do it, your being so important and all."

Harry glanced at Frederick, who stroked his beard thoughtfully. "Let's say that Harry will think about doing that for you," Frederick said. "How about that?"

Casey narrowed her eyes. "Why don't you let Harry decide?"

"I am. I am. I just do not want poor Harry to feel pressured, that's all. Assistant directors are often pressured by precocious starlets." He winked at Sandra.

There was an awkward pause during which she stared at her sandwich, fuming. The whole reason she went on this date was to ask Harry this favor. Frederick knew that and now he was blocking her from getting an answer. And he was the one to suggest she ask in the first place.

"And you're an actor, Frederick?" Casey said.

"No. Photographer."

"I thought you met Sandra at a casting call."

"That," Sandra said with a toss of her head, "is because he only wants to be in cowboy pictures."

Frederick nodded as he chewed his sandwich. "That's right. I grew this beard so I could be in a Western. My dream is to be a cowboy. I mean, I would like to be in a cowboy movie, but I wouldn't mind being a real cowboy either. I may do it, too, one of these days—quit Hollywood and become a cowboy."

"But you're German," Casey said. "A German cowboy?"

"That's what I said," Sandra said.

"Sure, sure," Frederick said. "I am an artist too. I draw. I used to work in the art department at Disney, but I quit."

"Why would you do that?" Sandra said. "That sounds like a great job."

He made a face. "My boss was an idiot. Besides, I don't want to sit around drawing Mickey Mouses all day. That's what they have you do, you know. They make you draw the same thing all day, every day. It's like working in a factory."

"So now you're a photographer for a studio?" Casey said.

"I don't need the studios to be a successful photographer. I sell my work independently."

"To who?" Sandra said.

He popped the last bite of sandwich in his mouth and looked at Sandra as if to say, *Come again?*

"Who do you sell photography to?" she said.

Frederick waved his hand. "Whoever wants it. Advertisers and the like."

No one knew what to say to that. Sandra picked up her sandwich, then put it down on the plate again. She couldn't eat any more of it.

"I see you girls are finished," Frederick said, brushing his hands. "Shall we take a stroll down Hollywood Boulevard?"

Sandra agreed, if for no other reason than to leave the diner. It was still light outside, despite being late in the day. Though Frederick was taller than Sandra, she felt like a leggy colt beside him. He was chewing on a toothpick and had the purse slung over his shoulder. They passed a movie theater with Egyptian statues out front. On the roof, a man dressed as a pharaoh was shouting movie times, "*Love Me Tonight* at 7 p.m. *Horse Feathers* at 5:30 and 7:20 p.m." Ahead of them, Casey and Harry were walking at a companionable pace. Harry's arms were behind his back and Casey was looking at him as they chatted.

At Grauman's Chinese Theater, they walked the courtyard comparing their foot and handprints with the movie stars. Sandra lined her shoe next to Mary Pickford's footprint, whose tiny high heels were like the heads and tails of fish.

"You've got big feet for a girl," Frederick said.

Sandra swiped a curl behind her ear, irritated. Mary Pickford wasn't even five feet tall. Of course her feet were miniature. The last time Sandra checked, it wasn't a requirement for movie stars to have small feet.

Then Harry said he was still hungry and asked if they wanted ice cream from a cart. When he and Casey went to order, Frederick offered Sandra his hand with a look of lustful invitation. She didn't want to touch him, but she didn't want to offend him in case Harry could register her at Central. After some deliberation, she put her hand in Frederick's and they stood that way in front of a shop window full of Shirley Temple dolls.

When Harry came back, she tried to free her hand to reach for the ice cream, but Frederick anticipated the move and tightened his grip. Soon she found herself trapped with one hand in his and the other holding a scoop of vanilla. As they started walking again, Frederick used her hand to steer her so that they were almost touching. The purse flapped at his side.

"What do you have in there, anyway?" she said.

"A camera."

"That's a normal thing to bring on a date."

"It is if you're me. You never know when inspiration will strike. Say, you should let me take your picture."

Sandra stared through the picket of her lashes at Frederick. "Now why would I do that?"

"You've got a good face. You have a better chance of breaking into pictures than your friend. Of the two of you, you're the pretty one."

"Oh, I think Casey is very pretty," Sandra said loyally, though she was pleased by the compliment.

Frederick shifted the bag higher on his shoulder. "Nope. You're a little skinny but you have a good face. Your friend is plain."

Sandra frowned. Skinny was a euphemism for flat-chested, which she wasn't. She had perfect proportions for her size. She'd measured it according to a chart in *Ladies' Home Journal*.

"I bet I could sell your face. In fact—" Frederick said that last word in a trailing singsong as he looked over his shoulder. Then he let go of her hand and trotted off. Sandra whirled around in time to see him crossing the street, forcing the traffic to halt and cars to honk. Casey and Harry walked up, both still holding ice cream cones.

"What's he doing?" Casey said.

"I don't know," Sandra said. "He just ran over there."

Now Frederick was by a fountain covered in blue-and-white tile, waving and gesturing for them to follow.

"I think he wants us to join him," Harry said.

"I'm not jaywalking through all that traffic," Sandra said. "We'll get hit by a car."

"Me neither," Casey said and then pointed down the side-walk. "Crosswalk."

With a sigh, Sandra followed Casey and Harry to the inter-section and waited for the light to change. As they stood there, it occurred to her that this was her chance to ask Harry about Central without Frederick butting in.

"So," she said.

Harry looked away and Sandra had the sense that he didn't want to talk to her. She suspected it had to do with Frederick. When the light changed, he took the crosswalk in long strides, leaving Sandra and Casey to hurry and catch up.

By now Frederick was sitting on the fountain, fingering a camera. He pointed it at Sandra as she approached, his face a nest of metal, lens, and beard. "The light here is gorgeous," he said. "Why don't we have you stand here, *schatzi*, and I'll take your picture."

"What's a *schatzi*?" Casey said.

"She is," Frederick said. "It means sweetheart in German." He held up the camera again and clicked it. "Now I take your picture."

Sandra glanced at Casey's shocked face. "Are you crazy? I'm not fixed up for photographs."

"Nonsense. You're luminous."

"Oh, now I'm luminous. I thought I was skinny with big feet."

"Come on. You have a great face and this is perfect evening light. It's good practice for the movies."

Sandra scanned the other two, asking their opinions. Casey shrugged and Harry shoved his hands in his pockets.

"I will tell you what," Frederick said. "If you let me take your picture, Harry will call Central for you. Won't you, Harry?"

Harry looked sideways at the traffic. "Sure, I could do that."

That was all Sandra needed to hear. She handed her purse to Casey. "Where do you want me to stand?"

It was strange to have her picture taken. Frederick was doing something to her, but Sandra couldn't feel it. She tried to remember her poses, tilting her head to emphasize her bone structure and sucking in her cheeks. People glanced at her as they walked by and she knew they thought she was a real model. Maybe Frederick was right that this was good practice. She bit her cheeks, thinking, *Greta Garbo.*

Frederick went through a roll of film and like that, it was over. Sandra felt disappointed. She could have modeled for much longer.

"You looked so natural, Sandra," Casey said. "Just like a real model."

"Yeah, nice job," Harry said.

"Please," Sandra said. "You're embarrassing me."

As they walked along again, she found she was in a better mood. It was fun to have her picture taken and now she was going to be registered at Central, plus she had that audition for *Mysterious Mansions* coming up. Things were finally going her way.

"You were great," Frederick said. "I can sell those photographs. Would you like to be in an advertisement?"

"Sure, why not? Just make sure to send me my cut."

They split off again, Harry and Casey ahead and Sandra and Frederick following behind. The light had a soft, pumpkin-like tinge and Sandra wondered if that was what Frederick meant by good light. The sunsets were different in LA. In Healdsburg, they were blues and lavenders, but here, colors tended to go more tropical—flamingo pink, tangerine, raincoat yellow.

As she was thinking this, Frederick suddenly pulled her hand, swinging her to him like they were dancing. He clasped her body against his chest, his hand on her back, and Sandra thought, *Central Casting.* Then his lips were on hers. No one had kissed her since Billy, and it was strange, but nice. The beard felt odd, but not unpleasant. Softer than she would have expected. She liked his hand on her rib cage too, and the feel of his mouth on hers.

Then there was the sound of clapping and she pulled away. A crowd had formed to watch them kiss. As Frederick dipped his head in a bow, Sandra scurried down the sidewalk toward Casey. It was low class, kissing in public like that. At least a dozen people had watched, and that didn't count the four lanes of traffic. Why, she'd just been kissed in front of hundreds of people!

Frederick fell in step beside her. "You know, we could get away from those two. Get a drink somewhere."

The thought wasn't completely repulsive. She looked into Frederick's face, trying to see what he was like underneath the beard. She'd never met anyone like him before. Someone was playing "Oh, You Beautiful Doll" on a trumpet. Frederick caught her fingertips in his hand.

Then, like a sudden shifting wind, Casey stomped over to them. "You stop that right now, Frederick Bauer. I know your little secret. Harry doesn't even work at MGM anymore."

"What?" Sandra said, jerking her hand away and meeting Casey's furious eyes.

"That's right. He was fired for stealing film."

Frederick glared at Harry, who was coming up sheepishly behind Casey. "Why would you tell her that?"

"I didn't mean to. It slipped out."

"So it's true?" Sandra said to Frederick.

This man had manipulated her. He'd used her for a ride and

then conned her into this date, all the while telling whoppers about cowboys and drawing Mickey Mouse. And she'd let him kiss her in front of four lanes of traffic.

Casey slipped her arm in Sandra's. "Let's go. Right now."

Harry looked disappointed. "Don't you want to see a movie?"

"No, thanks," Casey said. "We wouldn't want to waste the time of important gentlemen like you."

"Yeah," Sandra said. "Isn't there some sort of industry party you need to get to?"

Casey and Sandra giggled. It all seemed preposterous—the cowboy beard, the camera, the crazy lies.

"Come on and give us another chance," Frederick called after them. "We'll pay for the movie."

But Casey was pulling on Sandra's arm now and they started down the block, laughing so hard that they bent over. Sandra was relieved that she'd been right about Casey all along. She was a true friend.

"Good night," Sandra called over her shoulders. "Say hi to Norma Shearer for me."

CHAPTER 8

In Nebraska, Vira was looking forward to seeing Chimney Rock. *The Emigrants Guide to the West* described the rock as "a must-see sight for the explorer on his way to California. Not to be missed."

As she rode beside Elmer in the wagon, Vira studied the drawing of the rock. Even though they were in Nebraska, it would be a week before they reached it. When they started for California, there were hills, forests, and farms to look at, but now it was all prairie. The center of the country was made up of endless grasslands that Vira must lurch through at three miles per hour.

So far, the journey wasn't the romantic trip Elmer had promised. Any excitement on the trail was men's excitement. Every morning Elmer woke up whistling. He went on and on about the fresh air and virgin land and spent every Sunday hunting buffalo or prairie hens and coming back with meat for her to clean and preserve. Vira did her best to go along with it, like a good wife. She tried to like sleeping in the tent. She tried to think of the bouquet of blooming grass he put on her pillow as a sweet gesture, even though it made her sneeze and left seeds in her hair. She tried not to miss comforts like a fireplace or a feather mattress or an outhouse. But she failed, at least in her heart. More than anything, Vira wanted to take a hot bath, but that wouldn't happen until they arrived in California.

Tonight, at least, there was the promise of civilization. They would stop at Fort Kearny, where they could buy supplies and send mail. It had been weeks since Vira had been near a building.

Shutting the guidebook, she swiveled her legs around to climb into the back of the wagon.

"Are you going to play piano for me?" Elmer said.

"I thought I might," she said, although she played for herself. Slipping between the trunks, she made her way to the piano, where there was just enough room for Vira to sit on the edge of a crate and move her hands along the keyboard. At first it had been hard to play with the sloshing of the wagon, but after a while, she got used to it. By now, she'd gone through her songbooks so many times, she had them memorized.

Launching into "Faith of Our Fathers," Vira tried to ignore the nagging thought that the rest of the wagon train could hear her playing. There was little privacy on the trail. A crowd followed them wherever they went. Closing her eyes, she shut the emigrants out of her mind. She was far away from the wagon, playing her piano in the beautiful mansion Elmer had promised her. And in this home, her mother was still alive. She'd been waiting there all this time, and now she was watching Vira play, proud to see that her daughter had grown into a graceful woman with her mother's same long, slender fingers.

Fort Kearny was a cluster of unpainted wooden buildings huddled together on the vastness of the plains. It was Saturday, and the place had the air of a carnival. Booths lined the walkways, selling pots and pans, beef jerky, fabric, salt, feed, and lanterns. Vira and Elmer meandered the aisles, viewing the goods and sucking on rosewater candies. The colored lanterns strung above their heads obscured the night sky, but the stars were out. Vira was wearing her finest dress, which was still clean because she hadn't worn it since leaving home. She felt almost cheerful.

"Shall we get more of these candies to bring with us?" Elmer said. "They'd be nice to have on the trail."

"Yes. And let's buy more flour while we can."

She felt him restrain a sigh. He didn't like it when she worried about running out of supplies. Even though Elmer said they had enough provisions for a journey twice this long, Vira still monitored their bacon, rice, dried fruit, flour, sugar, oil, and coffee. There were thieves to worry about. She and Elmer had one of the biggest wagons on the trail.

"All right," he said. "We can get a small bag if you like. I saw a booth with flour this way."

In the next aisle, a musician was playing "Camptown Races" on a banjo. They stopped to marvel at how quickly his fingers flew over the strings. Two little girls were dancing, the ribbons of their dresses flying out as they twirled.

Vira noticed a booth selling books and paused to look through a basket of sheet music. She found a piano version of "Oh Susanna" by Stephen Foster and looked through the chords, determining how hard it was to play. "Elmer, may I get this?" she said.

"Yes, indeed. It would be nice to hear you play something new."

He gestured to the man and woman sitting deeper in the booth, apparently the proprietors. The woman was noticeably thin. Her cheekbones perched over the hollow of her face and her eyes were as lifeless as an overplowed field. She could have been thirty years old, or fifty. Vira hung back, wondering if she was ill.

The man smiled at Vira as he flipped through the sheet music. "Do you play piano?" he said.

"No, no," she said, looking down.

"My wife is bashful," Elmer said. "In fact, she's quite the little musician."

"I'm sure she is," the man said, taking Elmer's money. "Are you folks going to California?"

"Yes, sir. We're seeking our fortune in the Gold Rush. And yourself?"

Vira was so used to this exchange, where two travelers agreed they were both going to the Gold Rush to make their fortune, that she was surprised when the man glanced at his wife and said, "We've been there already. We're going home to Pennsylvania."

Elmer shifted from one foot to the other. "May I ask why?"

"I'm sorry to say it, but there's nothing left in California. I've been telling people whenever I can. All the easy gold is gone and only mining corporations can get it out of the ground now."

Throughout the trip, Vira had been fighting the worry that they were doing this all for nothing. She tried to have faith in Elmer instead, but here was solid evidence that he was wrong.

"If you'll excuse me for saying so," Elmer said. "Maybe the fault isn't the gold. Perhaps it was your claim."

"I had several claims and I didn't make a farthing."

As the men continued to talk, Vira watched the woman, who stood with her eyes angled toward the ground. She seemed to notice Vira for the first time and a fitful smile crossed her face. Reaching out her hand, she said something in a whisper.

Vira stepped closer to her. "Did you speak to me?"

The woman was shorter than Vira. Her dress hung heavily on her slender frame, as if it used to fit her better. There was no gray hair on her head, so she couldn't be that old.

"Yes," she said in such a faint voice that Vira had to lean in to hear her. "I said, don't have any babies on the trail."

Vira was shocked. The banjo music started again, and Elmer was asking how the mining companies were getting gold when the average man couldn't. She nodded, wanting to flee the woman and her strange eyes, which were set deeply in her face.

"All right," she said, and then, because she knew she would always wonder, added, "Did you have a baby on the trail?"

The woman looked to the side again with that same sad expression. "Yes. We'll see his grave when we go through Missouri."

Vira held the sheet music between them as if shielding herself. She'd seen the graves, marked with wooden crosses on the side of the road. There was cholera on the trail, on top of the usual risks of having babies. Vira had been recklessly gambling by going along with Elmer's romantic trysts in the tent. It was better to stop all that—at least until they had a home again.

"Well, sir, I don't think it's fitting to blame others for your failings," Elmer was saying, anger in his voice. "Certainly, you're the first person to tell me the gold is gone."

The man shook his head. "I will not be the last, I'm afraid."

Other people were coming into the booth and the conversation ended. Elmer offered Vira his arm and they walked back onto the boardwalk.

"That man is deranged," Elmer said. "Of course there will be gold."

She could feel his eyes searching her face, seeking reassurance. Without looking at him, Vira nodded. "Of course."

It was a week before they finally reached Chimney Rock. That afternoon, as they approached the monument, Vira again rode beside Elmer in the front of the wagon. Other emigrants blocked her view of the scenery, so she found herself staring at an oil spot on her apron, a remnant from frying biscuits. She'd scrubbed it on the washboard until her hands were red, but the ghost of a spot remained. Again and again, Vira put her finger over the stain so that the apron looked clean, then moved it away so that it reappeared. Doing this elicited a slight emotional fluctuation, an increase and release of gloom or frustration. When everyone around her gave a shout, she looked up in time to see Chimney Rock jutting like a shark fin between the wagons.

"Will you look at that?" Elmer said. "Let's go see it before it gets dark."

They camped within view of Chimney Rock, which was less impressive than Vira expected. It was smaller than she'd imagined, and looked less like a finger reaching to God and more like a funnel tipped upside down. She and Elmer hurried through the now-familiar rituals of pitching the tent, feeding the oxen, collecting firewood, and setting up the stove. The afternoon was humid, with temperatures in the nineties, and Vira sweated through her dress as she squatted to make biscuit dough from flour, baking soda, salt, and river water she'd collected the day before.

The water was safe because she'd boiled it. Every night since she met the woman at Fort Kearny, she scrubbed and aired and boiled to ward off disease. Elmer said she worried too much, but in the last week Vira had counted six graves along the trail. The last one had been yesterday, near the campsite where she'd gathered the water.

"Vira?" Elmer said.

She looked up at him. Without realizing it, she'd stopped kneading the dough. It sat in the bowl, a shaggy mess.

He held out his hand. "Let's go see Chimney Rock."

Hand in hand, Vira and Elmer walked toward the site. Neither of them spoke, unwilling to spoil the temporary peace between them. In these moments Vira could see why Elmer liked the trail. The late-afternoon sunlight gave everything a bee-pollen spottiness. Sagebrush caught the hem of her skirt, and the landscape was dotted with purple flowers. The sky in this part of the country was larger and more immediate, somehow, as if it had been unzipped from a pouch and fallen over their heads.

Chimney Rock grew bigger until they were in its shadow. Other emigrants were already walking around the base in reverent silence. Vira pushed back her sunbonnet to look at the rock and frowned. Every inch of Chimney Rock that could be reached by human hand was pockmarked with the names of previous travelers. In the center of the column, written in two-foot-high letters, were the words, "Westward Ho! JMW 1849." Beside that was, "Go Willard, Boston 1850." Underneath, "California or Bust—W. Fouts, 1851." From there, the writing grew smaller until it became a scribble. It seemed that every man going to California had left a mark on the stone.

The forbidden thought popped into Vira's mind again: *How could there be gold if all these people went to California before them?*

"I'll be doggoned," Elmer said. "What do you think of that?"

"It's a shame," Vira said timidly. "The rock is being worn away from the carving."

Elmer's chest was still heaving from the walk. When his lips spread into a smile, Vira's heart grew leaden within her. "I think it's grand," he said. "A monument marked by the Argonauts, people, just like us, who are seizing life by the hilt."

But, Vira thought, there weren't supposed to be people like them. They were supposed to be special.

Around them, emigrants appeared like tumbleweeds rolling

across a plain and gathered around the rock. Someone's musty
stink wafted over Vira and clung to the air around her. A woman
wiped away a tear. "I can't believe I'm here," she said.

Vira thought Chimney Rock wasn't worth all the fuss. It
was just another rock, like dozens of formations she'd seen on
the trip so far. It was even a little ludicrous looking, a spindly
column sticking out of a hump, like a wart on the prairie. And
the graffiti was so much empty bragging, each signature a gesture
left on a monument to be worn down by time.

She turned to tell Elmer she wanted to leave, but he was
pulling a knife from his pocket. "What are you doing?" she said.

"Carving my initials. 'E. Sanborn, Portland, Maine.' And
his pretty wife, of course." He walked up the mound and joined
the men standing on the rock like mountain goats.

Vira walked a few yards toward camp and waited for Elmer.
From there, the wagon train looked like a string of beads on
the land. This was supposed to be a pristine adventure, just the
two of them, and here were all these other people, taking the
best camping spots, polluting the water, and assaulting her with
stink and sickness. She thought Elmer resented them too, but
now Vira saw that wasn't so. Yet it seemed ridiculous to her that
an uninhabited country could be so crowded.

CHAPTER 9

On the day of the *Mysterious Mansions* audition, Sandra left Casey on a bench reading a newspaper and marched through the Spanish-style courtyard of the auditorium, curls bouncing on her neck, thinking in time with her steps, *This is my chance. This is my chance.*

Then she stopped short. The line of redheads waiting to audition stretched out the door of the auditorium and around a camellia bush. Sandra never thought she was a "type" before, but here was evidence to the contrary. It wasn't just that the other women had red hair; they looked like her too, tall and thin, with long legs and high cheekbones. Like her, each one was wearing a white dress and black shoes. There was nothing to do but take her place at the end of the line.

She was assigned Group 17 and told to wait in the auditorium until her number was called. The girl next to her, who had an appalling rash of freckles on her face, kept claiming the armrest with her elbow until Sandra gave up fighting for it. At least she had a chair. Redheads filled the aisles and stood along the back of the room. With a sigh, she began filling out the audition slip they'd given her, fibbing where necessary.

NAME: *Sandra Sanborn*

AGE: *21*

PREVIOUS ACTING EXPERIENCE:

—Lead role in Santa Rosa Junior College's production of Medea.

[Here was the end of Sandra's (slightly exaggerated— she was in the chorus) acting experience, so she added a few more:]

—Lead role in Santa Rosa Junior College's production of Macbeth, playing Lady Macbeth.

—Lead role in Santa Rosa Junior College's production of Romeo and Juliet, playing Juliet.

—Singer in the Billy Guess Orchestra.

SKILLS:

Acting, dancing, driving, accents, piano playing, drawing, screaming.

The sheet was getting sloppy from all the cross-outs and additions, so Sandra forced herself to put down the pen. Was it too much to say she played both Juliet *and* Lady Macbeth?

Singing was risky too, since Sandra sometimes had trouble keeping tune, but musicals were all the rage these days and it seemed unwise to leave the possibility off the list. Besides she had to get *something* out of all that time watching Billy's band play state fairs and dances.

On stage, a pattern everyone knew repeated itself. A man with a clipboard called out, "Group 15." Around the auditorium, girls got up, climbed the stairs, and stood on the stage in a line. Sandra watched one woman in particular pick her way up the aisle. She was the type of girl Hollywood wanted—small waist, big eyes—but Sandra thought her nose was a little blunt in profile. Her own nose, by comparison, was much more elegant.

The man stood with his back to the audience and pointed at each woman. When his hand came down, she let out a scream. In this way, he went down the line, producing each scream like he was playing a scale on a broken instrument.

Sandra tapped the arm of the woman next to her. "Excuse me, will you watch my seat? I'm going to the powder room."

The girl sniffed. "One doesn't leave in the middle of a call."

"I have time. I'm in group seventeen."

The girl shook her head and returned to her magazine. "Suit yourself."

"How kind," Sandra said, pushing past her knobby knees.

In the bathroom, the line for the stalls was so long that Sandra decided to hold it. She pushed through the pale arms of the girls around the mirror and swallowed hard as she looked at the reflection of the bathroom. It was a line of paper dolls, and she was one of them. The woman next to her was even wearing a similar dress, white with a red ribbon around the collar and sleeves.

As Sandra fished in her purse for lipstick, she glanced at her shoes and remembered Frederick saying that her feet were big and that she was skinny. He was quick enough to grope her, though, despite all her faults. And all along he was lying about Harry being an assistant director. She'd have to be more careful when it came to believing the promises of strange men.

When Sandra put the lipstick to her lips, the reflection in the mirror didn't correspond with her movements and she realized that she was looking at the lips of the woman next to her instead of her own. A red loop was on the skin above her mouth. The woman moved away from the sink, her eyes passing over Sandra with an expression of concern. Sandra shuddered and used a handkerchief to clean off the smudge.

Back in the auditorium, she pushed past the girl with the freckles and sat down again.

"Glad you're back," Freckles said. "I had to beat them off with a stick to save this seat for you."

Sandra didn't respond. She wouldn't allow this girl to bait her into a catfight. Her good breeding was an edge in this competition. That, and her natural grace. Many of these girls clomped around like Clydesdale horses, while Sandra had the nimble carriage of a ballet dancer. No one could tell she dyed her hair either, which was more than she could say for some of these girls.

On stage, Group 16 finished screaming, and Sandra snapped to attention. She was next.

The man came up to the stage apron, clutching his clipboard. Everyone looked up, expecting him to call the group number. He straightened his shoulders as if about to confront a man much larger than himself.

"Ladies, thank you for coming this morning. It looks like we've found our extras for this picture, so we're closing the call."

Some of the women groaned. Sandra looked around, alarmed. This was supposed to be her chance. She'd worked hard, gone to the studios, and ruined her silk shoes, and now things were supposed to turn in her favor.

The women began gathering their things and clicking by in their high heels, shaking off the wasted morning. Others swarmed around the man on stage with appeals and explanations. Sandra had the urge to say something to him too. She could see herself on stage explaining something—anything—so eloquently that the man would say, "Wait here." Then he would go into a room, come out again, jut his chin at her and say, "Go get 'em, kid."

But what could Sandra say that would make him do that? Nothing came to mind.

The space of time where she could approach him grew smaller until only one woman held his attention. He nodded as she spoke, his arms crossed high on his chest, clipboard dangling from his fingers.

With a sigh, Sandra left the auditorium. She found Casey sitting on a bench, reading a newspaper.

"There sure are a lot of redheads in this building right now," Casey said, folding the newspaper. "I thought you came by twenty times." Sandra frowned and Casey recognized her mistake. "Of course, you're prettier than all of them. How'd it go?"

"Awful. They hired all the extras before I had a chance to audition."

Just then, two redheads walked by on their way out of the courtyard. The seam of one of their jackets was worn away to reveal the white dress underneath.

"Look at that one's jacket," Sandra said.

Casey shook her head. "Now why wouldn't you patch that up? That's plain low class."

Sandra snorted. The girl must be an Okie. The news was full of them flocking into California for work that didn't exist. Then, when getting a job didn't work out, they figured they'd become movie stars. Well, Sandra had more right to be in Hollywood than they did. Her family had lived in California for generations.

"I guess we'll have to wait for the next open call to come along," Casey said.

"You know what? I'm sick of waiting. Let's do something tonight. Maybe we can meet someone from the studios."

Casey opened her mouth and shut it. They looked at each other.

Sandra leaned over and picked up the newspaper. Flipping to the calendar, she ran her finger down the column. "Tonight there's a lecture on Freud, a jazz performance, an O'Neill play, no . . . here's a good one: A movie premiere at Grauman's Chinese Theatre. Let's go to that."

"We can't get into a movie premiere, Sandra. It's for the people who are in the movie."

That made sense. From what Sandra could tell from newsreels, film premieres were corded off and heavily guarded. "Okay then," she said, putting down the paper. "What about a nightclub? Everyone knows movie stars go to nightclubs."

Casey groaned. "I don't think I can stomach another date with Frederick and Harry."

"Not those guys. We'll go by ourselves."

"You mean, just the two of us?"

"Sure, we don't need dates. Let's get dressed and go."

Casey looked doubtful and Sandra's mind spun for arguments why they should go. Yes, it was unusual for two women to go to a nightclub without dates, but it wasn't illegal, was it? The nightclub would let them in. It was an elegant place and they would be safe. It was a daring thing to do, like drinking moonshine or riding in the back of a jalopy in the moonlight.

But then Casey's mouth spread into a smile. "Okay, I'm in. Which club should we go to?"

Sandra threw out her arms. "The biggest. The best one."

Casey laughed. "Sure, why not? I got paid yesterday too."

They settled on the Cocoanut Grove Ballroom because it was always in the newsreels for celebrity sightings and award ceremonies. It was located in the Ambassador Hotel, a pink rectangle of a building set off Wilshire Boulevard behind a golf-course-sized lawn. The nightclub had an awning out front with a scalloped edge that looked like dripping rain.

"Golly," Casey said as they walked in.

The room before them was designed to look like a tropical paradise. Full-sized palm trees dotted the dance floor, their fronds scraping the ceiling, which was midnight blue with canister lights for stars. Along the walls, red curtains hung over murals of tropical beaches and lush jungles. On stage, a band was setting up beside a white piano.

A waiter led them through a maze of round tables with low-glowing lanterns, and up to a balcony, where they sat at a table with a view of the dance floor below. A cigarette girl was winding through the empty tables. She wore a hula dress that plunged so low, her entire back was naked. Sandra wondered if being a cigarette girl was a way to meet Hollywood people. But no, she reconsidered, that was too close to washing dishes.

"Look at these prices," Casey said.

Mortified by Casey's lack of refinement, Sandra glanced to see if anyone had overheard. Mabel always said, "If you have to ask, you can't afford it." Luckily, they were alone in the balcony. The closest people were seated downstairs. When Sandra read the menu, she saw that Casey was right. Although she was hungry, she abandoned the idea of eating there.

"Forty-five cents for hearts of celery," Casey said. "Why, I can get a bunch of celery and cut the heart out myself for a nickel."

It was an inelegant thing to say, but Sandra chuckled. "Maybe we could share something. The salted almonds?"

"Thirty-five cents for salted almonds? I can't do it. It's highway robbery."

"We have to order something," Sandra said in a pert whisper. "We can't sit here for free."

Casey shut the menu. "I guess you're right, but I don't like it."

They settled on salted almonds and two glasses of grapefruit juice. The waiter laid the almonds on the table as if presenting caviar. They came in a crystal bowl shaped like a pineapple.

"I don't see why these almonds are so expensive," Casey said. "They have salt and something else on them. What's that flavor?"

Carefully aware of how to do it prettily, Sandra took one of the almonds and put it in her mouth. "Cinnamon?"

Casey looked at the almonds. "You don't say. I'd never had that on almonds."

Sandra's eyes drifted to the dance floor. There was more of a din now, with couples dancing among the palm trees, but the club was still empty. Maybe it was too early, or maybe it was because of the Depression. People had less money for going out these days.

The bandleader was tall like Billy, but with thinner hair. Sandra and Billy had fought all the time about his career. She still thought he was capable of playing the best clubs in the nation, but he was content to stay in Santa Rosa playing county fairs.

If he'd listen to her, would he be leading the band at somewhere like the Cocoanut Grove now?

"What's going on?" Casey said, breaking into Sandra's thoughts. "Is someone here?

Throughout the nightclub, people were glancing up at the balcony where they were sitting. Four waiters marched by so quickly that a breeze fluttered the sleeve of Sandra's dress. With jerky movements, the staff pushed two tables together and covered them with a tablecloth.

"Do you think it's a celebrity?" Sandra said.

"I hope so."

A moment later, a host led a group to the table. There were ten of them, all in their midtwenties and expensively dressed. They were chatting with a sense of ownership, as if they were used to taking over a nightclub with their presence. The men pulled out chairs for the women, who sat down without breaking the flow of conversation, their arms willowy under the golden lamplight. Sandra noted their fashionable gowns: chiffon with crystal beads, bias-cut velvet skirts, sea-foam netting. Her midnight-blue dress felt dowdy by comparison. She'd have to buy better clothes if she was going to be a Dress Extra.

Then someone moved, and Sandra understood why everyone in the nightclub was looking in their direction. In the middle of the group, as casual as could be, sat Imogen Beauregard.

Casey scooted closer to Sandra. "Do you realize who that is?"

"Yes. Can you believe our luck?"

Imogen Beauregard had made a sensation in the 1929 picture *Whirlwind Romance*. In a small but much discussed dream sequence, Imogen was arranged on an oversized fruit salad, naked except for the Eve-like hair covering her breasts and an artfully placed piece of lettuce over her nether regions. At the end of the dream, the star of the picture, Lance Barney, kissed Imogen on the lips. The scene had been written about extensively in morality columns as an example of why Holly-wood needed censorship via the Hays Code. Because of this, Imogen was one of the most famous starlets in Hollywood. And now, she was only a few feet away.

Wine and champagne were brought to Imogen's table. Even though everyone said Prohibition would end soon, it was strange to see the bottles Sandra remembered from child-hood out in plain sight again. Imogen was wearing a tight white satin dress and carrying a small dog. Her skin was the color of a white nectarine and her lips formed a plump red bow. Most striking, however, were her cartoon-like blue eyes, which she blinked and widened and rolled at everyone at the table. As she accepted a glass of champagne, she handed a half-finished cigarette to a girl they were calling Lulu, who seemed to be acting as her maid.

"The rumor is she's pregnant with Lance Barney's child," Casey said.

Sandra looked at Imogen's midsection and gave a start. A definite bulge swelled against the dress. It explained why the gown was so ill-fitting. "You would think she'd get a husband real quick," she said.

"Yes, but she makes things worse. Last week, she was seen dancing with a known gangster." Casey raised an eyebrow as if to say, *Yes, it's that scandalous.*

Sandra shook her head. How could anyone be so stupid? The thing to do was to hide the pregnancy, go to Europe, and come back with a "niece." Either that, or get married and hope that no one did the math. Didn't Imogen care about her career at all?

"Are we going to have a second round?" the waiter said, coming up to them suddenly.

She drained her glass and nodded. Expensive or not, she

wasn't leaving the club now that she was in the vicinity of a starlet.

The person nearest Sandra was a man her own age. She wondered if she could talk to him without Casey saying something inelegant. The last thing Sandra wanted was to look like a country bumpkin in front of Hollywood people. "Hand me a cigarette," she said to Casey. "Not the lighter, though."

Casey opened her purse and took a cigarette from the carton. Leaning over, Sandra tapped the man on the shoulder. When he turned around, he was disappointingly unattractive. His black hair met in a widow's peak in the center of his forehead.

"Excuse me," Sandra said. "Do you have a light?"

"Sure." He brought a lighter out of his pocket and popped up the flame. Sandra put the end of her cigarette in the flame, making sure to meet his eyes the whole time.

"Thank you, I seem to have forgotten my lighter."

"It's no trouble."

"Say," Sandra said, before he could turn back. "Isn't that Imogen Beauregard?"

"It sure is."

"Are you a friend of hers?"

"I wouldn't say that. I work grip for Paramount and someone invited me along. I barely know Imogen."

Casey scooted closer, her chair scraping the floor. "That's lucky, isn't it?"

It seemed like a silly remark, but the man nodded. "She wanted a big group tonight."

Downstairs the music stopped and the band said it was taking a break. In the hush that followed, Sandra could hear Imogen Beauregard speaking to the waiter.

"You know what I want?" she said in a thick Southern accent. "Grits. Good old homemade grits. Do you have that here?"

"I could consult the chef," the waiter said.

"Yeah, do that please, and get us some cheeses. Fancy cheeses. For the whole table."

"Very good."

"I've been craving grits for days," Imogen said, bending forward as if it were a naughty confession.

"I love grits," someone said. "They remind me of Savannah."

"What's your name?" Casey said to the man they'd been talking to. "I'm Casey Roberts."

"Dean Thaley." He shook Casey's hand. "Nice to meet you, Miss Roberts."

"Charmed, Mr. Thaley. This is my friend, Sandra Sanborn."

Sandra shook Dean Thaley's hand and was about to ask what a grip did when Imogen tapped the table and said, "Dean! Do you know why grits are so hard to find? I can't get them anywhere." Sandra was aware that she was in Imogen's field of vision.

"It's Southern food, isn't it?" said Lulu. "Is that why it isn't served here?"

"I think that should change," Imogen said. "What could be more wholesome than grits? Where did my cigarette go?"

"My goodness," Casey said in Sandra's ear. "She's tight, isn't she?"

Sandra nodded, eyebrow raised. It wasn't even nine o'clock.

Suddenly, a photographer approached and asked Imogen to pose for a picture. She stood up, clutching the dog under her arm.

"Do you want me to take Boodle?" someone said.

"No," Imogen said, jerking away. "No one takes my baby." She looked down at the dog. "Smile for the camera, Boodle." She spun sideways and looked over her shoulder at the man, smiling kittenishly. The flashbulb went off.

Here it was, then, right in front of Sandra. Fame. It felt so casual, like stardom was a matter of knowing these people and she could have it too.

Dean Thaley had his back to her again. He was talking to a girl with a dark finger wave about how the Depression was affecting Hollywood.

"There aren't any new contracts," the girl was saying. "It's getting difficult for actors to find work."

"Yes, it's trickling down to the techs too. There might be cutbacks."

Then Casey astonished Sandra by saying, "Excuse me, but I couldn't help overhearing your conversation, and I agree. Finding auditions is getting impossible."

"Isn't it?" the girl said. "It's especially hard if you can't sing or dance. All the public wants these days are musicals."

The band started up again, and Sandra couldn't hear what they were saying. Casey moved closer to the girl, and Sandra found herself jammed with her chair facing them, but at an angle that made it difficult to hear. Dean was talking to someone else. The two girls were having an animated conversation, their knees pointing toward each other. Sandra finished her cigarette and stabbed it out on the ashtray.

She was about to pull her chair around to force her way into the conversation when the girl poured something from a flask into Casey's grapefruit juice. Casey indicated that Sandra should hand her juice over too and the girl poured liquor into the glass, the pink drink rising steadily up. Sandra tasted it. Gin. So much that the grapefruit juice seemed like a formality.

When the song ended, Imogen called across to Casey and the girl, "What are you two talking about over there? I have to know what you're talking about." The table grew quiet while Imogen trained her big eyes on Casey. Sandra tensed, praying Casey wouldn't say something inelegant.

"We were talking about how tough it is to get work right now," Casey said.

"Isn't that the truth?" Lulu said.

The tone at the table became serious. Everyone began talking about how the Depression was affecting the industry. The average wage had dropped for actors. Well-known names were forced to take jobs that paid three dollars for a day's work. Some studios were rumored to be close to bankruptcy.

"People just aren't going to see movies," one woman said. "I was talking to Katharine about this the other day. She told me that movie attendance fell forty percent this year. Can you imagine?"

"Which Katharine?" someone said.

"Hepburn."

Imogen fiddled with her dog's collar, sliding it around and around its neck. Sandra watched her pout and look around the room.

"But that can't be right," said a girl with dewy brown eyes. "Everyone says the motion picture industry is depression-proof."

"I'm not so sure about that," said the man next to Imogen. "Is this how a depression-proof industry acts?"

Imogen whispered something in Lulu's ear. Promptly, Lulu whirled around and pressed her hands on the tabletop, elbows out. "We're going to Fresh Squeeze in a moment," she said. Her tone was prim, as if chiding everyone for being dull.

The man next to Imogen summoned the waiter, and people poured the last of their drinks down their throats and collected their things. It didn't seem to matter that their food had yet to come. In ten minute's time, the entire group was trooping out with Imogen leading the way.

Sandra watched them file by without a glance in her direction. She hoped Dean Thaley would invite her to Fresh Squeeze, whatever that was, but he simply nodded as he passed.

"Nice to meet you," he said.

"You too, Mr. Thaley," she said, trying not to show her disappointment. "Goodnight."

Casey put her hand on Sandra's shoulder and said, "I'll be right back." Then she hurried off, leaving Sandra alone in the balcony. A waiter was picking up dishes from the table like a vulture circling a carcass. Downstairs, the band was playing the Gershwin song, "Someone to Watch Over Me."

She was finishing the last of her gin and grapefruit juice when Casey strolled back upstairs and tossed some bills next to the empty almond bowl. "Get your things," she said. "Rachel asked us to come to Fresh Squeeze. It's a speakeasy."

Over the balcony, the girl Casey had been talking to was drumming her red fingernails on the polished wood of the railing.

"Oh," Sandra said, swallowing. "What fun."

The evening had cooled to a balmy sixty-five degrees. Rachel, who worked in costumes, was telling a story about dancers on a movie set who'd revolted against the director because he kept making them take off more and more of their clothes. Incensed, the girls had surrounded the director and pulled down his trousers.

"What did he do?" Casey said.

"He tried to slap at some of them, and then he fainted."

Casey and Rachel laughed, their voices echoing off the Grove's concrete walls. Sandra pulled her wrap tighter on her shoulders and trotted to keep up.

CHAPTER 10

For a speakeasy, Fresh Squeeze didn't seem that covert. Jazz filtered into the alleyway through an open door and there wasn't even a password to get in. In the hall, hundreds of orange Bakelite balls hung from wires so that the ceiling looked as if it were made of oranges. Inside, the speakeasy was jammed with people. Despite this, one of the dark-green booths along the wall was mysteriously open for Imogen Beauregard. She slid in and her party fanned out around her. Waiters brought chairs for everyone else, including Sandra. To her left, Casey was talking to Rachel. To her right, the girl with dewy eyes was pulling a compact from her purse. Dean was on the other side of the table, out of conversational reach. Sandra wondered how she'd ended up here, sitting across from one of the most controversial starlets in Hollywood.

A waitress with lemon-shaped earrings appeared at Sandra's right elbow. "Good evening," she said, her voice muffled against the uproar. "We have a special on mimosas this evening, half off. Do you know what you'd like?"

Sandra ordered a mimosa, although she wasn't sure she had

enough money for one. Imogen was laughing as Lulu lit the cigarette dangling from her fingers. The dog was trembling in her lap.

". . . *Safari Way*?" Casey was saying to Rachel.

". . . tall and skinny . . ." Rachel said.

Casey turned to beam at Sandra.

"What?" Sandra said, tugging on her sleeve. "Tell me."

Casey shouted in her ear. "A part you might be right for." After saying this amazing thing, Casey turned back to Rachel, closing Sandra out of the conversation.

The waitress walked up balancing a tray of glasses of fizzy orange liquid. She handed one to Sandra.

"Well?" Imogen said. "How is it?"

With a jolt, Sandra realized that Imogen Beauregard was speaking to her. She swallowed and smiled her most poised smile. "Delicious. It tastes like bubbly orange juice."

"Ooh, I will have me one of those." Imogen grabbed the mimosa that the waitress was handing Lulu and took a gulp. "Was this yours?" she said to Lulu as an afterthought.

"I'll get another," Lulu said.

The band started again and for a moment the room was taken over by drums and horns. On the dance floor, people were jerking their elbows as if to take flight. Sandra scanned for movie stars, but didn't recognize anyone.

"I do so love mimosas, don't you?" said the girl with dewy eyes.

Sandra was surprised the girl was talking to her. "I've never had one before, but I think it's delightful."

The girl smiled over the rim of her glass and flicked long eyelashes at Sandra.

"How do you know Imogen?" Sandra said.

"What?" the girl said, cupping her ear.

"How do you know Imogen?"

"We were in *Hijinks in Algoria* together. It's a comedy that came out a couple of years ago."

Sandra examined the girl with interest. Of course she was an actress. Every woman in Hollywood was an actress. "Who did you play in the movie?"

"The hotel maid."

"Ah," Sandra said, disappointed. She should have known the girl was just another bit player. She didn't have that "It" quality someone like Imogen, or Sandra, had. "That must have been exciting."

"It was. I got to ride in a limousine to the movie premiere."

"You must have a contract with the studio then."

The girl drooped at the question. "Yes. It's so hard. I have to take so many classes: speech, dance, manners. And they want to file my teeth because I have long incisors, but I don't think they're so long, see?" She opened her mouth and showed Sandra her teeth, touching her incisors with the tip of her strawberry tongue.

"No, they look great," Sandra said.

"That's what I told them."

Casey tapped Sandra's arm, and she turned away from the girl, relieved not to have to talk to her anymore. Rachel leaned toward Sandra. "Casey says you're an actress?"

"Yes?"

"Can you fit into a size twelve?"

"Yes."

"There's a part you might be right for. It's for a picture called *Down Safari Way*. We have a costume that no one can fit into it."

Casey's mouth was almost touching Sandra's ear. "They need natives for the movie to throw spears at a plane. Like Amazons." She mimed throwing something into the air.

Sandra grimaced. A native? She was the Greta Garbo type, not the . . . Sandra couldn't think of an actress who'd gotten a career from that kind of role.

Now Casey and Rachel were talking again and it was too loud to ask more questions. Sandra didn't know what to do. It seemed that Casey was getting her an acting job, but as a native—whatever that meant.

The dewy-eyed girl was being led onto the dance floor. Dean was dancing with someone too, but that was fine. He was only a little taller than his partner, which made him too short for Sandra. She needed a man to be at least 5'11" so she could wear heels around him.

As the table thinned out, no one asked her to dance and Sandra began to feel insulted. She was as pretty as these other girls, even if her dress wasn't as fashionable. She sucked in her stomach and straightened her posture, studying the girls around her. All she wanted was a straight answer of how she measured up. Surely there was a scale somewhere in this town, buried on some producer's desk, which put desirability into a simple mathematical formula. Sandra bent to glimpse her reflection in a spoon she picked up from the table.

When Sandra looked up again, she saw a man with thick black hair watching her. She met his eyes and a minute later he was at her table. He introduced himself as Diego Ramses. Although he was a stranger, Sandra agreed to dance with him. She was pleased to find that he was a great dancer, guiding her through a foxtrot and rumba before buying her a second mimosa, which they drank at his table.

Sandra hoped Diego worked for the studios, but soon learned he was another struggling actor. In fact, he thought that she was the one in with the Hollywood crowd. "How do you know Imogen Beauregard?" he said.

"Oh, I don't know her well," Sandra said, avoiding the question. "But in this business, you run into everyone eventually."

"I know how that is," Diego said, although he plainly did not.

He pushed a bowl of almonds toward Sandra. She took one and remembered that all she'd eaten so far were almonds and alcohol.

"Would you like another dance?" Diego said.

Before Sandra could answer, there was a halt to the music. The people applauded and looked up for the next song. Instead, a man in a brown-checkered suit hopped on stage and grasped the microphone like a cane.

"Folks, we want to welcome you to Fresh Squeeze," he said. "We appreciate your business and to show our gratitude, we want to give you the gift of a free item from a local patron. The catch is, you have to find it yourself. Take it away, boys."

There was a drum roll and the spotlight jerked from the man's face to the dance floor, lighting the blinking eyes of the dancers. Then the light reeled onto the ceiling, where a net had been stretched overhead. Inside trembled dozens of orange balloons.

The announcer fingered a rope hanging from the net. "In each of these balloons is a coupon for a free item. But there's a catch: You have to catch one of these balloons to get it." He yanked the rope and the net fell away so that the orange balloons sprang into the air. The band began playing "Turkey in the Straw" as people dove onto the dance floor, grabbing for balloons. They elbowed each other, and the dance floor was soon filled with the jumble of bodies silhouetted in the spotlight. The room filled with the *pop! pop! pop!* of bursting latex.

"Hot dog," Diego said. "I'll get you one." He jumped into the mob and disappeared from sight.

Sandra watched a man strangle a balloon like he was killing a chicken. It popped to reveal a white paper. Why was she wasting time with Diego when she could be talking to real Hollywood people? For all she knew, Imogen could have left without her.

Carefully, she made her way to the booth where Casey, Rachel, Lulu, and Imogen were sitting by themselves. Filled as she was with mimosas and gin, Sandra traipsed over and sat next to Casey.

"Here she is," Casey said. "She's the one I mean."

"Hi," Sandra said. "Mean what?"

"I work for First National and there's a bit part in a picture called *Down Safari Way*," Rachel said, even though she'd told Sandra this an hour ago.

"We need more champagne," Imogen said, banging on the table. Her fur stole had slid off and was lying in the booth. The dog was asleep on her lap.

"The original girl doesn't fit in the costume because she got herself in the family way," Rachel said. "You should take the part. Shooting starts Monday at eight a.m. I'll put your name on the list, if you want."

"You mean you can just give me the part?"

Rachel waved her hand. "As long as the director likes you, it shouldn't be a problem. It's just a bit part. I think there's a line, so it only pays twenty-five dollars."

Elation filled Sandra. A speaking part would solve her money problems—or at least relieve them for a while. "I'd love to take it," Sandra said. "But I don't think I could play a native, could I?"

"Nooooo, you're perfect for it," Casey said. "You're tall and thin, which is what they want, right Rachel?"

"Yes. I can already tell the costume would fit you. Stand up."

Sandra scooted out of the booth and rotated in front of them.

"Perfect," Rachel said. "You're about five feet seven inches, right?"

Sandra sat back down. "That's right. But I'm too light skinned to play a native, aren't I?"

At this, Imogen and Lulu laughed, their shoulders shaking. Sandra and Casey exchanged confused glances.

"Honey," Imogen said, aiming her giant eyes at Sandra. "All you gotta do is dye your hair to get the role you want. My own hair is as dark as a buckeye."

"That's true," Rachel said.

"Here's what you do," Imogen said. "You dye your hair dark and do your makeup so that they can't see anything but a native when you walk into that studio. They'll eat you up like honey on a hush puppy."

Sandra studied Imogen's platinum waves. "I guess that makes sense. I mean, it isn't as though there are any real natives walking around Hollywood, are there?"

There was a pause as the women took this in. Then Imogen started laughing again, and Lulu and Rachel followed. Even though Sandra didn't know what was so funny, she found herself laughing too.

"Aren't you all adorable?" Imogen said, wiping away a tear. "I declare. You all should come to my house. I bought it in the hills last year."

"We'd love that," Casey said.

"Good. Lulu, you remember to invite these ladies over sometime soon. We'll have a good old-fashioned ladies time. I never get ladies time now, like I used to when I was younger."

"What's your phone number?" Lulu said, pulling a notebook out of her purse.

"We room together," Sandra said and told them the telephone number at the boarding house.

"Mr. Boodle is tired," Imogen said, picking up the dog and waking it. "Aren't you, Mr. Boodle? Sweet widdle Mr. Boodle is sleepy, isn't he?" Then Imogen stopped talking. The simper slid off her face and for a moment, Sandra could see what she would look like when she was an old lady. Imogen lowered the dog onto the seat, letting go of it for the first time that night, and placed her hand on her belly. Everyone at the table remembered the unspoken reality of her pregnancy.

Without a word, Imogen got up and walked across the club. Her shoulders were hunched forward with both hands pressed to her stomach. Lulu began to gather their things.

"Is she all right?" Casey said.

"She'll be fine," Lulu said. "Feeling a little peaked, that's all. We'll be leaving now. Would you like a ride, Rachel?"

Rachel scooted across the booth to follow her. Lulu tossed a wave at Sandra and Casey. "Nice meeting you," she said, flouncing off with Mr. Boodle on her shoulder.

"Remember," Rachel said to Sandra. "Monday, eight a.m. I'll put you on the list."

In a blink, Sandra and Casey found themselves alone in the booth. The rest of the party had disappeared, either on the dance floor or out the door. The speakeasy would be closing soon and they might be stuck with the bill. Sandra wasn't even sure she could afford the one mimosa she'd had. "We'd better get out of here," she said.

"Yeah, I was thinking the same thing."

As they stood to leave, Sandra noticed one of the coupons from the orange balloons on the floor. She picked it up. It read:

GOOD FOR ONE FREE GLASS OF ORANGE JUICE
AT RAYO SUNSHINE'S HOLLYWOOD KIOSK
Have a glass of sunshine on us!

CHAPTER 11

Three days later, Sandra sat sunning herself outside the boarding house and going over the encounter with Imogen Beauregard in her mind.

If she held perfectly still, she almost couldn't feel the headache that had been plaguing her since the night at Cocoanut Grove. She wanted it to go away before she had to go to the studio. First National had confirmed that she was on the call sheet for *Down Safari Way*. Filming started at eight a.m. on Monday. Sandra was officially a working actress. It was simply a matter of meeting someone who would let her in, just as she'd suspected.

Every time she thought of the part, nervousness dripped through her like rainwater. She was hoping the sun would give her enough color so that she wouldn't have to put on too much makeup to look like a native. It was bad enough that she had to dye her hair dark brown or black; she didn't want to worry about her skin too.

The sound of footsteps made Sandra jerk around. Casey was there, holding a newspaper. "Should you be out here?" Casey said. "Don't you owe Mrs. Pickler a bunch of rent money? If she sees you, she's going to want you to pay up."

Sandra settled in her seat. "She's out shopping. I'll be inside before she comes back."

"Well, I wanted to show you something. There's an article about Imogen in the paper today." Casey handed Sandra a copy of *The Motion Picture Herald*. On the front was a picture of Imogen beside the headline, STARLET'S SCARLET DIARY KEY IN COURTROOM BATTLE.

In an emotional testimony, sullied starlet Imogen Beauregard told a judge that her scarlet diary doesn't include information about her alleged affair with actor Lance Barney.

"I didn't have an affair with Mr. Barney, so how could it be in my diary?" the stunning young lady was heard to say in the courtroom.

Dressed in a Chanel suit and blinking back tears, Miss Beauregard was the picture of maidenly sincerity as she testified. Rumors have circulated of late that she and the very-married Mr. Barney had an affair during her performance in the aptly titled, *Whirlwind Romance*. These rumors have been amplified by Miss Beauregard's sudden weight gain and the alleged contents of the scarlet diary, which is said to contain sordid details about the affair.

While Miss Beauregard is making headlines for her love life, studio heads are rumored to be close to releasing the starlet from her contract. The beauty from Mississippi may be too much for Hollywood to handle.

"No wonder she hasn't called us about coming to her house," Sandra said.

"Yep. She's been pretty busy."

Sandra studied the photograph of Imogen, which looked like a professional studio portrait. She was staring heavenward, a picture of innocence in a boatneck dress. Her eyelashes were as long as moth wings.

Casey picked up one of Sandra's curls. "When are you going to dye your hair?"

Annoyed, Sandra pulled her head until the curl slipped from Casey's fingers. "I'll get to it."

"You'd better do it soon. The dye needs to set."

"I know."

"Okeydoke. I'm going in for a while."

As Casey shut the door, Sandra gazed up at the enamel sky and wondered why dyeing her hair bothered her so much. She wasn't a natural redhead either, but this was different, somehow. *You're an actress*, she told herself. *Changing appearance is part of it. Stop being such a baby.*

She shut her eyes and began practicing her diction, whispering, "Kiss her quick, kiss her quicker, kiss her quickest." The words drifted over the cement lot like smoke. Sandra would like someone to kiss her. The last person had been Frederick Bauer, who didn't count. Although Sandra didn't want to admit it, she missed Billy. In some ways, she hadn't meant to leave him. Yes, she'd packed the car to drive away, but Billy was supposed to come after her. It was something they'd been doing for months. In the middle of a fight, she'd make a show of packing, saying that she could do better than a two-bit musician. Then she would snatch her suitcase and stomp to the car.

The first few times she did this, Billy ran after her and clasped her to his chest, saying, "If you go somewhere, let me go too, please, please, please." Every time, Sandra felt as she had the night they met, when she rose above everything else in Billy's eyes. She would cling to his neck, and he would carry her into the house, his every touch seeming to renew the passion between them. It was as good, or better, as when they first got together.

But the day had come when Sandra sat in the car by the apartment with the motor running, and Billy didn't follow her outside. So she drove to the coast and parked on a cliff to watch the sun sink into the sea. When she finally returned, Billy hugged her tightly and said, "I thought you were gone forever," and it was almost as good as before. Almost, but not quite.

Then one fight later, he laughed when she stomped to the door. "Here we go again," he said. "You're pretending to leave."

And Sandra had set the suitcase down so hard that it thumped. Billy had called her bluff.

For that was what it was: a bluff. It was a game designed to make him fight for something, anything. It was better to fight than have Mabel's prediction of the marriage come true—that Billy would never amount to anything and that Sandra had married a loser. He wouldn't listen to Sandra about his career, but he would listen to her when she threatened to leave. He didn't know it was a game, not until he said, "Here we go again." After that, the rules changed. The fights grew nastier and Billy grew less willing to chase her.

So when Sandra walked into a club and found Billy canoodling with some brunette hussy, she knew what he was doing. He was saying, *Look how easily I can leave you, baby. Who's the real heartbreaker here?*

Sandra responded by going home, beating Billy's trombone against the bed frame, and tossing it into the closet. When he discovered what she'd done, he waved the trombone at her, shouting, "How can you destroy the very thing that feeds us?"

In reply, she flung open the suitcase and marched around, taking whatever she wanted from the apartment—money from his wallet, his pocketknife, spare razor blades—half-believing she was actually leaving this time. With vengeful efficiency, she emptied drawers and shook out boxes, her mind reeling with things she needed to set up life in Hollywood. If he wouldn't be the star, then she would.

The whole time, Billy held the trombone in his hands gingerly, as if it had been heated up and was just now cool enough to touch. "Why can't you be happy?" he said. "We have a nice life here."

"It's nice all right," Sandra said, throwing a canister of change into the suitcase. "So nice that you're necking with some two-bit floozy behind my back. Well, I can do better than you, mister. Just watch me."

Clicking the suitcase shut, Sandra dragged it off the bed. As she put her hand to the doorknob, Billy said in a calm voice, "I'm not coming after you this time, Sandra. If you go, don't come back."

She knew Billy meant what he said. He was tired of this game. He never wanted to play it in the first place. All he wanted was a nice girl who would support his modest career, bake Sunday dinners with his mother, and walk his eventual children to school. He was tired of her nagging him to try harder, to socialize in San Francisco, and to find out about the music scenes in Hollywood and New York. He wanted her to say, *This is good enough. You are good enough.*

And as Sandra stood there, preparing to walk out of their apartment, part of her thought that she could be that wife for Billy. Maybe they could start over and be something close to what they once imagined they could be together—if only he would ask her nicely. If he would let her win this last round, she might agree to put the game away forever.

"I'm leaving you," she said. "If I walk out this door, I'm going to Hollywood to become an actress. I won't come back."

She stood in the doorway, waiting for him to react, but Billy said nothing. He just sat holding the trombone with that tired expression on his face, so Sandra had no choice but to walk to the car. When he didn't come after her, she backed out of the parking space and idled at the end of the street. She was sobbing so loudly that a little boy walking by right then stared at her. It was that look more than anything that made Sandra realize she'd packed everything she wanted. There wasn't anything left inside worth going back for, so she drove away, heading south toward Hollywood.

Now Sandra reviewed her actions as if they belonged to a different person. In some ways, it felt like she'd never been the wife of a bandleader, sitting on the sidelines through countless rehearsals and performances while Billy got all the attention. Their marriage had seemed like the beginning of a glamorous life, but he only earned enough for them to live in a cramped apartment, where he was always draining his trombone's spit valve into the sink. That alone was enough to make one loathe trombones. Sandra deserved better; she was certain of it. Still, she wondered, if he'd come after her, would they still be married?

On the street came the sound of an approaching car and Sandra popped up her head like a prairie dog to see Mrs. Pickler parking in front of the boarding house. Sandra swung up, headache sharpening, and hurried inside.

Behind her, the hinge of a car door squeaked. "Miss Sanborn," said Mrs. Pickler.

Sandra slipped into the house and walked as fast as she could without actually running to her bedroom. Flinging shut the door, she locked it and backed away. The words on the sign jumped out at her: OWNER RESERVES THE RIGHT TO INSPECT ROOM AT ANY TIME. She could hear Mrs. Pickler shuffling upstairs, keys jangling. Before she could find a place to hide, the lock turned and the door nudged open. Mrs. Pickler leaned against the doorframe, panting, hat askew. "Sanborn, why did you run away from me?"

Sandra sat down on the unmade bed and nudged a Coke bottle filled with cigarette butts under the bedspread. "I beg your pardon? I did no such thing."

"I called your name."

"Did you? How odd. I didn't hear you."

Mrs. Pickler wrinkled her nose as she took in the room. It *was* a bit cluttered, Sandra had to admit. Magazines lay on the radiator, clothes littered the floor, and silk stockings hung over the lamp to dry. Her evening dress was draped across the dresser where she'd laid it the night she came home from the Cocoanut Grove.

"This place is a wreck," Mrs. Pickler said. "And it stinks."

"Yes, it bothers me too. You should clean these rooms before you rent them."

The old lady put her hand on her hip. "Listen, girlie, you owe me two weeks' rent. That's twenty dollars. Right now."

There were twelve dollars of her Billy money left, and Sandra wasn't about to spend it on rent, but she made a show of feeling in her pocket. "I'm afraid I don't have twenty dollars on me right now."

"Then you're going to have to pack up and get out of here."

Sandra gasped. "Mrs. Pickler, you don't mean it."

"This isn't a sorority, Sanborn. I'm not a den mother. And I'll have you know I can rent this room like that." She snapped her fingers. "So pay now or get out."

Sandra took a deep breath. "If you'll be patient, I'll pay you in a few days. I have a part in a movie, a speaking part. I'm a working actress now."

"No. Why should I wait a moment more than I already have?"

"Because," Sandra said, grappling for an excuse, "I'll pay you more. I'll pay you the money I owe, plus the next week in advance. Please, Mrs. Pickler. Times are tough."

"They're tough, all right. So tough that you can spend every day lazing around outside."

"That's for the role! I have to tan for the part. I've been working every day to prepare. Look." She snatched her purse off the dresser and pulled out two dollars, leaving ten inside her wallet. Cupping the money like a baby bird, she offered it to Mrs. Pickler. "Take this. It's all I have, my last bit of money, but you can have it. I promise I'll pay the other twenty-eight dollars when I get paid."

Mrs. Pickler's mouth turned down as Sandra pressed the money toward her, and for the first time, Sandra was scared. She had no backup plan. There was no place to go if Mrs. Pickler kicked her out.

Then Mrs. Pickler took the cash from Sandra's hands and turned, waving her arm like she was pushing off an invisible person. "Fine, Sanborn. But this is your last chance. You pay me the twenty-eight dollars or you're out."

"Thank you, Mrs. Pickler."

"Yeah, yeah. In the meantime, clean up this pigsty." She slammed the door behind her.

Sandra sunk on the bed, realizing she'd promised her entire wage to Mrs. Pickler. And there were so many other things she needed. Like decent clothes. And food. All she'd eaten lately were peanut butter sandwiches and apples. She was so desperate, she'd stolen an avocado off a tree in a drugstore parking lot and eaten it in her car. It was a hard, mealy thing that she'd gnawed on for a few minutes before throwing it into an agapanthus plant.

But if she didn't pay rent, she'd be homeless. She'd have to go home to Mabel.

No. No matter what, she wouldn't go back to Healdsburg. She'd promised herself that in high school when Mabel used to make her get up at five a.m. to help Daddy Jones harvest prunes. Whenever Sandra complained, Mabel would say, "My daughter, we don't always get what we want in life. I certainly didn't." It used to make Sandra so mad that she would scream into her pillow. She swore that once she left Healdsburg, she would never come back.

Now Sandra lay on the bed, thinking that everything would be okay. There was always her car. At least there was one valuable possession that she could sell. Or drive away in.

Lifting her hand, she rubbed her aching temples so that the pain faded to a dull ache under her fingers. It was almost painless, as long as she held her arm in the air.

CHAPTER 12

Throughout the journey to California, Vira worried about crossing the desert. In Great Salt Lake City, they purchased a map of a shortcut through the desert that was supposed to take three days off the trip, but Vira had her doubts. The Mormon man who sold the map had shifty eyes. She didn't trust him. When he said something affirmative, he shook his head *no*.

In bed that night, Elmer showed Vira the map, pointing to springs and pastures along the route. "It'll be fine," he said. "We'll load up on water at each oasis and that'll get us through."

Vira's finger traced from green spot to green spot on the map. "Maybe we should follow the common route across the desert, the one most emigrants take."

"Argonauts, dear."

"Argonauts, then."

"This will take days off the journey. The sooner we get to California, the sooner I can start digging for gold."

"If there's still gold to be had."

Elmer rolled up the map noisily and put it beside him on the ground. "Of course there'll be gold. Don't listen to gossip.

I've planned this trip in detail and it has been as smooth as a Swiss clock so far, hasn't it? So believe me when I say we'll be fine in California. All right?"

But the trip hadn't been smooth. They were a month behind schedule because of rains that fell for weeks, soaking through the canvas and dripping onto her piano. When Vira made dinner, she crouched with an umbrella over a sputtering fire, only to bring in lukewarm beans that crunched in her teeth. They had to sleep under the wagon to keep dry.

"All right," Vira said.

Elmer blew out the lantern and turned over on his side. Vira stared, dry-lipped, at the tent wall. Not a day passed where she didn't think about the woman from Fort Kearny who warned her not to have babies on the trail. Remembering her lifeless eyes, Vira wondered what, exactly, had happened to her in California. She pulled the blanket over her head, huddling against Elmer's sleeping back for comfort.

At daybreak, the wagons entered the desert. The distant ring of mountains was as white as salt next to the pink ground. As the hours passed, the temperature rose until it was 104 degrees by midday. The emigrants soon learned that the map wasn't accurate. Pastures were ten miles off from where they were marked and entire mountain chains weren't on the map at all. It appeared that the map seller had been making a fortune bamboozling people with his fictional shortcut.

At first Vira felt vindicated about her opinion of the shifty-eyed Mormon, but by the second day in the desert, her vindication turned to apprehension. They started passing furniture by the side of the road: a table, a stool, an anvil, a wooden cradle. The desert had enough furniture to fill several houses. Vira added empty beds to the tally of graves in her head: seventeen graves, eight beds.

Then they began seeing dead cattle. Their stench lingered like clouds of gnats above their bodies and she added them as well. Seventeen graves, eight beds, six dead cattle.

On the third day, water levels ran down. The oxen dropped their noses so low that they bumped against stones as they walked. At night, they bellowed for water. From filthy pans, Vira and Elmer ate dried beans and dough made with bacon fat. When she tried to brush the grease off her apron, it drove it in further. Dirt caked under her fingernails, between her toes, and in the creases of her mouth.

On the fourth day, a meadow appeared where it was marked on the map and the emigrants camped for two days, draining the shallow creek to a puddle. Once they started again, the oxen looked sickly right away. Soon the wagon train was lurching along like a large, dying creature.

On the seventh day, Elmer called to Vira, who was in the back of the wagon, avoiding the sun. "Dear, the oxen can't pull this weight anymore. You're going to have to get out and walk."

Vira, who'd been playing piano, abruptly stopped so that the sound died in the buzzing heat. Dragging back the curtain, she looked out at the desert. The other women were already walking. Sarah Brecknell was wearing goggles under her sunbonnet to keep the dust out of her eyes, which made her look like an insect.

Elmer stopped the wagon and she climbed to the desert floor. It was disorienting to be exposed to the sun, which was white in the sky.

If she were going to die, Vira resolved, she would die like a lady. She opened her parasol and walked in as stately a manner as she could, ignoring the dust, which kept making her sneeze. As she approached the other emigrants, she overheard Jack Cooper telling his son that they would soon find another meadow. "And when we get there, there'll be a cool stream, and we'll be able to get enough water for the cattle and ourselves."

"What will we eat?" the boy said.

"We'll hunt something. Don't you worry."

We're all going to die, Vira thought, veering away. *We're all going to boil away here and no one will know what became of us.*

Her skirt felt heavy, like rocks were sewn into the hem, but she was also alert, as if her senses were tuned beyond their highest level. It reminded her of when she had scarlet fever as a child and climbed out of bed one night, looking for water. Her mother's steady breathing had wafted from the bedroom down the hallway. Though Vira's body had been weak, in that moment, her mind felt eerily active. It was a little how she felt now.

To distract herself, Vira decided to list the people who'd wandered the desert in the Bible. There were the Israelites, of course. Elijah. Jesus. Hagar, the mother of Ishmael. The story of Hagar had always bothered Vira. First, Abraham's wife, Sarah, had told her husband to get Hagar pregnant so he could have an heir. He did, and Hagar gave birth to Ishmael. Then, at the age of ninety-something, Sarah gave birth to Isaac. And all Hagar did was make one tiny joke about Sarah being old, and she was banished to the desert.

And Vira didn't understand why God had allowed it. He told Abraham to obey Sarah and cast Hagar and his son into the desert with only some bread and a skin of water. To treat Hagar that way after she'd done everything she could to please Abraham. It was no wonder she'd given up and put the child under a bush to die. Vira wanted to lie under a bush too and let the heat bake her to bone, but she couldn't do that because the other emigrants were watching. She had no choice but to take herself out of this merciless place, one step at a time.

Now a man was approaching, his red beard licking his chin like flames. It took Vira a moment to recognize Elmer. She hid her hands in her skirt so he wouldn't see how dried out they'd become. They were old-lady hands, wrinkled and papery before their time. And her hair was oily and limp. It had taken three tries to get it into a bun this morning.

"What is it?" she said.

Elmer brushed the back of his hand across his forehead. "We're going to have to turn around."

For an instant, Vira thought he meant they were going home to Maine, but no, that couldn't be it. "Why?"

He pointed at the map. "We're here. About two hours ago, we should have come to this meadow." He pointed to a green spot. "But there was no meadow. The oxen aren't going to make it. We need to go back to the last stop, where there's water, and start fresh tomorrow."

That meant losing the ground they'd covered that day. It meant another day in the desert. Vira could cry, but she knew Elmer was right. They would have to go back. There was no choice.

"All right," she said.

"But," Elmer said, "my dear, there's something else."

Vira had never seen that expression on Elmer's face before. It was as if he were ashamed of what he was going to tell her.

No, that wasn't right. It wasn't shame on Elmer's face. It was fear. He was afraid of her, the woman who let him chase buffaloes in wild country, who watched him buy bad maps off shifty-eyed Mormons and never said a word, who let him trade their future for a pine wagon. *That* was the person who brought fear to Elmer's eyes.

"What?" she said, more sharply than she'd ever spoken to him. "Out with it."

"We have to leave the piano here. The oxen won't make it pulling all that weight."

"What do you mean, leave it here?"

"Leave it behind."

"Like the furniture we saw?"

"Yes, like that."

"Will we come back for it tomorrow?"

"No, we won't be coming this way again."

The idea of leaving her piano behind was the loneliest thing Vira could imagine. Lonely, like all the graves she'd passed; lonely, like the woman she met in Nebraska. Her mother's piano, which Elmer had promised would sit in their California home, would be left in this desert, by itself, for good.

She felt rage swim to the surface of her face, drawing her thin mouth thinner. "No. We'll have to make do with the piano in the wagon."

"We have no choice. The oxen can't tow it any farther."

And Vira wanted to strike Elmer in the face. He was talking about choice. Here they were in the desert, because of him, about to die, because of him, and he was talking about choice.

"No," she said again. The word was barely above a whisper, but it was also an order, a quick, sharp sound. Vira wouldn't allow it. She would refuse to let him leave her piano here. If he did, she would change into a pillar of salt in this desert, Lot's wife forever facing homeward.

Elmer swung around to the men. "Ned, Jack, help me unload the piano." He trudged toward the wagon.

Desperately, Vira followed. She couldn't believe this was happening. The piano was supposed to sit in the parlor of their California home. Elmer had promised. "Don't do this," she said. "Please." Her voice creaked out of her mouth, weaker than ever.

Swiftly the men put a ramp on the wagon and took out the

trunks. Without looking at her, they hoisted the piano and, in one motion, deposited it on the side of the road with a loud clangor and an echo of strings. A cloud of orange dust rose and covered the lavender glass.

Vira twisted away from the sight, but there was only more desert. She was making gagging noises. It was unladylike, but dirt was in her mouth and she couldn't breathe. Elmer picked her up, as he'd done once before under different circumstances, ages ago, but this time she arched her back and bucked. She never wanted him to touch her again.

And the emigrants saw it all, their ears pricking like a dog's for gossip. Vira was sorry she'd given them something to talk about and went limp in Elmer's arms. He laid her in the wagon, and they were pushing tepid water in a metal cup at her face. She drank, gulping in as much air as water. It splashed and someone said, "You're wasting it."

Then Vira lay down, grateful they were leaving her alone. She heard Elmer go to the front of the wagon, which started easily now that the piano wasn't weighing it down. "Don't leave it," she said. "Please, Elmer."

He acted as if he hadn't heard her, even though, in the new silence born from the absence of the piano, she knew he had.

She should never have married him. If she hadn't, she would be safe at home with her piano, living among friends and things familiar and clean. It was a bad match. If her mother had lived, she would have warned Vira against it. She would have explained that the lightning strike wasn't what Vira thought—it was a freak act of nature, not the finger of God pushing her toward Elmer.

It was too late now. They were married and there was no changing that. All Vira could do was make sure that nothing of hers was ever lost again because of Elmer.

CHAPTER 13

Sandra bit her lip to keep from crying as she streaked cold cream on her cheek. The newly dyed black hair flopped on her face, almost blue against her skin. She wished she'd listened to Casey and dyed it before now. Then there would have been time to fix it, but filming was starting in two hours and there was nothing she could do. Whether or not the studio had a costume, she had to dress for the role, or the director might not think she could do it. That meant going there in full makeup, and with her hair looking like this.

I'm going to have to make the best of it, she thought, and started crying all over again.

Casey came in, still wearing her nightgown, with a tube of foundation the color of pancake batter. "I thought you might have this problem, so I borrowed darker makeup from a waitress at work. I have powder and rouge too."

"Thank you," Sandra said, blinking back tears. Here she'd been annoyed all week that Casey was bothering her about her hair, and she'd gone and done this huge favor without Sandra knowing.

"Don't use it all on your face," Casey said. "We'll need some for your neck and arms too."

That was right! Sandra had to cover all her visible skin or she would look mismatched. That meant putting makeup on her hands, neck, arms, chest . . . "I'll never get ready on time," she said.

"Sure you will. Calm down. You have hours yet." Casey handed Sandra a grease pencil. "Here, line your eyes."

Sandra put on eyeliner and mascara, then applied rouge and powder. While Casey pinned her hair, she slathered her mouth with the Chinese-red lipstick. Finally, slipping into a red dress and her highest heels, she surveyed herself in the full-length mirror that Casey had brought up from downstairs.

The girl gazing back at her didn't look familiar. Her skin was a dull tan, like unstirred paint, and her cheeks had a peculiar orange tint. The black hair was pulled into a finger wave and tied in a bun.

"You look good," Casey said, handing Sandra brass hoop earrings. "You look the part."

"I look like a nineteenth-century immigrant."

"But Sandra, that's what acting is, dressing up like someone else."

Annoyed, Sandra tugged on her sleeves. As if she hadn't been telling herself that all week. "Tell the truth," she said. "You think I look okay?"

Casey nodded. "I do. All you have to do is act sultry and that part is yours."

She regarded herself again, trying to see what Casey saw. Her legs, at least, looked good. They always looked good, no matter how thin she got. She strutted toward the mirror, swaying her hips as she went.

"There you go," Casey said. "Now you're getting it."

Opening her purse, Sandra pulled out a cigarette and lit it. Casey was straightening the debris on the bureau, shutting compacts and putting lids on tubes. She'd been so kind when Sandra woke her up in a panic about her hair.

"Why are you helping me like this?" Sandra said. "You could be getting your own part in a movie right now."

"I don't have anything to do today, I guess," Casey said, laughing. "And, don't get me wrong, it's not that I don't believe in myself, but I'm not like you. I don't have the same star potential you have."

Sandra blinked. "You think I have star potential?"

"I do. It's like you're always saying, you have that royalty quality. What do you call it?"

"Aristocracy?"

"Yeah, that. You have that more than someone like Imogen Beauregard, I think."

Sandra returned to the mirror. The reflection seemed more acceptable now—French or Italian-ish. Exotic. She crooked her elbow, shifted her weight to one foot, and lifted the cigarette to her mouth. When she exhaled, she imagined smoke blowing from her lips in slow motion, suggesting a kiss.

Yes, she thought. *Maybe this will work after all.*

Morning traffic was worse than she anticipated. The four lanes were crawling, and all Sandra could see were other cars. She forgot to bring a watch, so it was impossible to tell how much time she was losing. Finally, her exit came into view and she sped up, passing illegally on the shoulder.

When she arrived at First National's gate, the guard looked up her name in a registry, and Sandra squeezed the steering wheel, certain he would tell her that she couldn't come in. But her name was on the list. He gave her a map, and Sandra drove into the studio, thinking that it couldn't be this easy.

The studio was made up of warehouses the size of airplane hangars. Sandra drove past them and ended up at a dead end, facing the legs of a water tower. She'd been holding the map upside down. Turning it over, she reversed the car and drove past a row of pastel-colored houses with flower boxes of perfectly groomed flowers. When she went around the corner, she realized that they were a façade propped against a wooden platform.

Finally, Sandra found the registration office on the other end of the studio. Dabbing her jaw with the powder puff, she whispered, "I'm okay, I'm okay. This is what I've been waiting for. This is what I should have been doing all along."

Taking a deep breath, she sailed across the parking lot. Inside a secretary was sitting at a desk, her burgundy nails clacking on the typewriter with knifelike efficiency. Her wavy hair was perfectly parted in the middle.

The clock on the wall said 7:15 a.m. Sandra froze. Somehow she'd gotten here forty-five minutes early. The secretary was looking at her, so Sandra sauntered to the desk, trying to project the image that she was the next big thing and that the secretary was lucky to witness her discovery.

"Hello," she said in a husky voice. "I'm here for filming of *Down Safari Way.*"

"Name?"

"Sandra Sanborn."

The secretary flipped through the pages on a clipboard and ran her finger down a column. "Here it is," she said. "You're early. The call isn't until eight."

"Yes, I know," Sandra said and opened her mouth to explain why she was so early, but the secretary didn't seem to care. She wheeled around in her yellow office chair and pulled papers from a stack behind her. Then she told Sandra to fill them out and report to Soundstage B at eight a.m. In the meantime she could wait in the women's dressing room located in a trailer outside.

Sandra thanked her and went to the trailer, which had metal stairs leading up to it like a fire escape. When she stepped into the room, she was confronted by her reflection in the mirror. Her green eyes were almost erased underneath the dark makeup and black hair. Again she was embarrassed by how she looked, but then, as Casey said, this was what acting was. Pretending to be someone else. She turned her attention to the script. It was one page. Her part, Native Girl Two, was underlined.

```
SETTING — A NIGHTCLUB IN A JUNGLE

White tables with lanterns. Palm trees and
tropical flowers. VICTOR FORESTER is sitting
at the table, waiting for the arrival of
LELANI LAURAINE.


                NATIVE GIRL TWO
    Would you like to try some monkey brains?

                VICTOR FORRESTER
    No thank you.
```

Leaning back, Sandra scratched her neck, then remembered the makeup and jerked her fingers away. Luckily, it hadn't smeared.

Well, she thought. *At least I won't have to throw a spear.*

"Would you like to try some monkey brains?" she said out loud. "Would you like to try some monkey brains?"

The makeup was itchy and Sandra wanted nothing more

than to slide her nails up and down her face. She crossed her legs and leaned back silkily, trying to appear poised and confident. "Would you like to try some monkey brains?" she said. "*Mon*-key brains. Mon-key *brains*."

The door squeaked and a woman stepped into the trailer. Her hair was cut into a black bob and the eyes under wisps of eyebrows were blue.

"Waiting for *Down Safari Way*?" she said in an English accent.

"You're in the right place," Sandra replied.

"Good," the girl said, bending to the mirror. She trembled as she pulled out a compact and applied blush to her cheeks. She had a nice face, but it was too broad to be classically beautiful, Sandra thought.

"I'm Peg, by the way," she said.

"Sandra."

"Have you worked with this director before, this Ub Winston?"

"No," Sandra said. "This is my first picture."

"Oh, very good," Peg said, looking at Sandra with new appraisal. "What role are you playing?"

"Native Girl Two."

"Ah. I'm Native Girl One. Do you have a line?"

"Yeah. It's 'Would you like to try some monkey brains?'"

Peg laughed. "Mine is, 'Please, mister, buy a beaded necklace? It look pretty on your lady.'"

Sandra laughed. "It's not Shakespeare, that's for sure."

"A fan of Shakespeare, are you?"

Sandra pulled a package of mints from her purse and popped one in her mouth, deciding to try her story out on the girl. "Sure. I played Lady Macbeth and Juliet back home. And Medea, although, of course, that's not Shakespeare."

When she looked up, Peg had a strange expression on her

face. At first Sandra thought she was impressed by her (slightly exaggerated) acting experience, but that wasn't it; the girl was staring at the box of mints.

"Want one?" Sandra said, holding out the box.

Peg grabbed three mints and shoved them in her mouth. The speed with which she moved, and the look on her face, made Sandra draw back her hand. This girl was hungry. The mints were food to her. She stood, repelled, and put the box on the table. "Have some more. I'm going to get some air."

When Sandra stepped outside, a breeze brushed against her, but there was also a haze in the air. The sun was a strange pinkish color, as if something was on fire. The only sign of life was a crow flying overhead.

She opened the map, found Soundstage B, and decided to wait outside. It had to be close to eight a.m. by now. Maybe it was open and she could finally go onto a movie set.

There was no one around as she wandered through the maze of warehouses—even the parking spaces were empty. The metal doors of the hangers were locked tight, including the sound-stage where she was supposed to report for work. A large red *B* was painted on the door, so she knew she was in the right place.

Sandra leaned against the wall of the building and tried to picture tropical things—palm trees, coconuts, pineapples—to have the right state of mind to play a native girl, but she kept seeing Peg's ravished eyes when she ate the mints. That girl must be desperate to be that hungry. It wouldn't be long before that became Sandra's future if acting didn't start taking off.

When no one came to open the doors, Sandra decided to check whether she was in the right place and walked back to the registration office. The clock said 8:15 a.m., but now the secretary's desk was empty. In fact, the entire building seemed empty, as though Sandra had come on a holiday and didn't know it.

Irritated, she drummed her nails on the desk. Was this the relaxed Los Angeles lifestyle they talked about in magazines—don't wear suits to the office, don't do any work during the day, keep people waiting for hours?

As she was thinking this, the secretary walked by, sat down, and began putting files in a cabinet.

"Excuse me," Sandra said.

"Oh my," the secretary said, fluttering her hand to her heart. "I didn't know anyone was there."

Sandra took a breath, trying to quell her anger. This woman had walked right by her. "I reported to Soundstage B for *Down Safari Way*, but no one was there."

The secretary raised an eyebrow. "I guess you don't know. The studio declared bankruptcy today. We just got the news. They canceled all pictures until further notice. I'm cleaning up and going home."

Sandra swallowed. Now everything made sense—the quiet atmosphere, the empty parking spaces, the shut soundstage. The studio was going bankrupt, so no one had come in for work. It must have been announced while she was in the dressing room.

"Are they going to reschedule the movie?" she said. "Maybe next week?"

The look on the secretary's face was of someone who didn't want to disappoint an excited child. "Honey, we don't know if we're going to be in business next week."

The door opened and they both turned to see Peg standing there. Evidently she'd overheard, because she sighed and leaned her elbows on the desk, cupping her face. "Not another bankruptcy."

The secretary smiled. "Hello, Peg. Are you going to play that silly part?"

Peg bent over and pulled at her hair so that it came off in her hand, revealing a crop of blond curls.

A wig, Sandra realized. Why hadn't she thought to get a wig?

"I *was* going to play that silly part," Peg said. "It appears as though a bankruptcy is stopping me."

"You're too good for that picture anyway. I saw you in *The Wild Duck* on Broadway. You were a wonderful Hedvig."

"Bless you."

Broadway! And here Sandra had bragged about junior college plays to Peg—and made up ones, at that. Hollywood must really be in bad shape if a Broadway actress could only get a small speaking part. Sandra sighed and started toward her car.

"Just a moment," Peg said. She headed toward Sandra, holding out the box of mints in her thin hand. With her overcoat and blond hair, she could be selling violets on the street in London.

"Your mints," she said. "You left them behind."

Sandra felt embarrassed, remembering the starved look on Peg's face. It was as if she'd witnessed something personal that she shouldn't have, like she'd walked in while Peg was on the toilet.

"That's okay," Sandra said. "Keep them."

"No, thank you," Peg said, her voice clipped. "They're yours." She shook the box insistently.

Sandra took the mints, shoved them in her pocket, and headed for the car, where at least she could scratch her face in private. This had all been a waste of time. She'd dyed her hair, put on a costume, driven all the way out here, and the movie was canceled. Now to get her hair back to normal, she'd have to bleach it and re-dye it, and even when it was red again, the texture would remain like crunchy animal fur for some time. And to think, she could have just gotten a wig.

Outside, more smoke lingered in the air. In the parking lot, Imogen Beauregard was sitting in a convertible not twenty feet away, talking to a man leaning against the car. Even with half her body obscured, Imogen looked pregnant. In the last week, her belly had grown round and hard, like she swallowed a cantaloupe.

"I don't understand why he won't see me," Imogen was telling the man. "I'm willing to screen test again. Did you tell him that?"

"Yes, I told him."

A tear slipped from Imogen's eye, and she brought a handkerchief up and dabbed at it. "Then why won't he see me? What did he say?"

Sandra shut the door to the casting office slowly, as if trying not to scare away a wild animal. She knew the decent thing to do was to get in the car and drive away. It was rude to bother Imogen at such a personal moment. And yet, if Sandra didn't talk to her, she would always wonder what might have been. She owed it to herself to try.

Taking a deep breath, she sauntered over to the convertible. "Imogen? What a surprise. It's me, Sandra Sanborn. We met at the Grove last week?"

The man and Imogen both looked at her, their faces inscrutable. Sandra remembered her black hair and touched it reflectively. "I usually have red hair," she said. "I was here to play a native in *Down Safari Way*. Do you remember talking to me about dyeing my hair for that?"

And it did seem that Imogen remembered. There was a glimmer of recognition in her eyes, as if the memory of that night at the speakeasy came back to her. With a dignity that Sandra would have thought impossible from this grits-eating country bumpkin, Imogen turned so she was looking through the car windshield. "Mr. Novelle," she said. "Would you kindly get this ridiculous person away from me?" Her Southern accent had disappeared. She sounded like Katharine Hepburn all of a sudden.

Mr. Novelle stepped forward, blocking Imogen from view. "Come on, let's leave Miss Beauregard alone."

"But I met you," Sandra said, leaning around Mr. Novelle. "The other night at Cocoanut Grove Ballroom. Don't you remember?"

"I'm sure I don't know what you mean," Imogen said.

The scope of the insult was becoming clear. Imogen Beauregard had called Sandra ridiculous. Imogen, with her pregnancy, her little dog, and her famous nude scene—*that* person had called Sandra ridiculous.

And Sandra wanted to say that Imogen was the ridiculous one. Here she was, plastered all over the newspapers for her salacious love life, pregnant out of wedlock, crying about her career in front of the registration office when there was a bankruptcy and people were losing their jobs. Who did she think she was?

Mr. Novelle was staring at Sandra as if daring her to do something. She ground her teeth, remembering when the man at Paramount Pictures made her leave for wearing the sandwich board. She never wanted to feel that way again.

Whirling around, she trudged to her car, slammed the door, and sat there, fuming while Mr. Novelle and Imogen put their heads together, murmuring. Every few moments they glanced at her, giving Sandra a faint feeling of power.

Then Mr. Novelle walked toward the casting department, and she supposed he was going to talk to someone about her. Putting the car in reverse, she backed out of the parking lot so fast that she brushed close to Imogen's car, meeting her eyes before tearing through the studio lot. She didn't even roll down her window to thank the guard when he opened the gate, but sped past him onto the street.

The sky was still hazy with smoke and she remembered now that the newspapers said something about a nearby forest fire. As she drove, Sandra imagined the entire city of LA on fire. The flames would pop from car to car like corn and move into town so that the movie theaters toppled and the Hollywoodland sign slid down the hill. Soon the whole sprawling city would rain ashes and it would all go, one by one—the studios, Cocoanut Grove, Rayo Sunshine, Central Casting, Mrs. Pickler's boarding house. And the people too, yes, they would also burn in a blistering inferno, the producers, casting directors, starlets, actors, and most of all, best of all, Imogen Beauregard.

Back at the boarding house, Sandra stripped off the red dress and ran to the bathroom, not caring who saw her in her slip. She scrubbed her skin with cold water, the makeup flowing down the drain in streaks, leaving orange water droplets on the basin.

When she looked at her reflection, she froze. Flakes of makeup stained the creases by her nose and her eyes, and the black hair had come loose and hung around her face in clumps. She looked small and white, like a child playing dress-up in her mother's clothes.

And Sandra then knew that Imogen was right. She was ridiculous. She was a migrant farmer's stepdaughter—not even his daughter—playing at acting. In a town where Broadway actors were starving, maybe it was true she didn't have a chance. Maybe she was ordinary after all.

Back in her room, Sandra was unpinning the rest of her hair when there was a knock on the door. She sucked in her breath, remembering that she didn't have rent money. Even if she gave Mrs. Pickler every penny she had, it wasn't enough for the twenty dollars in back rent, let alone the extra eight dollars she'd promised.

"May I come in?" Casey said, sticking her head in the room.

"Sure," Sandra said.

The mattress squeaked as Casey sat down. Sandra tossed a bobby pin onto the bureau. It skipped across the wood and fell on the floor with a small clatter.

"I take it the movie didn't go well," Casey said.

"I didn't get a chance to find out. The studio canceled the picture. They picked today to go bankrupt."

"I was afraid of that. After you left, I saw it in the newspapers. They want a government bail-out."

Sandra yanked a hairbrush through the black hair, enjoying the pulling on her scalp. She didn't want to hear about the studios. They could burn down for all she cared.

"I tell you, it's so hard right now," Casey said. "I might go home to Iowa for a while."

Sandra whirled around. "You can't do that. You're the only friend I have here."

Casey was wearing a plaid dress with puffed sleeves that looked like something Shirley Temple would wear. The face above it was sad. "I'm not like you, Sandra. You're here a few months and you're getting parts in movies. I've been in LA for a year and a half and all I have to show for it is one mob scene. And you can't even see me in the mob."

Again, Sandra heard Imogen calling her ridiculous. She remembered Mrs. Mel telling her that Hollywood didn't want her. She thought of Frederick saying she was skinny and had big feet. "I'm not doing so hot," she said.

"Sure you are. Oh, I know you're disappointed about today, but no one can help a bankruptcy. You're always saying you're going to be something, and you know what? I believe you."

Sandra wiped at her runny nose, touched. The fact that someone believed in her meant a lot. And Casey was right; it wasn't her fault that Hollywood was falling apart. No one could help a bankruptcy.

But right now, Sandra had more pressing concerns. Mrs. Pickler wouldn't give her anymore grace time on the rent. She was going to have to leave. And then what would she do, share a flophouse with five other girls? Get so low on money that mints would start to look like a promising meal?

She looked at the starlets pinned around her mirror. Where once they had appeared beautiful and aloof, now they looked smug and self-satisfied. It wasn't her fault, Sandra wanted to tell them. She'd tried in Hollywood, tried harder than she'd ever tried at anything in her life. If someone would just give her a chance, she would show him what she could do, but no one would do that.

With a little catlike cry, Sandra sprung to the bureau and tore down the pictures, jerking the pins with her fingernails so they slid down the frame. Then she tore the pictures until the beautiful faces were scraps in her hand and threw them up in the air like confetti.

When she turned around to face the bed, Casey had such a look on her face that Sandra laughed. A piece of Greta Garbo's chin had landed on Casey's shoe.

"Well," Sandra said. "I guess I'll have to figure out what's next."

CHAPTER 14

It was the first warm day of spring. The sun was making the water sparkle and birds were singing in the trees. Elmer was standing in a California river, panning for gold.

After five years, he was an expert at it. He lifted the pan from the water and shook it back and forth so that the rattling debris sounded like clothes being scrubbed on a washboard. Then he tipped the pan so that the gravel fell away and only a fine layer of silt remained. With his fingers, he sifted through the dust, looking for gold.

There was nothing, but he was having a good day. He'd found gold dust this morning and carefully stowed it in the inner pocket of his coat, where it was safe. It was spring that was causing the gold to appear. Snow was melting in the mountains and bringing it down to the river.

It wasn't much, but it was something to show Vira. This was Elmer's fourth claim, and it was getting harder with every failure to argue that he should continue mining. He wanted to move out of the hotel to a cheaper residence, but if he mentioned it, Vira would bring up his broken promises about the California mansion where her mother's piano was supposed to stand. At this point Elmer would do almost anything to avoid talking about that piano.

California had been difficult from the start. After dragging themselves out of the desert and over the mountains, they'd gone to the first gold strike they heard about, in a town called Rescue. When they arrived, it was deserted. The buildings stood empty, doors hanging open, furniture left to rot. The only resident was a man throwing loot from abandoned cabins into a wagon. He said that everyone had gone to a strike near Growlersburg, so Vira and Elmer went to Growlersburg. There they learned that the newest strike was in Sweet Springs, south of Hangtown. On the way, they ran into a standoff between the Americans and Mexicans over who owned access to the river. No one could pass until it was settled, so Vira and Elmer rode into Hangtown instead.

The first thing they saw as they entered town was the noose hanging from a scaffold. Mercifully, it was empty. Hangtown was comprised of saloons, mercantiles, and other buildings that seemed haphazard, as if they'd slid to their resting places on a tide of mud and remained where they landed. In the center of town, a horse auction was being held. The men shouted their bids while the horses jerked their bridled heads, white-eyed with fear. A woman in an orange dress was standing outside a saloon under a sign that said, DANCE THE FANDANGO! Seeing her, Vira blushed and looked down at her apron.

At the end of the street was the hotel, the first one they'd encountered on their journey. The walls of the room were made from the sails of ships that were abandoned in the San Francisco harbor, but there was a real bed and a floor and food that could be brought up from the restaurant downstairs. Compared to the wagon, it was luxurious.

Once in the hotel, Elmer hoped things would be better with Vira. Around Nebraska, she'd stopped having marital relations with him for reasons he didn't understand. That was before the piano. Since leaving the piano in the desert, she barely spoke to him. However, the hotel seemed to relax her. Sleeping in a real bed for the first time in months, Vira even let Elmer put his arm around her.

In the following days, he began preparing for his claim while Vira stayed in the hotel. Hangtown scared her. When she went out, the men stared at her in amazement, so rarely did they encounter a woman who wasn't a prostitute. Increasingly Elmer spent his nights in the restaurants, which were part-brothels, part-bars, relieved to be free of Vira and her constant worrying.

One night, he engaged in an indiscretion with a soiled dove, as they were called. She was a big woman with clay-colored ringlets who sat on his lap and giggled at everything he said. Vira wouldn't have found out about this act, which was natural enough for a man who'd been frozen from his marriage bed, if they hadn't happened to walk by one of the establishments he'd come to frequent. The doorman, a burly fellow in a patched waistcoat, winked at Elmer as they passed. "Got a pretty one this time, eh hombre?" he said. Elmer felt Vira's back straighten under his palm, but she said nothing.

That night, Elmer stayed at the hotel, telling himself he'd had enough revelry and it was time to work. He was crouching on the floor, polishing his boots, when Vira sat on the bed facing him so that he could see her button-up shoe in his peripheral vision. Folding her hands, she cleared her throat. "Elmer, I want to talk to you about this gold mining business."

He was surprised by the directness of this statement, which was unusual for Vira. "What about it?" he said.

"Don't you think it's time to give it up?"

Deliberately Elmer stroked his boots with the rag, letting a full minute pass before saying, in a casual tone, "But we just got here."

Her shoe ticked up and down like a horsetail flicking a fly. "Come now, Elmer. Be reasonable. Do you want to be like these other men, chasing every rumor of gold you hear? It's ludicrous. The smart thing to do is get a job at a bank in San Francisco."

Elmer sat back on his heels, flummoxed. More than anyone, Vira knew how much he hated banking, yet here she was asking him—telling him—that he should give up on striking it rich and go back to counting other men's money.

"Vira," he said. "I'd rather be hanged than work in a bank."

They'd had an awful fight then, the first real fight they'd ever had. It disturbed Elmer to see the change in his wife. She'd been so compliant when he married her, so gentle and sweet. Now she was as stubborn as a jar that would not be opened.

Though he'd gone out the next day and staked his claim, she hadn't changed her position one bit. For the last five years, she'd simply repeated that she wanted to go to San Francisco. With each failed claim, it became harder to say that he wanted to try again.

And yet, standing in the river with the sun beating on his back, Elmer was glad he hadn't given up. Today it was enough to be in this wild place and take what it offered with his pan. He'd purchased the pan in Maine and brought it across the country wrapped in a woolen blanket he'd been swaddled in as a baby. Now that same pan brought silt, gravel, and the occasional sparkle of promise out of this California river. With his own eyes, Elmer had seen a gold nugget the size of a frying pan in the assayer's office. These things existed, and if they existed, he had as much of a chance of finding them as anyone else.

A fish was swimming where he wanted to pan, hovering

almost invisibly above the gray stones. Elmer paused. The water was like glass, and the fish blended in with the river bottom, brown and taupe with speckles of silver. There weren't many fish in these shallow rivers.

As Elmer waited for it to swim away, the water grew more agitated. Waves splashed against his boots and the fish disappeared in a puff of silt. Elmer straightened to find himself standing by a river that was turning to mud.

He clamored up on the bank. On the mountain behind him, men blasted water so that mud flowed down like a second river. They were hydraulic mining—washing the dirt into a sluice to be strained and dumped into the water. It meant they would catch all the gold, making it impossible for Elmer to pan his claim.

He stalked toward the mountain, water splashing in his boots. Around a boulder, the sluice stretched like a miniature bridge into the water. Two men stood beside it, throwing rocks and dirt clods over their shoulders into a battered manzanita bush.

"What are you fellows doing?" Elmer said. "I was gold panning a quarter mile away from here, and your muddy water almost drowned me."

A man with a copper beard turned to study Elmer. He wore damp-looking long johns under overalls. Dirt cleaved to his face in patches like liver spots. "A quarter mile, you say?" he said. "That's part of our claim. We're the Davidson Mining Company."

"No, it's my claim. I've been here a week. None of this equipment was here when I staked it."

"I ain't going to argue about that," Copper Beard said. "Fact is, you're mining our claim, not the other way around."

"Yeah," said the little man beside him. "If you got any gold, it's our property."

"That's right," Copper Beard said. "Did you get any gold?"

Elmer thought of the nuggets wrapped in his pocket hand-kerchief and shook his head. "No, but if I did, it's my claim."

Copper Beard cupped his hands around his mouth and shouted over his shoulder, "We have a claim jumper here."

There was a commotion and a minute later, the rest of Davidson Mining Company rushed into sight. There were eight men—ten if you counted the first two—in threadbare shirts and exhausted trousers. Some carried rifles held aloft for Elmer to see.

"What's this?" said a man with a gun.

"This fellow is panning the river," said Copper Beard.

"Is that so?"

They moved nearer, and Elmer could smell their body odor mixing with something mineral, like ointment. He only had his pan with him, which he'd been holding it by his side all this time like a tambourine. It was useless, the wrong tool to have in this situation.

"I staked my claim last week," he said. "I was here first. By law, it's mine."

"Too late," one of the men said.

"Yeah, too late," said Copper Beard. "We staked the whole mountain six weeks ago."

But snow was on the mountain six weeks ago. The sluice hadn't been here, and there were bushes where now there were piles of rocks. Elmer knew he'd staked his claim first, but there was no way to prove it. The law would favor the word of a company over the word of one man.

And yet, if this claim failed, Elmer would have to give up mining for good. He couldn't put off Vira forever.

The little man, seeming even smaller beside his compan-ions, pointed at Elmer. "He won't say whether he got any gold from the claim."

Abruptly, Copper Beard slid to his knees and began patting

Elmer down, his hands running over his legs and diving into his trouser pockets.

"Hey!" Elmer yelled. "Get off me." He kicked at the man until someone cocked a gun and his spine twinged. If they found the gold, they might kill him. He'd heard of people getting shot for less—one miner was killed just for stepping on someone's claim while carrying a shovel.

Copper Beard felt down Elmer's sides, his fingers going over the spot where the gold was hidden. It was sheer luck that Elmer had put it in the inner pocket. He concentrated on not showing fear.

The man stepped back. "He's clean."

"Okay, you can go," said the short one. "But don't let us catch you here again. We don't take kindly to claim jumpers."

Elmer lifted his hands. "All right, I'm going." He backed away, arms still in the air, until he was behind the boulder. Then he limped toward camp and sat down on the riverbank to dump water from his boots. He was shaking from the close call. Glancing around to make sure he was alone, he took out the handkerchief and unfolded it. Gold crumbs glinted on the cotton. They'd almost cost him his life.

The river was turning the color of milky coffee again as the mining company resumed their work. The water rose so high that Elmer stood to avoid getting wet. The men were right—he was too late. If he'd left Maine when he originally intended instead of waiting around to marry Vira, he'd have arrived in California while the gold was still plentiful. He would have struck it rich.

The lightning strike had seemed like a sign to marry Vira, but maybe not. Maybe it was a warning to stay away from her.

With a set face, he gathered his supplies. Vira had won. He would go to San Francisco. He was too late. A pocketful of dust was all the gold Elmer Sanborn would ever get from the California Gold Rush.

CHAPTER 15

Sandra sat on her bed in her coat, hat, and stocking feet. Her shoes were on top of her blue Samsonite luggage, which was stacked by the door. The room was spotless. The curtains were pulled back and the sun shone onto the brown carpet, which she'd cleaned with a carpet sweeper. The pink bedspread was wrinkle free, the closet empty of clothes. She'd been unable to do anything about the smell, however. The window was open, but the stench of cigarette smoke lingered in the corners.

In a few minutes, Sandra intended to sneak out of the boarding house without paying rent. She had seven dollars to her name. There wasn't any way she could pay Mrs. Pickler the rent she owed, short of selling her car, which was out of the question.

The problem was where to go. Sandra had written to several insurance firms in San Francisco offering her services as a secretary, but that wasn't a long-term plan. The obvious solution was to get married, but it might be awhile before she could meet a quality man.

Casey was already gone. When Sandra had hugged her goodbye at the train station that morning, Casey had whispered, "Take some cash from Mrs. Pickler when you go. She won't notice."

Sandra had leaned back, hands resting on Casey's shoulders. "Did you—?"

The train whistle blew, interrupting the question. Casey picked up her luggage. "So long. I'll write you when I'm in Iowa."

Sandra remembered how Casey stole two quarters from Mrs. Pickler's desk. Maybe she'd been filching from Mrs. Pickler all along. She was always pretty solvent for a part-time dishwasher.

The room had filled with rosy late-afternoon light. Mrs. Pickler would be deep into a bottle of gin by now. It was time to go. Sandra checked under the bed and in the bureau drawers. On the shelf in the closet, she found the orange hatbox with the letters from John Hollingsworth. She'd almost left them behind.

It wasn't that Sandra had forgotten about John Hollingsworth. She'd meant to ask her mother about the letters, but it wasn't an appropriate topic for a postcard. She couldn't write, *P.S. I got letters from some guy claiming to be my father. You don't happen to know who he is, do you?* It occurred to Sandra that she could drive to Petaluma, track John Hollingsworth down, and ask him why he sent her the letters. It was better than asking Mabel about it. It was better than going back to Healdsburg. Or to Santa Rosa and her failed marriage. Or job hunting in San Francisco during a depression.

She tucked the hatbox under her arms, hooked her fingers in her shoes, picked up the suitcases, and tiptoed downstairs. To her immense relief, Mrs. Pickler was asleep in the parlor with her head slumped against the chair. Her mouth hung open and a snore drew in and out of her mouth like a feather in an updraft. *Amos 'n' Andy* was starting on the radio, and orchestra music was filling the hallway.

At the rolltop desk, Sandra felt for the key hidden underneath. She unlocked and lifted the lid, wincing at each click of the slats. As before, the cubbyholes were stuffed with money.

Sandra stood, flexing her hands open and closed. It would be a matter of slipping one roll in her pocket and going to the car. Mrs. Pickler wouldn't notice the money was missing until much later, and by then, Sandra would be halfway to San Francisco.

But it was one thing to stiff Mrs. Pickler on rent and another to steal from her. Mrs. Pickler had the ten-dollar deposit from when Sandra moved in, so she'd only be out a few bucks overall when it came to rent. To take more money was a low blow. Not to mention, the old woman might call the cops.

On the other hand, if Sandra took the money, she could go to San Francisco, check into a hotel, and figure out her next step. Maybe she could find a nice husband who would support her goals. She might not even have to get a job.

As she stood there equivocating, Sandra noticed a stack of mail on the desk. On top was a letter addressed to her from one of the insurance firms in San Francisco, an answer to her inquiry about employment.

Sandra glanced toward the parlor. If she got the job, there was no need to steal anything. If she didn't get the job, what choice did she have?

The envelope was covering the front page of yesterday's newspaper. When Sandra picked it up, she recognized the woman on the front page. It was Peg, from *Down Safari Way*, the one who'd eaten Sandra's mints. The headline read: PEG ENTWISTLE DIES IN HOLLYWOOD LEAP: ACTRESS ENDS LIFE BY JUMPING OFF FIFTY-FOOT SIGN AFTER FAILURE IN THE MOVIES

Sandra squeaked in surprise. The sound cut through the babble from the radio like a scratched record. Mrs. Pickler grunted and raised her head. For a moment, Sandra held her breath in the shadows by the desk.

Finally, Mrs. Pickler flopped her head back against the chair. Sandra waited, barely breathing, until she heard a snore. Then she picked up her suitcase, slid down the desk lid, and tiptoed outside. On the porch, she put on her shoes, ran to the car, and drove onto the first freeway she saw.

For several miles she sped in the fast lane, half-believing Mrs. Pickler or the police would appear behind her. From the passenger seat, Peg peered out of the paper with a pleading expression. Sandra took the next exit and pulled into a gas station to read the article. It said that Peg jumped off the *H* on the Hollywoodland sign. Sandra looked around as if expecting to be parked in front of the sign herself.

She read the article a second time. It covered Peg's early success on Broadway and the movie she'd been in that was delayed called *Thirteen Women*. There was no mention of *Down Safari Way*. Under the picture, the caption read, "Prefers death to failure."

Sandra shuddered. It was terrible. That poor woman. Sandra couldn't allow herself to end up like that. She must figure out how to get out of poverty once and for all.

And that meant she wouldn't go to John Hollingsworth. If the letters were a trick or a lie—which they were—then nothing good would come from such a trip. It might even be dangerous. Who knew what this man was capable of? Sandra had so little money, so little chance to keep herself from becoming destitute that she couldn't waste resources on a conman.

Picking up the envelope from the insurance firm, she opened the flap and pulled out a letter.

Dear Miss Sanborn,

We are hiring secretaries at this time. If you'd like to stop by, we'll schedule an interview.

Sincerely,
Wakefield Insurance

It was decided then. Sandra would go to San Francisco and work until she found a suitable husband. No one needed to know that she dropped out of college to marry Billy. For that matter, no one needed to know about Billy. She could say anything about herself she wanted. She could start over.

And Sandra was glad that she hadn't stolen money from Mrs. Pickler. She hadn't stooped to the casting couch either. She could say she left Hollywood with her integrity intact.

Of course, she'd stiffed Mrs. Pickler on the rent, but what was she supposed to do about that? That was an outrageous sum. For twenty-eight dollars, she could stay at the Wilshire Hotel.

Besides, Sandra thought, as she headed onto the freeway toward San Francisco, *that old woman would just spend it all on gin anyway.*

PART II

CHAPTER 16

When Mabel Sanborn was a little girl, her world revolved around her parent's house in San Francisco. It was a large-parlored, crown-molded manor where women in dresses with long trains moved like the flutter of moths. Surfaces were covered with fabric to muffle the sounds of everyday objects: cups placed on wood, forks put by plates, hairbrushes laid on dressers. There were many rules for being quiet in the house. Mabel must speak only when spoken to, tread lightly, use a ladylike tone, let Father think, let Mother rest. Sometimes, when she was in the parlor doing her lessons, the house was so still she could hear her own heart beating.

The home was on a hill overlooking the San Francisco Bay. Mabel's father was an important man at the stock exchange, so they lived in a good part of the city. There were bad parts, but Mabel never visited them. One day, if they all worked hard, Vira said that Elmer would be elected to the stock exchange board, and then they would move to Nob Hill, which was covered with palaces. Mabel had seen them herself. One had so many turrets and towers, it looked like a dollhouse glued to another dollhouse. Vira had taken her to lunch at that house once, and they'd eaten under a chandelier covered in crystals that reminded Mabel of a crown.

Her mother was on several morality committees to help clean up the city. Every week, ladies gathered in the parlor to drink raspberry shrubs and eat Vira's lemon cookies. The committees had names like "Women Against Pauperism" or "Ladies Aiding Lost Waifs." They were dedicated to ridding the city of "pestilence," a word that could mean anything from gambling to drunkenness to squalor, but usually meant prostitution. Mabel wasn't sure what a prostitute was, other than a kind of woman, but she suspected it was the reason she couldn't do what other children did. She could not, for example, go to school or join the children playing in the streets outside. Mabel could hear them singing songs or chanting while they skipped rope. One could hear everything in this house, which, aside from the habitual silence, had thin walls. Once, Vira heard the cook cursing in the kitchen and flew down from the second story and fired her on the spot.

"I heard that prostitutes run through the streets without any clothes on," Caroline Chase told Mabel. Caroline's father worked with Mabel's father at the stock exchange. Her brother Robbie was two years older and got to go to school because he was a boy. When their mothers met for committees, Caroline and Mabel played together in the nursery.

Mabel tried to picture a naked woman running through the streets. "But wouldn't we see them too?"

Caroline shook her head. "They come out at night. Then the men follow them into Chinatown."

Mabel didn't like that Caroline knew more about prostitutes than she did. It was her job to be the interesting one. Abruptly, she stood up with her legs apart and her fists on her hips. "I'm going on safari," she announced. It was something she'd over-heard her father talking about: people going on safari in Africa to see wild animals. Her mother had been outraged when he mentioned it. It was Mabel's new favorite game.

"I want to come," Caroline said.

"No. It's too dangerous for little girls."

"You're a little girl."

"But I'm trained to go on safari. My father knows about them."

Caroline rose. "I don't care. I'm coming too."

Mabel shrugged and Caroline grabbed the doll she carried with her everywhere. They weren't supposed to wander the house when the mothers were in a meeting, but Mabel did it all the time and never got caught. Near the parlor, they tiptoed by the door where the women sat with the bustles of their gowns rest-ing behind them on the chairs. The girls slipped into the dining room and scrambled underneath the table, which was covered with a long cloth. There they abandoned the safari game in favor of pretending they were trapped in a cave and running out of food. Just when they were about to die of starvation, their mothers came into the room. From under the table, the girls could see the hems of their dresses. Vira's dress was higher than Caroline's mother's dress. From that angle, Mabel could see the wooden heels of her shoes.

"She can be so willful," Vira was saying. "She doesn't listen. I'm afraid she'll lead Caroline astray with her behavior."

With a jolt, Mabel realized her mother was talking about her. She looked over at Caroline, who had buried her face in her doll.

"I wouldn't worry so much," Caroline's mother said. "They just get excited by their games."

"I hope you're right. Mabel is so inclined to take after Elmer, I don't know what to do with her sometimes."

Mabel was filled with injustice. She didn't understand what she did to make her mother say things like that. She wanted to be a good girl. She tried, hard.

"They're blessings, despite the trouble they cause us," Caroline's mother said as the women's hems moved toward the parlor.

"How true."

The door shut behind them, and the girls scuttled to the servants' entrance and through the back hallway. In the kitchen, the cook stopped mid-chop of an onion as they hurried past her and upstairs to the nursery. Collapsing on the bed, they burst into laughter.

"They didn't even know we were there," Caroline said.

"Yes, we got away just in time."

They lay on the bed, breathing heavily. The sun was drifting through the nursery window in a slanting line, highlighting the dust twirling in the air. Mabel wondered what her mother meant when she said she took after how her father "used to be." She couldn't imagine her father any other way than how he already was. Every night he read by the fire while drinking brown liquor from a glass. Sometimes she would stand by his chair while he admired her embroidery or asked about her lessons. Then he would pat her head, and Mabel knew she was free to leave.

Although Mabel loved her father, it was always a relief to get away from him. It was as if Elmer wanted something from her, but wouldn't say what. Whatever it was, Mabel didn't know how to give it to him.

Vira told Mabel that guests were coming and they needed to go to a bakery to buy a cake. That meant Mabel would ride in the carriage through the city, which was exciting, even if she had to be lectured first.

"You're not to leave my side," Vira said, kneeling by Mabel as they waited for the carriage. "You're to hold my hand the entire time we're on the street. You will not speak to anyone but me, and only then when you're spoken to."

Mabel didn't say anything because she was listening for the carriage wheels. Vira tugged so roughly on her skirt that she had to tilt back to keep her balance. "Will you mind me, Mabel?"

"Yes, Mama."

Vira sat on her heels so that Mabel was looking down at her. "I do all this to protect you," she said. "That's what mothers do, protect their daughters. You understand that, don't you?"

"Yes, Mama."

But Vira didn't say Mabel couldn't look, so that's what she did as they rode through the streets. The carriage went to the top of a hill and for a moment Mabel could see the city rising up and down like a seesaw. In the bay, clipper ships sailed in front of Alcatraz Island, which had a squat lighthouse like a half-burnt candle. Vira always said there were so many criminals in San Francisco that if the police caught them all, there would be no room in the jail. As they drove through the shopping district, with crowds bustling in and out of stores, Mabel wasn't sure if she should be afraid or not. It didn't seem like the people on the street would hurt a little girl.

On the sidewalk, Mabel saw what could only be described as a pet pyramid: a white rat on the back of a yellow cat, which in turn was on the back of a black dog. A man was squatting by this strange configuration and shaking a can for money. His eyes were white and Mabel understood that he was blind.

Vira leaned out the window and signaled for the driver to stop. For a moment, Mabel hoped her mother was slowing for them to get a closer look at the pet pyramid, but no, Vira was signaling to a police officer riding by on a horse.

"Excuse me," Vira said. "Do you see that beggar over there?"

"Yes, ma'am."

"I thought it was illegal to terrify people in this manner. I won't have my daughter exposed to such displays."

The horse was blocking Mabel's view of the pet pyramid, so she looked out the opposite window. Across the street, a woman was standing next to a carriage lined with sky-blue satin. Her hair was woven in braids and piled on top of her head, and she wore a dress made from yards and yards of eggplant-colored velvet that fell in elaborate folds over her bustle. When Mabel leaned forward, she could see that violet bows ran up the center of the gown. The woman's torso was so stiff that it seemed separate from her skirt, like a wooden carving on a ship, as she handed a bird cage to a boy sitting inside the carriage.

And Mabel realized that she was looking at a prostitute.

Her next thought was that the prostitute was the most beautiful woman she'd ever seen. It hadn't occurred to her that a woman could wear purple gowns or line a carriage with blue satin. Her own carriage was black and her mother wore a sober dress of dove gray. Mabel thought that she understood why men would want a woman like that, especially when you considered the dull colors respectable women wore. Given the two options, it wouldn't be so bad to be the other, even if it meant going to hell. But was there some way Mabel could be both things?

". . . out in broad daylight with vermin?" Vira was saying to the policeman. "There are children in that park."

"I will attend to it, ma'am."

"See that you do. Thank you, officer."

Her mother shut the window and rapped the roof. The carriage pulled into traffic, and Vira shifted her birdlike gaze on

Mabel. In the past when Vira looked at Mabel like that, it had felt like her mother could read her mind. But that was impossible, Mabel saw now. If Vira could see inside Mabel's head, she would know about the prostitute and she would be outraged.

Her mother sucked her lips into a line. "Mabel?"

"Yes, Mama?"

Vira turned her face away, and Mabel saw how uneasy she was. It gave her a faint thrill.

"Sit up straight," Vira said. "We'll be there in a little while."

CHAPTER 17

Sandra stood in a greeting line waiting to congratulate the bride and groom. Beatrice, the bride, looked slim and modern with her white-blond pageboy hairstyle. She was leaning against her new husband, Alvin, and gripping his bicep with both hands. A long veil curled like a cat's tail around her feet. Every time she moved, a bridesmaid adjusted the veil.

It was a nice wedding, Sandra had to admit. The ceremony was at a cathedral that emptied out to bells ringing and pigeons scattering into the sky. Now they were at the reception. The ballroom before her was full of tables of pink crystal dishes and vases of orange blossoms. It looked like something from a magazine.

This might have been Sandra's wedding if things had worked out differently. Six months ago, Beatrice and Sandra were secretaries at the same insurance firm. The two of them would commiserate over coffee about how few eligible men lived in San Francisco. Another secretary had wanted to set Sandra up on a double date with Alvin, a wealthy surgeon, but she already had a dinner scheduled that night and suggested that Beatrice go instead. Now Beatrice and Alvin were married, and Sandra was as single as ever.

When it was her turn to greet the bride and groom, Beatrice appeared overwhelmed and held onto Sandra's hand a little too long. "How nice of you to fit this in," she said. "None of the other girls from the office could make it."

Sandra felt vaguely irritated, as if Beatrice were suggesting her schedule was less important than the other secretaries, most of whom were recently engaged. But she smiled broadly. "I wouldn't have missed it. It was a lovely ceremony."

"Thank you." Beatrice leaned forward and said, "I've sat you by a single man. A doctor."

In the span of time it took Sandra to walk from the greeting line to her table, she allowed herself to hope. Weddings were one of the best occasions to meet quality men, something that was increasingly difficult these days. Since leaving Hollywood, there'd been many dates, and some almost-boyfriends, but no one who was husband material.

At her table, which was in a far corner, an old woman was sitting by a teenage boy with pimples on his forehead. Beside him was the doctor Beatrice had promised. He was short, with thick glasses and sparse blond hair that lay on his head like dead grass. His name, he said, offering his hand, was Wally.

Sandra was offended Beatrice thought Wally was the kind of man she would consider. Doctor or not, he was patently undesirable—tubby and thick, like a ham sandwich. And Beatrice must have mentioned Sandra to him too, judging by the lustful way he was looking at her. She was afraid she'd have to make small talk with him throughout the reception, but when she sat down, he took out a pen and began to write on a napkin. It was a strange thing to do, Sandra thought, crossing her legs and turning toward the room. At least she didn't have to talk to him.

Beatrice and Alvin sailed hand-in-hand toward the head table and everyone applauded. Beatrice's diamond was the size of a garbanzo bean. Sandra wondered if this wedding would be featured in "Women's World," the society section of the *San Francisco Chronicle*. Someone had told her that Alvin's family made their money in pear orchards, which made Sandra think of her father Arthur Beard's prune empire. Since moving back to San Francisco, she'd become aware of her rightful place in the city, had circumstances not worked against her family and forced them into poverty. She wondered where she'd be sitting in this room if her father had lived. Certainly not in the corner at the hangers-on table.

Wally stood up, revealing a large belly that had been hidden under the table. Sandra added "fat" to the list of things that were wrong with him.

"Excuse me, nature calls," he said.

She hunched her shoulders. A horrid phrase, "nature calls."

As Wally passed, he dropped a napkin into her lap. For a second, Sandra thought he'd forgotten it was there—perhaps his stomach had blocked it from sight—but then she saw there was writing on the napkin. It read:

> *A lovely day to wed*
> *Full of buds and bloom*
> *I hope a certain redhead*
> *Will rendezvous*

Sandra sighed. So that was what he'd been laboring on. He got points for the French word, she supposed.

Now waiters were bringing the food: chicken cordon bleu and asparagus, along with glasses of champagne. She kicked the napkin with the poem under the table.

When she moved to the city, she'd made a new plan:

1. Marry a good man, preferably a wealthy one.

2. Move out of her apartment and into a beautiful house.

3. Restore her place in the city that should have rightfully been hers.

The problem was that she couldn't get past the first goal. Now that she was thirty-four (although she told people she was twenty-eight), she found that most single men were either divorced or undesirable. And the situation would only get worse if the United States went to war. Already, magazines were urging girls to get husbands before the military swallowed them up.

Wally came back and shot Sandra an accusatory look. Apparently he felt betrayed that she hadn't followed him to the bathroom. The old lady and teenager had hobbled off somewhere and she was alone with him at the table. She stared at the dance floor, pretending to be engrossed by the band, and ignored his eyes on her face. It had been a mistake to come to this. She would say goodbye to Beatrice as soon as the cake was cut.

"Did you get my note?" Wally said.

Sandra blinked vacantly at him. "What note?"

He was a blusher. The blush went up into his forehead and made his head look like an Easter egg. Her eyes moved toward the dance floor again.

"Are you a model?" Wally said.

This guy didn't give up. Sandra turned toward him again with a smile on her face. "Why, no. How sweet of you to think so."

"I've seen you before though. Not in real life either. In a magazine or something like that."

She wouldn't wait for cake. After this song, she would say goodbye. There were no attractive men here, and this guy was depressing her with his attempts to seduce her.

Wally snapped his fingers. "It's that billboard. That's where I saw you. The one on Highway 37."

"No, sorry. I'm not on a billboard."

"Yes, you are. There's a billboard of your face by Vallejo. I'm certain of it."

Sandra laughed. "I think I would know if I were on a billboard."

Wally wagged a finger at her, a little smile creeping onto his lip. "It's you. I can see the ad in my mind. It's for antacid or something like that. It's just your face against the sky."

The music seemed to grow muffled. Wally was smiling with such self-assurance, that Sandra experienced a dizzy sensation, as if everything was going fast and slow at once. She had a sudden flashback of Frederick Bauer squatting by a fountain, pointing a camera at her face.

She couldn't recall going to Vallejo lately. It was too much like Healdsburg, a Podunk town with ranches and swamps and things like that. There could be many things she didn't know about, things that could have been there for years, waiting in the middle of all those salt marshes that surround the town. "Do you have a car?" she asked Wally.

"It's parked on the street."

He eyed her legs, and she knew he thought he was getting somewhere with her, but she couldn't think of another way to get to the billboard. She'd sold her car when she came to San Francisco, and since no buses went to Vallejo, Wally was her only option—or at least, the only one available. And if there was a billboard with her face on it, Sandra needed to see it right away. She couldn't sit here watching Beatrice's triumphant wedding while this outrage existed in the world. She stood up. "Take me to this billboard."

Wally's car had the antiseptic smell of a hospital. She wondered if his house smelled that way too. He had the clipped look she associated with doctors, as if he tweezed and scrubbed himself until he was thoroughly sterilized.

As he drove out of the city, he kept "mistaking" her knee for the gear shift, and she had to keep pushing him away and lean her legs against the door. They drove through Vallejo and toward a swoop of bridge that led farther north, where Mabel lived. Since moving to San Francisco, Sandra had been forced to visit her mother several times in Healdsburg. They had been stiff, uncomfortable visits and Sandra had avoided going there as much as possible. It wasn't her fault that her mother wouldn't visit her in San Francisco. Besides, Mabel loved to talk on the phone and called all the time. It wasn't as if Sandra were ignoring her completely.

On the bridge, the brackish water of the bay was brown and gray and blue all at once. To the left was the Mare Island Iron Factory, busier than ever because of the war in Europe. A forklift drove through the lot with a mattress-sized stack of sheet metal on its front. When the car crossed the apex of the bridge, Sandra looked through the hood of her cloak, over the front of the car, and through the lanes of traffic. There, at the bottom of the bridge, looming against the sky, was her face.

"Ah-ha," Wally said. "It *is* you. I never forget a face. I have a photographic memory."

She said nothing, just stared in horror as Wally pulled over and parked in front of the billboard. It was her face, all right.

She was gazing at the sky with an expression that could be interpreted as bliss or relief. It said, SWEETEN UP THAT SOUR STOMACH WITH STILLMAN'S CHEWABLE ANTACID.

"That complete and total rat," Sandra said.

"You really didn't know about this?"

"No. I never would have agreed to this. They can't put my face on a billboard without my permission, can they?"

"I should think not."

A red-winged blackbird landed on the top of the sign and stretched out its strawberry shoulders. The look on Sandra's face in the photo was humiliating. It was of someone utterly without guile or sophistication, like a young girl after her first glass of champagne or a country bumpkin looking at her first skyscraper. Or, it could be interpreted, of someone experiencing relief after chronic indigestion.

Sandra remembered how she used to hold that pose in the mirror every day. In her memory, it had been a wise and necessary practice for her acting career. It seemed impossible that this was what it actually looked like.

"Oh," she said, burying her face in her gloved hands. "What a day. Will you take me home, please?"

Through his thick glasses, Wally made amorous eyes at her. "Are you sure that's what you want?" He scooted closer. "Since we're out here, let's watch the sun set over the bay."

Of course this man was going to try some funny business now that she was alone with him. Normally she wouldn't go to a strange place with a man she barely knew. It never paid to break her codes. But how could she have waited, thinking there was a billboard of her face somewhere?

Wally reached for her again, his hammy palm cupping her kneecap. She could smell a scent like rubbing alcohol. There was such a thing as too much cleanliness.

Sandra picked up his wrist and put his hand back in his lap. "Take me home," she said firmly. "Now."

Wally didn't argue. His face went hard with anger, the way so many men looked after rebuffing them, but he started the car and did a U-turn. As they headed over the bridge, Sandra looked back at her sappy face at the bottom of the hill and balled her hands into fists. She would get even with Frederick Bauer if it was the last thing she did.

On Monday, Sandra was drumming her nails on her desk, waiting for the advertising agent at Stillman's Antacid to return to the phone. This was the third call with the company this morning. Now, finally, this Mr. Gaudry had put her on hold when she inquired why her face was on a billboard without her permission.

It was almost lunchtime, a slow period at the office. Sandra's finger hovered near the connector in case her boss, Randy Sloat, walked by. She didn't want him to know she was making personal calls during work hours. He was, by his own account, a tightwad. Every day he brought a Mason jar of milk from home and drank it while eating sardines that he got for a nickel a can from Fisherman's Wharf. That was his lunch, with the occasional addition of a roll or a piece of fruit like a persimmon or an orange. He liked to tell Sandra that a whole week of lunches cost him thirty cents, implying that he disapproved of her frequent trips to the coffee shop to buy premade sandwiches. It was her job to empty the trash after lunch so that his office didn't smell like fish.

The elevator door slid open and Sandra's finger twitched over the connector, but it was just the secretary from the next office. She waved as she passed, an engagement ring sparkling on her finger. Sandra waved back, thinking the insurance firm was going to have trouble getting secretaries if every woman in San Francisco got married—except her, of course. Maybe she could get a raise.

"Miss Sanborn?" said Mr. Gaudry on the phone.

"I'm here."

"I looked into that billboard. It seems we purchased the photograph from Frederick Bauer, as you suspected."

"I knew it. Look, he doesn't have my permission to use my image. I want that billboard taken down."

"That's just it. He submitted a photo release form that is signed by you."

"He did what?" she said shrilly. The light on the wall flickered, as if reacting to her voice. She looked over at her boss's office, but his door remained shut.

"I never signed any such thing," she said. "Not a thing, do you hear me? And I don't want my face on that billboard. I demand you take it down."

"Have you contacted Frederick Bauer? Perhaps you can take it up with him."

"I wouldn't begin to know how to track him down. He lives in Los Angeles."

"I don't think that's correct. He has a studio in San Francisco. Why don't you give him a call? It sounds like your quarrel is with him."

The elevator opened and the vice president of claims walked toward her, thumbs resting on his belt. Sandra clasped the phone to her shoulder. "Good morning, Mr. Walker."

As usual, he looked at her like property he could pick up or drop off anytime he wanted. That look seemed promising when Sandra was first hired, but she'd since learned that Mr. Walker was married.

"Morning, sweetie," he said. "Randy in?"

"Go right in."

She waited until he shut the door before putting the phone back to her ear. "Listen, Mr. Gaudry, my quarrel is with your company for putting my face on a gigantic billboard without my permission. I don't care what piece of paper Frederick gave you. I want that billboard taken down."

There was no reply. The other end of the connection was silent. "Hello?" she said.

The man had hung up. Sandra slammed down the phone, thinking that she now understood why men punch holes in walls. Marching to the kitchen, she stood in front of the water cooler, thinking through her options. So Frederick hadn't just sold her image, he'd forged her signature. She could sue him for that. For fraud, and defamation of character, and all kinds of things.

If only she had money for a lawyer.

"There you are Sandra. I was looking for you." Her boss, Randy, was standing in the doorway. White hair sprouted from his knobby head, reminding her of a potato.

She reached for a glass. "I was getting some water. What can I do for you?"

"I'm going on a long lunch. Can you reschedule my one thirty for tomorrow?"

"Certainly."

"Thanks very much."

Randy disappeared through the door. Sandra filled the glass, returning to the idea of hiring a lawyer. As she bent over to pick up the glass, someone pinched her butt. She spun around in time to see her boss dashing toward the door.

"Mr. Sloat," she said, her hand flying to where he'd grabbed her.

He giggled like a little boy. "Nice dress, by the way."

Sandra slapped her hands on her face. How she hated that man. She'd been working here much longer than she intended. She expected to be married by now, preferably to someone rich who could sue Frederick Bauer for her.

Back at her desk, Sandra pulled out the phone book and turned to the photography section. She found the ad for Frederick's shop right away. It was in a small box in the center of the page, where you had to pay for extra placement. It read:

FREDERICK BAUER
PHOTOGRAPHER TO THE STARS

CHAPTER 18

Mabel had disappeared. One minute she was in her room, embroidering a pillow sham, the next she was gone. Vira had combed the house and, when she confirmed that the girl wasn't inside, sent the servants out to search the streets. Standing on the second floor near the window, she could hear them calling "Miss Saaaaaan-born" with cringeworthy frequency. Vira hoped the neighbors wouldn't notice.

Even though Mabel was seventeen years old—practically a woman—she was still inclined to sneak around. When she was little, Vira would catch her in the strangest places: the linen cupboard, under the drapes, and, once, in the dumbwaiter. This behavior had seemed to stop, but now Vira wondered if the girl had just gotten better at subterfuge.

Again, the call floated up from the street, "Miss Saaaaaan-born." Vira shut her eyes. If Mabel didn't appear soon, she'd have to call the police and the matter would become public. She could see the headlines now: DAUGHTER OF PROMINENT FAMILY MISSING. And just when Elmer was up for secretary of the stock exchange board. His family must appear to have impeccable morals for the position, as the secretary was trusted to handle money. Mabel's nonsense was putting them at risk.

With a huff, Vira stalked to Mabel's bedroom. It was empty and spotless. The white quilt was pulled up over the bed and the only thing on the dresser was a bottle of rose perfume.

Outside, the acacia tree was covered with yolk-colored blossoms. Vira approached the window and looked at the balcony, which was as narrow as a row of encyclopedias, wondering if a girl Mabel's size could fit on a space that small.

As Vira tipped forward to look down at the yard, a floorboard moved under her foot. She knelt, skirts billowing around her, and pushed with her fingers so that it slid to the side. Underneath, in a grimy chamber, was a paperback book.

Vira put her hand to her throat as she imagined a book so illicit that her daughter had to hide it. The cover had a drawing of a man with a bag over his head, riding a horse and waving a gun. It read:

TALES THAT STIR THE BLOOD
~THE STORY OF BLACK BART~
Dangerous gentleman or gracious scalawag?

Flipping the book open, Vira read the words, "Zip! Zoom! Bullets flew aloft over my head as I whipped out my trusty pistol. 'Come and get me, you two-bit prairie dogs,' I shouted. 'You're no match for Black Bart!'"

She almost laughed. What a ridiculous thing to hide, a dime novel about Black Bart, that bandit the police captured a few years back. This was something a boy would read, not a well-bred young lady.

But as silly as the book was, it was proof that Mabel had snuck out of the house, for she likely bought it from a newsstand. Vira frowned as she nudged the floorboard back in place. It was Elmer's blood that made Mabel do such things. She was too like her father, too inclined to silly notions and foolhardy schemes.

From now on, Vira resolved that she would keep tighter control of the girl. They would be looking for her husband soon. Her daughter must not be distracted by fairy tales like Vira was when the lightning strike bound her to Elmer. Unlike Vira, Mabel had her mother here to guide her in such matters, and she would make a good, levelheaded match because of it.

Vira placed the dime novel in the middle of Mabel's bed so that it was the first thing she would see when she opened the door.

When the servants returned, Vira began to worry. Something could have happened to Mabel. Anything was possible in this city. In any case, she needed to tell Elmer about Mabel's disappearance before someone else did. She couldn't trust the servants to be discreet, so she ordered the carriage and went to the stock exchange herself.

Twice a day, before the morning and afternoon sessions, throngs of people roiled in front of the stock exchange building, spilling into the streets and blocking traffic. A policeman held back a path for Vira to make her way to the ladies' entrance, where she argued briefly with the man about the five-dollar admittance fee and entered the viewing chamber. There was no point in talking to Elmer until after the session. The appearance of a wife on the floor would point to an emergency, and that was the last thing Vira wanted.

She spread out her skirts and looked down into the chamber where the trading went on. The stockbrokers were milling among desks that fanned in a half-circle in front of the officers' rostrum.

"Are you bidding on California Consolidated?" a man near her said to his companion.

"Yes, sir. My broker says it's going to go to eighty dollars a share today."

"I heard higher."

Vira glanced at them out of the corner of her eye. Their top hats looked worn and threadbare. The last one who'd spoken had something crusted on his scarf. California Consolidated must be the latest mine to go public. A new type of mine went public every month, or so it seemed. First it was gold, then silver, copper, borax, limestone, and so forth. Elmer had made a fortune brokering mine stocks.

Below, Elmer was talking with Stanley Chase and a man Vira didn't know. Stanley, whose muttonchops fluffed from his cheeks like chicken down, shook his fist and shouted, "California Consolidated isn't worth the paper it's printed on." The unknown man said something Vira couldn't hear over the din and Elmer put out a restraining hand. There was a moment of tension, as if they might come to blows. Then the man yelled, "You, sir, are irresponsible," and waddled off.

Vira knew this was mostly theater—the brokers talked the stocks up or down depending on whether they were planning to sell or buy—but she loathed this behavior. It reminded her of Hangtown, where the men drank and caroused all hours of the day and the women were rough and fast. Vira had the double insult of learning that Elmer had been unfaithful while being mistaken as one of those women herself. That doorman had been standing outside one of those so-called restaurants, a large, slovenly fellow with a black beard, who'd winked at Elmer as they passed. "Got a pretty one this time, eh hombre?" he'd said. And Vira had known then what Elmer was doing while she was left alone in their hotel room.

She caught herself gritting her teeth and shut her eyes to relax her face. This habit of holding her mouth tight was making lines appear around her lips, but she couldn't stop herself. She even did it in her sleep, waking to find her mouth drawn into a line and her hands twisted like hooves against her chest. She must remember to steam her face tonight to combat wrinkles.

At the rostrum, the board president was adjusting himself and fluffing his beard on his plaid vest. One by one the officers sat beside him, glints of gold pocket watches or cigar holders appearing as they settled in their seats. An officer rang the gong, calling the session to order, and Elmer sat with the other brokers at their desks. The hall became silent.

The caller began reciting the stock offerings in alphabetical order. The proceedings were subdued as the As and Bs were read out, with only a flurry of interest for Bicoastal Pacific, with brokers shouting out whether they were buying or selling the stock. As they approached the Cs, the traders tensed with anticipation.

When the caller raised his eyes and said, "California Consolidated," the room erupted with excitement. Brokers scrambled over each other, shouting at the rostrum. The man to set the price first would buy at the lowest rate and make the most money from the stock. Vira watched in amazement as the fat man who'd been arguing with Stanley Chase knocked over a chair with his belly. Meanwhile, Elmer darted through the assembly, ducking under arms and coming right up to the podium.

"Buy 180 at $50," he said.

Chase was right behind him. "Buy 200 at $51!"

They argued about who said what first until the president banged the gavel. There was a sudden hush as he deliberated with the officers. "Buy 180 at $50," the president said.

"Buy 180 at $50," the caller repeated. The secretary recorded the number in a ledger.

Elmer slapped his hands together in victory. He'd set the price. Everyone else would pay more for the stock. As the men continued to shout their orders, the price rose to $100 a share. Vira did the math in her head. Her husband had just made $9,000 for his client, and that was one of many trades he'd do today.

Just once, Vira would like Elmer to admit that she was right to insist he give up gold mining and work in finance again. If they'd done what he wanted, they'd still be destitute in the foothills. Now they were well on their way to the lifestyle that he'd originally promised her when they came to California, but it wasn't because of him. It was because of her.

At the break, Vira made her way downstairs. As soon as Elmer saw her, he steered her into a hallway, out of sight of the brokers.

"What is it?" he said.

"Mabel is gone. We haven't seen her all day. I've combed the neighborhood and she has vanished."

Elmer caught her hand in his. "All day? We must call the police at once."

"Are you sure that's wise?" She lowered her voice. "The newspapers."

"We'll have to risk that. Something might have happened to her."

His insistence shook Vira out of the cold anger that had sustained her thus far. Mabel could have been robbed or kidnapped or sold on a ship. Her virtue could have been stolen right there on the street. What kind of mother was she that these things were just now worrying her?

When they arrived home, they learned that Mabel was still missing. In the parlor, Vira stumbled, white-lipped, to a chair while Elmer wrote to the police requesting assistance.

For a moment there was no sound but the scratching of pen on paper. Then Vira heard something in the next room. It was a small noise, like a stifled cough.

Her eyes jerked to the brocade wallpaper and a tendril of relief spread through her. The girl was unharmed.

"You're right, Elmer," she said, raising her voice. "We'll have to contact the police, no matter the cost. If the newspapers write about Mabel's disappearance and ruin our family reputation, so be it. That's the price of our daughter's safety."

Elmer looked up, confused. Before he could reply, there were steps through the next room and Mabel appeared, looking charming in an eyelet dress and her hair pulled back with a ribbon.

"Hello, Father," she said, jerking up her chin. "Why are you home this early?"

"Because of you, my cheeky girl. You've been running your mother ragged with worry."

Burning resentment filled Vira. "Cheeky" was almost a compliment. It was no wonder the girl was so brazen when her father said things like that.

Mabel's eyes flitted to her mother as she lowered herself—slunk, more like it—into a chair. "I was taking a walk. I didn't think it would worry you."

Elmer glanced at Vira and realized his error. In a sterner tone, he explained that Mabel must never, under any circumstances, leave the house alone. "Young ladies don't walk around unchaperoned," he said.

"As you well know," Vira added.

Mabel glanced at her mother. "I just wanted to go outside. Surely a walk is harmless."

At this, Vira stuck her face next to Mabel. "It's not harmless. A lady doesn't wander about, flaunting herself on the street. The appearance of it alone could damage your reputation. And at a time like this, when we're under scrutiny for your father's position on the board."

"That's right," Elmer said. "They'll be looking into our family life. It's important that we do what's right."

"Yes," Vira said. "And if you can't understand that, your father will put bars on that window."

The girl's eyes widened and Vira leaned back, satisfied. So she was right. Mabel had gone through the window like some kind of monkey.

Elmer cleared his throat. "Mabel, please go to your room while I speak to your mother."

Vira waited until Mabel was on the stairs before whispering to Elmer, "I meant that about the bars on the window. We can't have her running off."

"Surely we don't need to go that far. Mabel isn't a prisoner."

"Why don't you let me be the judge of how far we need to go with her?"

When Mabel was born, Elmer had agreed that Vira would be in charge of their daughter. Now she raised her eyebrow and waited through the pause that followed, daring him to go back on yet another promise.

"I have to go to work," Elmer said at last. "If she does this again, we'll discuss bars. In the meantime, don't be so hard on the girl." He patted her shoulder and left the room. It was a relief when the front door shut, taking him away.

As usual, Elmer was wrong about how to go about things.

Vira would be harder on Mabel, not easier. The child's impulses wouldn't ruin her chances for a good life. Vira would make sure the girl behaved and marry her off to a good man. If she had to be strict to achieve that end, so be it. Mabel would eventually see that her mother was right and would thank her.

CHAPTER 19

Frederick Bauer's shop was located in the Sunset District between a Chinese grocer and a tailor. Sandra stood outside wearing a trench coat and wide blue hat, smoking a cigarette. The sign said FREDERICK BAUER PHOTOGRAPHY, not FREDERICK BAUER, PHOTOGRAPHER TO THE STARS. She'd assumed the ad was refer-ring to movie stars, but with Frederick, maybe not. It could mean astrology for all she knew.

Taking the last drag on the cigarette, she went over her plan once more: she would begin in a businesslike manner, then amplify her request until Frederick agreed to contact the antacid company and get them to take down the billboard. If he refused, she would threaten him with the police. Forgery was a crime. He didn't need to know that she couldn't afford a lawyer.

She ground out the cigarette with her heel and opened the door. The shop was a boxy room with a gray carpet and a display case on one end. Photographs hung in black frames on the walls. Sandra recognized Errol Flynn's face behind the counter. He was leaning forward as if to tell her a secret. She felt a tingle of excitement. So "stars" did mean celebrities.

The door behind the counter opened and a man came out. Sandra liked how he looked right away. His hair folded back from his forehead in a graceful wave and his nose was long and straight, like that of a matinee idol.

When he grinned, Sandra recognized him. "Frederick Bauer," she said, smiling despite herself.

He did the opposite of a blink, a kind of widening of the eyes in surprise. "Hello there."

"Do you remember me?"

"Sure, sure. *Schatzi.*"

She couldn't tell whether he was teasing her by not saying her name or if he didn't remember it. Irritated, she put one hand on her hip. "Sandra Sanborn."

"Yes. That is it. It has been a long time."

The German accent was as thick as ever. Sandra had never minded it, which struck her as odd given how much Frederick had annoyed her. She straightened her shoulders. "I'm here on business. I saw that billboard of my picture on Highway 37." She waited for him to apologize or look guilty or in some way acknowledge what he'd done. Instead Frederick tilted his head and gave her a quizzical look.

"Don't you remember?" Sandra went on. "You took my picture on that date we had in Hollywood."

He snapped his fingers. "That's right. They put it on a billboard?"

"You don't know?"

"No, I just sell the photograph. The company can use it however they want."

Sandra bit her lip. That jerk at the antacid company, the one who'd hung up on her, acted as if he had no idea how her face ended up on the billboard. He was probably the one who ordered it.

"I called the company," she said. "They claim to have a form with my signature on it giving them permission to use my image. I never signed any such form. Would you care to explain that?"

She crossed her arms. That beard must have been a monstrosity if she hadn't noticed how handsome he was when they first met in Hollywood. Either that, or he'd matured in the last few years. Some men looked better as they aged.

Frederick shrugged. "All right, I signed it. I thought I would never see you again. Do you expect me to never sell the photograph under those circumstances?"

"Yes," she said. "I do."

"All right, all right. But what can I do now? The billboard is up."

"You can ask them to take it down."

"Come now, *schatzi*. The company won't take it down because I ask them to. Besides, is it so bad? You always wanted your face big for the world to see."

Sandra tried to stoke up her anger about the billboard, but it had abandoned her. Now she found herself, if not inclined to agree with him, at least wondering if the billboard mattered. Highway 37 was one of the least traveled roads. The only people who lived out there were farmers. And Mabel.

She looked down to gather her thoughts. Inside the glass case was a row of bridal pictures, and one of the women looked familiar. Sandra had seen her somewhere before.

"I could sue you, you know," she said. "Or have you arrested for forgery."

Frederick leaned down with his arms across the case, hunching like a cat over the brides, and looked up at her with denim blue eyes. "But you wouldn't do that, would you?"

Sandra turned and ambled along the wall, trailing her finger underneath the photographs. She spotted more celebrities—Carole Lombard, Anna May Wong, a baseball player. They were mixed in with a bunch of nobodies, so you had to hunt for them. The smart thing to do was to arrange the movie stars behind the counter so that you saw them as soon as you walked in.

"Your ad in the phone book says you're a photographer to the stars," she said.

Frederick rubbed his chin. "I forgot about that. I called myself that when I lived in LA, but it seems less appropriate now that I've stopped photographing movie stars."

This was a disappointing answer. "Why would you do that?" she said.

He blew out a puff of air. "They're so picky. Always complaining about whether they're old, fat, young, thin. It's easier to work with normal people. Come. Let me give you a tour of the shop."

Sandra looked around at the room. "Isn't this it?"

Frederick waved her behind the counter. "Come, come," he said, opening a door.

She followed him into an office, where photographs were organized in boxes along a sideboard. Next was the portrait studio, which was empty except for lights shaped like blown-out umbrellas along the wall. Last was the dark room, which had a red bulb hanging above three bins of liquid. Newly developed photos were strung on a laundry line above the bins. As Sandra examined them, Frederick stood so close that she could feel the warmth of his body through her coat. He was as aggressive as ever.

She cocked her head at a picture of an older man with a patch of white hair. "He looks familiar."

"He's a state senator."

"So you don't just photograph regular people then."

"No, politicians too. Businessmen. I took a picture of Charles Howard, the man who owns Seabiscuit."

"Oh," she said. "I know of him. He's a big customer at the insurance firm where I work."

"Ah. I thought you'd be in the movies by now."

"Nope, secretary." Sandra moved to the next picture of a young woman at a garden party. "This looks familiar too. Not the woman, but the picture."

"It was in the society pages of the newspaper. I work for them."

Sandra shot him a look. "You mean 'Women's World' in the *Chronicle*?"

"Yes, that is what they call it. I freelance for them. I go to the functions, take pictures, and they print them."

That, she realized, was why she recognized the bride—she'd seen her in "Women's World" too. Sandra tried not to show how much this impressed her. She read the column every morning while drinking her coffee.

"Frederick Bauer, Photographer of the Wealthy?" she said.

He stepped closer to her. The red light emphasized his fine jaw and plush lips. "Sometimes."

Sandra reminded herself that he was not to be trusted. He'd sold her picture and forged her signature. In Hollywood, he'd lied about his friend being an assistant director so he could date her. At the time it was insulting, but now it seemed flattering. No one had worked that hard to date her in a long time.

Carefully, Sandra moved around him and walked to the front of the shop so that the counter was between them. She crossed her hands in front of her, businesslike. "All right, you don't have to get them to take down the billboard. But I'll be requiring my cut. I deserve to be compensated for my work."

Frederick wagged a finger at her. "You're a rather material-istic little minx, aren't you *schatzi*?"

Minx. She liked that. "That's funny coming from the 'Photographer to the Stars.'"

He chuckled. It was a pleasant sound. "All right, for me to give you a cut, we have to go to my house. That's where I keep the old ad invoices." He yanked a coat off a rack and swung it on his shoulders. "It's up the hill. Let's go."

Something had shifted. Sandra was interested in dating Frederick but not going to his house. No self-respecting girl did that. He could get the wrong idea and think he could get whatever he wanted from her without even taking her out to dinner first. Besides, she hated walking up San Francisco hills.

On the other hand, he wouldn't invite her to his house if he were married.

"Is it far?" she said.

"No, no. Five minutes from here."

"How many blocks? I'm wearing heels."

Frederick took a paper from his desk, scrawled "Be Back Soon" on it, and taped the paper to the door. When he pushed it open, the mineral smell of fresh air flowed into the room. He grinned at her. "Come on *schatzi*. I don't bite."

The door shut, leaving Sandra alone in his shop. She glanced to either side, as if asking the pictures what to do. There was only one choice, or at least only one that interested her, and that was to follow him.

As Sandra suspected, Frederick was the type of San Franciscan who believed a mile up a steep hill was "a couple of blocks." She trailed behind, breathing hard, and thinking that while she was bending her code by going to his house, he definitely wasn't allowed to touch her. They weren't going to kiss, or anything like that. This was purely business. He would have to ask her out on a date if he wanted more.

They stopped on a hill overlooking the bay and she panted, wondering whether it was unladylike to have a cigarette. It was definitely unladylike to be sweating like this.

"Here it is," Frederick said.

Beside her was a blue Victorian with a postage stamp yard. Sandra was pleasantly surprised. "You own this?"

Frederick jingled his keys in answer. Inside, an entryway opened into a living room with a view of the bay. Sandra was still breathing hard as she stepped toward the window. "Nice view."

When Frederick didn't reply, she turned toward him. The expression on his face made her heart sidestep within her. "What?" she said, suddenly shy.

"Nothing. I like how your cheeks are pink. Here, let me show you the rest of my home."

Sandra never would have thought that Frederick would end up so respectable. The house had a sunny kitchen, dining nook, one and a half bathrooms, two bedrooms, and a small backyard with a neglected shed in the corner. He also had an office, which was neat and modern with a desk and more photography equipment. She preferred the homes they were building on the south end of town, modern places with washing machines, barbecue patios, and wall-to-wall carpeting, but Frederick's house was a good start. And you had to start somewhere.

They returned to the living room, and Frederick said, "Wait here while I see about your cut."

He left her alone beside a hideous couch. On the wall was a painting of two cowboys roping a bull. Although Sandra didn't care for the subject, she knew from years of sketching and reading art magazines that it was a good painting. The composition was complicated, one figure roping the bull, the other mid-lasso. Even the background was well done, with deep purple shadows under the trees and a yellow sheen on the distant pasture. When Frederick came back, she said, "Who painted this?"

"I did."

Sandra looked at the painting again, hardly believing him. Then she remembered how he used to work at Disney "drawing Mickey Mouses." She'd assumed that was one of his lies, but maybe not. "Did you ever end up in a cowboy movie?" she said.

He glanced at the painting, confused.

"The beard," Sandra said, miming hair on her chin. "Remember? You had one when we met because you were auditioning for cowboy movies."

"Yes, that's right. No, no one wanted me in their cowboy movies."

Sandra laughed. "I can see why. Frederick Bauer, German cowboy."

"Yep. I may still do that someday."

"Be in a movie?"

"No. Be a cowboy."

She looked up to see if he was joking, but there was no trace of humor on his face as he opened the file. Before she could question him further, he handed her the photograph of her face. Again, she cringed in embarrassment. Her expression was so goofy, so excessively fake and blithe, it was no wonder he'd sold it to an antacid company.

"Let's see," Frederick said. "The photograph was reprinted at fifty dollars. Your cut at ten percent would be five dollars. Does that sound fair?"

"No," Sandra said, laughing at the paltry amount. "Not at all."

Frederick pulled out his wallet and handed her a $5 bill. "That's showbiz, kid."

"I would rather you give me the negatives so I can make sure I don't end up on anymore billboards."

He shook his head. "I'm sorry. I can't part with it."

"Why not?"

"You have your face every day. This is my only way to look at you."

Even though Sandra knew this was a line—he clearly hadn't seen her face since the last time he sold the photograph—she was pleased. "I bet you say that to all the girls you sell images of without their permission."

"No, I always thought of you. I wish I had not behaved the way I did on our date. I felt that I blew it with you."

Again, her face grew hot and she hated that it showed how he was affecting her. Then she remembered his compliment about the pink cheeks and met his eyes. "Perhaps you could see my face more often," she said. "If you wanted."

As she spoke, the fog went over the sun, darkening the room. They were standing by the window and his face was bathed in shadows. She remembered her code and also knew that she wouldn't stop him from kissing her. This was another reason she didn't go to the man's house—so she wouldn't be tempted. It was her own fault coming here, because she was a goner now.

Instead of kissing her, however, Frederick reached out and wound his fingers with hers. Lifting her arm, he pressed his lips to the top of her hand.

"I'd like that," he said.

CHAPTER 20

Mabel could hear Vira's step on the staircase, *squeak, creak, squeak, creak.* She held up the needle and focused on the eye, willing herself to thread it on the first try. By luck, or force of will, the thread slid through. She bit it off, shoved the needle through the torn camisole, and waited.

Her mother was on the landing now, shifting from one foot to the other. Mabel took a stitch with the needle. The Women Against Pauperism committee murmured downstairs like a brook. She'd been about to sneak out the window when she heard Vira walk upstairs to check on her. Luckily, she'd managed to shut the window, dash to the bed, and thread the needle before Vira reached her door. Mabel imagined her mother standing in the hallway and thought, *Go away.*

Instead, the door swung open and Vira sailed into the room. She looked at Mabel, sitting on the bed, sewing a pinafore.

"What's wrong, Mama?" Mabel said.

Vira scanned the room. The window was shut, the curtain pulled back to reveal the tree outside. "I heard you open the window."

Mabel lifted her chin. "I don't know what you're talking about."

Her mother was starting to doubt herself, Mabel could see it. Vira examined the needle she held mid-stitch in the air, a convincing detail. It was all about the details when you wanted to deceive someone.

Vira's gaze fell on the floorboard where Mabel hid her Black Bart dime novel. Mabel had a long-standing crush on the outlaw based in large part on that novel. Ever since her mother left the book on the bed, Mabel had been waiting for the lecture about it, and now might be the time. She braced, anticipating a scolding.

But her mother's face relaxed. "All right. Remember the rules."

"Yes, Mama."

"You don't want us to put bars on that window, do you?"

"No, Mama."

Vira shut the door and headed toward the stairway. Mabel stood and waited until her mother started droning on to the committee downstairs, then opened the window and threw a leg over the sill. On the balcony, she peered at the grass below. The house was not so high up, really. If she fell, the worst thing that would happen is that she would break a leg.

Besides, Mabel had been climbing out of the window since she was a child. First she went into the backyard, poking among the rhododendrons, then down the street to Caroline's house, sneaking in through the servant's entrance. By now, Mabel had covered everywhere within a walk of the house. She'd even ridden the cable car a few times.

When Vira had discovered Mabel was gone, everything had changed. She started checking on Mabel every few hours and kept threatening to put bars on the window. It only made Mabel want to go out more. She must have fun while she could. Soon Vira would marry her off to a boring businessman and her freedom would be permanently limited.

Hiking up her skirt, she climbed down the trellis and slipped out the gate. Down the block, Caroline was standing by a rock wall holding a hooded cape. Without a word, Mabel pulled the cape around her shoulders and the two girls walked the block as quickly as they could. When they rounded the corner, they ran down the hill in giddy freedom.

Caroline flashed her father's pocket watch, the gold glinting in the sunlight. "How much time do you have?"

"About two hours. She won't check on me for a while."

It seemed a pleasant flood of time, an acre of freedom in which to do whatever she wanted. She suggested they go to the Chinese laundry where Black Bart had been caught. A sheriff had tracked a stamp on his handkerchief to the laundry and determined that the notorious stagecoach robber, who left poetry at the scene of his crimes, was Charles E. Boles, a former gold miner who lived in San Francisco. The laundry was located on Geary Street, within walking distance from Mabel's house.

In the shopping section, stray dogs ran by and carriage wheels tossed sprinkles of ditch water onto pedestrians. Vegetable carts lined the sidewalk, the cabbages spilling out like severed heads. Mabel caught Caroline's arm and they crossed the street, dodging traffic until they stood in front of the laundry.

It was closed. Mabel pressed against the glass and peered into the dark window. A ghostly dress form lurked behind the counter. She imagined Black Bart standing there, talking to the launderer. Even though she knew he was an old man with a handlebar mustache, she preferred how he was described in the novel, with flowing black hair and eyes the "color of the raging sea."

"The paper said that when Black Bart was arrested, he exhibited 'genuine wit under the most trying of circumstances,'" Mabel recited as they walked on.

"I'm not surprised," Caroline said. "He's so gentlemanly. I bet he's even a gentleman in prison."

"And he never took a lady's wedding ring, even when he was robbing her."

"It shows he was raised well," Caroline said. "He must have been forced into a life of crime against his will."

"That's the kind of man I'd like to marry."

Caroline glanced sideways at Mabel. "You wouldn't really, would you? He *is* a criminal."

"I would. Life with him would be thrilling."

"Your mother would disown you."

Mabel didn't reply. She knew how her father had saved her mother from the lightning in the most romantic way possible. The two of them had crossed the country together in a covered wagon, facing the elements and wild animals with nothing but their wits. If anything half that exciting ever happened to Mabel, the last thing she would do would be to hide it. Yet her mother acted like it was the biggest mistake she'd ever made.

When Mabel fantasized about her future, she imagined marrying a dashing man who would take her on adventures all over the world. It was nothing like the quiet life Vira wanted for her, the endless tea parties and charity meetings. And while the practical side of Mabel knew that she would have to marry a respectable businessman eventually, she wanted to have some excitement first.

In front of a store, the girls sifted through a table of goods that had been pulled onto the sidewalk. Mabel picked up a pincushion from the table. It was a tomato with people clinging to the edges. She studied their embroidered faces. "Have you talked to Robbie about the fight?" she said in a low voice.

"Yes," Caroline said, moving closer so the shopkeeper wouldn't overhear. "He says he'll take us to Donald Shannon's Villa if we can get out without our mothers knowing."

Mabel put down the pincushion. "That's good news."

Donald Shannon's Villa was a boxing ring in Sausalito, the town across the bay from San Francisco. Mabel was desperate to go to a fight. First of all, Robbie made boxing sound exciting—men matched by nothing but their strength, fighting until one of them collapsed. Secondly, she'd never been out of San Francisco, and even though Sausalito was only across the bay, it counted as a new city. Third, Sausalito was a place where the vices banned in San Francisco still went on, which sounded like something Vira would hate.

And now there was a fight worth seeing: Jimmy "Crushing" McNear vs. Samson "Stone Hands" Chang. According to Robbie, it was the most anticipated match of the year, and the best one to see. That same night there would be a church meeting for young ladies lasting the length of time it would take to see the fight and come home. If she timed everything the right way, Vira would never know she left.

"Did your mother say you could go to the church meeting?" Caroline said as they started down the street.

Mabel plucked a rose from someone's yard and put it to her nose. "Not yet, but she will. She'll want to walk me to the church, so we'll have to meet there and go to the ferry together to Sausalito."

"I don't know if I would like being on a ferry. It sounds frightening."

She tossed the rose away. Caroline was afraid of everything. The other day when the neighbor's poodle ran up to them, Caroline had almost fainted. She said the dog startled her, but Mabel knew it was because she was scared of animals. Caroline frequently fainted when she was afraid.

"We should go back," Caroline said, consulting the watch.

Mabel groaned. It felt like fifteen minutes had passed, not two hours. "It can't be time already?"

Caroline tucked the watch into the sleeve. "I'm afraid it is."

As they headed home, they passed a woman gardening in her yard. She was putting in a plant with leaves the size of hymnals that looked like it came from a tropical jungle. It was a bizarre sight next to the woman's white cottage. That was what Mabel loved about San Francisco, the mixing of everything—jungle plants next to cottages, criminals who were businessmen, prostitutes who dined in the same restaurants as the mayor. Why couldn't her mother see? California was neither good nor bad. It was both.

At the corner of Caroline's house, Mabel removed the cloak and handed it to her.

"Goodbye, Caroline," she said. "Tell Robbie that we are going to that fight, no matter what."

CHAPTER 21

Sandra and Frederick were married in a burst of warm November weather eight years and one month after first meeting in Hollywood. The wedding was held in a Methodist church that had been built after the San Francisco earthquake. Sandra stood in a back room waiting for the deacon to come get her for the ceremony. In the courtyard, wind moved the yellow leaves in the trees so they jangled like hundreds of gold coins. It seemed like a good omen for Sandra's wedding day.

She drifted away from the window and studied herself in the mirror. The wedding dress looked good on her. The white skirt hugged her hips and the Peter Pan collar framed her face. She bent to study her skin in the mirror, thinking that she could pass for much younger than thirty-four—twenty-eight, or maybe even twenty-six or twenty-five? Frederick hadn't seemed to notice that her birth certificate said 1906 when they got their wedding license. Maybe he thought she was still in her twenties.

It wasn't going to be a big wedding. She'd invited fifty people but only twenty-three were coming. Most of the invitations were to wealthy acquaintances, so she didn't take it personally that they couldn't come. Frederick had been taking her on assignment with him to shoot society events. She'd been to a ball and on a yacht, drinking martinis as she sailed underneath the Golden Gate Bridge.

Her calves ached from standing so long, but sitting would wrinkle her dress. It would be nice to have someone to wait with her. Most girls had bridesmaids in this circumstance, but Sandra didn't have any friends, at present. How could she make time for friends when she was preparing to start a new life with a wonderful man? It was understandable that she'd let that part of her life slip. Still, it would be nice if someone, anyone, were here with her.

After I get married, I'll make some friends, she promised herself. *Maybe with some society women. I might as well have rich friends as poor friends.*

In any case, this wedding felt fated, as if Sandra were returning to the life she was meant to have all along. It wasn't like when she married Billy, with Mabel in the courthouse chain-smoking cigarettes until the room got so smoky the judge told her to stop. With Frederick, everything would be different.

Sandra remembered the night they fell in love. They stayed in bed all day, tangled together, and she found herself marveling that she'd struck gold. Frederick was the perfect man: handsome, stylish, European, and an artist who was sensible enough to earn a good living. How blind she'd been in Hollywood not to see it. Of course, he was horrible when they first met, manipulating and lying to her, but the potential had been there all the same.

That night, Frederick had told her that as a young man, he couldn't wait to leave Germany. Early on, he'd been precocious in art and his mother had latched onto it, insisting he draw and paint instead of playing with other boys. Though Frederick had gone on to an apprenticeship with a well-regarded photographer, it never felt right. Artistic skills were like having a woman's eyelashes or lips, he said, beautiful but shameful.

"But being artistic is manly," Sandra had said. "I think it's manly."

"You do?"

"Yes, it's so technical. You have to have an analytical mind to do it. All those light readings and dial adjustments and everything."

Frederick hugged her with his arm around her waist and kissed the top of her head before going on. He was supposed to stay in Germany and become a photographer, but instead he hopped a boat for the United States to see about a job in Hollywood. After deciding against drawing Mickey Mouse, he tried his hand at celebrity portraits, then started photographing generic images of fruit, telephones, and typewriters to sell as advertising. It was lucrative, so he moved to San Francisco to be closer to the advertisers. Taking photos for "Women's World" was one of the best gigs he'd had. All he had to do was go to the event the newspaper sent him to, and they always took what he gave them. "Although," he added, "those rich ladies think too highly of themselves."

This point Sandra found silly. "They should. Rich people are the best kind of people, by definition."

Frederick chuckled. "Then I should have tried to get a hold of the silver mines my father's family owned in Germany. They were located deep inside a mountain, a heap of minerals glittering like Ali Baba's treasure. My family was known throughout Europe for their wealth." He grinned at her in a way that made her think he was teasing.

Sandra moved closer to him. "Why aren't you rich, then?"

"Very simple. My father's family never acknowledged his relationship to my mother."

Sandra's jaw dropped. "That's amazing. My mother was abandoned by her family too." She told him about Mabel losing the prune empire when Arthur Beard died.

"So we both have lost fortunes then," Frederick said.

It was then that Sandra considered telling him about the letters from John Hollingsworth. She'd never told anyone about them, and now seemed like the time to bring it up. Instead she said, "Do you believe the story? Do you think there was a silver mine?"

Frederick shrugged. "I don't know. Does it matter? What is past is passed. We have only the present, *schatzi*."

Now, standing in the church on her wedding day, Sandra considered what a wise answer that was. What did it matter about John Hollingsworth, whoever he was? Her future was with Frederick. She was on the verge, the very cusp, of getting everything she wanted.

There was a knock on the door. Frantically Sandra turned toward her bouquet, which lay on a chair, a cascade of peach roses touching the floor. She would have reached for it, but the door opened, and she dropped her hand against her skirt. Mabel sailed into the room.

It had been more than a year since Sandra had seen her mother, and she was startled at the change in her. Mabel's steely hair was pulled back in a Gibson bun and there was a fragility about her that hadn't been there before. Sandra thought, *Why, she's an old lady.*

"Emma," Mabel said, opening her arms.

Sandra couldn't remember the last time her mother had offered to hug her. Awkwardly, she stepped into the embrace and folded her arms around Mabel's lumpy midcenter.

"Mama," she said. "I was wondering when you'd arrive. How did you get here?"

Mabel released Sandra and stepped into the room, eyes darted from the vanity to the desk to the window. "I drove."

Sandra widened her eyes, imagining her mother hurling down the freeway. "I didn't know you knew how to . . . Whose car did you take?"

"I borrowed the neighbor's truck. I would have been here sooner but I had to guess the time of the ceremony. I never received my invitation."

Casually, Sandra moved back to the mirror. "How strange. I'm certain I addressed one to you. Maybe it fell behind the desk."

"That must be it. Because even the worst daughter in the world would invite her mother to her wedding."

Sandra avoided her mother's sharp eyes and studied her own reflection. The cigarette she'd smoked a few minutes ago should have smudged the lipstick, but it was still perfectly applied. This was a good lipstick then. She would have to remember the brand.

"You look nice," Mabel said with formality.

"Thank you."

"Although you're not helping yourself with that red hair. In my day only loose women dyed their hair, Emma."

There it was. *This* was why Sandra hadn't sent the invitation, to avoid comments like that. "I'm called Sandra now, as you know very well."

"Well, I don't like it. I named you Emma and that's your name."

And what Sandra wanted to say then, was that if her mother had gotten a wedding invitation—which she *hadn't*—she would see that it said, "Mr. Frederick Bauer to marry Miss Sandra Sanborn." Not Emma Sanborn. Never Emma Sanborn. Why couldn't her mother respect Sandra's decision to choose a different name?

"Have a glass of champagne, Mama," she said, gesturing to the bottle chilling on the bureau.

Mabel poured the champagne and took a sip. Then she held
the glass up and studied the bubbles. "Very nice. What are you
serving at the reception?"

"Roast beef and butter cake with cream frosting."

"Good. Not too much, but acceptable. You don't want to
appear to be trying too hard in front of your wealthy friends."

Sandra liked the way her mother said "your wealthy friends."
Ever since Mabel found out that Frederick was photographing
for "Women's World," she'd been mentioning Sandra's rise in
society with increasing admiration.

"I've noticed that," Sandra said. "They recognize good taste."

"That's what I mean. I'm glad I spent all that time drill-
ing these things into you. They're paying off now, aren't they?"

Sandra rolled her eyes. As if her life had anything to do with
her mother's old-fashioned ideas. If anything, Mabel had hurt
Sandra by letting Daddy Jones drag her into the fields to pick
prunes all those summers when she should have been practicing her art.

"Who did you invite to the wedding?" Mabel said.

"Kermit and Judith Hopkins, but they can't make it. But
we're going to their twenty-fifth anniversary party. Frederick is
photographing it for the paper."

"I remember the Hopkins family. They were in railroads."
Mabel said this casually, as if she were in the habit of offering
information about her past.

"Did my grandfather know them?"

"I have no doubt. Your grandfather knew everyone."

Sandra slipped her fingers under the collar of her dress to
warm them. Mabel never talked about her father.

"It's too bad there isn't anyone to give you away," Mabel
said. "It doesn't look right to walk down the aisle by yourself.
Even your Daddy Jones would be better than nothing."

Sandra made a face. If Daddy Jones were here, she would make him an usher, not let him give her away. Only Arthur Beard should have that privilege. If he couldn't walk her down the aisle, no one could.

For a moment Sandra felt something like nostalgia for the life she would have had if her father had lived. She would be wealthy, for one thing, as wealthy as Beatrice Bartlett was now. In fact, she would have a life a lot like Beatrice's, full of fine clothes and trips to Europe. And, as Mabel pointed out, there would be someone to walk her down the aisle.

She regarded her mother, who was wearing a lavender dress that Sandra remembered from when she was a teenager. The lace on the sleeve was tattered. It occurred to Sandra that this was the time to ask her about John Hollingsworth. She'd always meant to tell her mother about those letters, and here they were, alone, and Mabel was in a chatty mood—for her, at least.

"Awhile back," Sandra began. "I got a letter I've been meaning to ask you about."

Mabel stiffened. It was a trick she had, as if without moving, she'd somehow grown taller, like a plant unfurling in the sun.

There was a knock on the door. The deacon was on the other side, smiling behind wire-rimmed glasses. "We're ready for you, Miss Sanborn," he said.

Sandra's heart swelled. It was the last time anyone would say that name, Sandra Sanborn. From here on out, she would be Mrs. Frederick Bauer. Sandra Sanborn was a person of the past.

Mabel glided over to Sandra. Her fingers lightly tugged the tips of the Peter Pan collar. "There," she said. "You're perfect."

And suddenly Sandra felt like she might cry. Everything was so right this time around. Even Mabel saw that. She picked up the bouquet. "Thank you, Mama."

"I hope he'll be good to you."

"He will be. He's a good man."

The deacon offered Sandra his arm and she took it gratefully. Her dress felt like it weighed a hundred pounds. Piano music reverberated through the walls of the church and the two of them hurried toward the sanctuary.

As she moved down the hallway, Sandra heard her mother mumble, "They all seem like good men in the beginning."

CHAPTER 22

Mabel stepped out of the carriage and looked up at the building in front of her. The words DONALD SHANNON'S VILLA were painted on a brick wall. Men were leaning against the building and Mabel could feel their eyes on her as she stood on the sidewalk. She straightened her spine and reminded herself that this was what she wanted. This was real life, what her mother had been keeping from her.

Caroline came around and regarded the building. "It looks rather rough. Are ladies allowed inside?"

"Of course they are, Caroline," Mabel said, although she wasn't sure that was true. As they waited for Robbie to talk to the driver, she moved so she could see the men along the wall with her peripheral vision. They were dirty, as if they'd been walking behind a carriage. Their jackets were patched and their caps were pulled low over their eyes. One man, who looked about Robbie's age, had a broad face that came to a point at his chin like a cartoon dialogue box. A crooked grin spread across his face as if to say, *I see you*. Mabel jerked her eyes away.

"Ready for the fight?" Robbie said as the carriage pulled away.

"Are you sure Mabel and I can go in there?" Caroline said again.

"Of course. You're accompanied by a gentleman, aren't you?" Humorously, Robbie straightened his tie. He'd recently grown a mustache that, along with the pimples on his chin, made him appear younger than he was.

In front of the building, Robbie left the girls to buy tickets. As they waited, Mabel studied the poster plastered to the side of the building. A white man with a drooping mustache faced a Chinese man with a black braid hanging down his back. The poster said:

THE FIGHT!
JIMMY "CRUSHING" MCNEAR vs. SAMSON "STONE HANDS" CHANG

Robbie came up with three tickets and led them inside. It was so packed that he had to force his way through saying, "Excuse me. Excuse me." When the men saw Mabel and Caroline, they were taken aback, tipping their hats or mumbling something in Spanish or English. One man with greasy hair smiled lasciviously at Mabel, his lips peeling back from a horsey overbite. Caroline cast her eyes down when he did this, but Mabel tilted her chin up even more. Let this riffraff look. If she and Caroline were going to be the only women here, she would accept that fact with dignity.

"Do you think we're safe?" Caroline said.

"Yes, Caroline, I'm certain we are," Mabel said, annoyed and uncertain at the same time. "Robbie's here."

They seated themselves on benches near the aisle. A ring stood in the center of the room, surrounded on all sides by benches. The man in front of Mabel lit a cigar and she hoped her mother wouldn't be able to smell the smoke on her clothes, which would be hard to explain after claiming to be in church. The meeting Mabel told her mother she was attending was supposed to go on all evening. If they made sure to get the last ferry, there should be enough time for the forty-minute ride and walk home before the service ended.

Near the ring, some white men were chanting, "The Chinese must go!" Their voices were weak against the racket and no one seemed to pay attention. A few of the chanters were waving their pipes back and forth, as if keeping time with a band.

"What does that mean, 'The Chinese must go'?" Mabel said.

Robbie craned to look. "They must be Irish. They think the Chinese are taking their jobs because they'll work for lower wages."

Mabel watched the men with new interest. "*Are* the Chinese taking their jobs?"

"Well, naturally the companies want to hire the cheapest labor. Who can blame them?"

Before Mabel could ask anything else, the audience erupted in cheers. A man with woolly sideburns climbed into the ring. Mabel guessed it was the owner, Donald Shannon. He was a big man with a gut like a bag of peanuts trapped under the high waist of his trousers. Wrapping his arms around his front, he glared at the audience, allowing them to froth. The longer he stood there, the more excited they became. Finally, he swung out his arms wide and boomed, "Welcome to the final championship of the season!"

The audience roared so loudly, Caroline put her hands over her ears. Mabel had never seen people behave like this. The room was on the edge of something, she didn't know what, but it seemed like it could drop off at any time.

A man in front of Mabel leaned over to talk to his companion, blocking her view. When he moved back again, the boxers were in the ring on opposite sides of Donald Shannon. They were naked from the chest up, their skin reflecting in the lantern light. Mabel wasn't sure if she should be looking.

"In this corner," Donald Shannon said, "is Crushing McNear."

The people around Mabel leapt to their feet, forcing her to stand as well. In the ring, McNear clasped his arms over his head and shook them back and forth as if shaking his own hands. His gut was spotted with curly hair.

"And in this corner," Donald Shannon said, "is Stone Hands Chang."

The mighty roar from the Chinese drowned out the boos from the Irish. Chang was the tallest person Mabel had ever seen, taller than McNear, but thinner. His hair was shaved close to his head, except for a black braid hanging down his back.

"A champion fighter, Chang has won six matches this season alone," Donald said before his voice was drowned out again. He talked for so long that Mabel looked at Robbie.

"He's telling them the rules," Robbie shouted. "They have to wear gloves, they can't wrestle or hit below the belt, things like that."

Mabel stood on her toes to get a better view. Between the shoulders and necks of the men in front of her, the boxers were hunched with Donald Shannon between them, his fingertips spread on their backs as if balancing something. They shook hands, their leather gloves colliding like loaves of bread. In one swift move, Donald Shannon backed off and the bell rang.

The boxers advanced on each other, both holding their arms

up to shield their faces. McNear began wheeling one arm in a circle like a gear in a machine. Chang blocked his fist with his forearm and staggered into McNear, ramming him against the ropes. The man in front of Mabel said something to his friend, again blocking her view. When he moved back, McNear had slid under Chang's arm and was in the center of the ring again. He slammed his glove into Chang's face. Mabel covered her mouth to keep back a cry. It seemed that no one could survive such a blow, but Chang moved backward, bouncing on the balls of his feet.

There was a break. The bell rang and a boy mopped up the sweat in the ring. The boxers retreated to stools on opposite corners and people draped towels on their shoulders and doused them with water. No one sat down, and Mabel found herself in the middle of a crowd with little to see. Caroline was fanning herself with a handkerchief, and Mabel wasn't in the mood to hear about how she felt faint.

Then, like static prickling her skin, Mabel felt someone watching her. She turned to see the young man from earlier, the one who'd been staring at her outside the villa. In this one, heady night of freedom, Mabel did something daring—she looked right into his eyes. It was supposed to shame him for his lack of respect, but he cocked his head as if impressed. The grin spread across his face again, and Mabel pulled her eyes away, annoyed that she'd given him the satisfaction of acknowledging him.

The bell rang and the boxers resumed the fight. Donald Shannon hovered in the corner, stepping in and out, counting and jerking his arms. The noise was so loud it was like being inside an ocean wave. McNear and Chang were somehow isolated from it all as they jabbed at each other. Their gloves gave the blows a peculiar softness, as if the boxers weren't really touching each other's flesh. Yet bruises formed. Blood coated

McNear's nose and Chang's left cheek. Sweat flowed in streams
from their bodies.

"Mabel, shouldn't we go?" Caroline said, tugging on Mabel's
sleeve. "The church meeting will be over soon."

Mabel put her hand on Caroline's elbow, alarmed. She was
perspiring so much that an unladylike sheen covered her face,
giving it the appearance and color of a raw oyster.

Robbie noticed too. "Caroline, are you ill?"

At that moment, Chang raised his glove and slammed it into
McNear's chin. The audience froze as everyone stared at the ring.
In the seconds that followed, McNear shut and opened his eyes,
then tilted backward to look at the lanterns hanging above the
ring. His chest convulsed, as if he were laughing, and, reeling
from the middle of his body, he swooned and crashed to the floor.

The instant his head hit the ring, Chang raised his arms in
triumph. Donald Shannon began counting, but it was obvious
that McNear was unconscious.

When Donald Shannon said "ten," there was a roar from
the Chinese people in the audience, many of them thrusting
their arms into the air like Chang had done. From other sections
came grumbling. The room had a strange air, both angry and
jubilant at once. People rushed the ring and Donald Shannon
put his arm around Chang to protect him. The man who'd been
blocking Mabel's view began to argue with someone she couldn't
see. He thrust his body forward, his head bobbing up and down.

Mabel watched a derby hat sail through the air and land by
two men who appeared to be hugging. Or so it seemed until
Mabel realized that one of them was trying to rip the other's
shirt off. Caroline shrieked. Someone else's hands snaked around
the neck of the man in front of Mabel and Robbie shouted that
they must leave. All Mabel could think was, *So this is why Mother
doesn't want me to come to these places.*

Robbie moved with Caroline toward the door, which was blocked with people. Mabel tried to stay close, but men kept pushing against her or stepping in front of her.

"Caroline," she said. "Wait for me."

Caroline's head was lolling against Robbie's shoulder, and her eyes rolling toward Mabel, who was pushed back as more people forced themselves toward the door. Caroline's mouth fell open and she said something, but all Mabel could focus on were her bottom teeth, which were small and yellow.

It was the last sight of Caroline that Mabel had before the fighting closed in around her.

CHAPTER 23

Kermit and Judith Hopkins's twenty-fifth anniversary party was held at the Conservatory of Flowers, a greenhouse in Golden Gate Park that looked like a wicker birdcage. When Sandra walked in on Frederick's arm wearing her new moss-green dress, a butler was standing there holding a tray of cocktails. Each glass had a star jasmine floating in it.

"Stand up straight," Sandra whispered to Frederick. "Remember not to slouch."

He shot her a look.

"What?" she said. "You're always slouching."

The greenhouse was humid. The glass walls were shaped like an inverted spade, and the foggy night pressed against them as if trying to get in. Planters were filled with hydrangeas, begonias, and snapdragons. Along the wall, Greek statues were surrounded by lilies.

As Judith approached, her silver hair metallic in the warm light. Jewels bunched at her throat, ears, and fingers.

"My dear," she said, her voice like sour cream. "Such a cunning dress. Really, there's something so stylish about you two."

Sandra beamed. The compliment meant more coming from Judith, who had the money to know what stylish was. "Thank you. What a wonderful place to have an anniversary."

"Yes, it is rather magical, isn't it? I'm happy the *Chronicle* sent you to photograph the event, Mr. Bauer. We loved the portraits you did of my cousin's wedding."

"Please, call me Frederick."

"Such a German name. You are German, aren't you?"

Sandra shifted. She and Frederick had agreed that it was better he distance himself from his homeland. People were boycotting German businesses because of the war, and Sandra saw no reason why Frederick should suffer from that kind of prejudice.

"Not Germany," he said. "Austria."

"I beg your pardon. I thought you were from Germany."

"No, Austria. I came over after the first war."

Judith tilted her head, seeming to compare this information with something in her mind. There was a pause during which Frederick met her eyes, unblinking.

"Well," Judith said. "Don't work the whole evening. Make sure to enjoy yourself."

He thanked her and turned to set up the photography equipment. Behind a banana plant, a quartet was playing Bach.

Sandra had nothing to do but watch the room fill with elegant strangers. Judith greeted a young man, a nephew or cousin, Sandra guessed, with long arms that dangled at his side as if he hadn't grown into them yet. When Judith pinched his cheek, he batted her hand away.

"Do you think she believes you're Austrian?" Sandra said, stepping closer to Frederick, who was peering through the camera.

"Sure, why wouldn't she? She doesn't know the difference." He was always saying how ignorant Americans were about geography, which was true enough. Before Frederick, Sandra had never thought about the difference between Germany and Austria. Why should Judith be any different?

"Look," she said, yanking Frederick's arm. "That's the mayor of Oakland. You should talk to him." She indicated a grim man with round glasses who was standing beside a portly woman.

Frederick moved the light so that it was more angled. "What do I have to say to the mayor of Oakland?"

"I already told you. His daughter is getting married. You could do the wedding portrait. Judith said she'd introduce you."

"I'm working right now."

"Not now. After you're done."

Frederick was looking through his camera again, testing something. She didn't like how he ignored her when he took photographs.

"What do you think you'll say to the mayor when you meet him?" she said.

He threw back his head toward the ceiling. "Again, I'm trying to work. Go enjoy the party. We will talk about it later."

Sandra was tempted to argue with him but didn't want to start a fight, so she went to the bar to get a drink. Sipping a Brandy Alexander, she watched the other guests move in closed circles that seemed difficult to approach. This was the world she was meant to be in. She *would* be in it, once Frederick's career took off. She'd made a new plan:

1. With her help, Frederick would become a famous photographer.

2. She would be his assistant and glamorous wife.

3. They would be rich and have many important, influential friends.

She imagined life in a beautiful house with modern furniture, tall ceilings, and sculptures and art in the background. Friends like Judith would swing by before or after events, coming into Sandra's sitting room and surprising her with a peck on the cheek.

Bored, she wandered into the rest of the conservatory. Weak light illuminated the path between the shadowy clumps of plants. Pushing open a door, Sandra went through rubber flaps like the ones that hung in industrial freezers. The ferns clustering beside the walkway were so tall, they scraped the glass ceiling. Outside, the fog had cleared so that the moon was shining through the glass like an alligator's eye.

A moth was puttering against the moon. At first Sandra thought it was outside the glass, but then another moth joined it and they twirled around a fern. Moths were all over the room, flapping and knocking against each other and floating among the leaves. Sandra didn't know whether they'd been put here or come in on their own.

For a moment, the only sound was her own breathing. It was like being back in Healdsburg on a warm August night. While that thought normally would have disgusted Sandra, she found herself caught in a sense memory where something from her youth—a happy period with Billy, or moments of freedom wandering country roads with her sketchbook—was tied to the moths.

Then there was the noise of women's laughter, and the feeling vanished. Beatrice Bartlett burst through the rubber flaps, followed by another woman.

"Sandra?" Beatrice said. "Look who it is!"

Sandra was pleased to see someone she knew at the party, even though Beatrice hadn't talked to her since her wedding. "Hello, Beatrice. What a surprise to see you here."

Beatrice looked the same in a long-sleeved gown, her hair still in a perfect pageboy. She introduced the other woman as Eva, her sister-in-law and a semiprofessional swimmer. Sandra eyed the girl's narrow figure in layers of ruffles and asked Beatrice how she knew the Hopkins.

"Alvin is Mr. Hopkins's doctor. I didn't know you knew them."

"I don't, really. My husband is the society photographer with the newspaper."

"Do you mean 'Women's World?'" Eva said brightly. "I read that every day."

"Yes, that's it. The paper sends Frederick to events all over in the city and I go with him when I can. He needs me to assist."

On hearing this, the women seemed friendlier, as if Sandra had passed a test. Beatrice lightly touched her arm. "Congratulations on your wedding, by the way. I'm sorry I couldn't make it."

Sandra waved her hand as though it hadn't bothered her. "I completely understand."

"How did you and your husband meet?" Eva said.

"We met back in Hollywood. Frederick was a celebrity photographer and I was a starlet."

Eva clasped her hands together so that a breeze made her ruffles shake. "Were you in the movies?"

"Only a bit," Sandra said, waving her hand.

"She's being modest," Beatrice said.

The women crowded nearer, and Sandra was surrounded by their ruffles and purses. Beyond, she was dimly aware of the fluttering moths.

"I did play a maid in a movie called *Hijinks in Algoria,*" she fibbed. "I got to ride in a limousine to the opening, which was something for a twenty-year-old from Healdsburg, let me tell you. And I auditioned for *Bride of Frankenstein*, but lost the role to another girl."

It wasn't *Bride of Frankenstein*, but Sandra couldn't remember the name of the picture she'd almost auditioned for. Something about mansions?

"Is that why you left Hollywood?" Beatrice said.

"No. It was the Depression. One day I was on a studio lot and I overheard Katharine Hepburn herself complaining about how hard it was for actors to get work just then. And I said, 'If it's hard for you, Katharine, what chance do I have?'"

"Wow," Eva said. "Katharine Hepburn."

"Yes, she was even prettier in real life. Anyway, after that I came home to San Francisco and then met Frederick again by chance and, well, here I am." She shrugged modestly.

They might have asked more, but Eva let out a little shriek. A moth was perched on her shoulder, moving its antennas as if trying to communicate something. Eva hopped up and down, flapping her hands. "Get it off. I hate it, I hate it."

"Don't look at it," Beatrice said, batting at the moth with a handkerchief, which pushed it under a ruffle on Eva's shoulder.

"Don't move," Sandra said. "I'll get it."

Eva sucked in her breath as if willing herself not to scream. Gently, Sandra lifted the lace and scooped out the moth so that it perched on her fingers. It was gray with a white puff on its neck like a poodle dog. She moved it to a leaf, wondering if it was dead.

"Revolting," Eva said.

"My word, this entire room is full of moths," Beatrice said.

"I know," Sandra said. "Isn't it odd?"

For a moment the three women stared at the moths, which

had gathered near the ceiling like dust motes. Eva shivered. "Let's get out of here."

Back at the party, the Oakland mayor was by the bar in a circle of light surrounded by a group that included Judith. The low laughter of refined people rippled through the room. Frederick was nowhere in sight. The photography equipment was still set up, but the lights were off.

Brimming with fury, Sandra marched through the conservatory looking for her husband. He should be standing with those people, being charming and holding a Manhattan, not doing whatever it was he was doing. She headed toward the door, thinking he might be smoking outside, but found him talking to a man wearing a thermal shirt and khaki pants who looked like he belonged in one of Frederick's cowboy paintings. Lights from the lawn bathed them both in a marmalade glow.

"Ah," Frederick said, drawing her close. "Ben, this is my wife. Sandra, this is Ben. He works on the conservatory."

"Hello, ma'am."

She dipped her head in acquiescence. "Hello."

"Do you know that they have to climb the roof every week to clean it?" Frederick said.

"Have to, else the glass gets dirty," Ben said.

"Fascinating," Sandra said. "Frederick, would you get me another drink?"

He looked at her empty glass and nodded, reluctantly. As they walked away, she clutched his sleeve. "Honestly. I don't know what you're doing talking to that man when you could be talking to potential clients. Let's go, while you can still meet the mayor."

She jerked Frederick's hand, but he pulled back and dragged her beside a rubber plant. "Listen," he said sternly. "You cannot drag me through this party like a child."

Sandra was taken aback. He'd never used that tone before and she glanced around to see if anyone had heard.

"The mayor's daughter is getting married," she said, slowly, so it would sink in. "Taking her portrait is the kind of thing that can make you into a prominent photographer."

"Is that what you're trying to turn me into?"

Just then, Eva walked by, happy and jangling beside her husband. They smiled as they passed and Sandra and Frederick smiled back. She heard Eva say, "She used to be in Hollywood."

"You see?" Sandra said. "We've made a positive impression on these people. It'll be good for your business."

"I don't need a woman to tell me how to do my job."

"Well, yes, you do. Otherwise you're out here talking to some window cleaner instead of making lucrative connections with our city leaders."

Behind them came the sound of clicking high heels, and they turned to see Judith approaching. Sandra plastered a smile on her face, hoping Judith wouldn't sense the tension between them.

"Frederick," Judith said. "Let me introduce you to Mayor McCracken. His daughter is getting married and he's looking for a photographer."

Sandra raised an eyebrow in a way that she hoped indicated to Frederick that she told him so. For a moment, he paused, then nodded.

"Yes, that's thoughtful," he said. "Thank you. I'll be right there."

Judith smiled and turned around. When she was out of earshot, Frederick whispered, "Don't look so smug. I always wait for the customers to come to me in these situations. Your way looks too desperate."

Sandra sneered. "Desperate?"

"That's right. But if you want to assist me, as you keep saying, you can carry some equipment to the car." Seeing her reaction, Frederick grinned. "But you don't want to do that, do you *schatzi*? Never mind. Have another drink. We'll go home soon."

He walked away, leaving her standing there, fuming. Somehow Frederick always got the upper hand, even when she was right.

CHAPTER 24

Not long after the party, Beatrice began inviting Sandra to go shopping. Sandra had never been inside the high-end boutiques in Union Square before, but now, with Beatrice by her side, she walked in and out of Maggy Rouff, Pierre Balmain, and Jacques Fath with all the authority her high heels clacking on the marble floors demanded. These weren't the stores Sandra was used to, with racks of dresses and tables of folded blouses and skirts. Entire rooms contained only three or four beautiful things—a leather purse with wide zippers, a suit sewn with gold thread, an ermine coat as silky as a high-end hotel bed. Chandeliers dangled above Sandra's head like earrings and people chatted about touring Europe "before all this trouble." Someone was always playing piano.

With Beatrice, Sandra sat in a private room at Christian Dior, drinking free champagne while models put on an exclusive fashion show for them. Beatrice bought not one, but two, fur shoulder capes. At the jeweler, Eva, Beatrice, and Sandra picked out a platinum baby rattle for Eva's niece and Beatrice bought sunglasses with jade starbursts on the side. She paid for it with a Charga-Plate, a metal card that meant she had credit at the store. The jeweler trusted her that much.

Every time Sandra went shopping, she reminded herself that she wasn't going to buy anything. She was just going to look. It was good for her to be exposed to fine things as practice for when she and Frederick became wealthy, but they weren't there yet. Therefore, she could admire a fifteenth-century French armoire or hand-painted jewelry box that cost more than Frederick made in a year, but she couldn't buy them *yet*.

Still, as a newlywed, she had to purchase a few things. She and Frederick picked out a dining table and a bedroom set together. And she talked him into a sofa, matching chairs, and a coffee table for the living room. As Mabel said when she called on the telephone, it was a wife's privilege to set up her home. It should reflect her taste and station in life.

But that didn't excuse the mink muff that Sandra purchased one afternoon at Bergdorf Goodman. She'd wanted a fur for as long as she could remember and the store was having a sale, twenty percent off all furs. The salesgirl told her that the muff would last a lifetime if she took care of it, which made it sound like an investment. She'd been so good, denying herself so many things on these shopping trips that buying the muff felt like a reward for being restrained. So, Sandra wrote a check for seventy-five dollars and trotted toward home.

On the way she stopped at the bank to make sure they had enough money to cover the check. Standing at the deposit table, Sandra was shocked to see that Frederick's savings account had dropped significantly. Most of it was the furniture, but it was also her new red watered-silk dress, embroidered evening gloves, and patent-leather purse. And now, a mink muff.

Sandra experienced a new emotion: guilt. Not only had Frederick given her a generous monthly allowance, he'd handed over his checkbook to her. In return she'd been steadily draining all his money. She looked at the Bergdorf Goodman bag with black-and-white stars on front and sighed. The muff had only belonged to her for a few minutes and now it must go back. She picked it up and retraced her steps.

At the department store, she stopped on the sidewalk, remembering lunch yesterday with Beatrice's friends, wives of shipbuilders and strawberry growers. Sitting at the table, eating chestnut quiche and a nasturtium-flower salad, Sandra had the sense of reaching her station in life. Or almost reaching it. It was within reach, anyway. At the same time, being around those women made Sandra feel like she was back in grammar school, a skinny girl in a homemade dress eating prunes. She couldn't help noticing how much more traveled the other women were, and how elegant they looked with their well-tailored clothes and expensive salon haircuts. She wondered when she would be the rich woman in the room already. It was something she'd been waiting for her entire life.

The muff had seemed like the first step in attaining that lifestyle, and already it was slipping away. Sandra would have to look the salesgirl in the eye and admit, however indirectly, that she'd overstepped her finances. Even if she claimed to have changed her mind, the girl would know that Sandra wasn't the kind of woman who could afford a mink muff.

Then another thought occurred to her: Beatrice shopped at Bergdorf's all the time. What if, somehow, she found out that Sandra returned the muff?

She hugged the bag and whispered, "No." Then she turned toward home, slinging the muff on her arm and promising herself that this was the last splurge she would make. From now on, she would live frugally. She'd been planning to go out to dinner tonight, but she would cook instead. And she would do other things too—wear sweaters when she got cold and turn off the light whenever she left the room. And she wouldn't go shopping with Beatrice anymore, not even once.

Resolved, Sandra veered into the grocers to buy ingredients for dinner. With the muff tucked safely in the grocery cart, she strolled the aisles pulling food off the shelves until she had a week's worth of ingredients. Then she went home and prepared a stew, the cheapest meal she could think of. She even pulled out *The Joy of Cooking* and made dinner rolls.

At seven p.m., Frederick came into the kitchen where Sandra stood on tiptoe, peering into a pot.

"It smells odd in here," he said. "Is that food you're making?"

"Hardy, har, har."

He hugged her from behind, his hand traveling up her front, but she shooed him out and told him to sit at the dining table. Brandishing a potholder that had previously hung untouched on a nail, Sandra pulled a cookie sheet of freshly baked rolls from the oven and pursed her lips. The rolls looked lumpy and indents from her fingers were still visible. She didn't know what was wrong. She'd put yeast in the dough and left it on the counter to rise, like the recipe said.

Shrugging, Sandra decided to focus on presentation and lined a basket with a red cloth napkin while explaining her newfound love of thrift to Frederick. "I'm making lots of changes around here," she said. "I don't want you to think that because I go shopping with the girls that I don't care about our finances."

"That's good, *schatzi*. I'm glad to hear it."

Sandra picked up one of the rolls and frowned. It felt hard. When she tapped it on the cookie sheet, it made a distressing clicking noise. But presentation made up for a lot, she reminded herself. Thank goodness she could rely on her artistic skills in any situation. Laying the rolls in the basket and smiling confidently, she placed them in front of Frederick. "I mean, we may be going to war here soon," she said. "I need to do my part like everyone else. Now wait, there's stew."

Back in the kitchen, she ladled the stew into a casserole dish someone had given her as a wedding present. It was the first time she'd used it.

"I want to talk to you about finances as well," Frederick said. "You took more money out of the savings account?"

Sandra halted mid-ladle, thinking he'd found out about the muff. But he couldn't know about that since the check hadn't had a chance to clear. Mentally, she ran through her recent purchases. "Oh. That's for the herringbone chairs in your office."

She carried out the casserole dish and presented it to him, opening the lid with a flourish. Frederick leaned toward the stew. It was brownish gray with a sheen of oil on top. Ghosts of potatoes drifted underneath.

"Maybe you should make noodles," Frederick said.

She held out her hand for his bowl. "Give it a chance."

As she ladled the stew, he returned to the topic at hand. "This is the third time you've removed money from the savings account this week. You have to stop spending so much."

"The house has to be presentable, Frederick. That requires purchasing new furniture."

"Not this presentable. Seventy dollars for chairs I don't even sit on? Come now."

Sandra said in a this-should-be-obvious voice, "You have to spend money to make money."

"What does that mean?"

"It's an American expression."

Frederick shut his eyes. "I know that. How does it apply to chairs?"

As Sandra filled her own bowl, she repeated her rational-
izations for the chairs: furniture was an investment, it was
important to have a tasteful home in case clients came by, a
house was a showcase for success. They'd sounded reasonable
when she discussed them with Mabel, but Frederick just shook
his head.

"I don't care about that when I have to shoot extra portraits
to pay bills this month," he said.

Sandra sunk into her chair, irritated and guilty. "Fine, I said
I was cutting back, didn't I? I won't buy anything when I go out
with the girls for a while. All right?"

Frederick seemed doubtful. "All right." He tasted a spoon-
ful of the stew. Then he lowered the spoon and sat looking at
the bowl like a cat looking into a pool.

"What's wrong?" Sandra said.

"Is this finished?"

She geared up to be offended, but the memory of the roll
clicking on the cookie sheet made her stop. Fishing out a carrot
with her spoon, she tasted it, then forced herself to swallow. The
stew tasted like pork-flavored water. "Well," she said brightly.
"I guess there's bound to be a few rough meals until I learn
how to cook."

"That sounds like fun." He picked up a roll and tried to
break it. Then he picked up the butter knife and pried at it.

After dinner, Sandra threw the stew down the sink, stabbing at the lumpy potatoes with a spatula until they broke apart.
She'd never thought of herself as much of a cook, but she'd never
tried before. Frederick was disappointed, she could tell. His
eyes had asked, *Shouldn't a woman your age know how to cook?*
He was always complaining about the unwashed laundry and
messy house. At some point she would have to tell him about
the muff and then he'd be disappointed in her all over again.

Increasingly, Sandra seemed to fall short of Frederick's ideas of how she should be. He wanted her to be a housewife, a boring and lonely endeavor full of cleaning and laundry. Here she was, elevating his career and bringing sophistication to his life, and he hardly noticed. Or he told her that he didn't want a woman interfering with his work, which cut her deeply. If he listened to her, they would have plenty of money for fur muffs, but he resisted her suggestions. Sometimes she wondered if Frederick appreciated her at all.

CHAPTER 25

As Caroline disappeared outside Donald Shannon's Villa, the wave of fighting swept against Mabel and she was caught upon it like a cork. She ran to the nearest wall and stood facing the rioting men, unsure whether to wait for Robbie to come get her or to try to push to the door herself.

Nearby a man was slumped on a bench with his head between his legs. Blood was dripping on the wooden planks under his feet. She looked away in time to see two men coming toward her while clenching each other's heads, like mating insects. They crashed into the wall beside Mabel and she shrieked and looked for Robbie, but he wasn't there.

Just as she was about to plunge into the mob, someone embraced her. She looked up at the young man who'd been staring at her during the fight, the one with the crooked smile. His arm was a rope of muscles around her waist. "When I say to," he said, "walk as swiftly as you can."

Mabel nodded, her eyes never leaving his. He led her through the riot, pushing her with his palm when he wanted her to go and tightening his fingers on her ribs when he wanted her to stop. In this way, they sidestepped a shouting match, slipped out of range of a fistfight, and dodged the bell when it fell off the wall and clanked to the ground beside them.

Behind the boxing ring was a door that Mabel hadn't seen before. The man ushered her into the alleyway and released her. Cold air rushed around Mabel's waist where his arm had been. She straightened her skirt, waiting for him to attend to her nerves, but he didn't move.

"Thank you," she said. "I believe you saved my life."

"It was nothing," he said in a lilting accent. "My pleasure."

Why, he's Irish, Mabel thought. Now that she was calming down, she saw how inappropriate this was. She'd let a strange man put his arm around her, and now she was in an alley with him. The stench of garbage wafted out of a bin, and there was something slimy near her shoe. If they didn't leave right away, Vira would learn that she'd lied about going to church. Considering that walking down the street had made her mother threaten to put bars on the window, Mabel had a feeling this would be her last taste of freedom for a long time.

"I must find my friends," she said in a commanding way.

The man settled himself on a crate. "Yep, they're probably worried about you."

In the parking lot, there was more shouting and commotion, as if the riot had spilled outside. Inside the Villa, the voices of the men roared like fire. The alley was a pocket of peacefulness in the chaos.

"Usually a gentleman introduces himself to a lady," she said.

"A gentleman, am I? Pardon me. My name is Jared Smith. And you are?"

Mabel had never seen a man act like this. He was at once a dashing hero who had saved her from destruction and a cad with no manners. *Like Black Bart*, she thought. "My name is Mabel Sanborn."

"It's a pleasure to meet you, Miss Sanborn. And what might a fine lady like yourself be doing at Donald Shannon's Villa?" His lilt sounded musical all of a sudden.

She felt flustered, unsure how to explain it. "We were trying to find a little excitement," she said.

Jared chuckled. "You got that, didn't you? Come on. Let's find the people you came with."

In front of the Villa, they were confronted with a bottle-neck of carriages filling up the parking lot and road. Drivers were shouting out of their windows, their horses skittish. From inside the Villa came chants of "Chang! Chang! Chang!" Caroline and Robbie were nowhere in sight.

"They're not here," Mabel said. "I don't see them."

"Let's see if they're in the parking lot."

They picked their way through traffic and over horse drop-pings and gopher holes to the field that was used for carriages. Caroline wasn't in any of them. Mabel caught a glimpse of McNear standing by himself underneath an oak tree with a towel around his neck. He was smoking a pipe.

"We're not finding them," Jared said. "Let's see if they're in front of the Villa."

As they approached the Villa again, two men rushed by with an unconscious man slung over their shoulders. His face was so bloody, Mabel wasn't sure he had a nose anymore.

They left me, she thought. *Caroline left me here by myself.* Tears sprang to Mabel's eyes, but she wiped them away. She wouldn't cry in front of strangers. She had put herself in this situation and she would get herself out.

Jared waved at two men coming out of the Villa. Like Jared, they looked to be in their late teens or early twenties. One was tall with freckles and red hair and the other had ears that stuck out from the side of his face. He had the beginnings of a bruise on his eye.

"'Tis a sad day for the Workingmen's Party," said the tall man, shaking Jared's hand.

"Aye. It's a shame McNear lost. It was a good fight."

The tall man patted the other man's back. "Clancy got a couple of licks in tonight. Splattered one of them coolies on the floor."

"Well done," Jared said.

Clancy shrugged. "Doing my part for the cause."

Mabel had never seen Irish people up close before. She watched them out of the corner of her eye, struggling to comprehend what they were saying over their thick accents.

"Excuse me," Jared said. "Gentlemen, this is Miss Sanborn. Miss Sanborn, these are my friends, Mr. Séamus Reilly and Mr. Clancy Sullivan. Miss Sanborn here has lost her companions."

"I'm sorry to hear that," Séamus said, tipping his hat. "We're about to go for a beer. Will you be coming, Jared?"

"Aye. Won't you come with us, Miss Sanborn?

She was shocked. "To a saloon?"

"Sure. I can take you home afterward if you like."

"You mean you'll take me all the way to San Francisco?"

"Sure, sure, since your friends have gone, I'd be happy to accompany you home. But I'd like to grab a pint with my fellows here first."

It was a scandalous thing to suggest, which may be why Mabel's heart thumped at the thought of it. She did some calculations. If she went home soon, there was a slim chance that she could make it back before her mother found out. But Jared wasn't going to accompany her unless she went to the saloon and let him have a drink first. Her other options were to stay here alone to see if Robbie came back, or try to go to the ferry herself. However, she didn't have much money and wasn't sure how to get to the ferry without a carriage. The ferries stopped running at some point, and what would she do if she got there and they'd closed for the evening?

Jared was smiling again, but it was kinder before. "Won't you come, Miss Sanborn? I'd be honored to have your company."

Mabel decided to trust him. After all, he'd saved her life. Her father had saved her mother's life and look at how that had worked out.

"All right," she said. "I'll go, as long as you promise to take me home after."

"You have my word," he said.

The saloon was filled with men clutching glasses to their bruised faces and yelling about the fight. Mabel tensed, wondering if she was safe here. Maybe this place would riot too. She sat down at a table in the corner with the three men, who ordered beers, including one for her. She'd never tasted a beer, or any alcohol for that matter. It was bitter, but she found that if she took small sips, she could swallow it.

Slamming down his empty glass, Séamus said, "I tell you, we need to get rid of these coolies once and for all."

"Right you are," Clancy said. "Root them out at their source, in Chinatown."

"Why?" Mabel said.

Jared leaned closer and she could feel the heat from his body. "To keep them from taking our jobs."

"It's time for payback, you might say," Séamus said. "We Irishmen have been taking the shaft long enough from those buggers. You'll have to excuse my language, miss, but I get quite passionate when I talk about the cause."

Clancy raised his glass. "To taking back our jobs."

The men clinked, drained their beers, and ordered whiskey. When the bartender brought the bottle, Mabel was intrigued. It looked the same as her father's liquor, and nothing bad ever happened when he drank it. The small glasses reminded her of the cups she and Caroline used when they played tea party in the nursery. But Jared passed one to everyone but her.

"Why am I not allowed a glass?" she said.

Jared looked at the men. "Maybe you shouldn't. It's not the thing for ladies."

Mabel tilted up her chin. "I'd like to give it a try."

This statement made Jared's eyes light up, and she felt she'd done something to impress him. He gestured to the bartender for another glass and filled it with the mahogany-colored liquor.

"See, what you do is take this glass and drink it." He emptied the liquid in his mouth. "Quickly, like that."

Mabel picked up the glass. When the fumes reached her nose, she drew back, feeling like she might sneeze. The men were watching her, so she tossed the whiskey in her mouth as she'd seen Jared do.

The whiskey burned her mouth. She hadn't swallowed it and now she was suspended between spitting it out or forcing it down. It rolled on her tongue like a marble and she thought she might gag. Squeezing shut her eyes, she pulled up her chin to force the liquid down by pure gravity. It fell reluctantly down her throat. When she opened her eyes, the men were laughing so hard, they were bent over the table.

"Lord, if that wasn't the funniest thing I've ever seen," Clancy said.

Jared pushed a smudgy glass of water to Mabel. "Go on,

clean your mouth. I can't remember the last time I laughed so hard."

"Ladies shouldn't drink whiskey anyway," Séamus said, pouring a round to everyone but her. The remark seemed presumptuous, as though everything in the world was off limits to Mabel, even on her one night of freedom.

"Just a moment," she said, sitting up straighter. "Let me try again."

The men looked at Jared as if asking what to do. "Aye," he said. "Let her try it."

Séamus poured another shot and this one Mabel sipped, finding that the whiskey went down better that way. As the night wore on, she stopped worrying about what she would say to her mother when she got home. Instead, she watched the people in the bar. Musicians were playing a wild kind of music and people had started dancing. The women sat on the men's laps and laughed in a loud, coarse way. Their hair was singed from hot irons so that the ends splayed like sparks. One of them had a dress made from burlap, like a flour or sugar bag that had been dyed and fashioned into a garment. Mabel had never heard of such a thing before.

"What time is it?" she said after a while, almost out of curiosity.

"Time for me to go home," Séamus said, standing.

Mabel flicked her eyes up at him. Was it so late that these men wanted to leave? If so, she would have to go back to San Francisco and face her mother. Vira would know by now that she was gone.

"Yes," Clancy said. "It's time, I think." He drained the last of his glass and set it down. "Coming, Jared?"

Jared was gazing at Mabel. "No, you go ahead."

"All right then." Séamus bowed to Mabel. "It was a pleasure to make your acquaintance, miss."

"Goodbye, Mr. Reilly, Mr. Sullivan," she said. When they were gone, she shifted toward Jared. "What time is it, really?"

"Twelve thirty," Jared said, glancing at the clock behind the bar.

Hearing the time startled Mabel out of the trance she'd fallen into. The situation had gone beyond being jailed in her bedroom. If she went home now, her reputation would be ruined. Vira was always warning her that could happen, and while she wasn't sure what that meant exactly, one thing was for certain: the longer she stayed here, the worse the situation got.

But what could she do? The ferry had stopped running and she didn't know another way to the city. The only possible solution was for Jared to marry her. It wasn't an ideal situation, but at least it would make everything decent again. Wouldn't it? Jared moved closer so that his thigh was touching Mabel's thigh. In the candlelight, his eyes were like pieces of onyx. Of course, he was rather dreadful. Irish rabble, Robbie had called them. Maybe that didn't matter. Vira always said how rough Elmer was when she married him, and now he was about to be elected to the stock exchange board. Maybe Mabel could mold Jared the way her mother had molded her father, making him worthy of her hand.

Gently, Jared drew Mabel's face toward him. She liked the way his fingers cupped her chin, as though her face was small and precious. Then he kissed her, his ropy arms crushing her against him. A sense of abandon slipped over Mabel and she rested her hand on his chest, taking in the gentle insistence of his mouth.

Later, when they left the bar, he pushed her against a wall and pulled down the collar of her dress so he could kiss her neck. As his lips moved against her body, she looked into the streets of Sausalito, which were deserted and dark. It was peaceful after the noise of the bar.

Now she was stumbling through the streets with Jared, the two of them laughing, their voices bouncing off the houses. "I can't understand you," she kept saying. "Speak English." This was funny to both of them. They came down to the water, and Mabel tried to focus her eyes, which were blurry around the edges. Across the bay, San Francisco was clustered on the hills, the firelight of hundreds of windows twinkling. She'd never seen San Francisco from this side, unless you counted the moments when the ferry docked in Sausalito and Caroline shrieked with fear. That felt like days ago now.

A cold breeze slapped at Mabel's face, and she was grateful for it because now she wanted to be sober enough to know how they would get to where they were going. She couldn't go home because Jared hadn't asked her to marry him. It was important for her reputation that they get married. The foggy circumferences around her eyes made her feel like she was looking through thickened ice at Jared, who was grinning crookedly at her. Her feet were sore from walking in her little heels. She was tired, and Jared knew where she could sleep. Tomorrow, she would figure out what to do. Tomorrow, she would marry Jared and go home a wife. Then her mother would forgive her. But that was tomorrow. Tonight, she would let Jared take her arm and lead her away from the city, into Sausalito, and into his bed.

CHAPTER 26

One morning in January, Sandra walked out of her bedroom determined that today she would work on her art. Her New Year's resolution was to become an artist. It seemed that art had been there since childhood, back when she used to pretend she was Amy in *Little Women*. Art was like something firm and shiny underneath all the distractions—Daddy Jones, Billy, Hollywood, finding a husband. Now that the struggle for security was behind her, she could give it the attention it deserved. And so, a new vision of her future had emerged:

1. Frederick would be a high-profile photographer.

2. Sandra would be an artist with gallery shows in San Francisco, New York, and London.

3. They would live a glamorous, cosmopolitan life with many important friends.

While she'd bought art supplies and set up an easel in the living room, getting motivated to paint was difficult. The question of whether she had "It"—the ability to be great—came up every time she touched a brush. She'd never heard of a great woman artist before. There weren't many women artists, period, and no one ever compared them to geniuses like Michelangelo or Leonardo Da Vinci. If Sandra wasn't going to be a great artist, she didn't want to paint, and yet she would never reach greatness if she didn't work at it. But whenever she tried to paint, she couldn't shake the feeling that she should be farther along by now. At her age, she should know which brushes to use for what effect, or how to shade a natural-looking shadow. What she needed were lessons, but the good art school in the city only enrolled men. Sandra wasn't interested in learning from a second-rate class for old maids.

However, today she would ignore all that and just paint. No more dawdling, no more procrastinating. Even though it was winter and the light wasn't as good, that was no excuse. If she didn't produce work, she'd never be an artist. It was as simple as that. She would brew some coffee and get right to work.

Or maybe, Sandra thought, as she stepped over the basket of dirty clothes, she should go to the bakery for a pastry first. That's what a French artist would do. And what could be more appropriate for an artist than to imitate the French way of living?

In the living room, Sandra stopped in her tracks and stared out the window. The entire San Francisco Bay was full of liberty ships. They were so closely jammed together that it looked like a prisoner from Alcatraz could reach land by jumping from boat to boat. Blimps hung over the scene, their roaring engines ticking faintly through her window pane.

She sank on the window seat, feeling as though her legs had turned to twigs beneath her.

The war.

Last month, the United States had declared war when the

Japanese bombed Pearl Harbor. On Christmas Eve the whole city watched as boats carrying the injured rushed into San Francisco. Not long after, the blackouts started. The first time Sandra didn't understand what was happening. The radio went dead and sirens began shrieking. Frederick thought there was a fire at the radio station and they went to the window to look for flames. Outside, a figure with a megaphone was yelling "Lights out!" at the houses. They turned off the lamps and stood in the window, looking at the darkened city until the sirens stopped wailing.

At the time, Sandra was comforted by the thought that the war wouldn't affect her because Frederick was too old to serve. Now, looking at the ships in the bay, she saw that the war would change everything. The United States would never be the same.

Sandra removed the blanket that was over the easel, looked at the blank canvas, and covered it again. How could she paint with a war going on? Instead, she curled up under Frederick's jacket, which was comforting because it smelled like him, and listened to the radio. "Rolling blackouts are expected on the following dates," the announcer said, reminding Sandra that she had to make blackout curtains, which would look hideous next to her new toile drapes. And just when she was getting the living room the way she wanted it.

Everything in the city seemed wrapped in fabric these days. The news said that they were going to cover the Palace of Fine Arts so it couldn't be seen from above. Sandra wondered what it would be like to camouflage her house and stay in a subterranean world for months, even years. It sounded like an awful way to live.

Later, Beatrice called to see if Sandra wanted to go to lunch and shopping in Chinatown. Even though Sandra was trying to be frugal, she agreed, but left the checkbook at home so she wouldn't be tempted to buy anything.

At lunch, she told Beatrice about her scrapbook of her appearances in "Women's World." Since Sandra went to so many events with Frederick, she was often in the background of pictures—wearing a ball gown at a benefit, sitting at a luncheon, smiling at a statue dedication. She saved the clips and had collected them in an album.

Beatrice took a sip of the white burgundy they'd ordered. "That's something to be proud of. I know a woman whose husband was appointed an ambassadorship because his wife was in 'Women's World.' They did a feature on her work with orphans."

"Isn't that something?" Sandra said.

"Yes, and another gal told me her friend got married after being in the paper. The man, who was very rich, was taken with her picture."

"I wonder if Frederick took the photo," Sandra said.

She felt proud to be married to a man who could exert so much influence just by taking a picture. People were always impressed when Sandra told them her husband was a society photographer, but it hadn't been clear what "Women's World" could do for them before.

After lunch, they went to Chinatown. Giggly from wine, they walked through the busy streets, under signs advertising chop suey, past groceries selling dead ducks in the windows, and in and out of stores full of furniture and fine china.

It was in one of these shops that Sandra saw it: a vase sitting on top of a red stacking table. Carefully, she picked it up. It was made of china as fine as molded sugar. A perfect lotus flower bloomed on its side. Sandra caressed the bumps on the seed pod with her fingertip, thinking that she knew just where she would put it. It belonged on the mantel above the fireplace. She could picture the living room in one panoramic shot, sweeping past the low-back velvet sofa, wingback chairs, and coffee table before landing on this simple, well-chosen vase above the fireplace. It would be an elegant, understated focal point, a period in the perfect sentence of her décor.

"That's bewitching," Beatrice said, coming up beside her. "Look at the details on the leaves."

Sandra turned the tag hanging on the side and dropped her hand. It was $100, two monthly allowances put together. "I love it. Unfortunately, I don't have that much money on me right now."

"You could put it on a tab, if it's just a matter of time. The owner, Mr. Lei, is very reasonable about that sort of thing. I'll ask for you if you like."

It hadn't occurred to Sandra before to open a tab. No one she knew bought things that way. You saved your money, paid for it in cash, and that was that. But Sandra didn't want to seem like she thought a hundred dollars was a lot of money in front of Beatrice, so she agreed. Before she knew it, Beatrice was gesturing to an older Chinese man and explaining that her friend would like to purchase the vase, and would he be willing to put it on layaway for her?

The man studied Sandra for a minute as if trying to read something in her face. Then he said that he'd be pleased to give the lady the vase, providing she was willing to pay a $10 service fee for the convenience. Sandra agreed and he was sweeping it off the shelf, wrapping it in a veil of tissues, and putting it in a chic box. The vase had gone from untouchable to hers in seconds, and all she had to do was sign a paper promising to pay the man in ten neat installments of eleven dollars. Broken down that way, $110 didn't seem like much at all.

And the best part, Sandra thought, as she stepped into the streets of Chinatown, *is that Frederick would never have to know about it.*

CHAPTER 27

In the parlor, the sap in the firewood cracked almost as much as Robert Chase's voice as he explained to Elmer why he left Mabel at the boxing ring. Elmer, sitting across from the boy on the sofa, listened with barely contained rage while Stanley Chase hovered protectively. Robbie's reason for leaving his daughter in the midst of a riot was that he was afraid his sister would faint. Caroline had turned white and Robbie was worried he would have to carry her if he didn't get out right away. He rushed to the carriage, expecting Mabel to follow, but she didn't. Then Caroline, who was no delicate daisy as far as Elmer could see, vomited out the window and begged to go home. Other carriages were rushing toward the gate and Robbie was afraid they'd be trapped if they stayed, so he told the driver to go.

"Why didn't you go back in for her?" Elmer said. "Why would you leave a helpless girl in the middle of a riot?"

"I don't know, sir. I panicked. I'm sorry."

Elmer leaned forward so menacingly that Robbie gripped

the arms of the chair. Stanley said in a voice like a dog's growl, "Come now, Elmer. Be calm."

He sat back, even though he wanted to strangle Robbie. That boy had filled his daughter's head with silly ideas about boxing matches and then, when the riot started, he panicked and left her behind.

Stanley put his hands on Robbie's shoulders. "We'll organize a search party. We'll find her."

Elmer shut his eyes, thinking of his wife upstairs, where she'd been lying since she learned her daughter was gone. Vira feared publicity almost as much as she feared for Mabel's safety, but the situation was beyond such concerns now.

"I'll contact the police," he said.

Soon, Mabel's disappearance was all over the newspapers. Caroline, dubbed the "recovered girl," was said to have been morally compromised and, it was implied, disgraced. Robert Chase was blamed for the whole thing. "The graceless scamp persuaded Miss Sanborn to leave the sanctity of her home and view the violent sport across the bay," one article read. "Thence she has gone, and now her fate is unknown."

Reporters camped by the house. One climbed into the backyard and the cook had to chase him out with a broom. At all hours of the day, young men came to Elmer's door and volunteered to rescue Mabel, as if she were a kidnapped princess. But searches came up with nothing. Three days after Mabel ran away, she was still missing. Flowers and condolence cards began appearing and people talked as though she were dead.

Finally, Elmer visited Donald Shannon's Villa himself. The old boxer greeted him in his office, which was a table surrounded by athletic equipment. He said he had no memory of the girls at the fight. Women rarely came to the Villa, he added, and apologized he couldn't be of more help. Elmer knew how he must appear to the boxer: a man with so little control over his household that his daughter could pull off this scheme without anyone knowing. He found that there was nothing else to say, so thanked him and walked to the ferry.

On the boat back to San Francisco, Elmer stood on the deck holding his hat in his hands. The fog was a wall around him, a comforting blankness as he considered for the first time that Mabel might be gone forever. And if that were true, who had he been building a legacy for all this time? Not himself, surely. Not for his wife, who coldly detested him. Then who?

For his entire life, Elmer had tried to make a mark on the world. He believed that he was a special person, a rare breed destined to do something remarkable with himself. Now that seemed like a trivial and childish goal. He could have spent his life differently. He could have invested in other things—his daughter, for one.

When Vira was pregnant, she informed Elmer that since he had the bad judgment to bring them to California, he couldn't be trusted with a child. It had been easier to give in than fight her. The last time he put up a fight, it was over the gold mining. That went on for years, and he lost in the end anyway. So he gave the child over and found focus in work while Vira focused on Mabel. Things had been harmonious between them, if never exactly happy. But while Vira was harping on about morality committees, she was driving the child away. He should have suspected as much—she'd driven him away years ago, and Mabel was just like Elmer. Everyone said so. Yet he did nothing, and the child roamed increasing distances. Now she might be gone forever.

The docks of the city came into view and Elmer smashed

his hat on his head. Vira could lie in bed for as long as she liked.
He wouldn't try to comfort her.

At home, white flowers sat on every surface—tables, floors, even
the chairs. A funeral wreath was propped up like a painting on
an easel. In the entryway, the servants were huddled under the
teardrop-shaped light. "There's news," the cook said. Elmer took
the stairs two at a time, the boards sounding like they might
crack under his boots, and burst into Vira's room. She was in
bed, her body dwarfed by the rosewood headboard, clutching
a letter in her hand.

"What is it?" he said.

She thrust the paper to him. He didn't recognize the hand-
writing, so it wasn't until he read the words "Dearest Mother"
that he understood he was holding a letter from Mabel.

Dearest Mother,

*Can you forgive me for the fright I have caused
you? You must have turned San Francisco upside down
looking for me. I'm quite well. In fact, I'm wonderful.
Mama. I have fallen in love and gotten married.*

*Here's the truth: I went to that fight out of the re-
bellion of my heart, the one thing that you have tried to
beat out of me. It was wrong and I have suffered for it.
But even in our darkest moments, there is hope. It came
to me in the form of my husband, Jared Smith, who took
me under his wing that night. By the end of that evening,*

he proposed marriage. And, because circumstances beyond my control prevented me from returning home, he took me to the parson that very night. We were married before morning.

I know this isn't the marriage you dreamt for me, but Jared is a good man. Although he was born in Ireland, he's a true American who will rise out of meager circumstances. I know that you won't turn us away but will help us begin our new life together. So, Mama, when may I bring my husband home to meet you and Papa?

Your daughter,

Mrs. Mabel Smith

Elmer sat down on the bed. It felt like a stone had been removed from his chest. "She's alive. Thank God."

"Yes. And married, or so she claims. What are we going to do?"

He knew what Vira meant. Thus far, Mabel had been free of the shame Caroline had brought upon her family by living through the riot. Because Mabel was seen as the victim of the tragedy, she appeared unblemished compared to Caroline. Now it would come out that their daughter was not only alive, but in the bed of an Irishman.

Elmer paced the room. "I'd like to have him jailed," he said. "I should have him jailed."

"And bring public disgrace upon us with a trial?"

He stopped pacing. "What's your solution then?"

"We're not going to have him jailed."

"All right," he said, squeezing his fists.

"And we're not going to meet him. That would seem like we approve."

"No, definitely not."

Vira lay back against the pillows, her silver braid snaking around her neck. For a moment, the only sound was the ticking clock on the wall.

Now that Elmer knew Mabel was safe, his perspective on the situation shifted. She was no longer a little girl lost in the world, but a married woman living with a strange man. She'd made an adult decision and must live with the consequences of her actions. They must all live with the consequences of her actions.

"I didn't mention it before, but I've learned that they're planning to appoint me secretary on Monday," Elmer said. "The vote is a formality at this point."

Vira watched him through weary eyes. "That's good, I suppose."

"Yes. We're close, Vira. So close to finally achieving the kind of wealth I talked about as a young man."

She nodded. A heavy fact lay like something leaden and metal between them: If Mabel came home, the narrative would shift. They would go from an upstanding couple with a martyred daughter to parents of a fallen woman. It could put everything in jeopardy.

"There's only one thing to do," she said. "We'll go on as if she were dead. No one needs to know about this added shame."

Elmer stared at his wife's face against the pillow. He knew the wisdom of what she said, but his heart fought against the idea of pretending Mabel was dead.

"Have you considered that if you hadn't been so hard on the girl, this might not have happened?" he said.

"No. Have you considered that if you had put bars on the windows like I wanted, this might not have happened?"

Elmer sighed. He didn't want to argue. Vira would never forgive him, and Mabel had chosen her path. She couldn't be allowed to destroy everything Elmer had worked for in the last thirty years.

On the wall was a portrait of himself. It was strange that this picture hung in Vira's bedroom, a place to which he was rarely invited. As he examined the tired face in the portrait, another image appeared in his mind, like a photograph glimpsed through a stereoscope. It was of a young man riding a horse into a valley to chase wild buffalo. It seemed like a different person, but he'd once galloped into the wilderness to kill a beast twice his size. At the time, it had seemed like life would go on like that, and it was the start of many adventures. In fact, nothing exciting had happened to Elmer again. He would never be that young man on horseback again. His life had been lived for the most part. And no one would remember him when he was gone.

The clock chimed one p.m. It was almost time for the afternoon stock exchange.

"All right," he said. "Mabel made her choice. We'll go on without her."

Vira straightened the blankets and asked him to fetch the stationary from the desk. She would write and tell Mabel that they wouldn't see the new husband. After time had passed and she didn't appear, people would assume the worst.

As Elmer left for the stock exchange, he turned for a last glimpse of Vira. She was sitting up in bed, writing, her blue eyes snapping over the lines that flowed from her pen. Her lips were sucked into a straight, tight line. And Elmer knew he would never forgive her for driving the girl away.

CHAPTER 28

Judith invited Sandra to her house for a luncheon celebrating the victory garden she was planting. "A little soirée," she said when she called. She sent her town car to pick up both Sandra and Beatrice. The driver wore a black jacket with gold buttons running down the front. They sat in the backseat while the car glided through the city.

As they chatted, Sandra scrutinized Beatrice's clothes. Her ensemble, while still expensive, had a jaunty, sportswear look to it. Sandra worried her mink muff was too formal for a luncheon. Beatrice always had the more appropriate clothing, and it filled Sandra with restless insecurity.

But when the car pulled up to Judith's house on Nob Hill, Sandra was glad she'd brought the muff. Before her was a four-story Queen Anne sitting on an artificial hill. Spiral-cut topiaries lined the walkway to the door. As Beatrice rang the bell, Sandra glanced out to the street. The porch looked down on the other houses, like a castle lording over a village.

A maid opened the door. She wore a black uniform under a spotless white apron. To their right was a parlor with gold and crystal accents. The maid led them through the house, out onto a deck, and down a staircase that emptied into a walled-in garden. Judith, wearing a blue skirt and matching poncho, was pleased to see Sandra and Beatrice. She squeezed their fingers, saying, "I'm so glad you could fit this in." Sandra wondered what "this" was exactly. Judith had said something about a victory garden, but there were no plants to speak of, just raised beds made of volcanic rock. Dozens of women were milling among the beds. Fog floated through leafless wisteria vines.

The other women were dressed in expensive clothes, and Sandra held her muff in front of her as they trooped behind Judith, who explained that she'd had her roses removed to make room for a victory garden.

"In this bed, I'm planting peas, spinach, broccoli, cabbage, onions—and that's just early spring," she said. "My aim is to provide for all my family's needs as well as to produce five hundred pounds of food for the soldiers."

The women applauded. Sandra remembered Daddy Jones's rows of cabbages, which they ate even when worms chewed so many holes in the leaves that they looked like netting. And in late August, when she picked tomatoes, how the stems stained her skin yellow so that she had to scrub her arms with soap afterward. And that time Daddy Jones got a load of horse manure from a friend. When he came in after digging it into the garden, the crevices of his fingers were caked brown. Sandra had a vivid memory of his filthy fingers holding a greasy chicken leg.

Judith clapped her hands. "I have a surprise for you ladies."

On cue, a line of maids came down from the mansion carrying garden supplies: cotton smocks, gloves, trowels, and packets of seeds.

"I thought it'd be fun if you would help inaugurate the garden by planting some seeds," Judith said. "And you may keep these gardening supplies as my gift, so you can start your own victory gardens."

The women made pleased noises, as if they were getting favors at a wedding shower. Reluctantly, Sandra handed her muff over to a maid and took a pink smock.

The bare yard became more lifelike as the women, wearing their pastel smocks, seated themselves along the garden beds and dragged the trowels through the dirt. Judith was at the end of a planter with her hands folded, watching her guests plant her garden for her. Sandra was confused why Judith was doing this in February. Even with San Francisco's mild climate, frost could kill the seedlings. Maybe Judith didn't know that because she was a beginning gardener. Well, Sandra wasn't going to tell her.

The woman next to her had already dug a trench in the soil and was meticulously depositing seeds in a perfect row. "Isn't this fun?" she said to Sandra.

"It gives a whole new meaning to the phrase 'garden party,'" Sandra said.

The women laughed and Sandra supposed that was a positive sign. If she had to dig in the dirt, at least she was making a good impression.

"This must be comfortable territory for you, Sandra," Beatrice said. "I bet you had to help out on your father's prune farm all the time."

The statement seemed calculated to make her look like a hick in front of Judith. In the daylight, Sandra could see how the liner on Beatrice's lower lip looked crooked when she smiled.

"No, no," Sandra said. "That was before I was born. I get freckles after five minutes in the sun. Can you imagine what I would look like after a day in the fields?"

Again the women laughed. "You're quite a card," Judith said, wagging a finger at her.

Sandra smiled. The scent of cooking food wafted out of the house and she remembered that this was a luncheon. Everyone else had finished planting their seeds and maids were coming down the rows with watering cans. When no one was watching, she dumped her seeds in the hole and covered them with dirt.

Afterward, they ate chicken sandwiches from silver platters in a room overlooking the garden. Before Sandra had a chance to finish her second *petit four*, it was time to leave. Soon the women were trooping toward the door, folding their gardening smocks and collecting their furs. Luxury cars were pulling up on the streets, one after another. Judith stood by the door, thanking each woman for coming.

When it was Sandra's turn, Judith said, "Will you wait a moment? I want to ask you something."

Although Sandra couldn't imagine what this was about, she stepped aside and watched Judith and Beatrice say goodbye. As Beatrice walked toward the waiting town car, she glanced back wistfully at the house. Then the maid shut the door and Sandra and Judith were alone in the hallway.

Now Judith sighed, visibly relaxing. She took a cigarette case from her pocket and motioned for Sandra to follow her to the deck. The high railing was positioned so that a person could enjoy the view of the city without being seen from the street. Judith held out the tortoiseshell case and Sandra took a cigarette. It was an expensive kind she'd never had before.

Judith blew out the smoke and smiled apologetically. "I can't smoke inside anymore. The smell gets in the curtains."

Sandra nodded. "I know how that is."

For a moment they stood looking at the city. The sun was peeking through the clouds, lighting the sailboats in the bay with golden rays. This was the life Sandra wanted. It felt familiar, as if she'd lived this way some other time. Maybe her grandparents had a house just like this.

"Darling, I wanted to ask you," Judith said. "Do you think Frederick might photograph my victory garden for 'Women's World' when it's at full capacity?"

It took Sandra a moment to understand what Judith was asking her. The paper was running pictures of the war effort and as a result, every well-bred woman wanted to show that she was pitching in.

"I don't know . . ." Sandra said and stopped, confused.

"Am I mistaken?" Judith said. "Beatrice says you're running Frederick's schedule these days."

Sandra didn't know why Beatrice would say such a thing. She hadn't implied that—had she? Maybe she said she assisted Frederick, but not that she chose what went into the column. Even Frederick didn't decide what to photograph for "Women's World." His editor did.

But Judith had such an agreeable look on her face that Sandra decided to talk to Frederick about it. Judith was rich and powerful, and if Sandra could do her a favor, all the better. Besides, if Frederick photographed the garden, he'd have to come to this house, which meant that Sandra could spend time alone with Judith without Beatrice hovering around.

"Of course he could, for a friend like you," Sandra said. "I'll ask him."

As they rode home, Beatrice told Sandra about the scrap drive she was organizing, again. She'd been talking about it for weeks, and Sandra was worried she'd be expected to volunteer. The last

thing she wanted to do was to help sort trash, but she didn't
want to look unpatriotic either.

"It's amazing what they can do," Beatrice said as they reached
Sandra's street. "For instance, kitchen fat can make explosives.
Can you believe it?"

"I'll never look at bacon the same way again," Sandra said,
noticing a chip in her manicure. It was from all that digging.

"Do you think Frederick would photograph the scrap drive
for 'Women's World'?"

Sandra looked out the window at the passing sidewalk. It
seemed they all thought she could get them into "Women's
World." And she couldn't say no to Beatrice's scrap drive after
saying yes to Judith's victory garden. "Probably," she said. "I
don't see why not, for a good friend."

As they pulled up, an army officer was standing on the stoop
of Sandra's house. In most cases, a visit from an officer meant
a war casualty. Flags with gold stars hung in windows all over
town, each an emblem for a soldier who'd died.

"I hope everything's all right," Beatrice said. "I thought you
didn't have anyone fighting over there."

"We don't," Sandra said, opening the door. "He probably
wants us to donate to the war fund. Which we're happy to do,
of course." Breezily, she waved goodbye to Beatrice and walked
up to the officer. "May I help you?"

"Good morning, ma'am. I'm looking for Frederick
Bauer."

"I'm his wife."

"I'm Sergeant Bob McCoy from the US Immigration
and Naturalization Services. You should have received a letter
informing you that we would be coming by today to ask Mr.
Bauer a few questions."

The town car rounded the corner, taking Beatrice's curious

eyes away. Sandra clasped her hands inside the mink muff. "I never received a letter. What's this about?"

Officer McCoy was unattractive, with close-knit eyes poised to fall over his long nose. "We're interviewing enemy-born aliens associated with flagged activities. In Mr. Bauer's case, cameras can be used for spy purposes."

"Spy purposes? That's absurd. And my husband isn't German. He's Austrian."

McCoy consulted the papers under his arm. "Not according to our files. We have a copy of his birth certificate and a record of him coming to the United States from Hamburg."

"That must be a mistake," Sandra said, realizing that it was she who had made the mistake. Whether Frederick was German or not was an easy thing for the government to look up.

"Ma'am, is Mr. Bauer available?"

It seemed like a bad idea to have the officer come into her home, as if she would lose something if he did. She'd heard the government was locking enemy-born people in camps, but she didn't know if that applied to Germans or not.

"He's not here," she said. "He's working. He barely sees me."

This, Sandra noted, was true. When Frederick wasn't on assignment, he was shooting weddings or retouching photos in his office. Lately he didn't even want her to come to society events with him, which had caused some arguments.

"Mrs. Bauer, it's better for your husband to cooperate."

Sandra wished she hadn't lied to the officer about Frederick being Austrian. She might have made Frederick look guilty. "I suppose we can make time, if it's that important," she said. "We don't want to appear as if anything is wrong."

The officer agreed to come back a week later at two o'clock. Sandra chose the farthest date possible in case there was something she and Frederick had to do in the meantime—destroy papers or leave the city or something like that.

The kitchen clock said it was 2:45 p.m. She opened the breadbox where she'd been hiding bills from Frederick and flipped through until she found a letter from the government. She'd assumed it was another bill and hadn't opened it. Now, reading it over, she saw that the officer was supposed to come today to "interview Frederick Bauer about citizenship."

Below the letter was a bill for the vase she bought in Chinatown. Sandra turned it over in her hand. Had she really agreed to pay $110? That was an exorbitant sum, especially for that vase. When she put it on the mantelpiece, it had looked dwarfed and insignificant, as if it were not up to the task of being the focal point of the room. She relegated it to the bedroom where no one ever saw it except for her and Frederick.

Blowing out her breath, Sandra tried to remember how she thought she could pay that much in the first place. Frederick gave her fifty dollars a month as a household allowance, and Sandra figured that if she held back eleven dollars for the vase, that left thirty-nine dollars for everything else. That was plenty for food and household necessities, but the problem was, this wasn't the only bill she was receiving.

It was Beatrice's influence. When Sandra was with her, $110 started to seem like pocket change.

She ripped up the letter from the government, buried the scraps in the garbage, and took the bag to the curb. When she came back, she stared at the unpaid bills spilled on the counter like a spreading disease. There was something obscene about them out in plain sight, so she swept them back into the breadbox. Then she turned the radio in the living room to full volume and lay the newspaper on the dining table, looking for information on what the government was doing to German citizens.

She'd heard about something for Italians or Germans in the Mojave Desert, but the newspaper only mentioned camps for the Japanese.

The last time Sandra was on the Bay Bridge, the police had stopped a car of Japanese people, causing a huge traffic jam. When she and Frederick finally drove by, an officer was talking to a woman holding the hand of a little girl wearing a plaid coat. The child was shivering from the wind.

If Frederick were sent away, Sandra had nothing to fall back on, especially with all these bills coming in the mail. She would never go home to Healdsburg. The only thing she could do was to take whatever money there was, get in the car, and start over again somewhere else. At least that was always an option.

CHAPTER 29

Jared had been gone a week now. Mabel tried to reassure herself that he would come back but she was starting to believe that he might not. She had until the end of the week before she had to leave this house and she was almost out of the money Jared had left her. Séamus said he could get her a job at the restaurant he cooked for, but that was out of the question. The restaurant had dancing girls.

Outside a train went by. They went by day and night, horns blaring like elephants. Mabel went to the back porch to get away from the noise. From the chair, she looked through the neighbor's yard into the bay, where there was an island covered with trees. It was soothing to be out here, dressed in black for the mourning she felt, but technically didn't have a right to wear since Jared wasn't dead.

The mourning dress, which she'd dyed herself, was also protection. It filled in the story of Jared's disappearance without Mabel having to say a word. It was like the ring on her finger, which had no more basis in fact than Jared's death. When he'd said that he would never marry her, she insisted he buy the ring to preserve what was left of her reputation. It was the least he could do after getting her drunk and seducing her. It was a plain brass band, not even gold.

In the neighbor's yard, a ruddy-faced boy was playing with a mutt. He threw a stick for the dog and then ran after it himself as if he were the animal and not the other way around. To Mabel, it seemed like an idiotic thing to do.

The hovel the boy lived in was similar to the one she'd rented with Jared: four rooms and a yard filled with grass the color of a sunburned arm. No one did any gardening in this place. In Mabel's yard, the only plant was the brown remains of a Pride of Madeira, those purple flowers that died every year and renewed in the spring.

Her affair with Jared had been short, only a few months. Mabel didn't care to do the math just then. To think too hard would bring up emotions that were carefully packed inside of her like a folded wedding gown. Séamus said that Jared ran off to a Gold Rush in Canada, but Mabel thought he'd run off with that girl he was flirting with at the pub, the one who dangled her stocking legs in front of him. When Séamus told Mabel that Jared was gone, he seemed prepared for her to weep or faint, but she had erected herself into a pillar of dignity. A lady was a lady in every situation, as Vira always said. Even now. Even after all that had happened.

"What am I to do?" she'd said to Séamus. "Now that I have been abandoned by both my parents and Jared?"

Séamus turned his hat by the brim, as if to make sure it was still circular. Mabel wanted to snatch it from his hands. "You'd be welcome to work at the restaurant, if you like," he said. "I'm sure I could get you a job. Not as a showgirl," he added hastily, seeing the look on Mabel's face. "Waitressing. Good, honest work."

She thanked him and showed him out. Then she waited

for Jared to come back. When he didn't, Mabel thought of the words from her mother's hateful letter.

We have no choice but to allow you to lie in the bed you have made, Vira had written. *And I fear it's a wretched bed indeed. You will never get back what you have lost through your behavior. If you come here, I will not look you in the face.*

Mabel hadn't expected that kind of letter. She knew her parents would be angry but she thought she'd be allowed to go home if she had a husband. Even though Jared had refused to marry her, she was convinced that if her wealthy parents agreed to meet him, he would change his mind. But when that letter had come informing her that she was disowned, Mabel knew that Jared would never marry her and that her time with him would end sooner or later.

And it all happened because Mabel had chosen to do something on her own, for once. Her mother was a hypocrite. When Vira was Mabel's age, she'd abandoned her home and ridden across country in a covered wagon. That was easily as unladylike as going to a boxing match, especially when you considered the improprieties of living in a tent.

Vira may not believe in finding her way in life, but Mabel did. She would get back what she'd lost, despite what that letter said. She may have to do some unsavory things, but in the end, she would be triumphant.

Oh yes, Mabel resolved as another train went by, *I'll get everything back—and then some.*

CHAPTER 30

The typewriters were clacking throughout the newspaper office. The noise, along with the jangle of telephones, was giving Frederick a headache. He was grateful when his editor, Tom Broadbent, shut the door to muffle the racket. Sitting behind the desk, Tom pushed a file of assignments toward Frederick.

May 22: WAC ball, 8 p.m., black tie.
May 23: Connecticut Club picnic, 1 p.m.
May 27: Benefit for Wounded Soldiers tea, 3 p.m.

Frederick flipped the file shut. "Tom."

The editor held up his hands as if to say, *don't shoot.* "I know what you're going to say, Freddie, but these society dames love you."

He ignored the much-hated "Freddie" and opened the file again. "A picnic right after a ball? Two events in a row?"

"It'll be fast. Pop in, take some shots, leave. We're not even sending a writer to the picnic."

But it wouldn't be fast if Sandra came, and she always wanted to come to society events. It was a nuisance. The other

day, she'd asked him to photograph Judith Hopkins's victory
garden, as if anyone cared if a rich woman grew vegetables in
her backyard.

"What if I get you photographs of the city?" Frederick said.
"San Francisco at war, ships going out, weapon manufacturing,
the soldiers. It's them who should be in the paper, not these
society people."

Tom walked around his desk and opened the door so that
the noise streamed in again. "We have plenty of that. People
love the women's section. More importantly, our advertisers love
it. We need you on this beat, all right Freddie?"

Frederick felt such anger at this stupid man. Here he was
offering to take Pulitzer-Prize-worthy photographs and Tom
wanted him to waste his skills on tea parties. This would always
be a subpar newspaper with men like him in charge.

On the way out, Tom patted his shoulder and Frederick had
a hard time not smacking off his hand. "Stop by bookkeeping,"
Tom said. "Jennifer will pay you for last month's work."

After Frederick deposited the check at the bank, he stopped at
a diner for coffee. Opening the newspaper, he studied his latest
photograph in "Women's World," yet another tea party benefit-
ing the army. The women were toasting the camera with their
cups, their hair curled on their heads like sausages. All he did
these days was photograph women at tea parties, women in
gardens, women sewing quilts, women in ball gowns. Frederick
almost felt like a woman himself.

These rich women were a bad influence on Sandra.
She adopted their affected tones and coveted their furs and
jewels. Worse, she decided he was to become a "prominent

photographer" and tried to drag him around parties like a mother leading a child, expecting him to finagle work out of those people. Frederick wished Sandra were less interested in society and more interested in learning how to cook something other than watery soup.

He folded the newspaper and sipped his coffee. It was too bad Tom didn't want him to photograph the soldiers. It would be nice to have a patriotic activity to point to when the officer investigated him next week. Every time Frederick thought about the interview, a cool trickle of fear ran down his back. He was a citizen, but so were the other people being carted off to internment camps. Still, Frederick was careful not to show Sandra that he was worried. Her eyes, whenever the interview came up, were like flashlight beams on him. One wrong move might send her into hysterics.

Frederick wished he hadn't let her talk him into saying he was from Austria. The lie had had no effect on his photography business one way or the other, and now he would have to explain to an officer why he'd been claiming he wasn't from Germany.

It had been easy for Frederick to leave Germany, and he didn't miss it. By age twenty, life there had been planned out for him. As a photographer's apprentice, he worked all day doing whatever the photographer wanted, then came home to his mother, grandmother, and sister at night. It was an unhappy household, bone cold and poor, and he would slip in and out of it like a stray cat, cringing whenever his mother would turn on him. "You're acting like your father," she'd say, tugging on his ear. "Stop it."

How different the men were in the American cowboy movies he saw at the theater. They had found something that Frederick wouldn't have thought to want otherwise—a freedom or an authenticity that was linked, somehow, to their manhood or sense of self. Watching the vaporous men riding horses over the movie screen, it had occurred to Frederick that he could work in Hollywood. He had camera and art skills that would be useful on a movie set. Maybe, he thought, he could even work on a cowboy picture.

In secret, he wrote to every Hollywood studio, sending samples of his work and offering himself for employment. The only response was a letter from Disney saying that if Frederick were ever in Los Angeles, he should stop by for an interview. The next day, Frederick bought a ticket for New York. He boarded the boat and left in the wee hours of the morning without telling his family what he was doing.

When he arrived in America, he decided to cross the country before settling in Los Angeles. He went slowly and lived frugally, sometimes taking the bus, sometimes walking, sometimes earning money by washing dishes or selling photographs on the sidewalk. This was how, four months into his journey, Frederick found himself wandering through Texas in the middle of the night with nothing to eat. He knew there was a town somewhere nearby, but he misjudged the size of Texas, where everything, even the bus stations and post offices, seemed stretched out like chewing gum.

The air had cooled as the sun went down and there were no clouds, just a fat moon in the sky. Bugs were flopping around in the air and one smashed against Frederick's temple like a soft, dry kiss. He wanted to sleep and start fresh in the morning, but the hunger would keep him awake. It physically hurt, his gut clenching so that he doubled over. This wasn't the longest Frederick had gone without food since beginning his trek across America, but it was worse because he didn't know when he would see civilization again. The American wilderness could go on for thousands of miles.

He was calculating how many days a man could survive without eating when he heard a lowing coming from the left. Frederick held his breath, praying to hear it again. It had to be a cow, and cows meant people. There was a frustrating gap in time during which there were only crickets chirping. Then it happened again: a long, soothing moo.

Frederick groped toward the sound, tripping over stones and bushes until he was among what he thought were tree stumps. For a moment, he stared at the huge mounds, imagining a prehistoric forest that had been cut off by a disaster. Then one of the stumps moved, and he understood that he was looking at cows. A herd was scattered around him, flicking their tails in the darkness. It struck Frederick as pathetic that he, a starving man, couldn't eat one of these animals. The only tool he owned was his camera, which was more useless than ever at the moment.

Then the scent of cooking meat wafted over him and his stomach tightened as though someone had reached inside his body and squeezed. Frederick stumbled toward the smell until he saw a light. Within a circle of wagons, cowboys were sitting by a campfire.

Frederick had seen cowboys on his American travels before, but never in a bunch like this, and never out in the open prairie. It was just like in the movies.

He stood in the darkness, watching them. They wore chaps and Stetson hats and rested their guns and rope by their sides. One of them was playing a guitar and the rest were smoking or talking quietly. Behind them was a chuck wagon bulging with frying pans and pots like a peddler of yesteryear. A cook with a towel wrapped around his waist was tossing steaks on a grill.

Frederick stepped into the light. The cowboys stopped playing guitar and stared at the man with the suitcase who'd materialized out of the darkness.

"Pardon me," Frederick said. "I was wondering if I might have a bit of your meat to eat."

The oldest cowboy, who had a drooping gray mustache, sucked on his pipe and blew out smoke, assessing Frederick. "Sure you can. Go ask Cookie to cut you off a slab."

Frederick felt weak in the legs as he set down his suitcase. At the wagon, he repeated his request. The cook wiped his hands on a grease-stained apron and waddled over to the wagon where cuts of meat lay underneath an oil cloth. "Large or small?"

"Large," Fredrick said.

Cookie speared a steak as big as a frying pan, salted it, and dropped it on the grill. It sizzled and spurted, letting off the aroma of fat into the air.

My god, the riches of the United States, Frederick thought. During his youth, beef was reserved for special occasions. One Christmas when he was twelve, his mother served a steak the size of an American hamburger to the four of them. Frederick remembered watching his mother cut the steak and making sure that his serving was the same as his sister's. Now this stranger was giving him meat twice that size, for free.

Cookie loaded the steak onto a plate and handed it to Frederick. "Fork and knife on the end. Help yourself to beans and coffee too."

Frederick took the silverware from a blue-speckled coffee mug and walked with wobbly legs to the fire. The steak was tender enough to cut with a butter knife. He ate so ravenously that the cowboys laughed.

"Whoa, slow down there fella," one of them said. "There's plenty more where that came from."

Frederick grinned. Then he had a second steak, as well as a serving of beans. Full at last, he leaned back and talked to the cowboys. They explained they were in the middle of a cattle run, taking "those critters you saw out there" to market. They told him he could get lodgings at Shilo's Ranch, two miles away.

"You can get a short-term job there mucking stalls," said the one with the drooping mustache named Russ. "I'd jump at it if I were you. There's scarce work these days."

"Ain't that the truth?" said a young man. "Cowboying is going the way of the dodo."

"Times are rough," said someone. "My family says I should quit and get a job in a factory."

"Not me," said the young man, lying with his hands behind his head. "I love this life."

"That's because you're young," said Russ. "When you're my age, sleeping in a Tucson bed every night loses its romance."

"What's a Tucson bed?" Frederick said.

"It's a very special cowboy bed. You make it by lying down on your stomach and covering it with your back."

The men laughed and Frederick chuckled too. These cowboys were saying that life was difficult here, but that was because they were American and didn't understand how rich they were. Back home people were miserable because they had nothing. Frederick had been smart to go to a place where there were opportunities.

The cowboy with the guitar started singing, "The Yellow Rose of Texas." Soon they were all singing along, their voices lifting with the smoke from the fire and drifting into the sky.

Now, sitting in this San Francisco diner, Frederick found himself humming the song. He wished he'd stayed with the cowboys, casting aside his photography and Hollywood dreams. Everything he'd been looking for had been right in front of him, and yet the next morning, he'd gone on to California.

"More coffee?" asked the waitress, brandishing a pot. She had a round face and cornflower blue eyes.

"Yes," Frederick said. "And may I get some cream?"

"I'm sorry. We're out. It's rationing. We won't get any until tomorrow."

"Ah."

As the waitress walked away, Frederick shook out the newspaper again. His eyes fell on an article about more food shortages—RATIONING ORDERED ON CANNED FOODS: CURB TO HIT FRUITS, VEGETABLES.

He sat up straighter as an idea came to him. Sandra was always complaining about shortages for things she considered necessities: butter and milk, which came from cows, and eggs, which came from chickens. It occurred to Frederick that he could start his own ranch. All it would take was land, a barn, and a few animals and he could sell the food he produced at top dollar.

He flipped to the real estate section of the paper and scanned for affordable property. If you were willing to go a half hour out of the city, housing prices dropped dramatically. One property spanned six hundred acres and included a mountain. He could purchase an entire mountain! Frederick could see it now—a big house, children running through fields, cows and chickens in the pasture, and fruit trees, because you could grow anything in California. He would grow pineapples and peaches, his favorites.

But how would he talk Sandra into it? Here Frederick slumped back in the booth and took a sip of coffee. She wouldn't want to live on a ranch. She was always talking about how much she hated the country. But Sandra didn't know what she wanted. She hadn't wanted him, and now they were married. She wanted to be an actress, and now she didn't. She wanted to be an artist, but she never painted. Like most women, she needed a firm hand, which was why Frederick had always been able to bend her to his will.

So he would set up the ranch without telling her, then reveal it when he was ready. If he waited until Sandra had no choice but to move, she would come around. It would take a bit of convincing, but eventually she would grow friendly to the idea, especially when she saw that the ranch, and the lifestyle it represented, was something he'd always wanted, ever since he was a child—or so it seemed to him now. He was sick of photography. It was all empty images that meant nothing. The lack of authenticity in his life was the reason he was never quite happy, never quite satisfied. That was what the cowboys had that he didn't. He hadn't been smart enough to seize that lifestyle back then, but maybe he could re-create it now.

It wasn't too late. Frederick, too, could become a cowboy someday.

CHAPTER 31

The church picnic was held in the shadow of Mount Tamalpais. A breeze was ruffling the grass on the hills, which were turning from green to yellow. Arthur Beard stood by a tree, holding a china plate with slices of apples on it.

Although Arthur had made the long trip from Healdsburg to Larkspur to meet a woman at this picnic, now that he was here, he felt shy. His wife, Rebekah, had died almost a decade ago, and aside from the spouses of farmers he knew, he rarely spoke to women. But everyone agreed it was time for him to remarry. Rebekah hadn't given him children before she passed, and he was getting on in years. If he didn't marry soon, he'd never have a son to take over the prune orchard.

The women had prepared lunch baskets for a silent auction to benefit the new library. Arthur, who intended to bid on a basket, surveyed the ladies dispersed throughout the park, their skirts arranged in folds around their bodies like ribbons on Christmas packages. The source of their feminine grace seemed to Arthur to be anchored in their shoulders—the smaller the shoulders, the daintier the woman. And Arthur found himself favoring one pair of shoulders more than any other. They were the smallest and most perpendicular. The shoulders he favored were Mabel's.

His brother Charles approached, holding a glass of lemonade. For a moment they stood side by side without speaking.

"See anyone you like?" Charles said.

Arthur cleared his throat. "Do you know that one there, the one with the small shoulders and brown hair?"

"No, I don't believe I do. Nice eyes."

At that moment, Mrs. Brenson moved toward them in her wide navy dress like a barge approaching a pier. Earlier, Charles had introduced her as the lady in charge of the picnic.

"Mr. Beard," she said, wagging a finger at him. "What are you doing over here by yourself? Let me introduce you to some ladies."

"Speaking of that," Charles said, "Arthur was asking me about that lady in the purple dress. Do you know her name?"

Mrs. Brenson squinted at Mabel, who stood beside a group of women, listening to their conversation. "That's Mabel Smith. She joined the church recently."

"Ah. A married lady, then?"

"No, a widow, poor thing. She comes from good people, I think. Let me introduce you."

It was startling to Arthur how smoothly Mrs. Brenson interrupted the group's conversation to introduce "Charles's brother who's visiting from up North." The women clustered around him, except Mabel, who continued to stand slightly to the side.

"Mr. Beard, I want you to meet my daughter, Frances," said a lady, pushing forward a girl of about nineteen with a gigantic bow on her head. Arthur blushed at the thought that this young girl could be seen as a potential match for him.

"Nice to meet all of you," he said.

"What do you do for a living, Mr. Beard?" asked a woman, her thick eyebrows ticking up as if she were quizzing him.

"I own a prune orchard in Healdsburg," he said. "I've been meaning to visit Charles here in Larkspur for a couple of years now."

"And what do you think of our Larkspur?" another woman said, batting her eyes. "How does it compare to Healdsburg?"

"Well, now," Arthur said, "I suppose they're similar, both being country places, although you're closer to San Francisco, of course."

"That's so true," the woman said with a giggle.

An awkward silence fell. The four women, including Frances, were waiting for him to speak, but no words came to mind. Arthur wasn't used to so much attention.

"Whose basket are you bidding on, Mr. Beard?" Frances's mother said.

Before he could reply, Mrs. Brenson reappeared and asked the women for help setting up the auction. When Mabel started to follow, Mrs. Brenson stopped her. "Not you, my dear. You stay here and keep Mr. Beard company."

And like that, Arthur found himself alone with Mabel. She was older than she appeared from farther back, but lovely, with arching eyebrows and glossy hair. Neither of them seemed to know what to say. A choir was warming up for the afternoon entertainment, their voices trilling through the scales like demented birds.

"Are you enjoying the picnic?" Arthur said.

"I think," Mabel said, "it might be the nicest picnic I've ever been to." Her voice had a high-class trill to it, a tone of quality that impressed and intimidated him.

"Yes, it is nice," he said, rocking on the balls of his feet. "Very nice."

He saw her eyes dash over his old-fashioned suit and bushy beard. There was a sharpness in her look that seemed to dismiss him. "I understand you own a prune orchard," she said.

"That's right."

In the distance, a sheep bleated. Arthur reached up to fiddle with a hair under his chin, then caught himself. "Yep, it's a good old ranch, all right," he said. "I employ over two hundred workers these days at harvest time."

She flicked her eyes back to him. "That's a lot of people. Business must be thriving."

Arthur felt more at ease now that he was on familiar territory. "Yes, ma'am. My orchard ships all over the United States. Healdsburg is the prune buckle of the nation, you know."

The chorus began to sing "Yankee Doodle Dandy," indicating the auction was ready to start. Like the sun coming out from the clouds, a smile spread across Mabel's face. It was a dazzling change from cold dignity to girlish warmth.

"Well, I hope you'll bid on my basket. That way we can get to know each other better."

He nodded at her, smiling. "I intend to."

In front of each basket was a sheet for the bidder to write a name and amount. Arthur discovered he had a problem: Mabel hadn't told him which lunch was hers and there were no names on the sheets, just descriptions of what was inside, such as "roast beef sandwiches and peach cobbler" or "chicken salad and brownies."

People were watching him, which made him self-conscious. As he passed the woman with the quizzical eyebrows, she leaned forward and said, "Mine has a plaid bow, Mr. Beard."

"Ah," Arthur said, because he didn't know how else to respond.

Across the meadow, Mabel was talking to another lady,

seeming to have forgotten him. Mrs. Brenson was straightening a line of frosted cookies on a platter as Arthur jogged over to her.

"Excuse me," he said. "Do you happen to know which basket was made by Mabel Smith?"

Mrs. Brenson considered the question. "I believe it's that one."

She pointed to a hamper with a large pink bow. Arthur thanked her. There were already two names written on the bidding sheet, which said the lunch was turkey sandwiches and blackberry buckle. He wrote his name and a three-dollar bid.

For the rest of the auction, Arthur stood next to Charles watching people float around Mabel's table like gnats. At one point, a man picked up a pencil and seemed about to bid on her lunch, then changed his mind.

Finally, the pastor got up and said there would be five more minutes to bid.

"At this point, I'd like to ask the ladies to stand by their baskets," he said, and added, while wagging his eyebrows, "Let's see who made these wonderful lunches."

The chorus launched into "My Darling Clementine" as the women lined up. Mabel walked—glided was a better word for it—toward the tables, but didn't stop by the lunch Arthur had bid on. Instead she went to a smaller basket with a blue French ribbon.

Frances was standing by the basket with the pink bow, which, he saw now, matched the one in her hair. Arthur felt his face get hot. He, a man of almost fifty, had bid on a girl young enough to be his daughter.

The chirping chorus of the song seemed to goad Arthur as he rushed to Mabel's table. He only had time to write his name and a five-dollar bid before the song ended and the pastor called, "Time's up!"

Too embarrassed to speak, he slunk over to Charles. His

fingers riffled through the hair on his chin as the pastor asked the ladies to pick up their baskets and carry them to the top bidder. Mrs. Brenson weaved around, directing the women and pointing people out, oblivious to what she'd done to Arthur.

Mabel was reading her bidding sheet as if she hadn't seen him write his name a moment before. Frances, on the other hand, was looking at him. She put the basket on the crook of her arm and he braced himself, having no idea how he was going to explain bidding on two women.

But instead of coming to him, Frances veered toward a man with a bald patch on his head. They clasped hands and walked away, their arms swinging between them like a rope. Arthur didn't have time to be relieved, for Mabel was standing there, holding her basket. Her smile was radiant.

"It was kind of you to bid on my lunch," she said.

He offered his arm. "I can't wait to see what's inside."

Arthur and Mabel sat on a blanket apart from everyone else. Instead of the sandwiches and cakes, Mabel's basket had quail croquettes, lamb in mint sauce, and bottles of sparkling cider. The food was strange to Arthur, but he tried to like it.

"You're very popular, Mr. Beard," Mabel said. "I must be dining with the most eligible gentleman in Larkspur."

Arthur shook his head. "I don't know about that."

"Well, I do. It's not every day we meet a gentleman with a successful business like your prune ranch. Won't you tell me more about it?"

She seemed so interested that soon Arthur was explaining how California agriculture was having a renaissance. Farms were springing up all over, each area a pocket for a different crop, each farmer an entrepreneur, scientist, and philosopher rolled into one. The state was leading the way toward sweeter, healthier, bigger crops. Luther Burbank, the Plant Wizard, lived near Healdsburg and was splicing fruit and vegetables together to make food straight out of fiction—a fist-sized walnut, a stoneless plum, a white blackberry. There'd never been a more exciting time to grow food.

"What it gets down to is land," Arthur said. "It's remarkably fertile when irrigated. Everything grows here. Prunes, grapes, apples, hops. Everything you can think of." He stopped, feeling that he'd been going on too long and was boring her.

But Mabel's face was attentive, her knees pointed toward him like arrows. "I had no idea agriculture was so lucrative," she said. "And your orchard is behind your house?"

"All around it. I own five hundred acres."

There was the smile lighting her face. "That's a lot of land. And what's your home like?"

"My home? Well, it's a big house all right. It gets pretty lonely at night. When we built it, it was one of the nicest homes in town." He didn't add that it was also one of the first homes in town, so there wasn't much to compare it to at the time.

It was getting on toward evening. Mabel tossed bread to a blackbird, which hopped away on lacquered legs, its eyes like crumbs of glass on its head. Arthur could tell she was softly raised, from good people, but there was a stiffness about her, a regal distance that made her difficult to read. He wondered again about her age.

"Tell me, Mr. Beard," she said. "How is it that a man like yourself, with his own empire, isn't married?"

Arthur liked that word, "empire." "I was married. I'm a widower, I'm afraid."

"I'm sorry to hear it. I'm a widow myself."

"I know. Mrs. Brenson told me."

She looked down at her hands. "My husband, Jared, worked in railroads. My parents loved him very much. There was a fire. It took both Jared and my parents and left me penniless."

Arthur wanted to take her hand, but it seemed too forward. "I'm sorry you had to go through that."

Without his being aware of it, she'd moved closer to him on the blanket. "Do you have children?"

"No. That's my one regret, not having children."

He felt a weight slide from his pocket and they both looked down. The gold watch chain had slipped out and hung slightly above the basket. Mabel put her palm underneath the chain and lifted it so that it pooled in her hand. Gently, she tucked it into Arthur's vest pocket.

"That," she said, "is my one regret as well."

CHAPTER 32

Officer McCoy was supposed to come at two o'clock. Sandra cleaned as she'd never cleaned before, scrubbing and mopping the house so vigorously that Frederick said, "Where's Sandra and who are you?" She didn't have the spare energy to be annoyed. At 1:50, there was a knock. Wearing an orange dress, Sandra threw open the door with a wide smile.

The man standing on the stoop wasn't Officer McCoy. He was wearing a striped suit and a pork pie hat, and there was an unsavory air about him. "How do you do, Mrs. Bauer?" he said. "I'm here to collect payment for a vase you purchased from Old Shanghai Decor. The account is overdue."

Quietly, so Frederick wouldn't overhear, Sandra shut the door and stepped onto the stoop. "I know. I'm sorry about that."

Holding Sandra's gaze in a way that was both calm and threatening, the man extended his hand for the money. "You've missed three payments. That'll be thirty-three dollars."

"I don't have that right now, but I need you to leave. This isn't a good time."

"Ma'am, I can't leave unless you pay the money or hand over the vase."

Down the street, Officer McCoy rounded the block. He was whistling, which seemed out of character, somehow. Sandra had to get rid of the bill collector immediately.

"Wait here," she said.

Skidding into the kitchen, she called out to Frederick, "It's the milkman wanting payment." She thought of getting the vase and handing it to him, but Frederick might notice, so she grabbed what was left of her allowance and ran back to the door.

"Here," she said, thrusting out a handful of cash. "Now will you leave?"

The officer was a half block away now. He'd noticed Sandra talking to the bill collector and his eyes were neutrally focused in front of him, as if to give her a few last moments of privacy.

"This is only $7.50," the man said.

"I'll send the rest in the mail. Please apologize to Mr. Lei."

Officer McCoy was at the yard now, standing with hat in hand, waiting for Sandra to acknowledge him. Frederick stepped onto the porch.

"Good day, officer," he said.

Everyone looked at the bill collector, who moved his tongue in his mouth as if feeling for something. Pocketing the cash, he tipped his hat toward Sandra. "I'll be back, Mrs. Bauer. Good day."

"Bye, milkman," Sandra said. "Officer McCoy, how are you? Why don't you come in?" She stepped aside for the officer to pass, ignoring the curious look Frederick gave her. They went to the living room, which, now that it was clean, was attractive with its new furniture, gold candlesticks, and ficus tree in the window. It looked like the home of respectable people on the rise, Sandra thought. The government couldn't possibly find fault with it.

Of course, they might feel differently if they knew how much of it was borrowed on credit.

McCoy was businesslike. He wouldn't accept a drink, even coffee, and he wouldn't take one of the raspberry tarts Sandra bought from the bakery. They looked like something out of *Ladies' Home Journal* with each raspberry perched on the custard base. She wondered, staring abstractly at them, if she should have made a show of patriotism. Maybe she should have baked an apple pie.

Her mind wandered to the bill collector again. He was probably the first of such people to be coming to the house. There was something threatening about him. What would he do if she couldn't pay the money?

Frederick shot her a look, and Sandra realized she was rocking back and forth in her chair. She stopped herself and smiled. Officer McCoy asked to see Frederick's green card and birth certificate.

"Will you get them, Sandra?" Frederick said. "They're in my office."

On rubbery legs, she walked to Frederick's study. Behind her, McCoy asked, "What year did you come to the United States?"

For a moment, she stood in the office, breathing hard. Everything was in perfect order: the desk free of papers, the chair pushed in, the pens distributed evenly in a cup. She located the file drawer, but the green card wasn't in any of the files.

"What kind of photographs do you take with your camera?" the officer said.

Sandra made a noise of panic and went through the papers again. Why hadn't she gotten them out before the officer arrived? He would obviously want to see Frederick's papers. She was always focusing on the wrong thing or looking at things from the wrong angle.

Shutting her eyes, she willed herself to calm down. If Frederick said the papers were here, they were. He was absurdly organized. Breathing slowly, she flipped through the files one at a time, but no green card.

"Do you have them, sweetheart?" Frederick called.

It was odd to hear Frederick say "sweetheart." She supposed he was avoiding the German *schatzi* in front of the officer.

"Almost," she said.

The drawer opposite was also full of files. The first one contained the insurance policy to the house. Sandra glanced at the settlement number, then pulled the policy out in amazement. Frederick believed in a thorough home policy, but she didn't know it was like this. Even considering the San Francisco market, the house was worth more if it burned down.

It irked her. Why wouldn't Frederick discuss this with her before buying such a big policy? It was silly to pay so much for insurance, especially when they were low on money.

"Sandra, do you need help?"

"No," Sandra said, slamming the file shut. She found the immigration papers bundled together with his birth certificate, marched into the room, and handed them to the officer. While McCoy looked at the papers, Frederick smiled at Sandra, but she avoided his eyes.

"Now," McCoy said. "I hear that you've been saying you're from Austria. You admit now that you're from Germany?"

"That's correct," Frederick said, giving Sandra a warning glance to stay silent.

"But your wife told me the Austria story herself. So, would you explain why you've been telling people this?"

Frederick studied his hands a moment as though considering his answer. Then he looked into Officer McCoy's eyes. "To be honest, sir, I'm ashamed of my home country."

Immediately Sandra saw what Fredrick was doing. He'd come up with the perfect twist on the lie for why they were saying he was from Austria. It wasn't even that far off from the truth. Maybe it wasn't even a lie.

"I don't respect the political philosophies that pervade Germany," Frederick went on. "I wanted to live in the United States, where a man can pursue his dreams."

He spoke in a slow and steady way, imitating John Wayne. He did this when he wanted to appear extra American. Not many people would notice because of his accent, but Sandra heard it. She admired this about Frederick. It was like something she would do.

"And that's why you came to America?" the officer said.

"Yes. And, this is embarrassing, but I love cowboy movies."

McCoy chuckled. "Do you now?"

"Yes. We didn't get them often in Germany, but when I saw them as a boy, I would think to myself, I must go to this wonderful place."

Sandra could tell McCoy liked this answer. His face twitched as he wrote something down. "Have you been volunteering for war work?"

"No sir, not yet."

McCoy laid a pamphlet on the table. On it, a man stood with a shovel on his shoulder, a sunset behind him. The caption read, THE US ARMY CORP. WE CLEAR THE WAY. "You'll get good wages at the Army Corp. It would be smart to join."

Sandra met Frederick's eyes and shook her head. She didn't want him volunteering, especially when things were going so well with his photography.

"Sir," Frederick said. "I'm afraid I already have a full-time job."

"He's a photographer," Sandra said, shrilly. "He photographs very important people, like the Mayor of Oakland's daughter and Errol Flynn."

"I told him that already, dear."

"We must all make time to help," McCoy said. "We're only ankle deep in this war. If we don't all pitch in, we may not win."

Frederick folded the pamphlet. "You're right, sir. I'll consider it."

Sandra wondered if this was the real reason Officer McCoy was investigating them. Maybe it was all a trick to get Frederick to volunteer.

McCoy put his pen in his coat pocket. "I think we're done here."

"Already?" Sandra said.

"Yes, I don't see any problems with you folks. You get that job at the Army Corp, Mr. Bauer."

"I will, sir."

As Frederick showed McCoy out, Sandra flopped down on the sofa. It was over. The government was going to leave them alone. When she contacted Beatrice again, she could do so knowing that Frederick wasn't going to be sent away. Everything would go on as before.

That night, there was a rolling blackout. When it was over, Sandra and Frederick didn't turn the lights back on but sat on the floor of the living room, pressing their backs against the sofa.

"I'm proud of you," she said, kissing his neck. "He thought you were a model citizen. You were right that I should trust you."

"Yes, you should trust me. But I forgive you."

"I was so worried. You have no idea."

"Oh yes, I do. You talked of nothing else all week."

She stopped kissing him. She didn't know why he had to say things like that. Outside, a yellow light was blinking on and off, like the intake and release of breath. Sandra wondered if it was a warning she was supposed to know about.

"Honestly, I'm so tired of all this talk of patriotism," she said. "You can't see a movie without being made to feel guilty about your patriotic duty."

Frederick lifted his hand from where he was stroking her hair.

She pulled back to look at the outline of his face in the darkness. "I mean, what more can they expect of us? I'm even planting a garden when I hate gardening; and rolling tinfoil and reusing my stockings. Now they're expecting everyone to get factory jobs, when I already have a job. I'm an artist."

They both looked at her easel propped by the window. Frederick seemed not to reply on purpose, as if he were avoiding agreeing with her about being an artist, which was annoying. "I don't know," he said at last. "It might be a good idea for me to join the Army Corp."

Sandra groaned. She knew it. He wanted to join in the stupid war when he had a perfectly good job as a society photographer. "Do you want to spend every day working on boats with a boss breathing down your neck?" she said.

"No, but McCoy is correct that it's suspicious for a man of my background not to pitch in. You should volunteer too. What is it your friend does? The scrap drive?"

"That's sorting trash."

He threw his hands in the air. "I don't know what else we can do. You don't want me to be sent away, do you?"

Sandra tilted her head suspiciously, wondering if he was manipulating her again. When she first brought up him being sent to a camp, Frederick had scoffed at the idea but now that the investigation was over, he was talking like it was a real possibility.

"You told me that wouldn't happen and that I was being silly," she said.

"Well, we don't know, do we? The only way to know for sure is if we both volunteer to demonstrate our patriotism. Or else, we could move. The house is worth three times what I paid for it. We could get a big place somewhere out of the city and be free of scrutiny."

There was a long silence as Sandra remembered the insurance policy. It would be nice to have that money.

But he was talking about selling the house. It would have to burn down to get the insurance.

"Imagine it," Frederick said, holding his hands in front of her face like a movie camera. "A large house, bigger than this place. Easy parking. No more fog. You could have an art studio to paint in."

"I can paint here."

"No, picture it. A big studio, all your own. No cramped corner of the living room. With huge windows and beautiful nature to inspire you."

Sandra chuckled. It was a romantic idea. She could see herself painting in a mansion like the one her mother had had before the earthquake, only more stylish.

"A dream house," Frederick said. "With a backyard. And rolling fields. And horses."

"Horses?" Sandra laughed. "Frederick, stop."

"I'm serious. We could have anything we want. A place where you could put your antiques on display instead of shoving them around the house."

This was a good point. The house was getting crowded from Sandra's mistakes. The latest was the painting of the woman with smudgy eyes. Sandra thought the portrait would look good in the living room, but when she hung it over the fireplace, the woman's gaze followed her wherever she went. It bothered Sandra so much that she put the painting in the closet. Now every time she opened the door, the woman's eyes accused her of wasting money.

Maybe Frederick is right, she thought. *Maybe the face needs a taller ceiling to look down from. Maybe that's all that's wrong with it.*

"How could we afford this house?" she said, half-seriously.

"That's the beauty of it. Real estate outside San Francisco costs a quarter what it does in the city. We could sell this place and build whatever we wanted."

If they did that, Sandra could pay off her bills without Frederick knowing. If bill collectors kept coming to the house, he would find out about her debt for sure. "Maybe we could get another house in San Francisco."

Frederick dropped his head on the sofa and rolled it back and forth like a bowling ball. "No, no, no, *schatzi*. We can't afford that. It would only work if we left the city."

But if Sandra did that, she'd be giving up so much: her friends, Frederick's photography, their upswing in society. She was building the perfect life here, one where Frederick was a well-known photographer and she was an artist. She was so close to getting what she'd always wanted.

Sandra patted Frederick's hands. "It's a nice dream, isn't it?"

CHAPTER 33

Mabel and Arthur were married soon after the church picnic. A justice of the peace officiated the wedding with Charles as witness. The next day they honeymooned at the hot springs in Calistoga, where they rented a cabin with a private dining room and chef. This alone was ample proof that Arthur had the wealth he said he did—as did the clothes he bought Mabel, and the diamond ring on her finger.

Whenever Mabel thought about Arthur's wealth, she felt overwhelming relief. It meant so much not to have to worry anymore. The wedding was the fulfillment of the promise she made to herself that she would get back everything she lost when her parents disowned her. It was this promise that Mabel had held onto all this time. She'd held onto it when Jared ran off with another girl, leaving her penniless, and when she took shifts as a dancing girl and had to "make nice" to men who revolted her, and when she stayed up late washing people's clothes for extra money. It was that promise that led her to move to Larkspur and start fresh, spinning her good breeding around her like a web and waiting for the right opportunity to come along.

Here, at last, was that opportunity: a man with a thriving empire who needed a wife. Such men were rare, which was why Arthur had been so popular at the picnic, with all the women vying for his attention. He'd chosen Mabel out of all of them, changing her life for the better.

The longer she sat beside Arthur in the carriage, the more the folds of the gold hills around them reminded Mabel of something she couldn't quite pinpoint. It was a pleasant feeling, something from childhood that made her feel safe. She'd made a good marriage, as had always been expected of her. The wedding ring was an emblem of security encircling her finger and soon she would have a baby to further cement her status as wife. She'd allowed Arthur to think she was younger than she was, so it was important to get pregnant as soon as possible.

The pleasant sensation continued until they entered Healdsburg. The way Arthur talked, Mabel expected Healdsburg to be similar to an Italian village, with rolling vineyards, yellow homes, and little shops. But the town was plain. Women in calico dresses and men in overalls drove through the street. The plaza in the center of town was no more than a field of young trees surrounded by rectangular frontier buildings. When Arthur waved at a man missing a front tooth, Mabel stopped carrying on the conversation and sat stiffly, holding her bag in her lap.

They crossed a bridge and drove up a hill so that, for a moment, Mabel could see the forests beyond the town. Thousands of trees encased this hamlet. Her thumbs stroked the leather handle of the bag.

"What's that smell?" she said.

"They're fertilizing farmland by the river," Arthur said. "They spray steer manure, which makes the air a bit pungent."

"Does it smell like this all the time?"

"No," Arthur said. "Only now and in early spring."

They turned up a road and soon were surrounded by orchards. The trees shuffled by like pages in a book as the carriage rolled down the lane. Mabel could see plums dusky in the leaves.

"This is my land," Arthur said. "All of this is my orchard."

At this, Mabel felt hopeful. She wasn't going to live in the town, she reminded herself. She was going to live on his estate.

"We're almost there," Arthur said. "Shut your eyes."

Mabel obeyed. The crackling of the carriage wheels stopped and Arthur moved so that his chest was pressing against her back. She reminded herself not to move away from her new husband. He put his hands over hers, his fingers winding around the tops. Pulling down her hands, he said, "Welcome home."

Before Mabel was a yellow farmhouse with a porch and a dried lawn out front. It looked like every house Mabel had seen since leaving San Francisco, except that it needed a paint job. The trim was peeling and the hydrangea bushes by the porch were covered with dead flowers.

"This is your home?" she said, hoping there was some kind of mistake.

"Yep, this is the place."

A waft of the manure affronted her. It sunk in that she'd married a farmer. Mabel had been so happy the last few days thinking that she was getting her wealth back, but now it seemed that she'd made a mistake. There'd been many opportunities to marry farmers or shopkeepers in the past. She'd turned them down, despite her poverty, and held out for a man she could bring to her parents, if she so chose, one who would impress them with his wealth and position and make them sorry for disowning her. Arthur had seemed like that man, but now Mabel saw differently. After being so careful for so long, she'd married a farmer.

The inside of the house was as ugly as the outside. As Arthur held her bag, Mabel glanced from the metal stove to the quilt spread across the sofa to the rag rug on the floor. The ivy wallpaper creeping up the wall made the room feel smaller than it was. She could have married a shopkeeper and lived in a nicer home than this.

In the bedroom, Mabel was a pillar of stone crumbling as she sank on the bed. The ivy wallpaper was in here too. Arthur sat beside her, holding her bag with a concerned expression. She barely knew this man and his leg was touching hers.

"Don't you like it?" he asked.

Mabel continued looking ahead. "It's not what I expected."

"What did you expect?"

"You told me it was the biggest house in town."

"Oh," Arthur said. "It was when we built it. I haven't changed the house much since Rebekah died. I guess a lady like yourself would find it rather humble."

"Yes, I do." It was a blunt reply. She knew she was being ungracious, but he oughtn't have presented himself as an industry mogul when he wasn't one. She threw him an accusatory glance. "I thought your orchard was doing well. You said you ship nationwide and employ hundreds of people."

"I do." Arthur sounded shocked. He stood up and tugged her hand. "Come. Let me show you the orchard. You'll see I was speaking the truth. Not about the house, but the rest of it."

Mabel remembered the hope she'd felt a short while ago and relented. Behind the house, workers were harvesting prunes. Canvas lay on the ground below the trees and they were shaking the branches with poles so that prunes fell like large raindrops. The trees were so heavy with fruit that their branches sagged under the weight. Arthur said he was having one of the best years ever, with orders coming in nationwide. The biggest fruits would be graded "fancy" prunes, a luxury item on the East Coast. He estimated he would ship two railroad cars of fancy prunes and three cars of regular prunes.

"What do you do with the prunes once they've harvested them?" Mabel said.

"We wash and dry them. I'll show you." He led her through more trees to a red barn and showed her the well, which he called the dipper, where the prunes were washed. In the barn, workers were laying prunes on rectangular screens for drying. Through the open door on the other end, she could see the drying yard. Hundreds of screens were loaded with prunes withering in the sun, some as big as potatoes.

Mabel couldn't help smiling, the feeling of relief slipping back in stages. Arthur hadn't been lying about the business, at least. She put her arm through his as they walked toward the house, but when they reached it, she frowned again. It was a depressing sight in the middle of all this bounty.

"Mabel," Arthur said. "Charles is always saying I need a wife who can help me now that the business is reaching new levels. I suppose our home is part of that. So, if you want to change the house, I don't see why I should stop you."

She glanced sideways at him. "Change it?"

"Yes. In fact, I give the house to you as a wedding present. You have my permission to improve it as you see fit."

Mabel's face lit up. "And I can do anything I want?"

"Anything."

She looked around her with new eyes. The house was the reason Arthur gave off the impression of being a farmer instead of the head of an empire. It didn't have to stay that way. She had the taste to make it into something new.

"Change it," she murmured. "Yes, maybe it does have potential, after all."

CHAPTER 34

Beatrice and Eva left Sandra alone in the community center at the scrap drive while they got hot water for tea. Sandra stood with her hands in her pockets, looking at the piles of junk. All morning people had been bringing garbage to this room for the government to turn into weapons. Thus far, she'd managed not to touch anything. Pots and pans were piled near a mound of tires. Empty tin cans made up an enormous pyramid, like a used grocery display. The stack of newspapers was so tall, it threatened to landslide. Sandra wondered what the army was going to do with so much newspaper. She imagined them throwing spitballs at the Japanese.

Outside she could hear the music of the merry-go-round and the shriek of children. It wasn't until Sandra agreed to volunteer at Beatrice's scrap drive that she learned it was at the Alameda Fairgrounds. The scent of fried food drifted in through the open door.

Frederick had been coming to this side of the bay ever since he quit the society column and got a job at Kaiser Shipyard in Richmond. Sandra had been flabbergasted when he told her what he'd done. Evidently, Frederick didn't respect her enough to involve her in major life decisions. When she protested, he reminded her that it was important to do something patriotic. Officer McCoy might check in on them. So like that, the society column had slipped from her life, another casualty of the war.

In addition to a full-time job, Frederick was shooting weddings every weekend, which was good because they needed the money, but it also meant she rarely saw him. When he was home, they bickered over trivial things—who chipped the mug, what radio show to listen to, whether she did the laundry. She couldn't paint for some reason, and even her friendships felt at risk. Judith had asked through Beatrice when Frederick would be photographing the garden. "She said everything's in bloom and ready to go," Beatrice told her, and, even as Sandra worried how to explain about Frederick leaving the newspaper, she wondered why Judith hadn't asked her directly.

There was the sound of metal scraping on concrete. An old woman shuffled into the room, dragging a section of wrought iron fence almost as big as she was. She tottered and was about to fall, and Sandra had to drop her resolution not to touch anything and step forward to catch it. Together they threw the fence on the pile of frying pans, streetcar tracks, and church bells.

Sandra brushed her skirt and checked her shoes for dirt. "Thank you for your donation. I'm sure the army can use the iron."

"Come," the woman said in a thick accent. "There's more in car."

A station wagon was parked next to the community center. Over the wall, Sandra could see the Ferris wheel revolving to tinkling music. The old lady opened the door and they peered into a tangle of black iron. Every section of the car was stuffed with pieces of fence, like a mechanical puzzle.

"Did you pull this from your yard yourself?" Sandra said.

The woman took a handkerchief from the purse dangling on her arm and blotted her cheeks. There were bobby pins all through her hair. "My grandson is over there fighting. I must do something."

Sandra couldn't imagine this tiny woman dragging iron from her yard and stuffing it in the car. Beatrice and Eva still hadn't appeared and there was no one else around. It was starting to look like Sandra might have to unpack the fence herself.

"Would you like to take a rest?" she said. "We can get help from the other volunteers when they return. They're bringing tea."

In answer, the old woman began pulling at a piece of fence, her limbs shaking as if she might fall. Sandra caught the iron in her hand.

"Step aside, please. I'll remove the iron."

Sandra was dragging the last piece of fence out of the car when Beatrice and Eva returned. The iron pile was now the biggest in the room.

"My goodness," Beatrice said as she escorted the woman to her car. "I can't believe you brought all this yourself. How patriotic of you."

At that, Sandra let the last piece of fence fall with a bang. She was sweating and her dress had a brown spot on it. She batted at it, unsure if it was rust or dirt.

Eva handed her a cup of tea. "Can you believe what some people will bring in here?"

"I truly cannot. What took you so long?"

"We had to go into the fair to get water from a coffee stand. I'm sorry you had to unpack this fence alone."

Sandra sighed. "It's for the war effort, I guess."

For a moment, they both regarded the fence. Something about it made Sandra sad. It was a nice fence, the kind you saw around the better houses in the city. Now it would be made into ammunition.

"That woman's car is filthy," Beatrice said, coming back in. "I don't know how she'll ever get the dirt out."

"*I'm* filthy," Sandra said.

Beatrice tucked her straw-like blond hair behind her ear. "You poor thing. Why don't you go home and clean up? We'll finish here."

Relieved that she didn't have to touch any more garbage, Sandra began gathering her things. As she was powdering her face, Frederick strolled into the community center. He was strutting, unapologetically happy. He'd been happy a lot lately, even though he claimed to hate working at the shipyard. It was suspicious.

"What are you doing here?" she said.

"Hello to you too," he said and nodded to Eva and Beatrice. "Hello, ladies. Looks like you've been working hard."

Beatrice stepped forward. "Are you here to photograph the scrap drive for 'Women's World'?"

Sandra braced for Frederick to say he wasn't doing the column anymore, but instead he popped fair tickets from his sleeve like a magic trick. "Nope. I'm here to treat you to the fair, *schatzi*."

She cringed at the German word in front of her friends. Beatrice's face was unreadable, but Eva was smiling as though she thought Frederick was adorable. Sandra disliked fairs— they reminded her of Billy playing in the bandstand while she wandered around aimlessly—but she kissed Frederick's cheek. As she did so, she smelled whiskey on his breath. "How sweet," she said.

"Oh, the fair," Beatrice said. "That seems like something you'd enjoy, Sandra."

Again, there was something barbed about Beatrice's tone. Suggesting what? That Sandra was from some kind of carnival person?

Frederick pulled Sandra toward him and wrapped his hand around her waist. "Come. The fair awaits."

Beatrice shoved her hands in her jacket pocket. "Yes, Sandra, you'd better go. Frederick seems like he's in a hurry."

Before she could reply, Frederick pulled her out the door. At the fairgrounds, there were hay bales and barkers yelling about stuffed animals. Frederick was like a child, insisting on getting her cotton candy and trying to talk her into riding a giant pirate boat that swung high into the air. When she refused on the grounds that no one inspected those rides for safety, he pledged to do a shooting game to "win you a goldfish."

"What would I do with a goldfish?" she said.

He ignored her and spent way too much money shooting a tin gun at a bullseye. He was a terrible shot and missed the target entirely, but he didn't seem to mind. Next, he dragged her toward a building, saying, "They have prizewinning apples this way."

In a hall, slices of apples lay on plates with different colored ribbons on them. It appeared to be some kind of contest about who had the best apples. It reminded Sandra of cold mornings riding with Daddy Jones in the wagon to the orchards, prunes hanging like coal in the branches. Frederick tasted each apple, exclaiming at the differences. "This one is so much sweeter, and look, it's called Honey Sweet, and so it does, it tastes a bit like honey." He bit into another apple slice and said, "This one is very good too. Try it. Jonagold, it's called."

She bit into the apple slice and almost laughed at the

expression on Frederick's face as he watched her eat it. "It's an apple," she said.

He led her behind the building and toward the animal stalls. Seeing them, Sandra balked.

"No," she said, firmly.

"Come on. It'll be educational, *schatzi.*"

A child ran by as he said this, and Sandra cringed at the German word again. She thought of Beatrice's cold manner and wondered if this is what had caused the shift. "Frederick, you shouldn't use German words in front of my friends. We don't want people to think about where you come from, remember?"

He pulled her close. "*Du bist so hübsch,*" he said, though he knew she didn't understand German. "That means, 'You're so pretty.'"

"That's not funny. People can hear you. What has gotten into you?"

In answer, he pulled her toward the stalls and she found herself staring at sheep and goats. It smelled in there, and Sandra put her hand to her nose to block the stench. Frederick studied every animal.

"Can we go?" she said.

"Look at this goat."

She looked at the bony head of the animal. Its pupils were rectangles. "It's disgusting."

For the first time, Frederick looked serious. "You don't like goats?"

"Not at all."

"What about goat milk?"

Sandra made a face. "Not meant to be drunk by humans."

Frederick frowned at the goat. Then a rooster crowed and he brightened and pulled her toward the sound. At the end of the stall was a room filled with chicken cages.

She stood by the door near the fresh air. Behind her, she could hear the chickens scratching their beaks against the cage like prisoners dragging tin cups along a jail cell.

"This one is beautiful," Frederick said. "It won second place. I wonder how it does at laying eggs?"

A rooster screeched from somewhere, grating Sandra's nerves. When she was a child, the neighbor's rooster would wake her every morning with a gargling screech. Daddy Jones used to say he would sneak over there and make it look like a raccoon got in the cage, but he never did it. She took out a cigarette and stepped outside to light it.

"These are Rhode Island Reds, considered to be an excellent layer," Frederick said. "They lay six eggs a week per chicken. You'd never have to shop for eggs if we had one of those, eh, sweetheart?"

She ignored him. People were walking in clumps toward the stables. She wondered why so many people wanted to pay money to look at livestock. It seemed a supreme waste of time.

CHAPTER 35

Mabel waited until Arthur was out of town to place the newspaper ad for a builder to renovate the house. That way applicants would be forced to talk to her, not Arthur. The three men who responded to the ad were understandably confused. "Where's your husband?" they kept saying.

She expected them to react that way to a woman interviewing them for a job. What she didn't expect was for them to argue with her about the house. When she said she wanted to widen the staircase, they dismissed the idea out of hand. "Why don't you let me stain it a darker color?" one said. "It'll look good as new." Another said there wasn't room for a bigger staircase, and when she brought up knocking out a wall, he stared at her and said houses needed walls to hold them up.

Mabel showed them out and stood on the porch, wondering if anyone else would respond to the ad. The best way to find a good carpenter was to go to San Francisco, but she was too far away to make that practical.

The hydrangea bushes in front of the porch jiggled and Mabel put her hand to her heart. Beyond the railing, a man stuck

up his head and looked at her. Apparently, he'd been crawling
around in front of the house.

"Hello," he said, wiping off his knees. "I was checking the
foundation. Solid post-and-pier work down there."

Before Mabel could reply, he bounded up on the porch. He
was tall, with a wave of blond hair that rested on his forehead.
His limbs were oversized, like a puppy with large paws.

"The name is John Hollingsworth," he said, pumping
her hand. "I'm here to apply for the renovation job with Mr.
Beard."

"You'll be speaking with me. I'm his wife." John Hollingsworth seemed unsurprised, which threw Mabel off. She
continued, after a small pause: "I'll show you the house, then
you can present me with your ideas." She swept inside to explain
her plans for the fourth time that day. In the middle, she was
interrupted by a loud stamping noise.

John Hollingsworth was jumping so hard that the figurines
on the shelf rattled. He brushed back his hair. "No rotting wood,
I'm happy to report."

"As I was saying," Mabel said, "it's essential I have a proper
home. My husband's empire needs a showcase."

John smiled at her, and she averted her gaze. She had the
sense he thought she was cute, which was irritating.

"And for this room," she said, as they entered the parlor,
"I'd like to put in a wider staircase."

He nodded. "All righty."

"You think that's possible?"

"Sure. You'd have to make the room bigger, which in this
case means taking out the wall."

Mabel twisted her lips. She knew it could be done. Those
other men were incompetent.

He took out a tape measure and stretched it across the stairs.

"Yep, need to take out a wall. You'd want to do that anyway. We could double this house, no problem."

Mabel opened her mouth and shut it. She hadn't expected him to say that.

Now John was stalking around the staircase, looking underneath it and around the room. "Actually, you could take out the ceiling too and put in a grand hallway. That's what they're doing in mansions these days, making entryways with spiral staircases."

"Mansions?"

"Sure. A woman like you belongs in a mansion, that's plain enough. Look." John pulled a ratty notebook from his pocket and began to draw with it resting on his leg. He ripped off the page and handed her the drawing. It was the same room, with the same square windows and squat stove, but now there was a spiral staircase twisting to a newly formed second story.

She smiled. "You think you could do this?"

"I can do anything you want. For example, what about this?"

He sat on the sofa and began drawing again, his blond hair falling into his eyes. Mabel looked on as he started with the existing house and added to it, drawing a grander building around the old one. The parlor and dining rooms would become a front hall with a spiral staircase. The back of the house would become the new kitchen and parlor. Upstairs, there could be two bedrooms and a bathroom with indoor plumbing. There would be crown molding, stained glass, and gold leaf trim, he said.

"And a mural," Mabel said. "All the best houses have murals."

When John smiled, a dimple appeared in his left cheek that she hadn't noticed before. "I can do that for you, if you want. I'm a great painter."

Heat rushed through Mabel's body as she imagined the home he described. She thought of her mother envying the palaces on Nob Hill, the ones the railroad tycoons had built.

As a child she'd visited these mansions, with their columns and balconies and elaborate details. She could build such a place.

"Tell me about your experience," she said. "Have you led many jobs of this size?"

"Led? No. I was a carpenter on the Carson Mansion in Eureka. Heard of it?"

Of course the man with the best ideas would have the least experience. Mabel tried to listen as he described working on an eighteen-room mansion for a lumber baron up north, but her mind was filled with calculations. "If you've never led a job like this, why should I hire you?" she said, interrupting him.

John seemed taken aback by the question. "I may not have led a build of this size, but I can handle the job, believe me. I hammered my first nail before I was off my mama's—" He stopped, swallowing back a crass word. Mabel waited calmly as he gathered himself and began again.

"Mrs. Beard," he said in a humbler tone. "I've always wanted to build a house like the one I've described. A grand estate. And I can do it. I can make this place a work of art if you'll give me a chance."

While an hour before, Mabel would have been satisfied with a man who could widen the staircase and put in new floors, now it seemed she could never be happy with anything less than a mansion. She stood up to show John Hollingsworth out. "You may send me an estimate," she said. "If I like your numbers, we can go from there."

Soon after, construction began. The workers trooped into the house, filling it with sweat and noise as they unloaded their tools. Mabel and Arthur stood by the ivy wallpaper while John spread the final plans on the table for their approval. Mabel hoped Arthur wouldn't doubt John's ability to do the job. He'd gotten a haircut since they last met and it made him appear even younger than he was.

Arthur was quiet a long time as he looked at the plans. Once he reached up to fiddle with a hair under his chin. It was a bad habit of his. When he was nervous, he would yank at the hairs until they bled. Mabel was always pulling blood-dotted hand-kerchiefs from his pockets.

"What do you think?" John said at last.

"Well, now," Arthur said, "it's a bit more elaborate than I expected."

Mabel tensed, afraid that here at the last minute, with the men standing by holding their tools, Arthur would dash their plans.

Turning to her, Arthur looked searchingly into her eyes. "Is this what you want, my dear?"

"It is."

"Then do as she desires, Mr. Hollingsworth."

John rolled up the plans. "Her wish is my command, sir."

With impressive speed, the workmen picked up the table and moved it outside. Arthur led Mabel to the dining room, his hand on her shoulder, where he always wanted to put it. "I like that fellow," he said. "I think you made a good choice."

She straightened his tie. "I was afraid you were having second thoughts for a moment there."

"It's a bit more than I was expecting, but as long as you're happy, I'm sure it'll be worth it."

He kissed her forehead and returned to the orchard.

For a few minutes, Mabel listened to the workers in the next room. Soon they were banging and knocking so hard that the curtains shook. When she could stand it no longer, she slipped into the parlor to watch.

Already the room looked bigger. The men were slamming sledgehammers through the wallpaper so that the thin boards shattered into a hole.

John saw her and shouted, "Wait! Halt!"

They all looked at her. Feeling like a teenage girl again, Mabel lifted her chin, prepared to remind John that he was her employee and she could watch the construction if she wanted.

But John picked up a sledgehammer and held it with both hands, as though presenting her with a sword. "Would you like to take a couple of whacks, Mrs. Beard?" He smiled, the dimple inviting her into a conspiracy.

She found herself smiling back. "Yes," she said. "I believe I would."

John must have been strong, for he made the heavy sledge-hammer look easy to hold. Carrying it like a croquet mallet, Mabel picked her way across the room until she faced the partially demolished wall. She heaved with all her might so that the sledgehammer stuck in the ivy wallpaper. When she pulled it out, a round hole appeared.

"Push through with your body," John said, miming the swinging of an ax.

Mabel was aware that they were watching her and reminded herself that it was important to assert her authority, otherwise they would start answering to Arthur instead of her. This time, Mabel threw all her weight behind the sledgehammer and the wallpaper bent into the hole as if it were melting. The men applauded and she stepped back, elated.

The wall was filled with crumpled newspapers. John reached over her shoulder and pulled out a page. "It says 1883," he said. "That would be the year this house was built."

It was a copy of *The Healdsburg Examiner*. The headline read, THE SUPPOSED BLACK BART PLEADS GUILTY. Below was a picture of Black Bart with his white mustache and placid eyes. Mabel wondered why she'd ever fixated on this old man. It was ridiculous, as were all the preoccupations that had led to her ruin. They were the whims of a foolish girl, but she was a woman now.

Mabel handed the newspaper to John. "Then I'd say it's high time for a change."

CHAPTER 36

It was Frederick's birthday, and Sandra was on the cable car to get ingredients for a cake. Normally she would order one from the bakery on credit, but the owner was freezing her account until she brought in money to pay him. Since she'd paid all the bills she could this month, there was no option but to make it herself. It would taste wrong or be lopsided, but that was the curse of wartime, she supposed. One didn't get to have nice cakes when there was a war going on.

The cable car was crowded. It was always crowded these days. Not long ago, Sandra could get on at any time and have a choice of seats, but not anymore. The city had gained 150,000 people in half a year, causing housing prices to triple. The wait for a restaurant was forty-five minutes, movie theaters were always sold out, and if there was a city event—a parade or festival—it meant fighting through people just to get in. Clutching her handbag to her chest, she remembered Judith's town car and sighed.

Judith and Beatrice had stopped calling and Sandra couldn't think what she'd done to offend them. They didn't know that

Frederick had quit the society pages—at least, Sandra hadn't mentioned it—so the best explanation was that Frederick was German. The city was plastered with posters telling people to watch out for spies. In one, a Liberty ship was halfway under water, sinking like the *Titanic*. LOOSE LIPS MAY SINK SHIPS, it said. While Sandra had tried to think of whether she knew anyone who could be a spy, she never suspected that anyone could think that of *her*.

The line at the grocer's stretched out the door. Lines, lines, lines. Sandra was sick of "scrimp and save" and "have a stiff upper lip" and cancerous piles of soap ends in the shower and scooping bacon fat into coffee cans so that the army could use it in bombs. Most of all, she was sick of her victory garden. The price of food had gotten so bad that she finally broke down and put one in. The plants were healthy enough, but every time she went out to pick cherry tomatoes for Frederick's salad—the only kind that grew in foggy San Francisco—she thought about how she always seemed to end up back in the same place, worrying about money and growing things in the dirt.

In the store, Sandra wandered the aisles searching for cake ingredients with her ration book in hand. It was confusing. Was margarine the blue or red stamp? How many points was chocolate? Had she already used up the amount of coffee she was allowed to have? To make matters worse, she couldn't find sugar for the cake and had to go to the counter to ask. When the clerk told her that they were out of sugar, Sandra gaped at the girl. It was one thing to be out of chocolate or whiskey, but sugar was a basic thing, practically a necessity.

"What am I supposed to do?" she said. "I can't make a cake without sugar."

"You can plant beets," the girl said. "That's how some people are getting sugar."

This made Sandra imagine red sugar, which sounded like cooking with dehydrated blood. She made a face at the girl and left the store.

Sandra thought of going home, but sitting in the empty house with her painting supplies had started to remind her of when she was a little girl and Mabel would leave her alone for hours while she and Daddy Jones worked the harvest. This was before Mabel decided Sandra was old enough to pick fruit in her place. As a little girl alone in the house, Sandra used to get so afraid of earthquakes that she would hide in the closet until her mother returned. It was infuriating that even though she was a different person with a different name, she could still feel that same sense of overwhelming loneliness.

Instead of going home, Sandra headed toward the shopping district, which she hadn't visited since her trips with Beatrice. The French designers weren't making clothes since the occupation of France, so many of the stores she'd traipsed in and out of two years before were closed. But American designer Stella Larson was open, so Sandra swerved inside.

A saleswoman with a gold chain around her neck took one look at Sandra and turned to walk away. Sandra glanced down at herself. She was wearing a house dress, but it was ironed and clean. It was much newer looking than most of the clothes people wore these days.

There were no customers in the store except for a Chinese woman trying on a fur coat. Her husband was watching with an indulgent expression as she twirled, swinging the coat like a bell. Sandra straightened her posture and glided through the store, examining the clothes with barely disguised disapproval. It was offensive to charge such prices for garments with austere lines and boxy shoulder pads. The government had forced all kinds of rules on designers to save fabric—no pleats, pockets, or French cuffs—and it had made everything too spare and simple.

She circled around and was about to leave when she noticed, on a shelf, a black purse with a gold zipper running along the top. It was darling. She drew close to get a better look. Another salesclerk, a man this time, was standing behind the counter shifting through paper in a metal drawer. Sandra waited for him to acknowledge her. "Excuse me," she said. "I'm interested in that purse."

The man looked surprised. "Oh, you want to see it?" he said, taking the purse off the shelf and handing it to her. Instead of discussing it with her as he might have done with Beatrice, he went back to his receipts.

The purse was shaped like a seashell with a zipper set off by a row of rhinestones running along the frame. Sandra pulled the mouth open. A gold strap was coiled at the bottom of the bag. It was sleek and perfectly made. There was pointedly no price tag. If you had to ask, you couldn't afford it, Mabel always said.

Sandra wanted to buy the purse just to show the clerk that she was a person of quality who could afford an expensive item if she wanted it. "Excuse me," she said.

The clerk had stacked the receipts in neat piles on the counter and was stapling them with a small red stapler.

"Excuse me," she said, louder.

"Yes?" he said, drifting over. No, *ma'am. No, may I help you?*

"I'd like to hear more about this purse, please," she said.

The man looked at it, then at her, then listed off obvious facts in a bored tone. "It's silk. It has a gold zipper. The inside is also silk." He was young with heavy eyelids and curly black hair. She wondered why he wasn't fighting in the war.

"Is that all?" she said.

He studied his manicure. "It's part of our summer collection. It's for evening."

Sandra hated how he was talking to her. It reminded her
how, a long time ago, Imogen Beauregard had called her ridiculous. Even now, Sandra could picture the contempt on Imogen's
face when she said that word in the studio parking lot.

"Do you know who I am?" she said. "My name is Beatrice
Bartlett. I have a Charga-Plate with this store."

The young man blanched. "I'm sorry, I didn't know—"

"I was going to buy this purse, but now I will leave because
of your snide attitude." She set the purse in his hands and
marched toward the door.

Before she could reach it, the saleswoman who'd snubbed
her earlier slid in front of her. "Mrs. Bartlett, I'm sorry. We
didn't recognize you."

Sandra looked down her nose at the woman. Aside from the
gold chain around her neck, she showed no signs of wealth. She
was a glorified salesgirl, while Sandra was married to a prominent photographer and rubbed elbows with the elite.

"If this is how you treat your customers, I don't care to shop
here," she said.

"Please, ma'am. Brandon's new."

The clerk behind the counter looked aghast, and Sandra felt
a twinge of satisfaction.

"All right," she said. "Just remember, we're all Americans,
young man. We all deserve respect. Be more gracious next time."

She reached to open the door, but the woman laid a hand
on her arm. "Let us make it up to you. Brandon, get Mrs. Bartlett some champagne. Please, won't you stay?"

In this way, Sandra found herself in a private room drinking champagne and trying on Stella Larson's summer line. She
found that the austere fashions didn't look so bad on. As the
saleswoman said, Sandra had the figure for them. She agreed
that the diagonal-cut dresses made Sandra "look like a dream."

It was tempting to buy something, but she wouldn't actually charge anything in Beatrice's name and she had only enough money for a bag of sugar. So after several glasses of champagne—something she hadn't had since the war started—she told the salesgirl, "Nothing feels right today," and smiled sweetly at her shocked face. "I'll be back," she said in a singsong voice, sauntering onto the sidewalk.

In front of the store, a man with a large nose was holding a megaphone and yelling about the war effort. His eyes locked on Sandra. "Women are needed for the war effort. We need weapons manufacturers, drivers, cooks, typists, and clerks."

All Sandra's troubles came rushing back to her: the lack of money, fights with Frederick, the stupid cake she had to bake. She shot the man a look and hurried away. As she rounded the block, she heard him say, "I see you, lady. If you have time to shop, you have time to mop."

Sandra fought through a horde of people and got onto the first bus she saw. The poster in front of her seat had a woman with red hair clasping a letter to her chest. Below her, it said, LONGING WON'T BRING HIM BACK SOONER. GET A WAR JOB.

The bus was heading toward the beach and Sandra decided to take a walk by the ocean before figuring out what to do about the cake. It would be nice to see the water, and it was free, so she didn't even have to feel guilty about it. The crashing waves always made her feel like she was being pushed back together.

She got off by the zoo and walked the block toward the water. A light sprinkling of mist hit her arms, and she wished she'd brought a coat. When she reached the ocean, she discovered there was no way to get to the beach. The whole expanse of coastline was strung with fencing and covered with green fabric. A sign said, NO CIVILIAN ENTRANCE. She could hear the waves on the other side of the fence. When she pressed her eye to a dime-sized hole in the fabric, she saw that the hills along the coast were covered with camouflage.

Back at the bus stop, the schedule said Sandra had a forty-five-minute wait. The champagne had worn off and she felt heavy and dry. Tucking her hands under her armpits, she bent forward on the bench, thinking that this was how life would be from now on. No fun. No pleasure. Not even the smallest bit of joy was allowed to her, even if it was free.

CHAPTER 37

Mabel and John Hollingsworth were driving in a wagon to pick up the spiral staircase that had been delivered to the post office. It had taken six months for it to arrive from New York. It was supposed to be gold plated, like a gilded spiral in the heart of the house. Mabel was so impatient to see it, she was having trouble listening to John, who was telling her about the many jobs he'd had. In addition to carpentry, he'd been a seal trapper in Canada, logged redwood trees in Northern California, and shoveled coal in a steam engine in exchange for low wages and free travel. He'd even tried farming ostriches, although the venture was short-lived. "Ostriches are the meanest critters out there," he said. "Their necks remind me of snakes."

"Why did you want to farm a creature you didn't like?" she said.

He gave her a lingering look. "I enjoy a challenge."

Mabel averted her eyes, wishing he'd hurry up and get to the post office before people saw her riding alone with him in his wagon. If the staircase didn't meet her expectations, they'd have to halt construction until another could be found. She jiggled her leg, then caught herself and held still.

"Looking forward to seeing the staircase?" John said.

She hesitated, but could see no reason not to admit her feelings. "I am eager to see it, yes."

"Then let's speed things up." John flicked the reins, bringing the horse to a trot so that Mabel had to slap her hand on her head to keep her hat from flying off. The wagon, which was no more than a flat rectangle with seats, creaked and thumped in protest. John, who was jolting like a marionette, looked at her and laughed. As the trees rushed by and the wind blew at her face, Mabel found herself laughing too. For a moment, she felt like she used to when she would escape out the window as a girl—young and utterly without restraint. It had been her downfall, but it was also the only time in her life that she'd felt free.

The post office had arches that looked like hooded eyes. It was one of the busiest places in town, so Mabel had John park on the side, out of sight, and waited in the wagon while he spoke with the postmaster. She knew how ostentatious the townspeople thought she was. "Fancy" they called her. Arthur Beard's "fancy" wife. Not like Rebekah, the long-suffering first wife who'd helped Arthur build his business and then died just as it was starting to do well. "Poor Rebekah," everyone called her, who'd been cheated out of the success of her labor by dying young.

Well, they would soon see that Mabel knew what was best for Arthur. Throughout the country, industrialists and lumber barons were building mansions as a way of establishing themselves at the top of their professions. When John was finished, her house would be among the greatest homes in California, and that would do more for Arthur's reputation than anything Poor Rebekah had done.

"The staircase is behind the post office," John said when he returned. "They didn't know where else to put it. You have to sign for it."

Mabel took John's hand and dismounted. Inside the post office, the line for the clerk stretched across the room. Mabel recognized faces from the Fruit Growers' Guild as she passed through. Outside, her staircase was waiting in two wooden crates the size of bank safes.

"Shall I load them in the wagon?" John said, presenting her with papers to sign.

Mabel mentally stacked the crates, trying to imagine the staircase. The gilded railing was said to revolve around the stairs like vines. She couldn't wait another moment to see it.

"Perhaps we should look in the crates now," she said. "What if we get them home and the staircase isn't acceptable?"

The dimple appeared on John's cheek and Mabel knew he wanted to open the crates as much as she did. He waved at the postmaster. "Do you have a crowbar? We need to inspect the contents."

After some argument, a crowbar was fetched, nails removed, and the front of one crate taken off. There, shining in the box, was the lower half of the staircase, twisting like the entrance to another world. Clusters of grapes gleamed in the dark recesses of the box. It was beautiful, like something a god might own.

"Are you satisfied, Mrs. Beard?" John said.

Mabel ran her finger along the smooth metal. "Yes. Pack it up. It'll do fine."

She turned to see a crowd of people in the doorway, gaping at the crates. Two women from the Fruit Growers' Guild, who'd been friends with Rebekah, stared at the golden staircase, their mouths pulled into disapproving puckers. Mabel tilted up her chin and nodded to them as she passed, thinking that she should have waited and opened the crates at home.

She stood by the post office door until John brought the wagon around. The crates were loaded on the back and tied with ropes. Mabel climbed in, ignoring the passersby who looked curiously at them as they pulled away.

A week later, Mabel was walking up the driveway toward the house, carrying the newspaper. The orchard was in bloom and bees were darting so fast between the rows that she thought they might fly into her. As the house came into view, she stopped walking. The farmhouse had disappeared. In its place was the skeleton of the mansion that would replace it, with plywood instead of siding and holes instead of glass. It already looked far grander than any house in Healdsburg.

She found herself almost skipping as she continued past the orchards. Then she noticed a curious sight: John sitting on a kitchen chair in the middle of a row of trees, drawing on a notepad, hair hanging boyishly in his eyes. Mabel veered toward him.

"What are you doing, John?"

At some point, Mabel had started using his first name. It felt so natural, she often had to remind herself not to do it in front of the workers. Or Arthur.

"Getting inspiration for your mural," he said, thrusting out the drawing. On the page, the house—or what the house would look like when it was finished—was surrounded by so many plum trees, they stretched all the way to Fitch Mountain.

"That's excellent," Mabel said, grasping the notepad and pulling it close. John chuckled and she looked down at him. For a moment there was nothing but the sound of bees, the smell of the flowers, and his face. She cleared her throat. "This is perfect for the dining room. When can you start on it?"

John stood up and gestured to the chair. "I already primed the wall. Have a seat. I'll finish up and show you where it'll be."

Obediently, Mabel sat down and opened the newspaper, but she couldn't concentrate in her excitement. Last week, the staircase was installed. Next week, the master bedroom would be finished. It was all coming together: mural, crystal sconces, stained glass, high ceilings, and dozens of windows. She would soon be living in a box of light.

However, it also meant something else. When the construction ended, John would leave.

Mabel looked at him, bent over his drawing, and noticed how the skin on his arm was dusted with golden freckles. Jerking her eyes away, she directed her attention to the newspaper. She must not think about such things.

For several moments, there was silence. Then Mabel gasped.

"What's wrong?" John said.

She stood up. "I must talk to Arthur right away."

She marched to the orchards where Arthur was working with her head tipped back as if to hold the frown from falling off her face. He saw her coming and leaned against a wagon.

"This is pleasant surprise," he said. "You haven't visited me out here for a long time."

Mabel averted her eyes. "Wipe your forehead, will you please? You're dripping with sweat."

Arthur fumbled in his pocket for a handkerchief, which had dots of blood on it. She could see the scabs nestled in the wiry hairs under his chin. It looked like a bird that had plucked its feathers.

Her finger came down in a jab, like she was stabbing the paper with a knife. "Look at the lies the newspaper is printing about us."

The Healdsburg Tribune

APRIL 7, 1904

The Daily Tattle

Item: The Tattle muses about the spectacle on Gulch Road owned by venerable prune farmer Arthur Beard. The house has been torn apart and is being fashioned into a mansion headed by the new builder John Hollingsworth. Witnesses saw Mr. Hollingsworth pick up a solid gold staircase in the post office. In a time when many farmers are struggling, it's remarkable that Mr. Beard can fund this extravagance, which is said to be close to the heart of his wife, young Mabel Beard née Sanborn. Or is she young? But one should never question a lady on her age.

Arthur folded the newspaper. "Well, that wasn't very nice of them."

"Not nice? Arthur, it's outrageous. You have to make them stop writing about us."

"I don't think the newspaper would listen to me, honey."

"But they're lying about us. The staircase isn't solid gold, for heaven's sake. And it implies I'm misrepresenting my age."

Arthur was scrutinizing her face, and she regretted the bright sunlight, which would show the lines around her eyes.

"They tend to say things like that when a woman hasn't had a baby yet," he said. "If you want to stop tongues from wagging, we could start our family."

Mabel glanced to the side, toward the wagon. It had been her intention to have a baby as soon as possible after the marriage, but that was before John Hollingsworth and the mansion.

"We will when the house is finished," she said. "I can't have a baby on a construction site."

With a shrug, Arthur handed her the newspaper. "Then there isn't much we can do about the gossip, other than finish up the house."

Mabel couldn't believe Arthur's reaction. He wasn't outraged at all. He should defend her honor, or at least complain to the newspaper for her.

Weak. She'd married a weak man.

His fingers went to his face, touching the hairs again. Swiftly Mabel yanked his hand down and gave it a little slap. Arthur stared, shocked.

"I'll take it up with the builder," she said, turning to leave.

She marched underneath the orchard limbs, the skirt of her dress fluttering as she went, the newspaper crushed in a small, tight ball. At the front of the house, she sat on a pallet of lumber under a pepper tree, thinking about the gray hair she'd found recently. If people knew about her real age, perhaps they would find out other things too, like her parents disowning her, or Jared abandoning her, or what she'd had done to survive until she met Arthur.

But Arthur was right about one thing: Everything would be better once the house was done. People would see her good intentions, and even if they didn't, it wouldn't matter. A nice house was a fortress. No one could penetrate a cocoon of wealth. It was a barrier between the inhabitants and the world.

"What's this? A frown?"

John was standing there in the dappled light.

Mabel's pulse quickened to see him. Without a word, she handed him the newspaper.

He smoothed it out, read, and sat down beside her.

"Unbelievable," he said, "That *you* could be anything other than young."

Mabel smiled. He always knew the right thing to say. But he was too much like Jared, too inclined to drift on charm. Back then, she'd been a foolish child who'd thrown away all her security and wealth before she understood what she had. She must learn from her past mistakes. No matter what, Mabel couldn't risk her marriage to Arthur. She could never go back to the life she'd had before she met him.

"What did Arthur say about the article?" John said.

"He says to hurry up the construction so the gossip will stop."

"I see."

On the road, a carriage slowed and someone hung out of the window to gawk at her house. Was he looking through binoculars? It was hard for Mabel to tell from this distance. After a moment, he shook the reigns and the horses sped up, taking the carriage away.

"It appears people are curious," John said. "That's the second person I've seen gawking at the house today."

Mabel sighed. "The problem is that people don't have any imagination. When the house is finished, they'll understand what we're trying to do. If only there was some way to hide it until then."

John smiled at her. "Let me think on it," he said. "I may know a way for us to do just that."

CHAPTER 38

Like the parting of the clouds, Beatrice sent a note inviting Sandra to tea, along with Eva and Judith. "Just us girls for an intimate get-together," it said. Standing in her kitchen, Sandra hugged the note to her chest. She was invited back! They had invited her back.

She put on her most expensive day dress and rode the cable car to the Bartlett's house, a yellow Victorian near the marina. She was shown into the sunroom where Judith and Eva were already sitting with Beatrice. As soon as Sandra sat down, she learned that Judith's nephew had been torpedoed over the Pacific Ocean and was given up for dead.

Judith pulled a frame with a photo of the boy from her purse. Sandra recognized him from Kermit and Judith's anniversary party at the Conservatory of Flowers. He was the young man whose cheeks Judith had pinched.

"I'm sorry," Sandra said. "That's awful."

Judith stroked the photo tenderly. Instead of putting it back in her purse, she set it on the table, as if inviting the dead man to tea. Sandra found it hard to meet his eyes. He looked even more of a boy than she remembered, with the beginning of a mustache on his lip.

"You're so fortunate, Sandra," Beatrice said. "You're the only person I know who's untouched by the war."

Sandra chuckled wryly. "I don't know about that. Frederick is volunteering with Kaiser Shipyard. All that manual labor is touching our lives, believe me." It was meant as a joke, but the other women didn't laugh.

"That's hardly the same as having someone you love fight over there," Judith said.

She took a sip of the tea. "Of course not. I guess I am lucky."

"How is Frederick?" Eva said. "It has been awhile since I've seen him."

"He's well, thank you."

Judith cleared her throat. "I haven't seen his name in 'Women's World' lately."

Suddenly, Sandra knew for sure that they hadn't snubbed her because Frederick was German. It was because he wasn't working for the newspaper anymore. She decided it was best to act like there was nothing to hide. "For now, he's not photographing for 'Women's World,'" she said. "He doesn't have the time, what with the war."

The three women exchanged glances. "I was under the impression he was planning to photograph my victory garden," Judith said.

"And the scrap drive," Beatrice said. "Didn't you say he would photograph it, Sandra?"

It dawned on Sandra that maybe Beatrice wasn't really her friend. Maybe she'd just been using Sandra's connection as the wife of the society page photographer. It was all to get in the newspaper.

"I don't think I said that, no," she said. "I mean, I'm certain that if Frederick were doing the column, he'd photograph your projects, but he has to make boats for the navy. We all have to make sacrifices, you know."

There was a hush and Sandra felt her cheeks get warm. It felt cheap to bring up sacrifices with Judith's dead nephew staring at her from the picture frame. Instead of saying she would ask Frederick to photograph them, she should have implied that they might be able to get in the paper if they were nice to her.

"Frederick has a lovely accent," Eva said. "Where did you say he was from again?"

"Austria."

"Oh, Austria. That's a beautiful country," Eva said and then looked as if everyone had chastised her. "I mean, before the war."

Judith offered Sandra a cigarette from her tortoiseshell case. "But wait, doesn't Hitler come from Austria?"

"That's right," Eva said. "Hitler was born in Austria, wasn't he?"

Sandra put one elbow on the back of her seat and squeezed the cigarette between her fingers. "I doubt that."

"No, I'm certain that's correct," Judith said. "Austria was the first country to go over to Germany. It's right on the border, you know. They're practically the same."

"Italy is on France's border and you can't say they're the same," Beatrice said in a shocked—or was it theatrical?—tone. "My goodness, Judith; Sandra and Frederick are two of the most patriotic people I know."

"Of course they are. I didn't mean to imply otherwise." Judith put her hand on Sandra's arm. The ring on her finger had a round ruby surrounded by pearls. It looked like something Marie Antoinette would wear. "I hope you didn't think that."

"Of course not," Sandra said.

For the rest of the meal, she barely spoke. The women talked about how to have a war party at minimal cost and how to convert an old coat to a bathrobe—even the wealthy were practicing frugality these days. Sandra held her eyes open, willing the tears not to fall, but the roses on her teacup got blurrier and blurrier. When she glanced up, the eyes of Judith's dead nephew were peering from the frame as if asking what was wrong. A big tear rolled down her face and she excused herself to go to the restroom.

As soon as Sandra shut the door, she burst into sobs. To muffle the sound, she put one of Beatrice's washcloths to her face, but it was so thick it made her cry harder.

I'm being silly, she thought. *Everything is all right. I'm probably misunderstanding things.*

It was possible they'd asked her those questions because they wanted to get to know her better. Sandra never gave people the benefit of the doubt; that was her problem. It was Mabel's fault for teaching her that people were gossiping all the time and would lie to her. No wonder she was so distrustful.

Breathing deeply, Sandra reapplied powder and returned to the table where the women looked at her with concerned eyes.

"Are you feeling all right?" Beatrice said.

Sandra snapped her napkin and placed it in her lap. Who were they to eavesdrop on her private moment in the bathroom? "I'm fine," she said. "Don't let me interrupt."

The women communicated something with their eyes that excluded Sandra. Soon they were saying goodbye and Sandra was free to go.

In Beatrice's drawing room, she stood before the mirror over the fireplace, pinning on her hat. Her face showed no sign that she'd been upset. Thank goodness she wasn't one of those girls who got puffy when she cried.

Beatrice came up behind her, the column of her neck emerging from a boatneck black dress. "Don't worry about Judith, darling. That's just her way."

"It's her way to infer people are Nazis?"

Beatrice shook her head. "That was wrong of her. You have to understand, her nephew just passed away. I think she's looking for someone to take it out on."

There was an intimacy in Beatrice's tone that Sandra had never heard before. Apparently, while Sandra had been wandering around town for cake ingredients, Beatrice and Judith had gotten chummy.

Beatrice leaned against the back of the sofa, her ankles crossed, and watched Sandra in the mirror. "Frederick's a good man," she said. "It's funny, though. I swear his accent is German."

"No, you're wrong. He's Austrian. What's more, an officer came to our house to interview us and said that Frederick is a good citizen."

"Really? He was interviewed?" Beatrice said the word *interview* as if it were something dirty, and Sandra saw her mistake. Being interviewed looked bad, not good. She wanted to say that Beatrice didn't understand the full story. It wasn't that she wanted to lie about Frederick being German. She hardly ever lied, but she had to protect her husband.

"It's a matter of common protocol," she said. "They check all immigrants. I'm leaving."

Beatrice took a step toward her. "Wait. I don't want you to leave like this."

"Then stop implying Frederick is doing something wrong!" Sandra said. Her voice echoed through Beatrice's robin's-egg-colored drawing room and faded away. On the street there was the sound of a muffled car horn.

Beatrice looked down at her shoes. "I apologize. It's only that people were wondering about Frederick and your promises about the society column."

"Who? Judith?"

"And others."

Sandra didn't know who these "others" could be, unless it was Eva. Or the society women she'd met at Judith's house. "So you've been gossiping about me," she said.

"No, not at all. Judith was expecting the publicity for her garden, and so was I, for the scrap drive. It brought some issues into question, that's all."

It was out at last. They were using her to get into the "Women's World." All the shopping and parties and phone calls had been for Frederick, not Sandra. Mama was right. People were liars and backstabbers.

"I find this preoccupation with being photographed very self-serving," she said. "What's more, if you want to help with war effort, the first thing you should do is live less lavishly."

Beatrice raised an eyebrow. "Perhaps. But it's much easier to live lavishly if you don't have debts all over town."

Despite the blinding anger this brought up in Sandra, another thought occurred to her: Beatrice had been there when she paid for all those things on tab and was the only person who could guess the extent of her debts. She knew Sandra was lying about the bills, just as she knew Sandra was lying about Frederick being from Austria. What else did Beatrice know? Sandra thought of all the times she'd talked about Hollywood, knowing Katharine Hepburn and so forth.

"I can see you're angry," Beatrice said. "Let me have Bradford drive you home."

This meant Beatrice now had a chauffeur. Sandra straightened her shoulders with all the dignity her mother had taught her. "No, thanks. I'll take the cable car. It'll save fuel for the war effort."

She started toward the door, but before she reached it, Beatrice said, "By the way, Stella Larson called and told me that someone was pretending to be me at their store. This person had several glasses of champagne without buying anything."

Sandra looked down her nose at Beatrice, thinking how much she despised her. "How unfortunate."

"The funny thing is, the woman was a redhead. You wouldn't know anything about that, would you?"

Sandra laughed. "Me? That's absurd. Why would I pretend to be some gold-digging secretary who likes to put on airs? I have better things to do with my time."

Beatrice swallowed hard. With this parting shot, Sandra marched out into the street and toward the bus stop.

At home, Sandra drank some of Frederick's bourbon and listened to jazz records. The last insult to Beatrice had felt good at the time, but now she regretted it. It had been the death toll of her society career. Those women would never speak to her again.

Worse, what if Beatrice told Frederick about all her purchases made on credit? Sandra squeezed the bourbon glass until the tips of her fingers turned white. That must never, ever happen. She would have to keep Beatrice away from Frederick to make sure that it didn't.

Outside it grew darker but she didn't turn on the light. By the time Frederick came home from the shipyard, Sandra was sitting in the dark. He flipped on the lamp and looked at her on the sofa. "What's wrong now?" he said.

She scowled. No wonder they got in so many fights.

He took off his shoes and stretched out on the sofa so that his feet in their black socks were almost touching Sandra's leg. His body was lean and muscular from all the physical labor, the only thing she liked about his working at the shipyard.

She told him about Beatrice. "Why didn't you tell me Hitler came from Austria?" she said.

"He did?"

"Yes. Apparently, everyone knows that."

"I didn't."

"Couldn't you have said you were from Switzerland or something? I was so humiliated."

Frederick laughed. "My god, *schatzi*. The things you say. Do I look Swiss to you?"

There he went, going on about his superior European education again. Who cared what the Swiss looked like? That wasn't the point.

"Don't laugh at me, Frederick."

He patted her back. "I'm sorry, darling. They were cruel to you."

Sandra wasn't expecting this. It was unusual for him to be sympathetic. "They were," she said.

His two fingers rubbed the spine of her neck in little circles, and she bent forward so that it was easier for him to reach. "Which is why," he said, "we need to leave this city and get a house in the country."

For the first time, Sandra let herself consider that Frederick might be right. A big, beautiful house would show those society women that they were wrong about her. And, given how much their home had appreciated, she would finally have the money to make up for her mistakes.

"Okay," Sandra said. "You've worn me down. Let's start looking."

CHAPTER 39

There was scuffling above Arthur's head. The workmen were on the roof and it wasn't even seven o'clock. Sun was drifting through the windows that flanked the room, indicating it would be a warm day. Arthur, sitting across from Mabel at breakfast, glanced at the mural covering the wall. It was a painting of his house—or what his house was becoming—in the middle of a flowering orchard so big, it spanned all of Healdsburg.

Arthur was already looking at a debt that would take fifteen years to pay off, and Mabel showed no signs of slowing down. He had to tell her it was too much, but he was afraid of seeing the smile drop off Mabel's face. Her smile had become a way to measure how much she esteemed him, and she so rarely esteemed him. She was always urging him to sit properly, speak better, and to stop picking his beard. Just when Arthur thought he couldn't take it anymore, there was her smile, lifting her face and brightening her eyes, and he would forgive her anything.

The smile was there this morning. Mabel, in a diaphanous

yellow morning gown, was full of bubbling energy. It was a welcome change from the gloom that had surrounded her since the newspaper article.

Arthur cleared his throat. "My dear, I wanted to talk to you about the house."

"I want to talk to you about it too. I was going to ask you about converting the attic into servants' quarters. All the best families have the servants living upstairs."

Now Mabel wanted servants. Plural. Arthur didn't know anyone in the entire county who had more than occasional part-time help in the home. He picked a hair on his chin, then remembered she hated it and stopped.

"Well now, I don't know about that," he said. "I was doing the figures on the house and, perhaps you don't realize it, but the construction is getting expensive. For example, that staircase you bought came all the way from New York."

There it was, the smile fading, the mouth sagging at the corners. "You don't like the staircase, do you?"

"It's not that," Arthur said, although he didn't. "I don't think you understand how big this renovation is. There isn't any—" he paused, unable to say the word "budget."

Someone started hammering on the roof, the noise like a drumbeat echoing through the room. The crystals on the chandelier rattled.

Mabel began arranging the sleeves of her gown. "I thought you wanted me to be comfortable here."

"I do. Of course I do."

"Then you must trust me when I say the house will be worth it. After all, you married me for my refined taste."

Arthur's mouth dropped open. "That's not why I married you. I'd just be happy if we started a family."

As soon as the words left his mouth, he regretted them.

Mabel looked stricken, as if he'd insulted her womanhood. To make matters worse, the hammering started again and Arthur could only watch helplessly as moisture gathered in Mabel's eyes and threatened to overflow.

When the hammering stopped, she spoke in an uncharacteristically meek voice. "But I'm doing the construction for you, Arthur. I wanted to give you a showpiece to demonstrate what a great man you've become."

"I didn't know that," he said, surprised and flattered. "I didn't know you were doing it for me, honey."

"Well, I am. And after all the work I've done, all that planning and inconvenience, you're going back on your promise that I can do anything I want to the house."

The tears that had been gathering in Mabel's eyes spilled over and ran down her nose. It made her seem as delicate as a finch to Arthur. Before he knew what was happening, he was kneeling by the chair, promising that she could do whatever she wanted to the house. After many, many words, she let him stroke her slender shoulders in the yellow morning gown.

"And you promise you'll let me continue as planned?" she said.

"Yes, if it means that much to you. Your happiness is worth every penny."

As the words left his mouth, Mabel's face turned purple. Arthur's first thought was that she was ill, but then he saw that his hand was purple, and so was the chair. On the mural, every tiny tree was blossoming with purple flowers.

Behind him, a sheath of violet was covering the windows. It was as if a massive flower petal had descended over the house. Standing, he walked toward it, unable to understand what he was looking at.

"Good, it's up," Mabel said. "It's a curtain to cover the house during construction."

Arthur could hardly believe what she was saying. "Why would you want that?"

"For the element of surprise, of course. Our idea is that the neighbors will remember the house one way, and when we take the curtain down, it'll be completely different. Then we'll have a grand unveiling and invite everyone in town."

By "our idea," Arthur knew it meant Mabel and John Hollingsworth. "Our" never meant Mabel and Arthur.

He pressed against the window, trying to grasp what was happening. Scaffolding had been put in front of the house so that people could pass underneath. The curtain extended from the roof, over the scaffold, and to the ground, like a tent.

"But in the meantime, we'll have to live with a drape over the house," he said. "And construction takes months."

"Don't be so dramatic, Arthur. It's only over the front, not the whole thing. And it puts us in control of the gossip. If the newspaper wants to write about my house, they can write about it at the unveiling. I'm going to get dressed." With that, Mabel left the room.

He walked outside to see the curtain himself. On the roof, workers were positioning another enormous roll of cloth to fall over the remaining uncovered section. John Hollingsworth was shouting to his crew. "Use lots of nails, boys. We don't want it coming loose."

Arthur walked down the driveway and gazed at his farmhouse of thirty-five years, now flanked by a wooden scaffold and half obscured by a purple drape.

The construction had gotten out of control, yet stopping it meant going back on a promise he'd made to Mabel twice now.

And she said she was doing it for him, to prove what a great man he was.

The workers pushed the roll of fabric off the roof and it fell to the ground, unrolling and flapping so that the front of the house was completely covered with the curtain. Abstractly, Arthur lifted his hand to fiddle with a hair under his chin.

CHAPTER 40

Sandra was sitting at the kitchen table reading a romance novel and nursing menstrual cramps when Frederick burst into the house, grinning. Guiltily, she pulled the novel into her lap. "What are you doing home?" she said. He was supposed to be photographing a wedding.

Frederick put his hands on his hips, reminding her, absurdly, of an elf. "We are going for a drive."

"A drive," she repeated. She couldn't remember the last time she crossed the bridge going away from San Francisco.

He gestured for her to follow him outside. "Come on, come on."

"Frederick, I'm not dressed. Are we going somewhere nice?"

"No, you're fine. Let's go."

"I'm not fine. I'm wearing a housecoat. Don't you even look at me anymore?"

"Hurry up and change. I'll wait."

Sandra heaved herself up, got dressed, and met him at the car. They drove across the bridge and out of the city, where the fog that hovered like an umbrella over San Francisco suddenly lifted, revealing a summertime sky. Frederick drove one handed, going much faster than the thirty-five-mile speed limit. Soon the Bay Area was flashing by in a blur of green plants and white buildings, the sky a constant bluebell overhead.

Frederick's good mood was infectious and Sandra found herself smiling as they drove along. She knew he was taking her to look at houses and decided it might be fun. She hadn't gone shopping in ages. They would buy a big, enviable house with an art studio and a barn or whatever Frederick wanted. Then he would quit the shipyard and go back to the society pages and she would have the time and mental clarity to devote herself to her art. They could still go to San Francisco on the weekends for culture. Maybe they would even start a family.

They drove past Oakland and out where the hills were dotted by one or two buildings. Ahead was a tunnel, decorated with cement squares like an Aztec tomb. As they plunged into it, Sandra found herself digging her heels into the floor, as if trying to brake the car. This was much farther out than she'd imagined. She didn't even know what was out this way.

When they came out the other side of the tunnel, she was confronted with brown hills. Behind them, there was no sign of the cities they'd just come through, only the dark throat of the tunnel.

"Where are we going?" she said.

"You'll see."

She sat back uneasily. There were orchards on both sides of the road now, and Sandra wished she didn't know that they were almond trees. Frederick took an exit and they were speeding through Walnut Creek, which had nothing but a few saloon-style buildings, and then down a country road.

"It smells out here," Sandra said.

"Ranching. Some of the best ranching in the state is out here, and so close to San Francisco too."

But this place wasn't close to the city at all. There were signs of poverty everywhere—broken fences engulfed by blackberry briars, sheds with tarps for walls, rusty automobiles sunk in ditches. Around the bend, Mt. Diablo appeared on the horizon, its center split into two ridges like a woman's bullet bra.

"Diablo," Frederick said. "That means 'devil' in Spanish."

She shuddered. The car turned up an unpaved road, the engine growling over potholes. Soon the windshield was covered with filth and Frederick had to use the wipers to see. Outside were more brown hills, dry as paper bags.

"Isn't it beautiful up here?" Frederick shouted over the engine.

"How much further?"

"It's right here."

Ahead, there was a compound of buildings. Frederick slowed the car to a crawl and pulled to the side of the road. "Here we are," he said.

Sandra looked around. They had stopped in front of nothing in particular; just more land and dilapidated buildings. Cicadas buzzed in the trees.

"Where?" she asked.

"The house I wanted to show you."

Nothing met her definition of a house. "Where?" she asked again.

"Sandra, turn your head to the right and look."

She obeyed. A brown house with trim the color of corroded copper sat on a small hill. In front of it was an animal pen where two black goats were chewing on weeds.

"Now don't jump to conclusions," Frederick said. "Look at it and tell me what you think."

"It's a rundown shack."

"It's not a shack. It's a shell. It's 1,600-square-feet and has a sound foundation. And look at all the buildings that come with it."

"I thought you were going to build me a house."

Frederick let out a noise of exasperation. "This is more cost-effective than that. The house comes with fifteen acres of land. You see that rise over there? All that comes with the house." He pointed to a crest of a hill and dragged his finger over to a walnut tree in the distance.

Sandra shrugged. "So what?"

"So," Frederick continued in a patient voice. "This is an opportunity to have a ranch. We can have cows, chickens, even horses—there are stables."

She shook her head. This was disappointing. Frederick seemed to understand her so well and then he did something like this.

"Let's go," she said.

There was silence.

"Won't you at least look at it? Come on, give it a chance. It'll grow on you."

Clearly this wasn't going to end until Sandra looked around with him, so she jerked open the door. When she stepped out of the car, a blast of wind hit her. She held down her flapping skirt and followed Frederick up the hill.

Around the walkway, there was a bigger barn with a cactus growing alongside it. A prickly pear was split open on the ground and covered with ants. Across the goat pens were more paper bag hills against a pale blue sky.

Frederick stood with his hands in his pocket, smiling. "Look at that view."

"How many barns does this place have?"

"Three. It comes with these barns, the stables, a tool shed, and an outhouse."

"An outhouse. How delightful."

"Don't worry, there's plumbing and electricity in the house,"

Frederick said, starting up the path again. "And running water. Let me show you the old water pump. It's charming."

"Water pumps are not charming," Sandra said. "I'm cold. Can we go now?"

Frederick stopped. "You should see the house."

"I don't want to see the house."

"The house is a bargain. The whole house—which is structurally sound by the way—plus the land and stables, all for the cost it takes to build a house on a half-acre somewhere else."

Sandra waved her hand. "That is your idea of a dream house? Take me home."

"You are home."

The wind blasted Sandra's hair as she stared at him. She expected one of his joking grins, but Frederick's face was serious. In fact, it was struggling to remain calm.

"Realizing what a deal this was," he went on. "I decided to jump on it before anyone else did. I signed the papers this morning."

Sandra's mouth dropped open. "You bought this place?"

"Yes, I have been shopping on the weekends and trust me, this was something to jump at."

"I thought you were photographing weddings on the weekends."

"Well, no," Frederick said, rubbing the back of his neck. "I have been house shopping, and this is the one, Sandra. I promise we can start over, like we agreed."

She felt light-headed. She'd been counting on the extra money from his wedding photographs to pay bills. He'd been lying about that. What money they had was spent on this house. He'd lied to her when they first met, and he'd never stopped. The lies just got bigger and bigger. "I cannot believe you," she said. "What kind of man does this to his wife?"

The wind blasted a puff of dust against the back of Frederick's trousers. Behind him, the black goat was rubbing its head against a branch.

"Don't do that," he said.

"If you loved me, you wouldn't want me to live in a hole."

"I do love you, but I've already put a down payment—"

"Get the money back!"

Frederick didn't like this. She saw it in his face, the way his jaw got hard. "A deal is a deal," he said in his stubborn voice. "I gave my word."

"What about your word to love, honor, and cherish *me*?"

"That's what I'm doing!"

"By moving us to a hole?"

"Sandra, how *stupid* can you be? This place will be—"

She began to cry, drowning him out. The goat stared at them. "What about our future child?" she said. "Do you want your daughter to live in a place with broken glass and rusty nails? She'll get tetanus living here!"

"—everything we talked about. Horses, art studios, land."

"We're going home this instant!" Sandra ran to the car, the door shutting out the rushing wind. Sniffing, she smoothed her hair as he slammed in beside her. The fight continued the whole way back to San Francisco, shifting at one point to how Frederick was driving too fast and that they were going to get a ticket if he didn't stay under the speed limit. He pulled over to the side of the freeway and told Sandra to drive if she knew so much. When she refused, he threatened to get out and physically put her in the driver's seat. She dared him to do it and he squealed onto the freeway and almost got them hit by a truck.

At home, they screamed at each other in the car until they grew concerned about the neighbors overhearing. Then they went inside and screamed in the bedroom.

"You have forced us into this," Frederick said at last, pointing at Sandra.

"I'm the one who spent all our money on a shack in the boondocks?"

"No, you're the one who spent all our money! Before I met you, I had a savings account. Now we have no savings and debt. You have ruined me."

Even in her rage, the comment made Sandra falter. "Me? I have only helped you." She thought of the humiliation she'd endured, trying to be friends with awful snobs like Beatrice and Judith for the sake of his career, and all that cooking and cleaning and gardening she'd done to make him happy.

"Helped me into an early grave, you mean," Frederick said. "You've ruined me with your furniture and art supplies and frivolous clothing. You don't clean up around here. Look at this mess! You are a useless wife to me."

Sandra stepped back. He was the useless one. He'd been manipulating her since the day they'd met. "Bastard," she said, spitting out the word at him.

It was a sensitive point for him, an insult designed to hurt, and it met its mark. Frederick's jaw was as tight as a strung rubber band. He went to the closet, and she thought he was getting a suitcase, but when he came back, he had an enormous cowboy hat on his head.

Sandra put both hands over her mouth. "You have lost your mind."

Frederick stepped closer to her. "Now listen to me: the way out of this mess is for me to sell this house and go live in the country where we can build something together."

"No. I refuse to go back to that kind of life. You're a bastard for making me." It made him flinch to hear the word, so she shouted it again, "Bastard, bastard, bastard."

He grabbed her arm. His grip was not hard, but it was commanding. "Now look here. You are my wife. You go where I say. You live where I live. So, you will move to that house and you will like it."

Sandra ripped her arm away. She thought about spitting in Frederick's face, but decided against it. Snatching the $110 Chinese vase off the bureau, she threw it on the floor. Frederick stepped forward as if to catch it, but it had already shattered into dust.

It was so satisfying that Sandra grabbed the porcelain blue jay off the nightstand and threw it on top of the vase. Then she threw other things, the lamp, her silver mirror, an empty perfume bottle, the water glass—things she regretted getting, things she was sick of, things she had been wanting to get rid of for a long time. She didn't even stop when Frederick left the house, slamming the door behind him.

CHAPTER 41

Frederick didn't come back that night. Sandra broke everything in the house that was bothering her and cried and listened to the radio and wondered if they were getting divorced. She didn't want to divorce Frederick, but she felt such rage whenever she thought of that house. Never, no matter how many times he said it, had she believed Frederick would become a cowboy. What kind of knucklehead wanted to be a cowboy?

It was awful to be the one who was left behind. For the first time Sandra understood how Billy must have felt when she left him all those years ago. Sometimes she wondered where he was now. Maybe Billy was still in Santa Rosa, right where she'd left him. When she got around to thinking about the actual paperwork for the divorce, she discovered he'd already filed, citing "abandonment" as the cause. She wondered, not for the first time, what would have happened if he had listened to her about his career. Staring at the boats drifting into the bay, Sandra eventually fell asleep curled up on the window seat.

The next thing Sandra knew, there was hammering outside. She sat up and looked out the window. A man in a fedora was pounding a for-sale sign into her front yard. Leaping to her feet, she threw open the door. "What are you doing? Stop that!"

The man tipped his hat. "Good morning, ma'am. I'm from Barton Insurance and Real Estate. I was informed that Mr. Bauer has put this house up for sale."

"No that's a mistake. We're not selling the house."

The man resumed swinging the hammer. "All I know is I have to put this sign up this morning. The real estate agent thinks it'll go fast."

The red words *for sale* jumped out from the sign like a warning. Sandra hurried down the steps and touched the man's arm. "Listen to me. You can't put this sign up. It's my yard and I'm ordering you to leave."

He glanced at a car parked behind him. Stepping over, the man reached through the open window to pull out a copy of a document. "Here's the letter of intent to sell the house. Mr. Bauer signed last week."

Sandra took the letter, feeling betrayed all over again. Not only had Frederick bought that house without asking her, he'd signed the papers to sell this one too. He'd done it all in secret, keeping it from her, his wife.

"I'll tell you what," the man said, taking back the letter. "Let me put the sign up now and I'll contact Mr. Bauer. If he changes his mind, I'll come back and take it down."

Across the street, the neighbor was pulling back the curtain. Sandra realized how bad this looked, standing outside in her robe and bare feet, arguing with this man.

"I know what he'll say," Sandra said. "But doesn't it matter what I have to say?"

He picked up the sign and pushed it into the hole he'd made in her grass. "You'll have to discuss that with your husband."

She went inside and slammed the door behind her. The rug

was littered with parts of the Italian glass bowl that used to sit on the mantel. Sandra averted her eyes and walked to Frederick's office, the one room in the house untouched by her violence. "I should have married a doctor," she muttered.

There had been that doctor at Beatrice's wedding, the one who showed her the billboard. Wally was the doctor's name. He'd liked her too. At the time Sandra thought he was fat and dull, but now it seemed that she'd been ignoring the possibilities there: the security, the money, the reputation. How stupid to dismiss him so thoughtlessly.

She sat in the chair and looked up at her painting that hung above Frederick's desk, one of the few she'd managed to finish. It was an arrangement of apples on a flat surface. Now Sandra could see how flawed it was—one apple appeared to be floating on the table. Yet Frederick was pleased when she gave it to him. "*Schatzi*, it's your best work yet," he'd said.

It hurt that he'd gone to such lengths to deceive her. Gone was the elegant man she'd married, replaced by a stranger in a cowboy hat. Sandra almost felt as if she'd made that version of Frederick up. He, who was supposed to help her, was forcing her to go backward in life. If she went to the country now, nothing would ever happen to her. She would end up like Mabel.

There was a knock at the door. She hurried to the window thinking it was the realtor, then backed into the gloom of the house with a gulp. It was definitely not the guy from the realtor's office. Why did she ever answer the door anymore?

The bill collector thumped again. "Mrs. Bauer, I saw you in the window."

Sandra held her breath, hoping that if she were quiet, he would go away.

"Mrs. Bauer," the man continued, raising his voice. "If you don't come out, I will disturb this entire neighborhood if I have to. I will tell your neighbors that you bought a vase from Mr. Lei and have been shirking payment for over a—"

Sandra jerked the door. "What do you want?" she said, looking over the man's head into the neighbor's window. It was empty.

"I'm here to collect the $62.50 you owe for the vase or repossess it for Mr. Lei."

The cold air snaked around Sandra and she became aware that she was wearing little more than a robe. She felt in her pockets. "Unfortunately, I don't have any money on me right now. If you could come back when my husband is home—"

"Too late for that," the man said. Swinging up his arm, he pushed her into the hallway and stepped into the house.

"Hey," Sandra said. "You have no right to come into my home."

He ignored her and walked into the house as though planning to get the vase himself. Then he stopped as he took in the broken debris on the floor. "What happened here?"

In addition to the Italian glass bowl, the sculpture of a man's head that once sat on the coffee table was split open on the fireplace bricks. When Sandra threw it, the top of the head had rolled onto the carpet and landed upside down, like the top of a watermelon.

But it wasn't the sculpture the man was looking for. He wanted the vase with the lotus flower on it. That was in the bedroom, also shattered on the floor.

"There was an earthquake," Sandra said, nudging the plaster with her toe so that it was off the rug. "Didn't you feel it?"

"An earthquake? No."

"Oh." She leaned against the arm of the sofa. "It got us pretty good."

The man held out his hand. "The vase."

Sandra took a cigarette out of her pocket and lit it, then

exhaled to show that she wasn't scared of him. "That's what I'm saying. The earthquake got that too."

"You mean the vase is like that?" he said, pointing at the shattered sculpture.

"Unfortunately. I'm waiting for the insurance man to see if I can get anything for it." This was a bluff. Even if there had been an earthquake, Sandra couldn't afford to insure all the things she'd broken.

"Let me see."

"Mister, I'm not comfortable with you coming into my bedroom when my husband isn't here."

The man stepped close to Sandra and closed his hand on a clump of her hair. She shrieked and tried to stab him with her cigarette, but he grabbed her arm with his other hand and held it in the air. He was strong, and she found she couldn't move. Tugging her hair, he pulled Sandra's head down so that her ear pressed against her shoulder, then pushed his face close to hers. The irises of his eyes were a shade off from black.

"I know about you," he said. "You owe money all over town. Mr. Lei is one person you're not going to shirk. He hired me to get what you owe him and I'm not leaving until I do."

Sandra's hair was pulled so taut that the roots felt like they were on fire. "Stop," she said. "Please. I don't have the money and the vase is broken."

Roughly, the man released her and she staggered away, her hand flying to her scalp. It was hot to the touch.

"Show me," he said.

She led him to the bedroom and waved her hand over the scene. The sheets were torn off the bed and the nightstand was overturned. Crumbs of glass and porcelain glinted in the weak daylight. About two feet in, the vase spread like snow beneath the wings of the porcelain blue jay.

The man bent over to touch the crumbs of porcelain. "This is what you do to an antique vase?"

Tears fell against Sandra's will. She wiped them away with the heel of her hand, thinking that she would never admit she was lying to the man. Never.

"I told you, it was an earthquake," she said.

The man stepped close to Sandra and her hands flew to her hair, but he didn't touch her. Instead, he held out his hand. "It will have to be the $62.50 then."

"I don't have the money," she said, and winced, afraid he would grab her again. When he didn't, she went hastily on. "The house—the house is for sale. You saw the sign, didn't you? It's to pay our debts. If Mr. Lei will be patient, I'll pay him as soon as it sells."

As Sandra stammered this out, something changed in the man's face. It was as if he found what she said to be reasonable.

"Okay," he said. "You get one more chance, Mrs. Bauer." His hand popped in front of her face and she flinched as he extended one finger. "But just one." Like a shadow retreating, he pulled back from her. "I'll show myself out."

Sandra listened to the man retreat down the hall and shut the front door. Whirling around, she ran after him and slid both bolts. Then she ran to the bedroom, stepping over the mess in her bare feet and yanking a dress over her head. She had one thought: she wanted out of this city and away from these crazy people. If she had to go to Frederick's cowboy house to do it, she would think about that part later.

Shoving her feet into heels, Sandra snatched her handbag and ran to her car, stopping only to lock the door in case the man came back. She drove down the street to Frederick's studio, where she knew he'd been all along.

Parking on the street, she sat in the car trying to get control of herself. It wasn't a good idea to go inside shaking and crying like this. Sniffling, she took a brush out of her handbag and ran it gently over her sore scalp, then pinned her hair back in place.

Inside, the shop was transformed. The photographs had been removed from the wall and were sitting in milk crates and boxes. Errol Flynn's reassuring smile was gone. The room echoed in its bareness, and something about it drove home to Sandra how serious Frederick was about his plan. He was moving, with or without her.

A light was glowing under the office door. He was sitting at his desk, studying a negative. Sandra put her hand on his back and he jumped, startled.

"So this is where you've been," she said, picking up an empty bourbon bottle and throwing it in the trash can.

"As you see."

"What are you working on?"

"The Griffin's anniversary."

Sandra bent over a picture of an older couple holding hands, their fingers wound together. They were at least fifteen years older than she and Frederick.

"They seem happy," she said softly.

"They've been married thirty years."

The contentment of the old couple shone in their eyes, and Sandra found herself in danger of crying again. She wanted to be like the Griffins. She did. She wanted to be married for thirty years and have anniversary portraits of her and Frederick holding hands. She wasn't sure how things had gone so wrong.

"A bill collector came by the house," she said. "He wasn't very nice to me."

Frederick glanced at her, his jaw going hard. "What was it for?"

Sandra tried to remember which bills Frederick knew about

and which ones he didn't, but it was hard to think. She had a headache from her sore scalp.

"The sofa," she said, naming something they'd picked out together. "We still haven't paid it off, you know."

Frederick shook his head. "We need to sell that house. I can't keep up with the bills. I'm working fourteen-hour days. It's too much."

He didn't say things like that often. She looked at the dark circles under his eyes. There were streaks of gray in his hair that weren't there a year ago.

"That's why I'm here," she said. "I've decided to go to the new house."

Frederick held out his arms and Sandra climbed into his lap and buried her face in his neck. She sobbed, remembering the creditor. Her scalp burned from where he'd pulled her hair.

"Shhh," Frederick said, rubbing her back. "It's over now. We'll go to the new house and start over."

Sandra began crying harder, realizing she'd agreed to move into a shack. How could Frederick have thought such a place would appeal to her?

"I know it isn't your dream house," he said, as if he were reading her thoughts. "I know you don't want to move to the country, but this way we can have everything: the house, land, a family of our own, independence. It will be everything we ever wanted."

But that wasn't everything Sandra wanted. It wasn't even close.

CHAPTER 42

The wind swept tendrils of hair into Mabel's eyes as she watched John's foreman paint rectangles onto the side of the house. Five paint cans were open at his feet, each as smooth and untouched as a pool. John said the house should have five different colors to be considered a "Painted Lady."

Mabel was so cold from the wind that she couldn't concentrate on which color went on the scrollwork and which on the balustrades. The purple dress she was wearing, the one with scalloped ruffles on the neck, felt like a sieve. She should have dressed more warmly, but it was hard to judge the weather with the curtain outside her bedroom window. It made everything so dark inside the house that Arthur had moved out of the master bedroom to sleep on the sun porch. He said it was the only way he could tell when to get up in the morning.

"I think this color combination is the best choice," John said. "What do you think?"

"Yes," Mabel said. "Let's go with that."

"You heard the lady," John said to the foreman. "We'll go with light green, dark green, purple, beige, and gold."

When the foreman was gone, John turned toward her, his blond hair falling over one eye, and saw that she was shivering. "Come on," he said. "I've got a solution to your problem." With that, he vanished around the corner.

Mabel hesitated. She could hear the workers hammering, a constant rhythm that had underscored more than a year of her life. After making sure no one was watching, she slipped around the front of the house after John.

The wind was worse here, whipping the trees and causing the curtain to ripple and snap. He was nowhere in sight. When Mabel called his name in a hoarse voice, he stuck his head out from behind the curtain and held up his arm, inviting her underneath. She hesitated. Arthur was inside, getting ready for a trip to San Jose to meet with distributors. When the wind blasted her again, she rushed under John's arm like a duckling under a mother's wing.

Mabel found herself in the space between the wall and the scaffolding. It was warm under here, the curtain having absorbed heat from the sun.

"Better?" John said.

"Much better," she said.

She was unable to speak as she looked up into his face. They'd never been alone like this before. Usually they were in public, either in the wagon or working on the house in front of the crew.

John reached out his hand and seemed about to touch Mabel's breasts. She stiffened, preparing to stop him, but he brushed her décolletage instead. The ruffle of her dress had blown inside out, laying against her exposed chest. With his big thumb, he put the ruffle back in place and trailed his fingers across her skin.

With an intake of breath, Mabel caught his hand. She didn't

know if she did it to stop him or to keep him where he was. Delicately, John kissed each knuckle of her fingers.

Then came Arthur's voice from somewhere behind her. "Mabel?"

She snatched her hand away and hid it behind her back, rotating around, but Arthur wasn't underneath the curtain with them. The voice had come from inside the house.

"You need to leave," she said, pushing John. "Go."

John let Mabel push him, stepping backward with his eyes on her. She was aware, even in her distress, of her fingers sinking into the muscles of his chest. Finally, he disappeared, and she was alone under the curtain.

"Mabel?" Arthur called again.

She made her way toward the kitchen, her footsteps reverberating as she moved deeper into the house. When she opened the door, Arthur was standing on the other side.

"There you are," he said.

Mabel put her hand on the ruffle, covering the section of skin where John had touched her. She waited for Arthur to call her a prostitute and throw her out of his house.

"Have you seen my shoeshine kit?" Arthur said. "I want to buff my loafers before I leave for the train."

She let out her breath. "It's in the linen cupboard. I'll go get it."

After Arthur left, Mabel ate a solitary supper in the dining room. Every time she thought of how close she and John had come to being caught, she felt light-headed with guilt and fear. Arthur didn't deserve this kind of treatment. He'd been nothing but kind to her—doting even. And if she did continue with John,

Arthur would be justified to cast her out like her parents had done, and she would have nothing then. John wouldn't take her on. He was too flighty. The day would come when he would leave, like Jared had, and she would be destitute, again. She must not, *must not*, allow that to happen.

The next day, Mabel skipped her usual morning meeting with John and ordered the carriage to take her downtown to pick out a new dress for the unveiling ceremony instead. When the newspaper wrote about her house, she planned to anonymously send clippings to Vira to show how wrong she'd been about Mabel never getting back what she'd lost. Then it would be up to her parents to decide whether or not to contact her.

As she left, John was climbing a ladder on the side of the house and gestured for Mabel to come to him, but she averted her eyes and went to the carriage. She didn't look out the window until she was downtown.

The next day, she avoided John again, leaving in the morning and staying away until the workers were gone. On the third day, the marble tile for the hallway was delivered. Despite her resolutions, Mabel wanted to open the tile boxes with John and went to look for him, but couldn't find him. When she asked the workers where he was, they told her John wasn't coming in that day and that they were supposed to start on the tile without him. They opened a box so Mabel could examine the stone, which was cream with silver flecks. It was pretty, but looking at it wasn't the same without John.

When John didn't come the next day, Mabel began to worry. His absence revealed what life would be like once the house was finished and he went away. It was a lonely feeling. Life without him would be dreary.

That evening, as the sun was setting, Mabel was brushing her hair at her dressing table. When the sun hit the curtain at this hour, it gave the room a purple glow that felt like being inside a lavender bubble. She tried not to think about the minutes alone with John underneath the curtain, but the memory of his lips on her fingers filled her mind anyway. Shutting her eyes, Mabel pressed her knuckle to her mouth.

Someone opened the front door of the house, and she turned toward the sound, wondering if Arthur had come back early from San Jose. When John's voice drifted from the hallway, calling her name, Mabel was filled with joy. She put down the brush and went to the door.

The setting sun was hitting the curtain and shining through the round window on the opposite wall. The effect was a spotlight of purple in the hallway. Mabel stepped into the light, her arms stretched on the railing, long hair streaming down her back.

John was holding a sheath of papers. "I'm sorry for bothering you," he said. "I brought you papers to sign for the tile."

She looked into her bedroom, at the glimmering candles on her dressing table. Arthur wouldn't be back until tomorrow. They were alone in the house.

"Let me get a pen," she said.

In some part of her mind, she heard him bounding upstairs behind her. When Mabel reached for the pen on the dressing table, she heard his voice, close, saying her name. She turned to see John in the bedroom doorway. He filled it up, his masculinity jarring against the fairy garden of her room. She knew she should tell him to leave, that she was married, and that Arthur was a kind man who deserved a faithful wife, but she was so weak when it came to John.

"Where have you been?" she said, her tone biting.

He shut the door and came so close, she couldn't breathe. "You were avoiding me. I thought you wanted me to go."

"You must go."

"I will. But first, I want to try something."

Then he kissed her. Mabel's heart was pumping all through her body, and as he folded her in his arms, she could feel his heart beating too. In the stillness of the room, she was aware of the papers slipping from his hands and falling softly to the floor.

PART III

CHAPTER 43

The loan office had a narrow window that came to a point at the top like something from a church. It let a slit of yellow light onto the red carpet, the only warmth in this granite-lined room. Sandra crossed her legs and noticed a thread sticking up from her stockings. She bent to see whether it was starting to run, then sat back in relief. It was only lint. This was her last pair of silk stockings. Once they went, she wouldn't get another until the silk shortage was rectified—assuming Frederick ever gave her money to buy stockings again.

Mr. Fox, the loan officer, came in and crossed his legs under the chair when he sat down. "All right, Mrs. Bauer. I've read through the plan for your art gallery."

Since moving to Walnut Creek, Sandra had begun painting in earnest. She'd finally found her subject: things she hated. She'd covered canvases with cowboys, paper bag hills, and the rose teacups. They were the most interesting paintings she'd ever done, and she felt they had promise.

The problem was that Frederick wouldn't give her money for art supplies and she was running out of essential things, like white paint. He said she needed to use what she had first, as if he could judge what she needed. Being an artist required money for canvases, brushes, and lots and lots of white paint.

So she'd developed a new plan to make her independent from Frederick's whims:

1. Open an art gallery in San Francisco.

2. Become an artist.

3. Move away from Walnut Creek for good.

"What did you think?" she said to the loan officer.

"I'm afraid I can't help you."

Sandra had expected this answer, so she launched into her speech. "Mr. Fox, with the world at war, we need art more than ever. All I need are the funds to open my gallery, and I'm certain there would be interest in my work. I would pay you back from proceeds of the sales."

With enough money, she could leave Walnut Creek and get an apartment in the city. Then Frederick could stay in the country and visit her whenever he wanted.

"First, you don't have any collateral," Mr. Fox said.

"There's the jewelry I brought with me."

"We don't accept jewelry. As to the deed on your house—" Mr. Fox pulled out the deed, which Sandra had filched from Frederick's papers.

"Yes," Sandra said. "The house is worth quite a bit. We've fixed it up."

"As to that, it's under your husband's name, so I'd have to do business with him."

"That's impossible. My husband is . . ." she hesitated, thinking the word *dead* would be going too far, "serving in the war.

I doubt he'll be home for months, maybe years. So you'll have to do business with me."

"Then on that point alone, we couldn't proceed. We'll only sign a woman if a male relative will cosign with her. Do you have a father or brother who could do that for you?"

Sandra crossed her arms. "No. My father has passed. But surely you can make an exception."

Primly, the man slid the business plan over to her. "No, I'm sorry, we can't. And even if we could, we don't cover this kind of investment."

She lifted her plan from the desk. What was she supposed to do, go to a loan shark?

"Do you know of any institutions that will loan to women?" she said.

"I'm afraid not. It's the law. A woman can't borrow money on her own. You could get a war job to help fund your endeavor. They're desperate for help."

Sandra tapped the papers on his desk so they were perfectly aligned. Everyone was always telling her to get a war job, as if that would improve her situation in the slightest. She tucked the business plan under her arm. "Good day, Mr. Fox."

Outside, San Francisco was sunny, but chilly. She stood in the alcove and lit a cigarette, then walked toward the bus stop for the long ride back to Walnut Creek.

Sandra had heard that it was difficult for a woman to get a business loan by herself, but she didn't know that it was illegal. Frederick would never cosign with her. He wouldn't give her so much as a nickel since finding out about her debts. It was true she'd been irresponsible, but he was the one who bought an entire ranch without telling her. As far as she was concerned, they were even.

The bus, at least, wasn't crowded. A woman in the back

stared at her and Sandra glanced down at her clothes but saw nothing out of the ordinary. Slumping in a seat, she watched the city flow past her window. She'd been counting on that loan. Every penny they had was tied up in the house, and Frederick wouldn't sell it, no matter how many times she brought it up. They were so broke that he still worked at the shipyard so they could pay bills. "You'll get used to living here," he kept saying. As if she could ever get used to that shack with the wind blowing through the buckeye trees and all those animals Frederick bought squawking and rutting outside.

"If only I had some money," she whispered to the window. "If I had some money, everything would be different."

A blimp was floating by the window, drifting along like a drunken bee. After two years of war, Sandra was used to seeing blimps, but out in the bay, not in the city itself. It was only slightly above traffic, shaped like a bullet and shining like a new dime. The basket where the pilot should sit appeared empty.

Sandra turned to watch the blimp. The other passengers had noticed it too and were gathering around the back window. It was heading toward a Victorian house that was slightly taller than the buildings around it. The roar of the bus engine was the only noise as the blimp floated toward the roof, giving off the eerie sense that the passengers were watching a scene from a silent movie.

All at once, people began shouting.

"Where are the drivers?"

"It's an attack."

"Stop the bus!"

There was a jolt and a screech, and the bus stopped so hard that Sandra had to put out her hand to keep from slamming into the seat in front of her. People screamed. The driver, distracted by the blimp, had hit a pickup truck.

Now passengers were rushing off the bus and hurrying toward the unmanned blimp. It had narrowly missed the Victorian and was nosing toward low-hanging electrical wires. Sandra put her hand to her mouth as the blimp brushed against the wires so that the metal casing made sparks fly onto the roofs below. There was a moment where it seemed like the buildings might catch fire, but then the sparks went out and the blimp drifted between two anemic redwood trees.

Sandra found she was alone on the bus, except for the woman who'd stared at her when she first got on. The woman was wearing factory overalls with her hair tucked in a kerchief. As Sandra met her eyes, she opened her mouth to speak, then shut it again. Sandra stood up and walked onto the street.

The bus had dented the truck's fender. Cars were honking and passengers were scattered around the sidewalk staring at the blimp, which had risen so high that it looked like a child's balloon in the sky.

She clomped down the street, away from the disaster. Three blocks later, there was a gas station with a payphone, and she dug in her purse for a nickel. It took several minutes for Frederick to come to the phone at the shipyard.

"What's the matter?" he said.

"I'm stranded in San Francisco. The bus broke down and I need you to come get me."

There was a moment of tense silence. "Are you shopping again?"

"With what? You won't give me any money."

"Then why are you in the city?"

Beside her, a car pulled up to the gas pump and the attendant began washing the windows. A mother ushered her children, dressed in matching blue coats, toward the restroom.

Sandra lowered her voice. "I wanted to get out of the house

for a while. I didn't think a ten-cent bus ride made any difference. I brought a sandwich for lunch."

"Well, I can't leave work every time you get stranded in
the city."

"I suppose I could get a hotel room . . ."

"No, you will not. It's three o'clock. I get off at five. You'll
have to wait until then for me to pick you up."

Even though Sandra knew Frederick was mad at her, the
fact that he didn't care enough to come get her stung. Ever since
he found out about the extent of her debts, he'd ceased to do
anything for her at all.

"I'll see if I can take another bus then," she said. "I'll call
you back if I'm still here at five."

"I look forward to it," he said and hung up.

Sandra felt in her pocket for a cigarette, but came up empty.
The mother marched the kids back to the car and they climbed
in the backseat. The father of the family was talking to the
attendant and Sandra had an urge to tell him about the blimp.
A minor disaster was happening three blocks away, and these
people had no idea.

Back by the bus, police cars were parked on the road and an
officer was directing traffic around the accident. The bus driver
was talking to a woman wearing a tacky hat with a bird trapped
in a net. It was the kind of unfashionable clothing Sandra saw
all the time in Walnut Creek. She tapped him on the shoulder.
"Excuse me," she said. The driver ignored her. Sandra stamped
her foot and reached into her purse for a cigarette, forgetting
that she was out. As she rifled through, she heard someone say,
"Sandra Sanborn?"

Sandra's head came up, alert. She hadn't heard that name
since before she was married. Warily, she turned to see the same
woman who'd been staring at her earlier.

"It's me," the woman said. "Casey. From Hollywood."

Like cards being shuffled into place, Casey emerged before her—her eyebrows, freckles, nose, and mouth. It was all there, but different. Heavier. Harder. But Casey, nevertheless.

"My word," Sandra said. "Casey!"

The next thing she knew, she was embracing the strange woman, and laughing. For it was Casey, twelve years older and thirty pounds heavier. There was her voice, there was her bad taste in fashion, there was her thin hair. She even wore the same drugstore brand of gardenia perfume.

"Are you going to Walnut Creek too?" Casey said.

"Yes, I live there."

"So do I!"

"No, you don't."

"I do. I own horses there."

Although Sandra was smiling, underneath she was panicking. She and Casey had ended up in the same place. That couldn't be true. She was not the same as Casey.

"But you're wearing factory clothes," she said.

"Yeah, I decided to earn some extra money. What about you? What were you doing in San Francisco?"

"Wasting time, I suppose."

The bus was rumbling to life. Sandra and Casey moved toward it with the rest of the passengers, talking excitedly.

"And what are you doing in Walnut Creek?" Casey said.

Sandra shrugged, embarrassed. "You won't believe it when I tell you who I married."

As she stepped on the stair, she looked one more time for the blimp, but it was no longer in sight. The pickup with its dented bumper pulled onto the road and joined the traffic moving in a steady stream around a bus. Its turn signal went on, and a moment later, it was gone.

CHAPTER 44

It was nine a.m., judging from the sun's placement in the sky. Frederick rolled out of the cot in the barn where he'd been sleeping and washed his face with the hose, running his fingers through his beard, which was an inch long now. It was starting to look like it had back in Hollywood, except that there were a few more gray hairs this time around.

This was a Saturday, meaning he was free to work on the ranch all weekend. He put on boots and his cowboy hat, whistling "Tumbling Tumbleweeds," and took a slug from the whiskey bottle sitting near the stall door.

The barn held the industrial refrigerator for when his ranch started yielding food. It was a race to see what would produce first: the cows, which were pregnant, or the young chickens, which were almost old enough to start laying. Frederick was betting on the chickens. When they got going, they would make six dozen eggs a week.

Frederick slid open the door and stepped outside, deliberating whether to patch the chicken coop or fix the bathroom sink. Sandra, of course, wanted him to fix the bathroom. "I can't even wash my face here," she'd wailed. It wasn't his fault that the sink was broken. He expected to quit the shipyard when he moved to the ranch and spend all his time fixing the house, but unexpected changes in their finances (her fault, *her* fault) hadn't allowed for that, yet.

The cows, Lotte and Thilde, were grazing, their bellies swollen with pregnancy. At the coop, the chickens ran over each other in excitement at the sight of him.

"Good morning, *damen*," he said, scooping feed into a tin can. Opening the top of the coop, he scattered the feed and watched the chickens rush at it. Then he dragged the hose over to fill the trough. The cows ambled up and put their lips to the water. There were so many things about cows that Frederick hadn't known before, like how their jaws moved from side to side when they chewed, or how they could wind their tongues around an apple and pull it into their mouths. It was remarkable. He liked being around them. The stillness of their bodies made him feel peaceful.

He decided to fix the coop. Let Sandra use the kitchen sink.

But first he must change his shirt, if he could find one in all the mess inside. Sandra had refused to unpack when they moved in, just left their things flowing out of boxes. She informed him there was no point in cleaning "a shack." She, the queen of the realm, was too good to live in such a place.

When he stepped inside, he heard Sandra talking. "The blimp crashed in Daly City. I saw it in the newspaper. It landed in the middle of the street."

Frederick crossed his arms and tapped his foot. She was on the telephone again. Last month's phone bill had been fifteen dollars. As much as he controlled their finances, she still found ways to spite him. It was as if she were determined to spend his money, no matter what.

He started toward the living room, resolving to remove the phone from her hand and hang it up himself. Then he heard another voice reply, "I wonder what happened to the pilots."

"No one knows. It's a mystery. The parachutes were still on board. Even a pilot's hat was inside."

In the living room, a dumpy woman was sitting beside Sandra on the sofa. Both of them were smoking, the ashtray overflowing with butts. A cloud of smoke hovered over the velvet low-back couch, which, along with the glass coffee table, looked out of place beside the plaster walls and scuffed floors. The rug was rolled in the corner and several unpacked boxes were shoved beside it. The only other furniture in the room was a credenza holding some of Sandra's glass paperweights, which she called "art pieces."

Sandra surprised him by smiling. "Frederick, you'll never guess who lives down the hill from us—Casey."

He knew from Sandra's expression that she expected him to remember who this was. Someone from Sandra's past, no doubt.

"Casey Roberts," Sandra said. "From Hollywood, remember? She's my oldest friend."

Frederick had a vague memory of the girl who'd gone on that double date with them, the one who'd ruined his chances with Sandra. The years hadn't been kind. The woman, who was not so pretty to begin with, was chubby now. There was a glint in her eyes, a skepticism that he recognized from their date.

"Hiya, Frederick," Casey said. "I see you've gone full cowboy at last."

Sandra tapped the cigarette on the ashtray. "He insists that now that we live in the country, he can grow a beard again. Isn't that right, dear?"

He nodded, trying not to show his anger. "If you say so."

Sandra smirked at Casey. "My husband's happy you're here."

"Isn't that nice?"

Frederick left without excusing himself and headed toward the bedroom, thinking that maybe a friendship was a good thing. It might make Sandra happier about living here. In any case, it would distract her from talking on the phone all day.

He walked through the house, taking in the mess. There was a hole in the wall that he had to fix. Wires were dangling in the corner, and he wasn't sure why. In the bedroom, his shirts were hanging on the four-poster bed. The only things in the closet were Sandra's ball gowns.

Frederick found a work shirt and put it on. Then he noticed a pile of mail on the bureau, with the phone bill on top. He opened it and stood flipping back and forth through the charges. "Sandra," he said in a sweet voice, "could you come here a moment?"

The conversation halted and he heard her coming down the hall. She had an impatient smile on her face. "What is it?" she said.

"How on earth did you run up a thirty-dollar phone bill?"

She raised one eyebrow, which was harsh against her white skin. "I beg your pardon?"

Frederick flapped the bill under her nose. "Thirty dollars. On phone calls! It's like you're determined to run our finances into the ground."

"Shhh. Casey will hear you."

He lowered his voice. "We could have a year's worth of telephone calls on what you charged in one month."

"Perhaps if I lived in San Francisco and could see my friends, I wouldn't need to call so often."

"What friends? You don't have any friends. Besides, you're calling internationally." Fredrick flipped through the bill. "This one is to England. Who do you know in England?"

"Not that it's your business, but I wanted to see how one goes about selling paintings in Europe. So I made a few phone calls."

"Instead of worrying about paintings, you should be cleaning the house." He picked up the sleeve of his shirt and jiggled it at her. "Look at this. I asked you to hang up the laundry and I come in to see it on the bedpost."

A smirk crossed Sandra's face, then she quickly composed it. "You didn't say where you wanted me to hang the laundry."

She was mocking him. Frederick twisted the bill in his hands, making a strangling motion. "What kind of woman are you? You never cook, you never clean, the bedroom is a disaster, you run up a thirty-dollar phone bill. You're worthless."

And like a bomb exploding, she turned on him. "Worthless? You, who wants to be a cowboy, like a little boy, think I'm worthless?"

In the living room, Casey coughed. Frederick and Sandra both looked toward the door.

"May I get back to my guest now?" she said.

He waved at her. "Go. Go." He folded the bill and put it back in the envelope. Soon the chirpy conversation resumed in the living room, and he slipped back outside.

As Frederick approached the coop, the chickens were excited to see him all over again. He let them out into the field and pulled the tarp off the roof, dodging the dirt and dried leaves that slid to the ground. Placing the ladder on the side of the coop, he climbed up to look at the wood that passed for a roof, but more resembled a cracker. He began yanking up nails with a hammer and heaving them below.

He'd let Sandra run things for far too long. No more. He was the man. A man doesn't take pictures. He doesn't draw Mickey Mouses. He finds meaningful work that matters, and he does whatever is necessary to complete that work. His wife should support this. When, after months of fighting, he gets her to the house in the country, she should be cheerful. She should work hard at cleaning, cooking, sex, and childbearing. She should be his helpmate.

True, the house was in worse condition than he would like, but whose fault was that? The money he expected to use fixing up the house had gone to all her *secrets*. The secrets he'd been lied to about: the five-dollar lamp that turned out to be fifteen dollars, the twenty-dollar "bargain" desk that was ninety dollars. The things hidden in closets and drawers: handbags, jewelry, ball gowns, a mink muff. A mink muff! And all the things he'd ignored, like the full extent of her painting supplies: unused canvases, painting smocks, boxes of unopened paints. So many secrets came tumbling out that Frederick couldn't look at Sandra and see the same woman anymore. It was amazing that he'd felt lucky to have her. He'd once thanked providence that he, a poor immigrant, could attract such a vivacious American woman.

And yet, if only Sandra would help, if only she would try. But she never cooked, she never cleaned. When they moved in, she refused to unpack, just left everything overflowing in boxes and suitcases. And always on the phone, *yap, yap, yap, yap*.

And she had the nerve to say that Frederick was in the wrong because he hid buying the ranch from her. So he had, and he didn't regret it either. He was the one who decided their lives, not her.

A splinter went into his thumb and he stopped to pry it out so that it released a pinprick of blood. For a moment, Frederick sat on the roof, looking out over his land. The chickens were scratching under a live oak. The cows were on the other end of the field, surrounded by asters. One of them—Lotte— was peeing, the urine arching from her body and falling to the ground like an arrow.

This was his land. Like the early American pioneers, he would shape it into something worthwhile. Sandra was always complaining about the high insurance policy on the house, but she had no vision. The ranch would be something great someday. It needed protecting.

Eventually, Sandra would understand this. The practical side of her nature always won out in the end. She would come around. She would have no choice. As the man, he would make her.

CHAPTER 45

The lavender curtain over the house faded to the color of a hydrangea blossom and grew stiff from wind and rain. A storm blew dust so that a yellow smear stained the bottom of the fabric. Inside, the house was split in two. The front, which was covered with the curtain, ceased to have seasons. At night, the only light was the flickering of candles and red crack of the stove.

Arthur still slept on the sun porch. He needed to be near the orchard. Plum pox had invaded the trees, a virus that causes honeycomb rings to appear on the fruit and leaves. Once a tree had it, it would never produce healthy fruit again. There was nothing to do but pull it out by the roots. So far, he'd burned some of his best producers and vigilance was necessary to keep the disease from spreading.

So the house was divided into Mabel's half and Arthur's half. Mabel's half was a tinted world where things floated in dim light, like ghosts in photographs. Arthur's half was the everyday world of socks and teaspoons. In between was the knocking and sawing of construction.

For days, Arthur didn't see Mabel at all. Since he was

working such long hours in the orchard, they no longer ate together. When he did see her, she always wanted to discuss another project: remodeling the stables, wiring the home for electricity, installing a telephone booth, building a gazebo. Arthur despaired that the house would never be done, and he would never be rid of John Hollingsworth's presence in his life.

At night, Arthur wished Mabel would come to him, but she never did. Going to her room also proved difficult. At some point, Arthur began to find the purple half of the house hard to approach. It should have been simple to walk up the spiral staircase and open the door to his wife's bedroom, but it wasn't. The curtain made the house perpetually dark, and at night, it was as black as a cave. His footsteps echoed through the rooms, and he felt observed, even though he knew he was alone. The lantern he carried cast shadows of scaffolding and stacks of boards that looked like lurking rock formations. Then he came to the spiral staircase, his hand sliding up the metal handrail. At the center of the spiral, he felt trapped, as if caught in a cage.

At the end of the hallway was Mabel's door, always shut. It was heavy mahogany with a crystal knob. Every step closer dragged at Arthur's body until his feet felt like they were encased in concrete blocks and his hands had turned to sandbags at his side. He would order himself to enter Mabel's room. She was his wife. He had a right to open the door. Until recently, this had been his bedroom. Still, he didn't move. He stood there, sometimes for several moments, listening to the sounds coming from inside the room—a creak of the wardrobe door, a rustle of fabric, a whisper.

Often at that point, Arthur felt like a spooked horse, and the urge to flee would come over him. It was a childish impulse, born from a longstanding fear of the dark. As a boy, he was so afraid of a darkened room that his mother let him sleep on the floor by the fireplace instead of in his own bed. Standing in front of Mabel's door, the blackness curled around him, and he felt as if fingers would reach into the puddle of light cast by the lantern and grab him. Then Arthur would jog through the hallway and down the spiral staircase, turning in little circles as he went. Finally, he reached the other side of the house and stopped to catch his breath, feeling foolish and more than a little cowardly.

He couldn't understand why he did this. It was a force in his body that he didn't control. It was like his beard, which he picked without realizing until his fingers were wet with blood.

At night, lying in bed, Arthur practiced telling Mabel to take the curtain down. It wasn't having the effect she wanted. Instead of stopping gossip, it had become the town joke. When Arthur was out buying feed or overseeing shipments, people said things like, "When's the circus going to open, Beard?" Or, "Isn't that family of gypsies ever moving on and letting you have your house back?" They didn't say these things to Mabel, but she sensed their ridicule. It made it more frustrating that she continued with the ever-growing construction.

When Arthur had married again, it was because he wanted a wife and a family. Lately it felt like he had neither. And he didn't like the looks John Hollingsworth gave Mabel when he thought no one was looking. Something was going on there. Arthur wasn't a fool and he wasn't blind. The house was a place where anything could be happening in dark corners or behind mahogany doors. And yet, Arthur still wished that Mabel would come to him.

CHAPTER 46

Sandra felt a twinge of embarrassment as Casey followed her into the bedroom. It was a disaster. The bed was unmade, boxes were shoved in the corner, and Frederick's shirts hung on the bed frame. The rest of the clothes—with the exception of her ball gowns—matted the floor like a rug.

Casey blew air out of her mouth. "You weren't kidding about the mess."

"Yeah," Sandra said, kicking a path to the bed. "We could do this at your house."

"Nah, it's fine. Let's do your hair."

They cleared off the bed and soon enough, Casey was kneeling on the mattress behind Sandra, combing her hair. It felt like they were back at Mrs. Pickler's boarding house, where Sandra's biggest problem was how to get an audition. She found herself wondering if it was a mistake to leave Hollywood. She'd done pretty well there, it seemed now. If the Depression hadn't happened, who knows, maybe she'd be a movie star by now.

"Whatever happened to Imogen Beauregard?" she said,

fingering a string of beads that Frederick had given her for a birthday.

"I don't know. She stopped working around the time we knew her. I read in a gossip rag that she's an alcoholic."

"I believe it. Remember how she drank?"

"Yeah, that couldn't have been good for the baby she was carrying," Casey said. "There, now you look like Veronica Lake."

Sandra picked up the hand mirror. Her red hair hung in peekaboo bangs over one eye, as smooth as velvet.

"Thank you. Although I don't know why I bother getting spruced up for Frederick these days."

Casey made a strange noise and buried her mouth in her hands. For a second Sandra thought she was crying, but then realized it was the opposite: Casey was laughing. "I'm sorry," Casey said. "I can't believe you married that guy. I can't believe it!" She let out a loud, snorty laugh.

For an instant Sandra felt offended for Frederick's sake, then wondered why she had the urge to defend him when he was being so awful.

"He's very handsome without the beard," she said weakly.

"Still. Do you remember him dragging around that purse? And now he's dressing like a cowboy. And that hat!" Casey started laughing so hard, she shook the bed.

Sandra fingered the red beads Frederick had given her. They'd seemed so bright and lively before, but now they seemed cheap.

"I'm sorry," Casey said. "I shouldn't laugh. It's just that I pictured you with a doctor or a president of something. Not that I should talk. Lord knows I've had bad luck with men."

Casey had already told Sandra the trouble she'd had since leaving Hollywood. When she went home to Iowa, her kin weren't happy to see her. It was the height of the Depression and they didn't want another mouth to feed. After a few weeks of sleeping on the porch, Casey ran off with a guy she'd known since high school. Her son, Andrew, was from that marriage, which ended in divorce five years later. Her second husband had brought her to Walnut Creek to live on a horse ranch. Both husbands had been drunks. Andrew's father had beaten Casey. Since the divorce, she'd been living on the ranch, eking out a living by giving riding lessons and selling horses. Right now she had a pregnant horse that was going to give birth at any time.

Sandra wondered if all that hard living was why Casey looked so different. The winsome quality she'd had when she was younger was gone and was replaced by a hardscrabble grubbiness, as if she'd been exposed to too many harsh things: sun, wind, cold, men.

Casey said that Sandra looked the same as when they were in Hollywood, but she wasn't so sure that was true. There was something different about her face that she couldn't quite define. Not wrinkles so much as a thinning and narrowing. And was it her imagination, or was her neck looser somehow? And her eyelids—she was certain they were droopier than they used to be. Would they eventually drop over her eyes, like a basset hound's? She couldn't believe this was her life—thirty-eight years old, living in the boondocks in an unhappy marriage. She expected to be so much more by now. Sometimes she wondered if she would ever be anything at all.

"Let's try on hats!" Sandra said all of a sudden.

She had dozens of hats: fezzes, berets, shepherdess hats, pillbox hats, hats with birds, hats with fruit, hats with flowers. She wasn't sure how she'd accumulated so many, although the shopping trips with Beatrice may have had something to do with it. She gave several to Casey as a thank you for doing her hair. It seemed gracious and extravagant, like something a wealthy woman would do. And it meant fewer things to unpack.

"Do you think you'll ever marry again?" Sandra said, tipping a pillbox hat on top of her head carefully, so as not to disturb the hairdo.

"Nah, it's not for me. Men don't treat me right and I have my boy to think about."

"Men can be bastards, that's for sure."

"At least your men have been kind to you for the most part."

"A lot of good it did me. My problem is that I'm always attracted to artists. First a deadbeat musician, now a photographer who doesn't want to be a photographer. To think, I could have married a doctor."

Casey pursed her lips as she examined herself underneath a black hat. "Why don't you get the Reno Cure, then? That's what I did."

It was so simple that Sandra couldn't believe she hadn't thought of it before—she could go to Reno for a divorce. People did it all the time in the movies. She'd considered divorcing Frederick, but it hadn't seemed like a serious option until this moment. For one thing, she loved Frederick, or at least she loved the man she married—who, she now had to admit, she might have made up. And if Frederick didn't agree to a divorce, she would have to get a lawyer and fight him, which seemed daunting. But Reno didn't require a lawyer. Hollywood stars were always going there for quick divorces. And, just as often, they remarried someone else in a Reno wedding chapel.

"How long do you have to live in Nevada to get a divorce?" she asked.

"You have to stay six weeks to establish residency. In most states you have to wait a year."

"A year?"

"Yeah. Look, I did it both ways, the traditional way, which was a nightmare, having to air my dirty laundry in court and waiting for months, and him getting the upper hand with Andy in the end anyway. The second time, I went to Reno and had a little vacation."

"Vacation!"

"It was, though. They have gambling and dude ranches and music and dancing."

Sandra wondered what it would be like to live in Reno for six weeks. If she handled things well, she might be able to meet a recently divorced doctor or some other professional and be married again within the year.

Casey picked up another hatbox and peered into it. "Oh, this one has papers in it."

Seeing the orange hatbox was like receiving a small electric shock. Sandra picked it up, surprised by how shabby it had gotten in the past eleven years. The round lid was soft, the printing faded. She didn't understand how it could have aged so much just by sitting in a closet.

The letters from John Hollingsworth were still inside, waiting for her. She pulled one from the envelopes, the paper thin as onionskin, and suddenly, Sandra was telling Casey about the letters. It was the first time she'd shown them to anyone. It felt right, as if she should have told Casey about them back in Hollywood.

Casey turned them over in her hand. "I can't believe you've had this all this time. And do you think John Hollingsworth is your father?"

"I don't know," Sandra said, surprising herself with the answer.

"Wow. It's a mystery, like in *The Thin Man*. Maybe he's rich and wants to claim you as his heir."

Sandra read through the letters again. The sentence, "I'm a painter, and I have my own studio" leapt out at her. John was an artist, just like she was. Maybe *he* could help her career. Maybe the solution to her problems had been in these letters all this time.

"If it were me, I'd want to know who he is," Casey went on. "Why haven't you looked into it?"

Sandra fingered the picture of her mother. Now that she was older, she could see how young Mabel was in the photograph. Her eyes were clear, her mouth not yet frozen in a perpetual frown. "I used to think he was a conman," she said. "I thought he was sending these letters to take advantage of me. Now I'm not so sure."

"Well, there's a solution to your problem. Go to Petaluma and get to the bottom of it."

"You mean, just show up unannounced?"

"Sure. Let's jump in the car and go to his house right now. I'll drive."

It sounded so simple. All Sandra had to do—all she'd ever had to do—was ask John Hollingsworth who he was. Petaluma was north of San Francisco, not far from Healdsburg. They could get there in an hour.

But wouldn't it be strange to show up a decade after receiving the letters and demand answers?

Sandra pushed the whole thing off with a shudder. Damn these letters for causing this continual circle in her mind.

"That's okay," she said, standing up. "But you can drive me to the store for more cigarettes if you want. I'm out."

CHAPTER 47

The sunlight pierced the cracks in the curtains of Arthur's bedroom and touched Mabel's cheek. Arthur, propped on his elbow watching her sleep, kissed the warm spot.

She groaned. "Can't you close the curtains?"

"They are closed," Arthur said, rising from the bed. "I'll pull them tighter." He tugged the curtains until the sun was no longer on her cheek, then tiptoed toward the door. He would let her rest. She needed to now that she was having their child.

As he put his hand on the knob, Mabel rolled over and said in a voice heavy with drowsiness, "Don't go, Arthur."

He was flattered and surprised, and returned to the bed, lying on top of the blankets so that Mabel could rest her forehead against his neck. He'd almost given up on having children, when one night, Mabel left her half of the house and knocked on his door, entering in a cloud of charmeuse and perfume. "I'm sorry I made you wait so long," she said "Let's start a family."

He didn't ask what changed her mind. It was easier not to know. What did it matter, anyway? It had only taken a few tries, and now she was pregnant. Arthur felt as he had when they were first married—lucky to have her, proud she was on his arm. She was once again a precious gift to Arthur. A gift that required patience, yes, but one that opened life up at the most unpredictable ways.

When she fell asleep, he moved incrementally off the bed and left the room. As he walked through the house, he marveled at how close it looked to being finished. The floors were in, the wainscoting installed, the stained glass window panels painting orange and yellow patches on the floor. He couldn't wait for the curtain to come down and the gloom to be removed for good, along with John Hollingsworth.

Outside, he inspected the trees for plum pox. The orchard was starting to leaf out, and he held each branch in the light, studying them through a magnifying glass. So far there was no sign of the telltale honeycomb spots. If he kept on top of the disease, he had every reason to think the plum harvest would be back to normal this year.

Inside again, he was greeted with the smell of breakfast, meaning that Mabel was cooking—another rarity. She made his favorite, flapjacks with blackberry jam. As they ate, Arthur told Mabel that now that she was pregnant, she must stop helping with the construction. No more going to the lumber mill, no more overseeing the workers with their swinging hammers and sharp saws. It was time to take care of herself.

"You're absolutely right, Arthur," Mabel said, cutting into a flapjack. "I intend to stop all that immediately."

Arthur, who'd been expecting an argument, was surprised by her easy agreement. "Well, good," he said.

He was happy she had an appetite. Early in the pregnancy she'd had a difficult time keeping food down, something that happened to women in this state, he'd learned. Now the color was back in her cheeks, and Arthur could see the bulge against her gown.

"By the way," she said. "I thought May fifteenth would be an appropriate date for the unveiling ceremony. The house will be finished by then, and I shouldn't be too far along to host a party."

Although Arthur had no interest in the event, he viewed it as the last thing he would endure before peace came back to his life. He offered to go with her to the newspaper to pay for the unveiling announcement. After breakfast, they took the carriage into town and strolled through the plaza, making their leisurely way to the newspaper office. The hills in the distance were covered with yellow mustard flowers and looked like they'd been dipped in pollen.

At the newspaper, they placed an announcement to run closer to the date:

On May 15, come one, come all to the grand unveiling of the remodeled Beard Estate. Tour the grounds and enjoy refreshments under the cool shade of the prune orchard, courtesy of the Beard Prune Company.

Mabel was cheerful when they left the office. She was telling Arthur that the unveiling would be good advertisement for the orchard when she suddenly said "Oh!" and put her hand to her belly. Arthur bent over her, asking what was wrong, but Mabel flapped her hand and said, "Shh." Then she straightened and smiled.

"He kicked," she said.

Arthur looked at her swelling stomach, wanting to touch her but feeling like he shouldn't. As if sensing this, Mabel put his hand on the bulge. He flushed, aware that he was handling an intimate part of his wife's body in public. Then he felt it, a butterfly of movement beneath his hand.

"Well, now," he said. "That's fine. That's very fine."

Mabel squeezed Arthur's arm and started walking again, her hair lustrous on her head. "He's strong," she said.

"He gets that from me. I was climbing all over the house when I was little."

"I can't imagine. There it goes again." Mabel snatched his hand and pushed it on her abdomen. Again, he felt the bubble movement beneath his fingers.

"A regular New York Knickerbocker," he said.

They laughed and continued toward the fountain. On the opposite street, John Hollingsworth was sauntering along with a stack of library books. A dimple appeared in his cheek as he approached. As they made small talk, Arthur noticed that Mabel had gone rigid and worried she was tired. He was about to say goodbye and take her home when John said, "Since I have you here, Mr. Beard, I want to talk to you about the house."

Arthur put his hand to his chin and fiddled with a hair. Every time the builder wanted to talk about the house, it cost more money.

"I went through yesterday and took inventory," John said. "I think we can pack up and get out of there by the end of April."

"Well, now," Arthur said. "That's excellent news."

"Yes, it is. In fact, I can guarantee an end date of May 6. I'm leaving for Mexico on that date, so the house has to be done."

"You bought boat tickets?" Mabel said, eyes searching John's face.

"Yes, ma'am. I'm sailing on a boat from San Francisco to Los Angeles, and from there, to Mexico."

"We'll miss you," Mabel said to John, and a spasm of jealousy shot through Arthur. He took her arm.

"Well," John said. "You'll have me for a bit longer. If you'll excuse me, I have to get these books to the library." He strolled away, swinging the books as if Mabel and Arthur had already slipped from his mind.

She squeezed Arthur's arm. "Let's go home, I'm chilled through."

Eagerly, he rubbed her hands. "Right away. I didn't realize."

Walking backward, Arthur led Mabel through the park like a water-filled balloon. On the ride home, her head lolled against the seat cushion, her eyes on the road. She didn't speak, even when he made a joke about naming the baby Knickerbocker.

At home, he hoped they would continue to spend the day together, but she wanted to lie down, saying she couldn't sleep "with all the light in your room."

"I'll have someone make thicker curtains," he said.

"No need. I'll just go to the master bedroom."

Arthur watched her disappear into the curtained half of the house and knew he wouldn't see her again that day. He tried to regain the sense that they were a happy family, but something had shifted. He and Mabel had been so distant for so long that they didn't seem married anymore, not in the real sense of the word. Even while she was sharing his bed, something about it felt like a formality. He hoped things would change after she gave birth, but at this moment, he doubted they would. Even with his baby inside of her, to Arthur, Mabel was a stranger.

CHAPTER 48

The prunes Sandra was painting looked more like coals than fruit. She scrutinized the canvas, trying to figure out how to fix it, but no solution came to mind. Annoyed, she flipped on the radio and "Sentimental Journey" drifted through the speaker:

> *Why did I decide to roam?*
> *Gotta take that sentimental journey*
> *Sentimental journey home*

Sandra turned off the radio.

She'd commandeered the dining room as her art studio because it had the best light in the house. The walls were lined with canvases of things she hated: Mt. Diablo, cowboys, victory gardens. And now this still life of prunes in a wooden bowl, which wasn't going well. It would be easier to paint plums, which had speckles and color gradation, but Sandra liked plums. It was prunes she hated.

What she needed were art lessons, but Frederick said they

didn't have money for that. Every penny had to go to the ranch. What she wanted was unimportant.

One night last week, she'd asked Frederick what was wrong with the trees in her painting of a lake in Golden Gate Park, where she used to spend her lunch breaks when she was a secretary. Painting it reminded her of how much she had hated her boss, Randy, and how the office felt like a prison. In real life the cypress trees behind the lake lurked like evil gnomes, but in her painting, they looked like green clouds on stumps. She explained to Frederick that no matter what she did, the trees looked wrong.

Holding his second or third whiskey of the night, Frederick stood with his hand over his chin, considering. He didn't move for so long that Sandra started fidgeting.

"Well?" she said.

"Let me see. Paint a tree."

Sandra dipped her paintbrush and painted leaves on top of the green shadows that she'd placed behind the lake. Her painting books said that layering colors was the way to get a three-dimensional look, but it wasn't as easy as the illustrations made it seem.

"No, no," Frederick said. "Give me the fan brush."

He pointed to the brush lying beside her paint palette. Reluctantly Sandra handed it over and watched Frederick dab it on the canvas. He added green and purple to the leaves, then picked up a thinner brush and drew a brown line of a trunk down the center. When he pulled his hand away, a fully formed cypress tree had appeared. "And that, *schatzi*, is how you paint a tree," he said.

It was a good tree, she had to admit. But it wasn't her tree. "You're painting on my painting," she said.

He looked amused. "I'm showing you how to do it."

"Don't show me. Explain and let me do it."

"I am explaining. You make dabbing motions, like this." He flicked the fan brush over one of her shadows again, forming a second perfect tree. It was starting to make Sandra's look inept by comparison.

"You're painting my trees for me," Sandra said, reaching for the brush.

"Yes, because I do it better," Frederick said, swinging his arm out of reach. "I have some skills, you know, even if my wife wants to take up painting as a hobby."

Sandra paused, amusement draining from her face. "What does that mean?"

"Nothing," Frederick said, taking a swig of bourbon. "I'd just prefer you do some laundry before you do your art, that's all." He put the brush in her hand and left the room.

Dipping the paintbrush in the black paint, Sandra smeared it all over his trees.

Now, the painting sat behind her while she worked on the prunes. She could feel her face growing tighter, remembering Frederick calling her work a hobby. He needn't think so highly of himself. She had a year of college under her belt, which made her the more educated of the two of them.

As she was thinking this, Frederick came in carrying two rectangular tin cans of what looked like turpentine and set them down at her feet. Sandra stopped, paintbrush in midair.

"What's that?" she said.

"Linseed oil." He stamped the floor with his foot. "I was going to replace the floors, but we don't have money for that. So they need to be mopped and coated with linseed oil."

"And that does what?"

Frederick winked. "Makes them shine, *schatzi*."

He hadn't called her that in a long time. Sandra smiled and returned to her painting.

"The way it works," Frederick went on, "Is you coat rags or newspapers with oil, then rub it on the floor, like wax. The kitchen, dining room, living room, and bedrooms need it."

"You should get on that," she said.

"Not me. You."

Sandra laughed. "Sure."

"I'm serious." Frederick was standing beside her. She could smell whiskey on him. Again. He was drinking too much, even by Sandra's standards.

"The floors," he said. "I need you to sweep and mop them, then coat them with linseed oil."

"I can't. I'm working."

"I see that. However I have to get this ranch up and running, and in order for that to happen, you're going to help. We'll start with the floors."

Sandra stared at him, anger mounting inside her. "Again, I'm painting."

"Then you prove to me what I've suspected for a while now."

"And what's that?"

"That you're a rotten wife."

With that he marched from the room. Sandra squeezed the brush in her hand, looking at the cans on the floor. The smart thing to do was to stay here and cool down before pursuing this conversation. But the name he'd called her reverberated in her mind until she put the brush down and followed him to the living room. "Okay, I'll bite. How am I a rotten wife?"

Frederick grabbed an art magazine off the coffee table and flipped through it, stopping at an article on the artist Audubon. He rotated the page sideways to examine a painting of a bird. "It's simple," he said. "You don't cook or clean. You don't want to help me build a life here."

"I've been busy painting every day. Not that you care."

He shut the magazine. "You're right. I don't. You know what I care about? My house being neglected. My life falling apart. My wife avoiding responsibilities."

"Look who's talking! You're drinking every day. I bet they love that down at the ol' shipyard."

"It doesn't matter. Today I quit the shipyard. As of two weeks from now, we'll officially be dependent on this ranch."

Sandra experienced the familiar groundswell that happened when he did something without her knowledge. For the rest of their marriage, he would go on doing things without consulting her. That was what he'd done since the beginning, and he would never change.

"You go ahead and be a rancher," she said. "I'm going to be an artist."

"A woman pushing forty is too old to be chasing a career. And ladies can't do art anyway."

Sandra gasped. "I'm sorry I married you. I should leave you."

"Go ahead. Although I guarantee there's no money left for you to start over again, or whatever it is you want to do."

There was truth in this. Here she was, pushing forty, as Frederick had been so kind to point out. Her mother had never been able to start over after the earthquake. She'd been stuck in poverty.

"Then we'll sell the house and split the money," she said.

Frederick gave her a look of pure contempt. "I will never sell this house," he said. "It's my home, whether you're here or not."

In response, Sandra picked up a paperweight from the table and threw it so that it thumped and rolled under the sofa.

Frederick looked at her so intensely that she dropped her hand. "If you throw one more thing, you'll regret it."

It seemed like a dare, so Sandra seized the magazine and threw it with all her strength. The paper fluttered, hit the wall, and slid to the ground.

Without a word, Frederick walked to the dining room where she kept her art. She watched through the open door as he took out a pocketknife and flipped open the blade.

"No!" Sandra shouted, running into the room.

"You destroy my things, I destroy yours." Frederick moved toward a painting of a paper bag hill dotted with chickens.

She grabbed his arm. "Stop! That's my work."

"Work?" Frederick said. "You've never worked a day in your life. You're too lazy. You'll never do anything with yourself. Don't you know that by now?" He looked at her painting and snorted. Then he folded the knife and put it back in his pocket. "These aren't worth destroying." With that, Frederick left the room, and a moment later the front door shut.

Sandra looked at her paintings, stunned. But she would be an artist, she tried telling herself. Her mother had always said their family was destined for greatness. It was in her blood.

Wasn't it?

Putting her fingers to her temples, Sandra tried to follow through with her thoughts. Her father, Arthur Beard, had been a man of vision and she was destined to be a success too. For the first time, that didn't make sense. What did being good at business have to do with art? She certainly hadn't gotten her artistic talent from Mabel. Her mother couldn't even arrange flowers in a vase.

Then Sandra remembered something else: Mabel may not have been a painter, but John Hollingsworth was. She jogged to the bedroom, pulled up the hatbox, and fished out the letter. There it was, in John Hollingsworth's own hand: "I'm a painter, and I have my own studio that I'd like to show Emma."

It didn't sound like a sentence written by a conman. It was possible that John Hollingsworth might be a real artist. And if he was an artist, she could prove to Frederick that art was in her blood and that he was wrong about her.

Slamming the lid on the hatbox, Sandra hurried to get her coat. She would go to John Hollingsworth's studio and tell him about her work. If he was an artist, John could help her become the success she was always meant to be. It wasn't too late. She would get to the bottom of who she was, and then, finally, things would start to go right for her.

CHAPTER 49

It was almost five a.m., dark enough for stars but light enough to see the contours of the prune trees in the orchard. Arthur had been up for an hour, preparing for the day's work. There had been honeycomb spots on a tree near the house, which had put him on guard for plum pox.

Mabel didn't get up until nine a.m. most days, at least as far as Arthur knew. She'd moved back to the curtained side of the house because she said the bright light made it hard for her to sleep. Yesterday she'd brought up adding a nursery, saying that maybe Hollingsworth could be convinced to put off Mexico for a while. This time Arthur would say no. He would insist that the builder had until May 6 to finish the construction, as agreed. Then he would take down the curtain, go to Mexico, and Arthur and Mabel would be a family at last. The child would be the glue holding the two halves of the house together.

As Arthur was thinking this, there was a rumbling and shaking all around him. He looked up and the branches of the prune trees were undulating at the sky as though in worship. Behind him, the house had come alive, jerking as if to free itself from its foundation. There was a crash, like something collapsed. Arthur thought of his wife and unborn baby and ran toward the house.

In front, the scaffold had fallen to the ground, bringing the curtain down with it. The ornate two-story house was the color of a new dollar bill, but Arthur had no time to look at it. He threw open the double doors and careened inside.

Everything was sloshing and shaking. In the hallway, the railing of the spiral staircase had fallen to the floor. Arthur ran up the stairs, scurrying around the spiral like he was running up the center of a tornado. A ceiling beam crashed to the ground and his chest tightened. Mabel might be trapped under something, and she was pregnant with his child.

On the upstairs landing, Arthur shouted, "Mabel! Get out of the house!" There was no answer. He ran down the hallway to her room where, as usual, the door was shut. When he put his hand on the knob, the earthquake stopped. Immediately the door became foreboding, the crystal knob turning to ice in his hand. It all came rushing back, the feelings he experienced whenever he stood outside her room, a mixture of dread and desire. Blood draining from his head, he flung open the door. It swung on its hinges and settled halfway shut, partially blocking his view.

Inside, Mabel and John Hollingsworth were scrambling to get dressed. She was standing beside the bed, holding her lacy nightgown in front of her body, eyes wide, mouth forming a shocked "oh." He could see her naked shoulder, perpendicular and white.

For months, Arthur had been unable to enter this room. It had seemed foreboding, as if to open it would reveal something terrible. Suddenly, that seemed a petty concern. It had been easy to open the door, and now that he had, he didn't even want to go inside. He left it open and headed back in the direction he'd come from.

With the curtain down, weak beams of morning light flooded the hallway and he could see the damage. Chunks of plaster had come off the ceiling and cracks ran like veins throughout the house. Fresh air came floating up from below, indicating something was open to the outside. As Arthur reached the staircase, he saw that it had come loose. There was now a gap of six inches between it and the landing, and the only thing holding it up was its circular shape.

Downstairs, the house was in chaos, with piles of books on the floor and the remnants of the china cabinet glinting in the pale light. The door to Mabel's room was shut and he could hear them whispering inside. Arthur went to the nearest window, a polygon of glass that looked out at the orchard. How beautiful his trees were. The leaves were green and untouched, with no sign of the disaster that had just occurred.

Since the window didn't open, there was no other option than to take the staircase. He couldn't stay up here with two of them, half-naked and hiding in what had once been his bedroom. Walking back to the landing, Arthur looked at the gap between it and the staircase, and then at the twenty-foot drop. He glanced once more at the door, and put a foot on the stair.

Slowly Arthur made his way around the spiral, one step at a time. After three steps, the staircase creaked and he froze. When it didn't fall, he inched to the center so that it was balanced again. His eyes focused on the gold handrail that had fallen to the floor. One of the new tiles had flipped up revealing the original pine boards he'd put in when he was married to Rebekah.

As Arthur took another step on the teetering staircase, he remembered laying those floors one summer in his youth, sweating as the smell of lemon blossoms blew in through the open door. The lemon bushes were pulled out years ago, but he couldn't remember why. It seemed now that he'd lost something precious with them. As he laid those floors, Rebekah had brought him lemonade made from those bushes, which was fresh and light on his tongue. He'd never tasted lemonade that good again.

He remembered Rebekah, and the way her forehead crinkled when she listened to him and how her dusky hair fell on her face when she worked beside him in the orchard. He thought of her as the rumbling moved the staircase, sending it—with him on it—down to the pine boards below. They were the last things Arthur ever saw.

CHAPTER 50

During the drive to Petaluma, Casey and Sandra discussed Frederick. They agreed his offenses boiled down to the following:

1. He moved her to that awful place.

2. He constantly lied and manipulated her.

3. He insulted Sandra's art career.

4. He called her rotten and said she was pushing forty.

5. He didn't love her anymore.

"Sometimes I wonder what men are good for," Casey said. "They always treat you badly one way or another."

Sandra sighed. "I keep thinking that if that house would disappear, I'd be free."

"So get rid of the house. That would fix things, wouldn't it?"

"I don't know how that could happen. No one would buy that ranch. Only Frederick is that stupid." As she said this, she remembered the home insurance Frederick had taken out on the house. Even though money was tight, he'd purchased a full policy based on his fantastical ideas of what the house might be worth someday. The only way Sandra was likely to get money out of the ranch was if there was another big earthquake.

They were getting close to Petaluma. In fields, flocks of chickens were scratching in front of long industrial coops. A sign on the freeway declared Petaluma the EGG BASKET TO THE WORLD.

Frederick would love it here, Sandra thought.

At a drugstore, they went inside to use the payphone. Huddled in a booth near the cash register, Casey opened the phone book and ran her finger down the names beginning with H. There, printed on the page, was "Hollingsworth, John, 655 F Street."

Sandra bit her lip, looking at the name. "It's funny. I thought he'd be dead by now. Or maybe I thought he didn't exist."

"Well, he does," Casey said, ripping the page out of the book. "Let's go find him."

As they drove toward F Street, mansions started appearing on either side of the road. They passed vast houses with columns and towers and palm trees bordering neat green lawns.

Casey whistled. "I had no idea chickens were so profitable."

Sandra was too nervous to laugh. The houses surprised her too. She'd never visited Petaluma, even though it was only a few miles from where she grew up. She imagined John Hollingsworth in one of these large houses. If that were the case, she was going to need an explanation as to why she'd had to put up with Daddy Jones all those years.

But the house they parked in front of wasn't a mansion. It was a one-story mint green cottage with a flimsy metal porch. The yard was full of white stones and flanked by a chain-link fence.

"This can't be right," Sandra said.

Casey looked at the phone book page. "This is it. 655 F Street."

The white door of John Hollingsworth's house gleamed in the afternoon sunlight. Sandra twitched her lips.

"Do you want me to come?" Casey said.

Sandra nodded. The door creaked in the quiet street and she wished Casey had a nicer car. If John Hollingsworth was her father, she wanted to pull up in a Rolls-Royce, not a Chevrolet with a broken taillight.

Behind them, a voice said, "If you're looking for John, he's not here." A woman had come out of the house across the street. She was carrying a dishtowel as if she'd run outside as soon as she noticed a car.

"Yes, ma'am," Casey said. "Do you know where we can find him?"

"This time of the day, he's at work. John's Place. It's a bar on Petaluma Boulevard with a neon sign out front. Go south out of town, you can't miss it."

Casey and Sandra exchanged glances. Maybe they had the wrong John Hollingsworth.

"You say he owns a bar?" Sandra said. "I heard he was an artist."

The woman leaned back. "That does sound familiar. John has had many jobs, more jobs than anyone I know. These days it's the bar."

"Thank you," Sandra said, turning around.

"How do you know John?" the woman said, but they pretended not to hear her. The sun was sinking in the sky as they drove out of town. Soon they saw a building that said John's Place, just as the woman had described. It was set off the road in a gravel lot. A single car was parked out front.

Casey pulled beside it and they sat there while the engine cooled. A window revealed polished tables and a bar with shelves of liquor behind it. Neon beer advertisements cast the place in a squalid glow.

A second later, the sign outside lit up. The words JOHN's PLACE glowed beside a silhouette of a cocktail glass.

"Do you want to go in?" Casey said.

"I guess so."

Sandra reached into the backseat and opened the hatbox with the letters inside. The photo of her mother was on top. Sandra wondered whatever happened to the fur piece she was wearing. Her mother never got rid of clothes. She'd been wearing the same dresses for Sandra's entire life.

Even though it was evening, John's Place had the hushed, expectant air of early morning. Behind the bar, a man was writing something in a balance book. A thin layer of silvery hair clung to the back of his head. Sandra knew as soon as she saw him that it was John Hollingsworth.

"What can I get you ladies?" he said.

"I'd like a martini," Casey said, taking a barstool. "Dry, with an olive."

John's eyes shifted to Sandra.

"Me too," she said, feeling shy.

They watched him stir and pour the martinis into glasses, garnish with olives, and place them on square napkins in front of them. Then John began to wipe down the bar with a towel, even though there was nothing there that Sandra could see.

She whispered to Casey, "That's him. I know it."

"Me too. You have the same nose."

Sandra hooked her fingers around her nose. Casey was right. John's nose was a manlier version of her own.

"Say something," Casey said.

Sandra shook her head and took a long sip of her drink.

"Nice place you've got here," Casey said to John.

He began to move toward them, still rubbing the counter with the towel. "Thank you."

"Been here long?"

"I've owned the place about eight years."

"You must be John then."

"That I am."

Casey gave Sandra a look that said, *That's your chance.* Sandra shook her head and put her lips to the limpid surface of her drink.

"Are you ladies from around here?" John said.

"No," Sandra said. "We came to see you."

He moved back his head slightly. "Me?"

Reaching into her handbag, Sandra fingered the letters. She took a deep breath and laid them on the bar. "Did you write these?"

John was smiling as though he thought Sandra was playing a joke on him. He came closer and looked at the letters. Then he bent down to really look at them. "What the—?" he said, picking them up. He took out Mabel's picture and stared for a second, blinking rapidly. Then he looked at Sandra. "You're Emma."

"Yes," she said, finding it difficult to speak. "That's me."

He looked straight into her face and his eyes softened. "What do you know? How old are you now?"

"Thirty-eight," she said, wincing because she couldn't remember if she told Casey that she was thirty-one, which is what she usually told people. But John Hollingsworth would know if she was lying.

He whistled. "That long?" He looked at Casey. "And you are . . .?"

"Casey Roberts," she said, extending her hand. "Just a friend."

He shook Casey's hand, but he was looking at Sandra while he did it.

Casey said she would wait in the car so they could talk. John Hollingsworth locked the door and turned off the neon sign. Then he made himself a drink and sat with Sandra in a booth by the window. She fingered the napkin beneath her martini, folding the corners so that it was shaped like the bottom of the glass. Late afternoon sunlight filtered over the stained carpet.

"I didn't think you ever got those letters," he said.

"I did. I just didn't know what to make of them. Mama never told me about you."

"And how is Mabel?"

Sandra shrugged, unsure what to tell this man. A car on the road slowed, as if the driver was trying to see whether the bar was open.

"I thought you were a painter," she said. "The letter said you wanted to show me your art studio."

John slapped his forehead. "Right. I forgot about that. I wrote that letter when I was painting murals for a living. But it didn't make much money, so I switched to house painting instead. I had a pretty lucrative business going for a while there."

A house painter. Sandra should have known. This was no artist sitting across from her. His jeans sagged in the seat, as if the fibers were collapsing from overuse.

"And now you own a bar?" she said.

"Yeah. I've jumped around a lot when it comes to jobs. But you know, Emma, I like this bar. I think I might have finally found the thing I was always meant to do."

Sandra's eyes darted around the room. It looked like any other dive bar to her. The walls were covered with deer heads draped in team flags and the booth stank of stale beer.

John was studying her face again. On second thought, she wasn't sure if their noses were alike after all. Her own nose was small and elegant. This man's nose was large and ethnic looking, like a pirate's, or Mussolini's.

"Are you my father?" she said.

He sat back as if stunned.

"Yes," he said. "I am."

Sandra crossed her arms over her chest, unsure whether to believe him. "Then who was Arthur Beard?"

"Mabel's husband."

"Then who are you?"

"Not her husband. Didn't Mabel tell you any of this?"

"No. She told me that Arthur was my father and that he owned a prune empire."

John Hollingsworth almost choked on his drink. "A what?"

"A prune empire. That he headed an empire selling prunes nationwide, and that all his money was lost during the earthquake." She heard how naive that sounded, and her cheeks got hot. Picking up her drink, she took a long sip.

"Arthur Beard was a farmer," John said. "That's all. His prune orchard was a big one, but I wouldn't exactly call it an empire."

"So, it's not true that Mama lived in a big house with Arthur Beard?"

"No, that part is true. I worked with her on the house."

Things that had been unclear before were coming together. Sandra didn't know a lot about the house Mabel built with Arthur, but she knew one thing. "You were the builder."

"That's right."

"So the house was your idea."

"Part of it was my idea. The rest was your mother's. She wanted a mansion. But to tell the truth, after a while, all that expanding was our attempt to keep Arthur from finding out."

"Finding out what?"

"About our affair."

Outside Casey was leaning against her car, wrapped in a brown felt coat. Cigarette smoke streamed up from her fingers. Sandra was glad she couldn't hear the conversation.

"What happened?" she said. "Tell me, please." She met his eyes, hoping that for once, someone would tell her the truth.

He seemed to understand. "Okay, Emma. I will."

First, John explained, it had been a business relationship. Mabel had hired him to build a grand home. He loved the ambitious scope of the project, which was a great opportunity for an unknown builder, but his attraction to Mabel was there from the beginning. When townspeople started criticizing the house, he came up with the idea of putting a curtain over it to stop the gossip. The affair began shortly after it went up. John went to Mabel's room when Arthur was away.

"I had some excuse," he said. "Some piece of paper I wanted her to sign, even though I knew I had no business going to her bedroom. From then on, we were inseparable."

Sandra made a face. It was too much to think of her mother in love with this man. Her mother was incapable of loving anyone, even herself.

"What about Arthur?" she said. "Did he catch on?"

John shook his head. "If he did, he never said anything about it. Not until the end, anyway. I don't think he wanted to know."

Outside, a truck pulled up to the bar. A man wearing a cowboy hat got out and stared up at the extinguished neon light. He jiggled the locked door, then crunched back to his pickup.

"Why didn't you just run away together?" Sandra said. "If you loved each other so much."

"I tried, but Mabel wouldn't leave. She said she would never be poor again and that she wouldn't live in a hovel. So things just went on and on."

Sandra shut her eyes, but the smell of cheap beer seemed stronger that way, so she opened them again. "Maybe you're wrong about me," she said. "Maybe I'm still Arthur's daughter." She heard the wavering hope in her own tone. Again, she looked at the man's nose.

"It's me," John said. "I'm sorry to tell you. Arthur never touched Mabel after the early months of their marriage." He frowned, and anger seeped into his expression. "But when she found out she was pregnant, she made good and sure Arthur thought you were his."

"He knew she was pregnant with me?"

"Right. The pregnancy forced a decision about our affair. Mabel said she didn't want to be poor and was going to have Arthur raise you. And I was all right with that. I wanted to move on by then. I was going to go to Mexico and leave you with her."

"Why didn't you?"

"The earthquake happened."

Sandra bit her lower lip. All her life she'd heard about the great earthquake that killed Arthur Beard. "Where were you when that happened?" she said.

John sighed deeply. "I was in your mother's room."

"I thought you'd called the affair off by then."

"We had. I even bought a ticket for Mexico. But we were still seeing each other in the meantime."

With a grunt, John got up and walked to the bar. Sandra turned toward him, irritated that he was stopping in the middle of the story to pour whiskey into a glass.

"Do you want another?" he said.

"No, thanks. What happened with the earthquake?"

But John wouldn't be hurried. He pulled two cherries from a jar, plopped them in the drink, and returned to sit across from her. It wasn't until he settled back and took a sip that he continued. "I was asleep. It was early, maybe five a.m. I woke up to the house shaking and the curtain falling off." His eyes were looking inward and he shook his head as if he couldn't believe what he saw there. "It was so fast. Not even half a minute, and all that damage. The entire city of San Francisco on fire, half the population homeless. And my house—Mabel's house— damaged beyond repair."

"Did the house collapse on you?"

"No, it moved off the foundation, but we didn't know that at the time. The side of the house caved in."

"Where was Arthur?"

John swallowed hard. "We heard him running through the house, calling your mother's name. When he got to the bedroom door, he stopped outside. He did that lots of times; we used to hear him stand in the hallway by the door, but he never opened it. Usually I would run into the closet when he did that, but this time, with the earthquake and all, I didn't have the wits."

"So what happened?"

"He opened the door and saw us."

Sandra gasped. Her eyes pricked with tears for Arthur Beard, the man she'd long thought of as her father.

"Then he ran off," John went on. "I shut the door and when I turned around, Mabel grabbed me. I remember that so vividly. Her hand was like a claw on my arm. Then we heard this horrible crash." He put his elbows on the table and his head in his hands. His fingers wound through his sparse hair.

"Well? What was the crash?"

"It turned out that the stairway had come loose from the landing while Arthur was on it. It crushed him."

Sandra shuddered.

"After Arthur passed away," John went on, "Mabel was terrified that everyone would know about the affair. There was no hiding you, you see. And I'm ashamed to say it, but it was all a bit too much for me. I left for Mexico, like we'd planned. I never contacted Mabel again."

It was the end of the story. The room was silent. Even the busy road seemed hushed for a moment.

Sandra couldn't believe it. All this time her mother had said people would lie to Sandra, but she was the one who'd been lying. Mabel had said to trust only her when she was the last person Sandra should have trusted. "If you left the way you did, why did you write me those letters?" she said.

John shrugged. "I guess I wanted to make sure you were okay."

"Oh."

They sat looking at each other. John was nothing like she had expected. There was dirt under his fingernails. His hair was clinging in silver threads to the back of his head. For the first time, Sandra was glad she had Mabel's brown hair.

"I'd better let you open your bar," she said, picking up her handbag.

"Emma, I'd like to see you again, if that's okay. I'd like to get to know you."

Sandra looked at her glass, which was long emptied. This, after all, was her real father, the man she was related to. It was a strange thought. Arthur Beard, the man she'd always imagined as part of her, was a fantasy. Here was her real father, alive and well. But he was the kind of man who would cheat and lie and abandon her.

"I don't think that would be a good idea," she said.

John was looking at her with his blue eyes, so different from hers. She stood up and reached for her coat.

"But what's life like for you?" He said, "Are you happy?"

Sandra pulled her coat tightly around herself and buttoned it, then tilted up her chin. "Oh yes, very much so. I'm married to a celebrity photographer. I'm starting to see my art career take off. I'm an artist too, you know, the fine art kind. So things are going great for me."

A gleam of pride shone in John's eyes. Sandra lingered, looking at the old man with the familiar nose. Even at his age, he looked too big for the chair he was sitting in. She thought she might get her height from him too. "Well," she said with a bright smile. "Thanks and all."

"You're most welcome, Emma."

Sandra walked out of the bar and didn't look back as she got in the Chevy.

"What happened?" Casey said, eagerly. "What did he say?"

"It's like I always thought," Sandra said, yanking at the seatbelt. "He's just some man who knew my mother once. I think he thought I was wealthy or something and wanted to bilk me."

"Golly," Casey said. "How kooky can you get?"

"Yeah. Let's go."

Casey started the engine and pulled onto the road, heading toward the freeway. "It's funny how the mind tricks you," she said. "I swear you had the same nose."

The shadows had grown long and the sky had turned pale yellow. Sandra found herself touching her nose again.

She wished she believed what she'd just told Casey, but John Hollingsworth's story made too much sense. It fit perfectly underneath the stories her mother had always told her, a shadow of truth underneath the lies.

The car sped onto the highway, and Sandra rolled down the window so that wind rushed into the car.

"What are you doing?" Casey said, her hair flying from under her scarf.

Sandra picked up the orange hatbox, pulled out a letter, and held it out the window so that it wobbled in the wind. When she let go, the wind caught the letter and twirled it away. Then she held the second letter and watched it go too.

Next was her mother's picture. In it, Mabel was beautiful in a way that Sandra had never known her to be. She should keep the picture—it was the only thing she had of her mother before Sandra was born—but she found she didn't want to. So she let it go too, and the photo slid out of sight.

Finally, Sandra pushed the hatbox out and it rolled under the car. In the evening light, the box sat like an orange spot on the road. A moment later, a truck drove over it, crushing the box under its wheels.

CHAPTER 51

The next morning Sandra awoke still angry. The fury only worsened as the day went on. Digging through boxes, she found her old *Medea* script from college and read her favorite lines from the play: "Let no one deem me a poor weak woman who sits with folded hands, but of another mould, dangerous to foes and well-disposed to friends; for they win the fairest fame who live their life like me."

Sandra walked through the house, chanting the lines. They made her feel stronger. It was hot outside and she didn't want to leave the house, but she didn't want to be inside either. She stomped from room to room, picking things up, putting them down, opening boxes and shutting them again. Nothing in the boxes seemed good enough anymore. They were all mistakes. Everything she'd purchased was a mistake.

In the dining room, her paintings were stacked along the walls. She could hear Frederick saying, *These aren't worth destroying.* For the first time, Sandra saw the paintings as they were. It wasn't that they were bad, but they weren't good either. They had promise, but she could also see the bad color choices and

poorly drawn perspectives—the mistakes of an amateur. Whatever potential she had would take years to develop, and all for
the uneven gamble of making it as a woman artist. And here
she was, pushing forty, as Frederick had said.

The ringing telephone cut through her mind and shook
the stillness of the house. Sandra moved like one hypnotized
to the kitchen.

"Long distance call from Mabel Sanborn," said the operator.

The conversation with John Hollingsworth came back like
a wave of nausea. Sandra wanted to hang up, but Mabel could
hear her on the other end of the line, so she accepted the call.

"You decided to pick up, I see," Mabel said.

"Hello, Mama."

Sandra sank down so she was sitting on the kitchen floor.
She thought of Arthur Beard. He was never her father. There
was never a prune empire. Mabel had cheated and ruined him.
He'd died because of her.

It occurred to Sandra that she could ask Mabel about John
Hollingsworth. All she had to say was, *I met John Hollingsworth.
I know what you did.*

"What's wrong with you?" Mabel said.

"Nothing."

"You sound upset."

"Frederick and I aren't getting along right now."

"What did he do this time?"

The question felt bigger than Sandra. She buried her face
in her knees, peering at the scuffed kitchen floor between her
legs. "He thinks I'm a rotten wife."

"What?" Mabel sounded outraged. "How dare he say that?
He's a bad husband, dragging you to the boondocks and making
you live in a hovel."

Sandra nodded into her legs. "That's what I said."

"Don't listen to him. Men are selfish and controlling. Not your father Arthur so much, but Daddy Jones, certainly."

Despite everything, it was nice to hear some sympathy about Frederick. Even Mabel could see that he was the one who was wrong about their marriage, not Sandra.

"I should divorce Frederick," she said.

"Emma Jones, shut your mouth. No daughter of mine will have two divorces."

Sandra banged her head against the wall three times—not hard, but enough to feel it.

"Why not? Why shouldn't I divorce him?"

"I have to tell you? It's low-class. It will mark your reputation forever. Do you want to be known as a divorcée?"

But Sandra wouldn't be known as a divorcée because she would move somewhere new and start over. Besides, she intended to meet a man in Reno and get remarried right away.

"Those social rules are there to protect you," Mabel went on. "It doesn't pay to rebel against them, believe me."

"What am I supposed to do then?"

"I hate to say it, but you'll have to try to make the best of it with him. That's what I had to do with Daddy Jones."

Sandra shut her eyes and thought, *You deserve everything you got. You deserve worse than you got.* Again, she thought of telling her mother about going to Petaluma. All she would have to say were the words, *I met John Hollingsworth. I met my father. I know the truth.*

"It's too bad," Mabel said. "I wanted more for your life than I had."

Her eyes flew open and rested on the dingy wall of the kitchen. "But I'm not like you."

"Yes, you are. More than you know."

Sandra shook her head. She was a good person. The only

reason she was in this situation was because Frederick had tricked her and moved her to Walnut Creek against her will. He was like a Nazi in the way he controlled her, but like the American army, Sandra would fight back.

"It's time you learn that we don't always get what we want in life," Mabel said. "I certainly didn't. What have I always said?"

"People are liars," Sandra repeated.

Like you, she thought. *Cheater. Liar.*

"Yes, people are liars. Husbands can be liars as much as anyone else, Emma."

She squeezed her fists, thinking that once, just once, she wished her mother would call her Sandra.

"But don't worry," Mabel said. "No matter what, I'll be here. Your Mama will always tell you the truth."

I know what you did, she thought. *I know the truth now.*

"Are you still there?"

"Yes, Mama," Sandra said.

CHAPTER 52

The men were taking the tile from the floor to sell. All morning Mabel had been listening to them scuttling around the house like crabs. They took the gold leaf yesterday and the claw-foot bathtub the day before. It was John's idea to sell what could be salvaged from the house while they could. Many things were damaged beyond repair—cracked windows, broken sconces, furniture encrusted with fallen plaster. Mabel shouldn't even be in the house. It was dangerous. One side had collapsed and there was a hole in the kitchen. The wind blew through at night, echoing through the great hall. The stairs were destroyed, and Arthur . . .

But Mabel wouldn't think about Arthur right now, or how he'd known everything at the end, or the way he'd looked at her in those last moments before turning and walking away. Her pregnant belly swelled like a hill in her maternity gown. John said she needed to be peaceful for the baby, but it was so bright without the curtain over the house. Even with the drapes drawn, light burst under the cracks. Mabel hadn't slept for days.

Now the door to her bedroom opened and Mabel knew it was John.

"Here's the money," he said.

She looked at him. His handsomeness had faded with time, but the smile, that infectious smile, was still there. He was holding a clump of bills. "Sixty-three dollars."

"That's all?" she said, grabbing the money and counting.

"Most of the tile was damaged in the earthquake."

She groaned. "Like everything else."

John reached out and stroked her belly, but she stiffened, clutching the money in her hand. He had some sort of house-building material on him. Tar, perhaps. Nausea filled her. It was his fault that Arthur was dead. The house was poorly constructed, the stairs installed incorrectly. She should have found a builder with more experience.

"Do you want me to leave?" he said, formality in his voice.

"It would be best."

"Mabel . . ."

"Please." She moved her head toward the seam of light. "You've done enough."

He sighed. "It doesn't feel right to leave you like this and go to Mexico."

"If you stay, everyone will know. It'll be the talk of town."

He stood and went to her desk. She thought, *Go. Just go. I don't want you here.*

"May I have this?" he said.

He was holding a portrait she'd had taken a few years ago. She knew she already looked different—older and wearier.

"I don't care," she said.

John stuck it in his pocket, then kissed her on the forehead. He opened the door and she heard his feet shuffling down the hall. It was a familiar sound that used to send a low, pleasant thrill through her body, but now all she could think was how stupid they'd been not to put a lock on the door. All those times

Arthur had stood with his hand on the doorknob and she'd never thought to buy a lock.

The day after John left for Mexico, Mabel took the carriage downtown to see the lawyer. She sat in his office as he pointed to numbers indicating Arthur's debt.

"Are you sure the house must be sold?" she said, interrupting him.

"I'm afraid so. The bank has put a lien on it."

"How much can I expect to get?"

The lawyer shuffled through the papers for longer than necessary. It seemed to Mabel that he didn't want to answer the question. "It might go for $800."

Mabel blinked. The amount was paltry. "Is that all?"

"Yes, the house will have to be torn down. The real value is the prune orchard."

"But how can I live on $800?"

"No, I'm afraid that money will go to the bank. It's owed on the debts your husband took out."

Mabel put her hands on her stomach. "They can't do that."

"I'm afraid they can and will," the lawyer said. "They own the house."

Despite her state of mind, Mabel had the impression that the lawyer didn't like her. He didn't ask about the baby or how she was feeling. Perhaps he'd listened to the gossip too. The newspaper had been writing about the fate of her husband nonstop. BELEAGUERED PRUNE RANCHER ARTHUR BEARD DIES IN TRAGIC END, had been one headline.

"Can't you do anything?" she said. "What are we paying you for?"

As she said this, Mabel realized that whatever amount the lawyer had been paid in the past, there was no money to give him now. He was not such a cad to point this out, however. "Do you have any relatives?" he said. "They can be a comfort at times like these."

Mabel didn't reply, unwilling to admit she hadn't spoken to her parents in over twenty years. As the lawyer explained when and how the auction would be arranged, she looked at the leather-bound books displayed behind his head and felt numb. If it weren't for the baby inside her, she would have felt empty.

When the lawyer was done talking, Mabel faltered out into the Healdsburg afternoon. An unseasonable heat was beating on her black mourning clothes and she felt light-headed. Across the street were the remains of Fellowship Hall, transformed into a pile of white bricks by the earthquake. Mabel averted her eyes. She couldn't stand another ruin right now.

At the end of the block, she climbed into the carriage and sat, panting, as the driver—who would have to be let go—drove her home.

The buckeye trees were covered with shoots of pink flowers, like fairy wands. It should have cheered Mabel to see them, but the blur of scenery was making her dizzy and she looked at the blue silk lining of the carriage instead.

All that work, all that plotting and struggling, and she was penniless. This situation felt the same as when Jared had left her all those years ago, only this was worse because she was older, and pregnant. What was left of her looks would drain out of her when she had the baby. The house would have to be sold, and where would she go?

For the first time in years, Mabel wanted her mother.

CHAPTER 53

It was so hot on the drive home from the shipyard that Frederick had to roll down all the car windows to get a breeze. He was exhausted. He'd been up since three a.m. because his cow, Lotte, had given birth. There hadn't been much for him to do, so he'd crouched on his haunches and watched the hooves emerge along with a pool of steaming mucus from the cow's body. Soon it was out, and Lotte was licking the newborn all over. By the time Frederick left for work, the calf was standing on wobbly legs, nursing.

This evening, Frederick would try milking Lotte for the first time. In three days, he would be free of the shipyard forever and would become a full-time rancher, whether Sandra helped or not. He meant it when he said he would never sell the house. If she refused to give ranching a chance, she could leave. He would get rid of her junk and good riddance.

He was almost sick from the heat when he pulled onto the road. In the pasture, the new calf was standing in the shadow of its mother's legs. When Frederick parked by the barn, he noticed that the wingback chairs and coffee table were sitting in the yard. He thought Sandra was kicking him out and looked around for suitcases, but her clothes were there too, draped on a trunk. There was the sofa—how had she gotten it out herself?— the rolled rug, the radio, the credenza, and a milk crate filled with bottles of liquor from the bar.

The doors and windows of the house were open. As he came closer, Frederick saw something he never thought he'd see: Sandra, on her hands and knees, scrubbing the floor with linseed oil. The room was empty of furniture and she was kneeling beside a bucket of rags, muttering something in a singsong rhythm as she spread the polish in wide, arching circles. The diamond pattern of the inlaid floors shone with a warm glow.

"*Schatzi*," Frederick said.

Sandra was wearing old pants and one of his shirts, her hair pulled in a bun. She didn't smile when she saw him, just dumped more oil on the rag. "I did the kitchen already," she said. "I'll do the bedroom tomorrow."

He looked down, shaking his head. Those old floors looked pretty good. All they needed was some care and attention.

When Sandra stood, the knees of her pants were brown from oil. She picked up another tin and carried it over to the bucket. "You'll have to sleep in the barn tonight. I'll go to Casey's."

"Of course," he said. "That's no problem at all."

So, she was starting to accept living here. It was always that way with her—he could convince Sandra to do anything if he was clever and patient. No matter how she acted, in the end, all Sandra needed was a man's firm hand to guide her.

"What made you change your mind?" he said. "To help me?"

She looked at him oddly. Then she opened the new can, pouring oil on the rag. Dropping down, she resumed scrubbing, the diamond pattern gleaming more with every swipe. When it was evident she wasn't going to reply, Frederick decided to check on the calf. As he walked toward the field, Sandra began mumbling again. He heard her say, "For they win the fairest fame who live their life like me."

CHAPTER 54

Although Mabel worried her parent's house had been damaged in the earthquake, it was in the same place it had always been. The castles on Nob Hill hadn't fared as well. All four of the grand homes that her mother had coveted were in ruins, but Vira's house still stood. Mabel knocked on the door and waited. Emma, dressed in a christening gown, was asleep on her shoulder. She was growing heavy, but Mabel didn't want to move her. It was better that the child be asleep when she met her grandmother, than awake and cranky.

Mabel thought of the letter she'd received from her parents all those years ago. "If you come here, I will not look you in the face," Vira had written, and Mabel wondered if she would be turned away at the entrance. But the maid said to come in and just like that, after twenty years, Mabel stepped into her mother's home.

The house was full of light and opulence with lace curtains, toile wallpaper, and crystal sconces. Furniture that had been hidden in plain sight by tablecloths when she was a child had been uncovered and she could see that they were fine things, expensive things. Mabel was glad she was wearing one of the few nice dresses she had left. It was important to appear as if she didn't need her mother's help.

"Would you like me to take the baby?" the maid said.

Mabel shook her head, tightening her arm around the child. The maid led her upstairs, which still creaked, and down the hallway toward her mother's bedroom. Vira had always slept upstairs and Elmer downstairs. But Elmer was dead now, Mabel had learned from Caroline. He'd passed away from a heart attack years ago and she hadn't known.

Caroline came out of the bedroom. She looked so much like Mrs. Chase that for a moment, Mabel was confused about who was greeting her.

"It *is* you, Mabel," Caroline said. "Your letter was the greatest shock of my life. I thought you were dead."

How strange to see Caroline, still a child in some respects, with wide eyes behind her glasses. She never married but continued to live in this narrow neighborhood, taking care of her mother and Vira.

There was a friendliness in her face, and sympathy—even affection. After all this time, Caroline wanted to be friends. For a moment, Mabel considered it. It would be good to have someone to fall back on if Vira turned her away. But no, she wouldn't stoop to that. This girl had betrayed her. If Caroline and Robbie had waited outside the riot all those years ago, Mabel's life would be completely different now.

Caroline's eyes were on Emma, who was drooling in Mabel's shoulder. "Is this your little girl?"

"Yes, this is Emma."

"Do you want me to take her?"

"No. I want her to meet her grandmother. How is she?"

"The same as when I wrote you. She's not well. I can't

remember the last time she left the bedroom. Let me take you
to her."

Caroline led Mabel past a lacquered table with a vase of red
gladiolas. The flowers looked so lovely that envy and grief filled
Mabel. Even if her mansion hadn't been destroyed, it would
never have had the same fine-grained opulence as this home. It
came from the good taste Vira had carried with her from Maine.

It's not too late, Mabel thought. *I can make amends.*

At Vira's bedroom, Caroline stopped. "She knows you're
coming but I'm not sure she's pleased. Don't be surprised if she
doesn't react well."

The heavy rosewood bed frame still dominated the room,
as it always had, and Vira was propped up on several pillows.
She was a smaller, frailer version of the mother Mabel remembered, but it was Vira all the same.

"Leave us," Mabel said to Caroline, as though commanding a servant.

Caroline bit her lips, looked back and forth between them,
and turned from the room. Mabel hoisted Emma higher so that
the baby's head was balanced on her shoulder.

"Hello, Mother," she said.

Vira's eyes were like panicked birds as she took Mabel in. She
didn't say anything. Mabel wondered if she was able to speak.
Caroline had given the impression that Vira could talk after her
apoplexy, and yet her mother just stared.

"This is your granddaughter," Mabel said, nudging her
shoulder so that Vira could see the baby's face. "Her name is
Emma."

There was a flicker of emotion in some part of Vira's face.
That was a good sign, Mabel thought. This was Vira's blood,
after all.

Mabel picked up Emma's curled hand and extended it

toward her mother. "Piano-playing fingers, like yours." When Mabel released Emma's arm, the child pulled it into herself in one adorable, unconscious move. Again, there was a change in Vira's expression. It was the slightest movement, the pulling of the mouth from a frown to—not a frown.

This is working, Mabel thought.

And it had to. She was penniless. The house had been handed over to the banks and John was gone. No one in town would speak to her. Women from the Fruit Growers' Guild crossed the street when they saw Mabel. Even Arthur's brother, Charles, had turned his back on her. If this didn't work, she'd have to marry Ezekiel Jones, that ugly migrant worker. There had to be another option.

"Emma's father passed away," Mabel said. "I came home because she needs to know her family."

As Mabel spoke, she was distracted by a picture of her father on the wall. He was the same as how she remembered him, with white hair and tufts of eyebrows, but the sadness in his eyes was new to her. She wondered about this man she'd never known. If there was some disappointment in his life, she couldn't think what it could be.

"I wanted you to know there was an heir, Mama," she said. "Someone to carry on after us when we're gone."

Vira's hand, covered with liver spots, closed on the bedspread. Slowly, she turned her face to the wall. It was the wrong thing to say. The word "heir" implied money, which meant gold digging.

"Mama," Mabel said, clutching the child's legs. "I'm sorry. I misspoke. I meant that she's your blood."

Vira's eyes remained fastened on the wall. Mabel thought of the words in that letter of many years ago: *If you come here, I will not look you in the face.*

But there was still hope. There was the way that Vira had

looked at Emma, the way she'd almost smiled. She couldn't still blame Mabel for something she did as a child. All the people whose opinion Vira had cared about were dead. The stock exchange was a relic. The earthquake had changed the city, and it would change how people remembered it, erasing everything from the Gold Rush to the earthquake, from one uprising to another. Mabel and Vira could start over.

She laid the sleeping child on the bed next to her mother. Emma stretched out her legs, her wet mouth slack with sleep.

"Mama," Mabel said. "Please. She's your granddaughter. Do you want to be cared for by an old spinster when you could be cared for by family?"

In the hall, Caroline was pacing and Mabel remembered how you could hear everything in this house. She looked at the hand clutching the bedspread and decided to wait out the old woman. Eventually she would have to look at Emma, and when she did, Vira would soften again.

Then Caroline opened the door. She looked from Mabel to Vira and said, "Maybe it's time for you to go."

Mabel leaned forward. "Mama, if I leave here, you will never see me again. Your only child won't be coming back and I'm taking your only grandchild with me. You'll be stuck here with Caroline."

The room grew quiet. Mabel could hear the faint chopping of a knife in the kitchen.

Then Vira moved. She opened her mouth and her tongue snaked out to lick her lips.

"My only child," Vira said in a raspy voice, "is dead."

Before Vira had finished the last word, Mabel was scooping Emma up and walking past Caroline to the hall. The child awoke and began to cry.

"Mabel," Caroline said, jogging after her. "She's very old. She doesn't know what she's saying."

It was the silliest lie Mabel had ever heard. Vira knew exactly what she'd said.

"She can die alone for all I care," she said.

She jogged down the creaky stairs, carrying the crying child, and wondering how it was that everything else could change, yet these stairs were the same.

The maid held open the door as Mabel sailed through, carrying the baby into the San Francisco streets. As she marched away from the house, the child's eyes focused on the door. When the maid shut it, the child stopped crying and stared back at the big house.

At least there's Ezekiel Jones, Mabel thought. *At least there is that.*

CHAPTER 55

At eleven a.m. Frederick's supervisor told him that Sandra had called. There was an emergency and Frederick needed to come home right away. Though he was considering divorcing Sandra, Frederick was surprised by the depth of fear he felt as he careened toward home. He must still love her if he was so shaken up by the thought of her being hurt.

Near the house, the sky turned gray with smoke and Frederick had to roll up his windows so he could breathe. The smoke grew thicker the closer he got to his home. On the hill, fire engines blocked his path. His chickens were wandering in the road. Behind a tree, a billow of smoke rose like steam from a locomotive in a children's book.

No, Frederick thought. *She wouldn't do that. Not even Sandra would go that far.*

He pulled the parking brake and ran the rest of the way up the hill. His house was on fire. Orange flames were coming out of the roof like tissues from a box. Firemen were idly streaming water onto the blast as if it were already lost.

Frederick whirled away to breathe air free of smoke. He felt

dizzy. The rest of the property—the barns, the chicken coop—
were safe, but the animals were scattered. He saw more chickens
on the hillside. Lotte and the calf stood behind a car and the
other cow, still pregnant, was grazing land he hadn't yet fenced
for pasture. Police cars were parked by the barn with their doors
open, radios squawking. There was an assembly of policemen
standing under a walnut tree. Casey was beside one of the officers, and in the middle of it all, was his wife.

Frederick knew Sandra had done it. He knew it as much
as he knew the shape of her breasts or how she would act if he
brought her flowers. She was crying, clutching a handkerchief,
but they were beautiful tears, the actress at work. She looked
beautiful, in fact, and much younger than her thirty-eight years,
wearing a green dress that accentuated her slender figure. Her
long legs tapered to matching high heels. She was smiling hope-
fully at the police officer through her tears. Fredrick had seen
her smile like that in a hundred situations, to get a discount on
a dress she wanted or to impress those society women. She'd
smiled at him like that for the entire first year of their marriage,
it seemed to Frederick now as he strode over to her.

"You," he said, pointing. "You have destroyed me. You have
destroyed everything I've worked for."

The police officer stepped in, saying something in a commanding tone. Sandra crumpled like a piece of paper, sobbing into her
handkerchief and Casey put her arm around her.

"How can you say that?" Casey said. "It was an accident."

But Frederick spoke only to Sandra. "You did this, didn't
you? Admit it."

She shifted her face away. "This is what I mean," she said
to Casey.

"That's enough," said the officer, whose nametag said QUINN.
"I assume this was your house?"

Frederick looked at the box of flames behind him. Smoke rose in dark torrents, billowing and twisting like a tornado. "Yes," he said, looking away.

"And you think your wife is responsible?"

"Yes."

"She wasn't even here," Casey said. "She was with me, weren't you, honey?"

"I was. Casey's horse gave birth this morning and I went over to her house to see the baby."

"That's right," Casey said. "Sandra wanted me to tell her as soon as it happened."

Frederick was pacing back and forth, his eyes glued to the burning house. The wind blew smoke toward them, and he batted at it and coughed.

"Okay," said Officer Quinn. "Mrs. Bauer, what happened before you left the house?"

"Well," Sandra said, hooking her fingers together. "I was making tea on the stove and the phone rang. It was Casey telling me about the colt, and I was excited to see it, so I rushed to get my shoes and hurried out the door."

"I see. And did you turn off the stove when you left?"

At this, Sandra's eyes got huge. She lifted her hand and put it over her mouth. "No," she said, her voice muffled. "I don't think I did." She lowered her arm and stared at Casey. "I must have accidentally left the pan of water boiling on the stove. That had to have caused the fire. Frederick installed the stove himself and he's not much of an electrician."

"You dare pin this on me?" Frederick said.

Officer Quinn thought Frederick might get violent and nodded to his partner, who took the man's elbow and said he wanted to talk to him in private. Sandra was holding a handkerchief over her nose as her friend supported half her weight. She looked as delicate as a gardenia on a stem to Quinn.

"Now, Mrs. Bauer," he said. "Your husband seems to believe that you lit this fire."

She shivered. "He hates me. You see why I'm leaving him now. I was planning to tell him this evening."

Quinn looked over at the house behind them. It seemed unlikely that a kitchen fire could get so out of control, even on a hot day like this. On the other hand, it was more likely this woman had gotten distracted and accidentally left the stove on, no matter what the husband thought.

One of his officers approached carrying two large paper bags, which he set in front of Quinn. "I found these out by the rubbish bin," the officer said. "There are three more just like it."

The bags were full of rectangular metal cans. Quinn pulled one out and read, "Thermo Treated Linseed Oil." On the label was a picture of a drop of oil, but the yellow teardrop shape looked as much like a droplet of flame.

"What's this?" he asked Sandra.

"Oh," she said, wiping away more tears. "That's the linseed oil I've been using to help fix up our home. I spent all week oiling all the floors in the house. Frederick said he wanted me to make them shine."

"Linseed oil. Did you know that's flammable?"

"Flammable?" She blinked rapidly at him. "And I did the kitchen just this morning!"

Officer Quinn shook his head. This explained why the fire spread so rapidly. She'd covered the entire place with flammable oil.

Frederick was waving his arms as he talked to Quinn's partner. Then he wheeled around and marched over to them. "Ask her why she saved her things," Frederick said. "Why is her friend's car filled with art supplies and photo albums and clothes?"

Quinn stepped between Frederick and Sandra. "Your wife has already explained that before you arrived. Mrs. Bauer, would you care to repeat yourself?"

Sandra was twisting the handkerchief. "Frederick, Casey's car is packed because I'm leaving you. I want a divorce. I was going to tell you tonight but then this awful tragedy happened."

Frederick's jaw was tight as he stared at her. "I wish you were dead."

Everyone cried out. Sandra reeled back as if she'd been slapped.

"That's enough," Quinn said. "Let's separate these two for now."

His partner tried to escort Frederick away, but he threw up his arms and ran over to the firemen, shouting at them about the water. Officer Quinn looked back at Sandra. She was trembling, despite the heat.

"Can she go now?" Casey said.

"All right, Mrs. Bauer, I have a statement from you."

"Come on, honey," Casey said.

Officer Quinn watched Sandra leave, looking for signs of suspicion. She kept looking over her shoulder at the house, an expression of bewilderment on her face. He shook his head. Another one of those nasty divorces. Here the country was at war and these petty people couldn't get along.

As they walked away from the fire, Sandra brought her arm to her nose and smelled the smoke on her skin. There was no mark of ash on her, just the stink of smoke. It didn't matter. The smell could be removed. She would take a bath and wash it all away: her marriage, the house, the last few years of her life. Tomorrow, she would start fresh.

For that was what Sandra needed, a new start. She was becoming an expert at it now. It would hurt for a while, yes, but soon this would be just another episode in her life, like Hollywood, or Billy. It would be something forgotten and distant, with people she would never see again, and stories with endings she would never hear.

This time though, everything would be different. Even if Frederick fought her, she was entitled to some of the insurance money, which would be enough to float her until she could meet a politician, or a mortgage broker, or someone else with a lucrative job. Then, finally, things would be the way they should have been if Sandra didn't keep getting dragged down by circumstances beyond her control. For the first time in months—years, even—a familiar sense of resolve settled over her.

"You know, Casey," Sandra said. "I think things are going to be better now."

"You bet they will, now that you have that man out of your life," Casey said, swinging her arms.

But that wasn't what Sandra meant, so she didn't reply. They had come far enough down the road that the house was blocked from sight by trees. Above her head, mistletoe had taken over an oak tree, clinging like steel wool to the branches. The last puffs of smoke were dissipating into the air. It wasn't so much a cloud anymore as a stream, like a recently extinguished match. When the smoke got high enough, it would become part of the air itself, climbing on the wind to the top of Mt. Diablo. Soon Sandra wouldn't be able to sense it, but it would be there all the same. The air would move in and out of everyone's lungs, the chemicals from the smoke joining their blood streams and becoming part of them, and their children, and the atmosphere itself, until it was so broken up, so infinitesimal, that it would be impossible to trace it back to the source. It would be almost as if it were never there at all.

ACKNOWLEDGMENTS

This book would not exist if not for my agent Susan Velazquez, who remembered it from a slush pile and tracked me down to see if it had representation. I also want to thank the people at Blackstone Publishing, especially Addi Black, Josie Woodbridge, and my editor Holly Rubino.

Thank you to my dad, Rudolf Lanzendorfer, and my uncle, Richard Lanzendorfer, for letting me borrow family stories to write this work of fiction. I'm deeply grateful to Marcia Simmons, my best friend and reader, and my husband, Kyle Rankin. Your patience, unflinching honesty, and faith in me is the foundation on which this book stands.